KU-250-249

THE
CONTEST

By Karen Hamilton and available from Wildfire

THE PERFECT GIRLFRIEND
THE LAST WIFE
THE EX-HUSBAND
THE CONTEST

London Borough of Tower Hamlets

91000008170644

KAREN HAMILTON

THE
CONTEST

WILDFIRE

Copyright © 2023 Karen Hamilton

The right of Karen Hamilton to be identified as the Author of
the Work has been asserted by her in accordance with the
Copyright, Designs and Patents Act 1988.

First published in 2023 by
WILDFIRE
an imprint of HEADLINE PUBLISHING GROUP

1

Apart from any use permitted under UK copyright law, this publication may
only be reproduced, stored, or transmitted, in any form, or by any means,
with prior permission in writing of the publishers or, in the case of reprographic production,
in accordance with the terms of licences issued by the Copyright Licensing Agency.

All characters in this publication are fictitious and any resemblance
to real persons, living or dead, is purely coincidental.

Cataloguing in Publication Data is available from the British Library

Hardback ISBN 978 1 4722 7943 9
Trade paperback ISBN 978 1 4722 7944 6

Typeset in Bembo by Palimpsest Book Production Limited, Falkirk, Stirlingshire

Printed and bound in Great Britain by Clays Ltd, Elcograf S.p.A.

Headline's policy is to use papers that are natural, renewable and recyclable
products and made from wood grown in well-managed forests and other controlled
sources. The logging and manufacturing processes are expected to conform to the
environmental regulations of the country of origin.

HEADLINE PUBLISHING GROUP
An Hachette UK Company
Carmelite House
50 Victoria Embankment
London EC4Y 0DZ

www.headline.co.uk
www.hachette.co.uk

For my father, Clyde

Prologue

I'm a killer. The wrong-fork-in-the-path kind. Not the cold-blooded, have-been-planning-it-for-years type. But hindsight is the real torture. In my recurring nightmares, I'm forced to relive the moment when it all went horribly wrong.

The last climber was awaiting their turn in the cool darkness below. We caught a flash from their head torch every now and then, or maybe it was the glow worms. I've repeatedly lied to myself over the passing months. So much so that it's hard to know which of my memories are real. As I ran my hand over the rock, moss brushed my fingers. To our right, daylight shimmered tantalisingly beyond the entrance to the cave, calling to me as if it knew how desperate I was for it to be over. That memory is true, I'm sure.

A last double check of the ropes.

'Rope free!' a voice echoed.

Two words, innocuous enough.

Only this time, they were a lie. After, on the ground, only visible by torchlight, was a twisted, terrifyingly still body.

Time slows in these moments, filled with eerie silence. Until the brain catches up, all you can do is hope without hope that it somehow hasn't happened. Then realisation hits like a smack in the face. There's

1

no going back. Only the fevered dream that your mistake might be buried, might not be discovered.

Now, the last climber is a free spirit. Unlike me.

ONE

Florence

Nairobi

My socials were showered with balloons and noti-
fications yesterday, so naturally my colleagues
assumed it was my birthday. Reluctant to correct
the misunderstanding, I accepted their kind wishes and downed
multiple cocktails at the hotel bar. In the heat of the moment,
I lost sight of the fact I was on a business trip, not a holiday.
I regret it now. Images of the previous evening flash like film
trailers through my semi-conscious mind. The basement night-
club: hot, busy, dark, noisy. A live band. A vicious argument.
The extortionate bar bill (which ended up on my company
credit card because Mandy, aka Mandy the Manager, had come
down with food poisoning). We were asked to leave after one
of our clients shook a bottle of champagne like a Grand Prix
winner.

Oh, God. Fresh dread hits. My professionalism will be under
even closer scrutiny. As key employees of Blackmore Vintage

Travel, we're expected to maintain a professional front. No exceptions. The mosquito net brushes against my face as I roll over and plump up my pillows. My mouth is desperately dry, the first warning of a hangover. Thirsty as I am, I can't summon up the energy to rise and hunt for the minibar. The hotel is so swish that everything is hidden behind panels in shades of slate and black.

It's still dark outside. Good. It means I have time to mentally prepare for the big breakfast meeting to go over the fund-raising challenges on this important annual trip, nicknamed the Great Escape. I rarely shut the curtains or blinds completely; I like to be woken by natural light. Sunrise offers hope and possibility for the day ahead, before I must face the consequences of yesterday's multiple screw-ups. Most of which were not my fault, yet I predict that the blame will be dumped on my shoulders. If I don't smooth over the damage in an expert and seemingly effortless fashion, heads will roll. I don't intend one of those to be mine, ever. The humiliation alone would kill me. As the king of bespoke travel and opulence, the award-winning BVT (founded by Hugo Blackmore in the eighties) has introduced me to a world of luxury and privilege. Now, without work tentacles seeping into every area of my life, I'm not certain who I'd be any more.

Habit makes me reach for my phone beneath my pillow, my heart rate already up a notch. Good day or bad day? Disastrous or manageable? I feel instantaneous relief the moment I grab hold of its familiar shape and slide it out. Problems can arise worldwide at any time, and it fills me with fear that I could potentially wake up one morning to an absolute shitstorm, having slept through it, whether I'm on call or not.

I remember, I'd only been at BVT for a fortnight when a

freshly promoted manager strolled into the office at nine, coffee in one hand, a paper packet speckled with spots of grease in the other.

'What?' he said, noticing Mandy the Manager's stern expression.

She named one of our biggest clients and explained that they'd had to spend the night *curled up in a bloody chair* in a regional European airport after an unexpected flight diversion.

'No one answered the emergency number,' she added. 'They were left stranded. All the hotels they called – *themselves* – were full.'

The man placed his breakfast on his desk and took out his phone from his pocket, staring at it as though he'd be able to disprove Mandy's accusations. He went pale, his hands shaking. I remember thinking he was hung-over. With the benefit of hindsight, I now appreciate his fear. I soon learned that there was no way any of us could get through a night on call without something going wrong.

'There must've been a problem with my phone,' he said.

'Hugo is waiting for you,' she replied.

He lasted five minutes in Hugo's office before storming out, avoiding all eye contact and throwing the coffee at the window. The thud made us all jump and we stared at the brown liquid sliding down the pane. I leapt up to clean it. A mistake, I also now know. Hugo emerged from his office on the way to one of his many brunch meetings and caught me dabbing at the glass with kitchen roll and tissues. Judging by his look of disgust, I assumed that I'd be joining the rest of the heads on stakes.

'For Christ's sake, someone tell Florence we have a cleaning firm on speed dial.' 'On speed dial' is classic Hugo-speak. I grab a pillow and prop myself up as I scan my inbox. Fourteen work-related emails, twelve of which can be dealt with by those manning the fort back in Kingston upon Thames. I forward them on with comments like: *To be actioned by midday* and *Keep me posted*. I used to worry that I came across as terse or demanding, but having Hugo as a boss toughens you up. BVT doesn't employ shrinking violets. Hugo-speak, again.

Two personal texts. One at 2 a.m. from my colleague, Jacob – Hugo's slippery son – clearly off his head. I do my best to interpret his nonsense. The last sentence gets to me. '*Stop acting like bloody Miss Marple.*' He's scared I'm going to pin some of the blame for yesterday's mistakes on him. The second is from Mandy, who must be feeling more like her old self as she also messaged in the early hours, which is normal for her. All BVT employees do this and most of the time, if we're honest, we expect a reply. Putting our phones on silent would be breaking an unspoken expectation. Broken sleep is part of the job. The message is typical Mandy, and by that, I mean she's fishing for information.

I'd have bought you a gift in Duty Free if I hadn't been ill. A nice perfume or an eyeshadow palette, perhaps. Clearly, it's the thought that counts in this case! Anyway, just checking something. I thought your birthday was tomorrow?

Wrong date on my social media. Long story. How are you feeling? I reply.

Much better. The wrong date on all of them??? Are you going to correct it at some point? It would do my head in to have everyone wish me happy birthday on the wrong date.

It *was* mildly annoying but a small price to pay. I prefer not to give out information online unless strictly necessary. The thought of lurkers knowing random stuff about me gives me the creeps. Someone sent me expensive gifts anonymously for my thirteenth, sixteenth, eighteenth, twenty-first and thirtieth, all wrapped in crimson paper, tied with black ribbon. My mother said it was exactly the type of thing my absent father would do.

'Grand gestures. That sums him up perfectly,' she said.

She always refused to tell me anything about my 'father unknown', saying that we were better off with him out of our lives. *'No point inviting darkness in.'*

Except I have vague memories of good, not bad. Random things like, the sound of a male voice reciting a nursery rhyme, the smell of cologne, seeing a pair of feet wearing large, black shiny shoes walking up the stairs. Even laughter. Plus, those gifts proved that he wasn't out of our lives; he was on the periphery, in the shadows. Watching. Lurking. I pretended to my mother that I didn't care for the presents – a Burberry handbag, a Gucci watch, a Tiffany pendant, a crate of vintage champagne, a hamper of luxury goods. But she knew I was acting, just as I knew the gifts unsettled her. She died last year before I was able to extract the truth, quashing the fantasy that we could have a proper heart-to-heart one day. I hate that I left it too late to push for information because I always thought that we'd have plenty more time together.

A parcel arrived the day after her funeral, wrapped in the same crimson paper with black ribbon as my birthday presents. A thoughtful gift – a framed picture of my mother. She was young, happy, smiling on a beach. At first, I didn't recognise her. Since then, nothing. I posted the picture online hoping it would draw him out of the shadows. I monitored the likes and comments for weeks, hoping he'd be unable to resist revealing himself. After a fruitless week, I deleted the post. My grandmother claims she doesn't know anything either.

'Your mother was always secretive. Even as a child.'

Every Christmas after cheese and port (the only time she'd drink) I'd press my grandmother while my mother cleared up after lunch.

'Was he tall, my father, do you think?'

'Maybe. You're taller than your mother was at your age.'

I used to cling on to these tiny pieces of non-details as though they were nuggets of information gold.

This bittersweet wistfulness isn't new. I feel the same every year as my birthday in early March approaches. A familiar, crushing sense of loneliness threatens to take hold, which I usually bury by focusing on something work-related.

A flash of light on the other side of the room catches my eye. The TV? My laptop charger? Something feels off. Probably alcohol-induced paranoia; I'm not a good drinker. Silence. I feel grateful for the shield of the mosquito net, however flimsy.

I remove my earplugs (a traveller's godsend) and check the time: 4.41 a.m. Two hours and nineteen minutes until *the* meeting. Being alone with Hugo is not enjoyable. He's one of those people who uses silence to get his opponent to say more than they intend. I'm more nervous about the meeting than I am about climbing Kilimanjaro in five days' time as part of the Great Escape.

I'm psyching myself up to get out of bed when the unmistakeable thud of something dropping on to the carpet on the far side of the suite makes me freeze. What the—? Please God, no. I can hear breathing. Not mine. Child-like, I squeeze my eyes shut, willing the monster to go away. Above the sound of my heart's *thud, thud*, I listen, praying that I'm wrong. *Think.*

Another flash of light, then it's gone. My heart rate revs up yet another notch as I imagine a machete slashing the mosquito net open. I twist my head slowly to the right and see a thin line of light beneath the hotel room door. It's reassuringly close, bright, like an emergency exit sign. I can charge for safety.

I tense my body, ready to move. *Now!* I drop to the side of the bed and crouch to scramble beneath the sheer fabric, but the netting pulls taut against my face. Despite my panic, I hear a door opening somewhere, then softly closing. Free from the goddamn net, I aim for the door, one hand groping for the handle, the other clutching my phone. I twist then yank it open. The door jams. The chain is still on! What the hell is going on?

I fumble against the wall for a light switch so I can see what I'm doing, but my hands are trembling so much it feels like an age before I locate it. My eyes blink as brightness floods the room and I struggle to scan my surroundings. No monsters; no one. It doesn't make sense. My bag on the luggage rack appears untouched. A thief would've done some rifling, I reason. I'm not an unpacker, my nomadic childhood made me that way. My breathing still heavy, eyes wide open, I scour the room, still convinced I will see someone.

The door leading to the bathroom is shut – I'm sure I left it ajar with the light on – and there's another door which leads to the living area, also closed. I definitely didn't close them. I hover indecisively, before I step towards the bedside table, pick up the hotel phone with my hands still shaking, and press the *Guest Services* button. No answer. I try again. Bloody hell. Too agitated to stay in the room, I pull on some trainers without socks, zip up a hoodie, pick up my key card, slide back the chain and step out. The door closes with a gentle click. Along the corridor, scattered service trays lie abandoned outside various rooms; mounds of silver domes on white plates, wilting salads, pools of sloppy yellow, melted butter, plastic ice containers and abandoned beer bottles.

I jump as a uniformed hotel employee appears from around the corner. Likewise, he starts at the sight of me.

'Good morning,' he says.

'Good morning,' I repeat as he carries on with his job delivering newspapers, carefully placing them outside each door.

As he hands me a paper, I'm about to blurt out that I thought someone was in my room to explain why I'm just standing here, but decide I'd rather discuss my fears with security. I glance down at the dramatic newspaper headlines in bold capitals listing ROBBERY and ASSAULT before I stride towards the main staircase. Just as I reach the stairs, I catch sight of the golden lettering on door 332 as it opens and someone peers out at me. Behind them is darkness; I can't make out their features. I have a sudden urge to get far away from them. I run down the main stairwell, concentrating on the gold and navy swirled carpet patterns.

The main lobby is ghostly empty, apart from one man with a floor polisher, who is making back and forth arc motions on the marble floor, coiling the cable around his wrist. He ignores me.

The reception desk is unattended. A column vase of red lilies dangling claw-like over green leaves rests on the counter.

I hit a silver bell. *Please Ring for Attention.* The rings echo and fade. No one appears. I look around. The person cleaning the floor has disappeared. I am alone, in a vast space of marble and mirrors.

'Hello?' I call out.

Silence.

But then, a uniformed member of staff appears from a nearby door.

'Good morning,' I say.

As I begin to explain the situation the obvious hits me. I remember the sound of a closing door as I grappled with the bloody mosquito net. Jacob and his girlfriend have the suite next to me and we have interconnecting doors – my pet hotel hate. I know it's customary to play tricks (or pranks, as Hugo refers to them) on opposing team members, but someone creeping around my room is taking it too far.

'I'm sorry to have disturbed you. I thought there was an intruder in my room but now . . .' I stop, feeling foolish. 'I don't think I need anything after all.'

God, Jacob is such a constant bloody thorn in my side. As this is my first time on the Great Escape, I suspect he's just trying to unsettle me. Typical hazing, the kind I've heard plenty about.

Back inside my room, still slightly mortified by the memory of the quizzical look on the hotel receptionist's face, I rush around, flinging open doors, switching on lights. I check my essentials: passport, purse, credit cards. All there. Untouched. I rummage inside my handbag. Perhaps the stress *is* getting to me. Still, I can't shake off the feeling of not being alone.

Without waiting to talk myself out of it, I open my connecting door and rap loudly on the second.

'Jacob! Open the door!'

Silence.

I try the door. It opens, swinging in the opposite direction to mine.

'Jacob?' I call out. Nothing. I try his girlfriend's name. 'Clarabelle?'

I shine torchlight from my phone around the room. It's unoccupied. The mosquito net dangles above the rumpled bed in a neat knot. A half-filled bottle of water rests on the bedside table. Odd. I switch on the main light. Nothing and no one. I try Jacob's number. Voicemail.

I lock my side of the interconnecting door, cursing my stupidity at not checking whether it was locked. And yet . . . maybe I did imagine it all. Jacob was very drunk when he left the message for me. He'd have been like an elephant crashing about my room had he actually done so. I'm tired – no, exhausted – and stressed. Being here, accepting the challenge of team leader is a double-edged sword. Not that saying no was an option. The ins and outs of the company need to be fully appreciated to understand what this means. My long-suffering friends – who are used to me cancelling arrangements at the last minute – still don't get it. It's an honour, like drawing the ultimate golden ticket.

I select a coffee capsule – the strongest blend on offer – and inhale the aroma as the machine steams. I wash the mug in the bathroom; I never trust that hotel mugs are cleaned decently. Thank God the minibar has proper milk. It's always the little touches that can make or break a hotel.

My hands wrapped around the mug, I sip the coffee, enjoying the warmth. I step out on to the balcony and gaze at the city lights beyond as Nairobi gradually awakens.

Daybreak lines the horizon in a burst of peach pastels, a glorious Kenyan sunrise.

Excited as I was when Hugo picked me this year to head a select group of VIPs, I knew it would be more than just about winning. Especially as Jacob is the other team leader. It will also be about surviving, in more ways than one. Being here, in the heart of the action, will finally give me the opportunity to ask questions that need asking.

My phone rings. Hugo's name appears on the screen. I take a deep breath to calm the tingling sensation in my chest.

'Florence?' He clears his throat before continuing. 'I appreciate that it's early, my dear, but I need to bring forward our breakfast meeting.'

'Sure.'

It's not as if I can say no. I have asked him not to call me *my dear* but he says it's a habit he can't break. Funny that he's never slipped up with any of the clients. I hope my voice came across as confident, in control, someone who isn't worried that their career is on the line because of a few hotel room mix-ups, missing luggage and some airline cabin downgrades.

'Meet me in the business centre in ten,' he says. 'In the meeting room next door to the gym. The staff promised to have it ready for us.'

He disconnects and I stare at my phone. I reassure myself that I came across just fine, as always, before I rush to the bathroom to clean my teeth, tie my hair up into a bun to pretend that I spend my life looking professional and work-ready, even at ungodly hours. I open the wardrobe and pull on a navy jumpsuit. This is typical Hugo, keeping us on the hop. Although it has its benefits. Clients regularly tell me that they love working with me because of my calmness under pressure. They trust that I won't abandon them in the middle of the night if their travel plans have gone awry.

I take the lift. The door opens to a deserted lower ground floor. It makes me do a quicker than normal scan of my surroundings. I was mugged at knifepoint one night a couple of years back when I worked as a tour guide after saying goodbye to my clients outside a lonely (supposedly haunted) pub. Ever since I've always carried an unhealthy amount of paranoia around with me. The business centre reception is unmanned, which doesn't help, and the lights are dim. I open the door to the gym, relieved to see several early birds running and rowing. Normally, that would be me.

After knocking and receiving no answer, I open the door adjacent to the gym. It's dark, so I switch on the light. On the desk are a basket of croissants, a flask of tea or coffee, two notepads, a pen beside each and two bottles of water.

I sit down, help myself to a coffee, even though I don't normally drink more than one cup a day, and wait. Five minutes. The air conditioning is too cold and as I get up to adjust it, Hugo steps into the room. He's tall, but that's not what gives him his presence. Nor is it his bespoke work suits, handmade shoes and neatly trimmed grey beard. It's because he carries himself with the confidence of someone who rarely hears the word 'no'.

'Good morning, Florence.'

'Good morning.'

'Pour me a coffee, would you?'

I sit down again and lean across the table to do as he asks. There's no point in suggesting he does it himself, it wouldn't achieve anything.

He sits opposite me.

'Right, let's dive straight in. I have several important things on the agenda, which is why I'm speaking to you first, and Jacob later. I require your undivided attention.'

I can feel my heart beat a little faster as Hugo slides a sheet of A4 paper across the table. I glance down at the list detailing the four challenges. His PA has already emailed them to Jacob and me but Hugo is old school; he likes 'to see things in print'. Climbing Kilimanjaro alone simply wouldn't be enough. It's the norm for these annual trips to test leadership skills in multiple ways. In typical Hugo-speak, the challenges are to:

Wow each client on the first day in Tanzania. Keep at the forefront of your mind that the aim is to retain and gain future business.

Arrange a unique extra-curricular activity at camp during the climb. Remember – always think outside that box!

Raise £25,000 each in sponsorship to be split between a climate change charity and a serious sporting injuries charity, as chosen by our special guests, the Armstrongs.

Write a blog and post on all platforms as best you can, Wi-Fi permitting. Make your followers utterly sick to their core with envy. Aim for over ten per cent engagement. You love to insinuate that I'm behind the times, so now's your chance to prove to me what I've supposedly been missing!

The winner will be the leader who completes all challenges successfully and summits with the highest number of team members.

As leaders, it will be up to Jacob and me to ensure the wellbeing of our team to the best of our abilities. The fact that the winner needs to summit with the highest number of team members is a stark reminder that not everyone will necessarily make it to the summit. The success rate for summiting varies between forty-five and sixty-five per cent. Anyone – marathon runners, athletes – can succumb to altitude sickness or other misfortunes. If it can happen to Martina Navratilova, it can happen to any one of us.

'A little bird has told me that Ethical Getaways is about to pull a big publicity stunt,' I hear Hugo continue. 'Consider it a mini challenge to find out what they're up to and upstage them. I have my suspicions, but I need them confirmed.'

Ethical Getaways is a rival firm who set up shop nearby in Kingston upon Thames three months ago. They've already made a dent in our business because they're focused on the latest environmental issues, have a dedicated social media team and an impressive marketing budget. They also appear to be working their way through our VIP client list by enticing them with a decent reward system and charity-of-their-choice donations. Hugo thinks they're gimmicks.

'Has your little bird shared any further details?' I say.

'They're planning to demonstrate that it's possible to enjoy long-haul trips yet minimise the environmental impact,' he says. 'Guilt-free travelling or something along those lines. They make it sound like a box of sugar-free chocolate brownies, although, joking aside, I suspect they're about to publicly throw down the gauntlet. It's ridiculous to think they can become as big or as exclusive as us. They'll learn. I've seen off many so-called rivals in my time, and Ethical Getaways are not going to be any different.'

I'm not sure how to respond. He stares at me. I wish I wasn't on the back foot because of all the mistakes from the beginning of this trip. On the bright side, one of the missing suitcases has turned up although another one belonging to a client, Casper Jackson, has seemingly disappeared. I worked bloody hard to resolve things and smooth away any bad impressions, but still I know that Hugo won't let me forget it.

'Are you up for proving your loyalty by accepting this challenge?'

I hesitate.

'Unless, of course, you're not up to the task?'

There's only one answer I can give.

'Of course—'

But his phone rings. Hugo glances down at the screen and dismisses me with a wave of his hand. He swings round in his chair, turning his back.

I'm left in the dark wondering what else was on his agenda.

TWO

Jacob

Nairobi

Cloudless sky – tick. Clear blue swimming pool – tick. This is why Jacob does what he does. He loves the smell of chlorine; it whisks him back to one of his family homes in Sardinia. It's gloriously cool in the shade of the hotel veranda but he can tell that today will be a scorcher. There's a simmering sense of the approaching heat and with it, the promise of a wonderful day. A bird with long, skinny legs and cloak-like wings struts across the grass. Jacob googles it. A Marabou stork, sometimes referred to as the undertaker bird. It has disappeared by the time he looks up from his phone. Jacob stares at the gardens beyond the pool – neat rose beds and rock features. Sprinklers spray the lush, rainforest-green lawn although random dry patches are visible despite the best efforts of the gardening team. Nothing's ever perfect.

Take last night, for example. One moment he was on a

winning streak at the casino, the best in a long time. The next, he was conned and the shame of his latest loss is still smarting. *Blank it out*, he tells himself.

Jacob takes a sip of espresso and savours the peace, before wolfing down more of his full English even though he's starting to feel full. He's not into fruit or yoghurt or continental breakfasts. He wishes he had more time to mentally prepare for the pre-climb meeting with his father. It's the first time he's been selected to run a team in BVT's annual competition, and this could be his last chance to prove to Hugo that he's not the teenager his father still thinks he is.

He picks up his phone. Jacob tends to pass on the more mundane work to others, leaving him free to do what he's good at: making clients believe they are important and valued. They trust him. They're loyal, on the whole. His sales figures reflect that. He can't rest on his laurels though. He'll need to put in extra groundwork and pay more attention to detail. There have been rumours of belt-tightening, even among his wealthier clients. It's Jacob's aim to ensure that his remaining customers continue to believe that bespoke travel is essential, not a luxury. It could be disastrous if some of them decided to cut costs by booking directly online. Or worse, even more of them directing their business Ethical Getaways' way.

Jacob checks his mails, messages (even the sent ones, aware that he can be his own worst enemy after a few too many), but there's nothing of immediate concern. He switches to the web browser. Lately, a slew of disparaging comments have appeared anonymously on a site which claims to give the nitty gritty on what it's like to work for various travel companies nationwide. Disgruntled ex-employees can air their grievances and receive validation. Like that can only be done on a public forum. Jacob thinks the clues are in the very words *disgruntled* and *ex*. Point is, BVT has featured a lot in the past few months. He finds the forum strangely compelling.

To accept a job there is to sell your soul to the devil.

No examples given, Jacob notes.

No customer care, it's all about the money.

Same as most companies.

Florence needs to watch her back.

He half wonders whether he should mention this new comment to Florence but talks himself out of it, because from time to time individual employees are 'named and shamed'. There's no point in alerting her because nothing has ever come from it. He deals with his gnawing anger that people can write anonymously online without a care for the conse-quences by reporting the comment to the website's admin team. It's surprisingly satisfying.

Has anyone been following the comments written by the Anonymous Traveller? he reads next.

He clicks on the link.

So, it's that time of year when a certain travel company sends the crème de la crème of their staff and clients on an annual jolly. There's been speculation that this year will be the toughest yet . . .

Jacob skim-reads. There's nothing of great interest that stands out and he closes it down. As he's about to press on the next app, his favourite gambling one, a new comment catches his eye on the anonymous work travel site.

Senior management have blood on their hands.

For the first time that morning, Jacob feels cold. He looks

up and sees Luke approaching his table wearing the mirrored sunglasses he'd bought specifically for the climb and had delivered to the office.

'No Clarabelle?' Luke says, sitting down and removing his glasses before placing them down carefully on the white tablecloth. 'In the doghouse?'

More like dog eat dog, Jacob thinks.

Clarabelle had slept with her back towards him last night after their argument over his casino visit.

'Seems I upset a few people with my honesty last night,' he says.

'There's honesty and there's being a total arse.'

'Look, it came out all wrong,' Jacob says. 'Let's forget it and move on.'

Tension fills the air. The unspoken is as loud as if they were both still shouting their grievances.

Luke had better not expect an apology, thinks Jacob. *He is a traitor.* Luke had blatantly lied and told him that Hugo had insisted he be in Florence's team.

'News to me,' Hugo had said when Jacob had confronted him over the decision on their flight from London to Nairobi. 'Luke put in a special request and asked to be on Florence's team.'

Whatever Jacob thinks about his father, Hugo doesn't lie about business decisions. Hugo believes in his judgement wholeheartedly.

Luke and Jacob should be working together. Luke doesn't do anything by half measures – he's an all-or-nothing type of guy – and Jacob needs people like him on his team. This year is their most important yet. They've had to pull out all the stops because a firm they never even considered a rival is making waves. Jacob's impressed upon Hugo that they need to outsmart Ethical Getaways from the off. Modernise, be mindful of climate change and excessive air travel for short trips, pay staff a fair wage in all countries and increase their social media presence. And does he listen? No. Hugo mimes a 'shoo, shoo!' motion with his hand every time Jacob brings it up. Tough times don't exist in Hugo's mind.

Luke looks like he's got a lot more to say, but Florence chooses that moment to appear through the glass doors opening on to the patio area. She's wearing pink and purple gym gear and looks unruffled, which is quite the transformation from last night.

'Morning!' She sits down beside Jacob without going through the whole 'Is this seat free?' façade. Flo assumes a lot of things.

'Good morning,' says Luke, looking way more pleased to see her than he did Jacob.

'Green tea, please,' she orders when a member of staff approaches. She looks over at Jacob as if she's wondering how to word something. 'I thought you were in the room adjacent to mine? Apparently, it's unoccupied.'

'Upgrade,' Jacob replies.

She looks puzzled, as though this piece of information isn't what she expected.

'Oh. All right for some,' she says glancing down at the menu.

Yesterday Jacob had taken pleasure in her discomfort and panic as realisation had dawned that her meticulous planning was coming apart at the seams. Although, credit where it's due, she had stayed calm enough to sort out the room mix-ups. Jacob's favourite part was at Heathrow when the airline ground staff had broken the news in front of Hugo that one of the VIPs had been downgraded to economy. Once onboard the flight Florence had ordered two large vodka and Diet Cokes and downed them with uncharacteristic speed. He knows because he took a stroll from his Business Class seat to economy to spy on her. It was a mistake, in his opinion, that she had allowed herself to be banished to the back of the cabin. Hugo takes careful note of how people who work for him let themselves be treated and asks Mandy to type every little piece of information he discovers about them on a spreadsheet. Jacob has spent too many years learning that the hard way. *If you don't value yourself, Hugo won't either.*

An awkward silence falls. A man wearing a grey suit at the adjacent table is on a video call with his children. Jacob wishes someone like Casper or Casper's partner, Jonessa, would join their table. He keeps looking across at the double glass doors in hope. There are things everyone pretends not to see or brushes under the luxury wool carpet in the BVT offices, one being a noticeable gap at the table, both at the office and today. George. His absence is the elephant in the room. Or on the veranda. The four of them were an ambitious managerial team, as well as being the top salespeople. *Call it leading by example*, Jacob thinks. All of them – himself, Luke, George and Flo – were very good at their jobs, although Jacob still considers himself the best when it comes to attracting new clients. Jacob even liked George outside work. He was a good laugh. He wasn't too uptight, and he'd lend him money – unlike some – without making him feel crap for asking.

'Have you had your meeting with Hugo yet?' Florence asks him.

It's none of her business.

'Why?'

'Just curious,' she replies with an impressive poker face.

Jacob's dying to ask if she's had hers, but manages to resist.

They're interrupted by the arrival of his father. Hugo steps out through the double doors and on to the veranda, dressed in a crisp linen suit and – Jacob can barely believe his eyes – a matching Panama hat. Lord knows what he'll wear on the actual climb. At least they'll have experienced guides who will hopefully talk some sense into him. Jacob cares because Hugo is on his team. At first, he was pleased because Hugo is most definitely one of life's winners. But now, he's not so sure. Despite hinting several times that this was Jacob's sink-or-swim opportunity, it also seems Hugo doesn't fully trust him. Or he's keeping score, preparing to list Jacob's supposed failings if they happen. They won't. This is his chance to show Hugo that he's been wrong about him. By God, Jacob is going to make his father eat every belittling word that has ever spewed out of his mouth.

He no longer feels hungry and pushes away his half-eaten plate of bacon and eggs. The yolk has run, and a couple of wizened mushrooms lie pooled in yellow.

'Morning, morning, morning!' Hugo says, sitting opposite Florence.

Jacob watches their exchange closely, expecting to see Florence looking a little sheepish after all the booking errors. But no, disappointingly, she remains as poised as ever. Mr and Mrs Armstrong, Hugo's first ever clients and long-term friends, are on Flo's climbing team. They were supposed to be whisked to the hotel via limousine and allocated the honeymoon suite. Instead – Jacob tries to suppress a smile every time he recalls this – they ended up in a minibus with the rest of them. Mrs Armstrong sat at a strange angle, an oversized handbag on her lap, clutching on to the back of her seat as though her life depended on it. Upon arrival, the honeymoon suite had already been allocated – to Jacob – under Clarabelle's surname. No one put two and two together, and if they had he'd have pretended that it was part of the annual pranks the two teams traditionally play on one other. Round one to Jacob. If he is going to spend a week hiking and camping, he can't resist surrounding himself with as much luxury as possible before-hand. A proper rest is the best preparation and might give him just the edge he needs.

Silence descends on the table as Hugo picks up the menu. By force of habit, Jacob finds himself sitting a little straighter in his chair. Hugo can't stand slouching. Yet every time Jacob does something purely to keep on his dad's good side, a little piece inside of him dies.

'What's everyone having?' Hugo asks, without looking up from the menu.

'I had the full cooked breakfast,' Jacob says. 'Thoroughly recommend it.'

Hugo glances down at Jacob's half-eaten plate before summoning a waiter.

'Muesli and fruit salad, please,' he says, patting his stomach. 'And a black coffee.' Then he looks over at Jacob. 'We'll bring our meeting forward. Twenty minutes.'

'That suits me well,' Jacob says, avoiding Flo's eyes. He has perfected the art of nonchalance. 'Has anyone heard if Mandy has recovered from her food poisoning yet?'

Hugo's expression doesn't falter. Jacob would love to know if any of Hugo's secrets ever eat away at him.

'I've just spoken to her,' Florence jumps in. 'She's almost as right as rain. She'll be fine to make the climb.'

But surely Mandy will be weakened by her stomach upset, thinks Jacob. Mandy has told him something in the strictest confidence recently. He's glad she confided in him, because it's usually Florence people turn to because she's a good listener. Jacob doesn't intend to reveal what Mandy told him, but he will use the information if he has to. It might be too good not to.

Hugo digs into his cereal, his spoon gently clinking against the bowl. A group of tourists at a nearby table burst into raucous laughter.

It's unfortunate for Mandy that her name begins with 'M', because not only is she Mandy the Manager, she's also Mandy the Mistress. It's an open office secret that she and Hugo are having an affair, which is why Mandy has to be on Flo's team – because Sara, Hugo's third wife, is climbing too. Jacob is fond of Sara and Mandy, and hates the situation. They both deserve better.

Florence stares at her phone, her hands shaking slightly. She's more hung-over than she's letting on, Jacob thinks. She tops up her cup from the silver teapot, pressing her finger against the lid with her spare hand. Even so, she spills some into the saucer and on to the pristine white tablecloth. Brown dots seep and spread. Flo dabs at the tablecloth with her napkin, while Hugo stares at her with what Jacob hopes is disgust. His father has a thing about table manners. He has a thing about a lot of things.

Jacob struggles with silence so his prayers are answered when another client, Imogen, steps on to the veranda. Imogen – 'If you're going to shorten my name, please make it Ginny, not Immy' – wouldn't be his number one choice to join them. But anyone who can change the atmosphere at the table is a welcome sight right now.

'Hi,' she says. 'May I join you?'

'Of course,' says Luke. 'It's lovely to see you.'

He stands up to pull back one of the wrought-iron chairs for her. It scrapes against the floor tiles, setting Jacob's teeth on edge. Imogen smiles her thanks and sits down. If Jacob had done that, he reckons it would have been the wrong thing to do. Luke gets away with stuff.

It's only the second or third time Jacob has met 'Ginny not Immy', because he doesn't mix with the less important clients at Blackmore Vintage Travel. To be fair, maybe he hasn't warmed to her because she's an old friend of Flo's. Hence the reason she was afforded VIP client status. Her company doesn't meet the minimum annual spend criteria. Florence and Imogen were colleagues in a previous work life, prior to securing themselves the comfy positions they both now hold. God only knows how they slipped through their respective recruitment nets.

Mandy had met Flo at a tennis club and the next thing, Florence had a much higher-level entry position at BVT than Jacob did when he started. She was head of a team of over thirty staff, whose roles were primarily to attract and retain premium business travellers, as opposed to the luxury end of the leisure market, which is Jacob's area of expertise. Although Jacob prides himself on being able to harness his talent to focus on both. He has, on average, over fifty separate clients travelling at any one point – while most of BVT's dedicated travel managers are allocated a mere twenty clients at a time. Jacob can guess how Mandy got Hugo to do what she wanted him to. What he's never got to the bottom of is why she was so keen for Flo to join them.

'I could sense she had ambition and was a hard worker. You can tell the sort of people who are going somewhere in life,' Mandy had said when Jacob had asked her.

It never rang true. BVT have a long waiting list of applicants, desperate to set foot through their door. They don't need to find employees; future candidates find BVT and are willing to come and work for lower salaries than they'd prefer.

It has backfired for Mandy, given that Florence, Luke and Jacob have become heads of international operations. Mandy is still the office manager, and her work days appear to be a stream of never-ending admin. She claims to love it. George hasn't been replaced. Jacob thinks it's because if they appointed someone else, it would be an admission of sorts that he might never return.

Imogen now works for a global, all-terrain travel clothing chain and is head of social media.

'I'm a natural,' Imogen says. 'If you'd like me to help you with the fund-raising promotion on your socials, I'm happy for you to make me your go-to person.'

As if, thinks Jacob. If only people knew what Imogen was like offline. Mind you, people probably wouldn't like him much in real life either. He picks up his phone and posts an update on how much his team have raised for a carbon offset scheme and environmental charity so far. He adds #paradise for balance. There's no point in denying that what they're doing most certainly isn't suffering. Yet. He wants to give an impression of authenticity and 'keeping it real'. Their social media followers must believe that they are sharing the rough and the smooth.

Excitement replaces his earlier unease. Their first challenge is to wow the clients in Tanzania before the climb. Easy. There's no way that Florence will be able to beat him on this one. He's pulled out all the stops, excelled himself. He can't wait to see Hugo's face. Or Flo's, when she realises she's lost the first challenge.

Jacob can't sit still any more. He needs to get this meeting over with.

'Shall we head off to your suite now?' he says to Hugo. 'Or we can use the meeting room I booked. That way, we don't have to disturb Sara or Clarabelle.'

Hugo points to a spare table at the far corner of the veranda.

'Let's order a fresh cafetiere of coffee and we can take our drinks over there.'

'Sure.'0

They excuse themselves as some of the other clients step on to the veranda.

'Fire away,' Hugo says, before Jacob's even sat down.

Jacob gives updates on the total raised by his team so far, an impressive fourteen grand, give or take. Not bad for the first five days.

Hugo's face remains impassive. Fresh paranoia takes hold. Has bloody Flo raised more than that already? *She can't have.* Jacob clenches his fists. Since Flo's arrival at BVT things have felt slightly off. She's a shark in quiet waters. Jacob knows from diving trips what to do in a shark scenario: distract them. And that's what Flo needs.

They pause as their coffee cups are placed in front of them. Then Jacob starts to go through the timings of the day ahead. Their itinerary is organised by the hotel. A trip to the Karen Blixen Museum, an elephant orphanage, a village market and a nearby church. Hugo believes that sightseeing is a good appetiser before what he considers to be the real event. 'Trips are like books,' he's fond of saying. 'They should have a beginning, a middle and an end.' BVT is the ultimate in luxury travel and extreme sports; extreme anything, in fact. Their motto is that there's no limit, and Jacob has never failed to give his clients exactly what they desire.

'And what do you have prepared after our arrival in Moshi?' Hugo says.

Jacob's heart pumps faster. This is it. Challenge one. There are three acclimatisation days in Moshi before the climb, because if they are well rested it will increase their chances of success. Every little thing helps. Nonetheless, the clients must still be wowed and entertained without becoming exhausted. Free time by the hotel pool with two-for-one cocktails at happy hour won't cut it.

Jacob can't stop himself from smiling. 'A trip to the Serengeti,' he says. 'Glamping, but at hotel standard which obviously offers the best of both worlds.' He passes over his phone to wow Hugo with some pictures. 'They can watch the Great Migration when the zebra and wildebeest cross the Mara River, trying to avoid the crocodiles.'

Hugo doesn't respond.

'Like *The Hunger Games* but in the wild,' Jacob adds.

Hugo frowns. 'I know what the Great Migration is. But *camping* before seven nights of *camping* on Kilimanjaro?'

'Luxury *glamping*. Proper beds.'

'Every single client has done multiple safaris,' Hugo says.

'Not like this one,' Jacob counters.

'The Armstrongs took their eldest daughter on a safari for her twenty-first,' Hugo says. 'Remember Janey?'

A bad feeling starts to unfurl in the pit of Jacob's stomach, a sickening realisation that this meeting isn't going the way he expected. He glances over at his colleagues and clients. They're too far away to overhear, but it's still obvious that their exchange isn't going well. How stupid of him not to consider the Armstrongs' daughter, Janey, who was killed in a white-water rafting accident on that trip. They blamed BVT, and Hugo promised that a decent amount for a charity of the Armstrongs' choice would be raised in her honour every year on the Great Escape. It was a tragic accident, but Hugo said that he understood that when tragedy strikes, people need an outlet, someone to blame. The Armstrongs have been invited on every single trip since, as Hugo is a keep-your-enemies (AKA people who could potentially sue him or spread bad publicity) -close type of person. He's persuasive. He made them believe that Janey would've wanted them to live their lives, and it was a nice way to honour her memory.

Hugo has said more than once that Jacob doesn't have what it takes to win. He's wrong. Jacob assumed that because Hugo had picked him as this year's leader, he'd changed his mind. Or that he'd only said it to push him. Hugo is more stick than carrot.

'It's not the best time of year,' Hugo points out. 'July to September is better.'

'It's good to go now,' Jacob pushes. 'Less crowded.'

His father doesn't look convinced. 'And that's it? That's all you've planned?'

'It's a two-day trip.'

'Our clients need relative rest, not more hotel-hopping and travelling.'

'It's not that far. Plus, it's luxury *glamping*,' Jacob repeats patiently. 'They can leave most of their belongings in their hotel room in Moshi.'

'And why would they want to do that?' his father says.

'Because . . .'

The words stop, despite all of his prepared speeches. His mind freezes.

'What's Flo arranged?' The question bursts out before he can stop it.

His father looks pleased. 'A visit to several local schools and a tour of a coffee plantation. She asked for some suggestions from a friend of mine, who lives in Tanzania. Florence genuinely wants to make a positive impact on the communities we visit and to be a traveller rather than a tourist. I admit, in some of our clients' cases – no names mentioned – they need steering in the right travel direction, but I agree with Florence that it's important that we become less inward-looking. We've been international leaders for a long time now and we need to diversify to maintain our place at the top. Ethical Getaways is giving back to the planet and making travel morally OK.'

He looks at Jacob sorrowfully. It makes him want to punch Hugo in the face.

'We should've acted first,' Hugo continues. 'It's about being better than the competition, Jacob. It's about always staying one step ahead. That's your job. I built this company up. You, Flo and Luke have one job: to move with the bloody times. I'm old. You're young. It shouldn't be this difficult. We must be seen to be doing whatever the right thing is at the right time. Our – your – finger should be on the pulse.'

He always does this; he twists things round. Jacob wanted BVT to modernise and had been suggesting exactly these types of changes, long before Saint Bloody Florence appeared on the scene.

'There's more to this, isn't there?' Jacob says. 'Why did you pick me when you're always so ready to tear my ideas down? Sustainable travel is a subject I've brought to every strategy meeting for years now.'

'Well, perhaps you didn't explain it well enough. And, as I reiterate every year to everyone who is picked, and I'll repeat it again as you don't seem to fully grasp what I'm saying: success is about leadership and making the right decisions at the right time. It's not gambling, it's about calculated risks.'

And there we have it, yet again. That very fine line between love and hate that Jacob so often experiences.

'Why don't we take it a step further then,' he jokes, 'and couch-surf? That way we'd be proper travellers, not tourists, by meeting and staying with locals rather than lining the pockets of big hotel chains.'

Jacob knows full well that Hugo will avoid this approach at all costs.

'And have you planned such a thing? I'm not messing with itineraries in an ad-hoc fashion. It's not how we roll; it's most certainly not professional and you jolly well know it.'

Jacob takes a sip of coffee. Already, it's cold.

His father is wrong. The clients will love his glamping trip. Florence is blatantly virtue-signalling and Hugo's too blind to see it. It's got eff all to do with supporting the local community. He's conveniently forgotten that Jacob ran the London Marathon last year and raised a small fortune for ActionAid. He reckons that even if he wrote a list detailing all he's done for BVT, Hugo would still expect even more from him.

'By the way,' Hugo says, standing up, 'find out what Ethical Getaways' latest game is. I've also mentioned it to Florence because I need to know as soon as possible. Now, we need to prepare for today's trip. Chop, chop. I'm glad we're visiting a museum and a church – it's too hot to spend all day outdoors. I believe it was Florence who suggested these ideas to the hotel concierge.'

Does Hugo believe that by visiting a church his sins will be cleansed? Jacob has only been inside a church once (weddings, funerals and christenings aside), when he was desperate. He'd planned to slip in unnoticed, but a priest tried to make sympathetic eye contact. It was intrusive, not comforting. Too self-conscious to attempt a prayer, he lit a candle, silently wishing for some solution to his problem. The candle expired in a pool of wax.

So, it definitely didn't help. Then again, sometimes, nothing or no one can.

THREE

Florence

Nairobi, Kenya to Moshi, Tanzania

O ur party of seventeen is stuck in an executive airport lounge, having already eaten our complimentary second breakfasts. The flight is delayed by over two hours. It's not how I anticipated our stopover in Nairobi would end. Three of the clients have asked me if there's anything I can do to speed up the Wi-Fi.

Answer? Nothing.

Acceptance has finally filtered through that we're here for the duration, and they've all settled down with movies, books or phones to while away the time. I sink into a chair in front of a window facing the runway, my back to everyone.

A moment's peace. Thank God.

I take a sip of my second coffee – so far – while eyeing the Buck's Fizz on the menu and wondering whether I can order one out of Hugo's earshot and pretend it's an orange juice. It's actually my birthday today. I unzip my handbag and take out the card my grandmother posted to me before I left home. Before I tear open the envelope, I study her familiar handwriting, feeling a rare pang of homesickness while trying not to think about the cards I won't receive this year.

To a wonderful granddaughter.

Inside is a voucher for a spa treatment. It makes me smile. She thinks I work too hard and don't spend enough time looking after myself. She's right, but I love my lifestyle and ambition is a good thing. 'Life will reward you if you work hard and take control of your own destiny,' my mother used to say. That all-too-familiar pang of loss and grief hits. Sometimes, I worry that I will forget the sound of her voice over time.

I'm in the middle of composing a thank-you text to my grandmother when a voice makes me start.

'Happy birthday, my dear,' says Hugo, taking the chair next to me.

'Thank you. How do you know it's today?'

'Ways and means.'

Mandy must have mentioned the date to him as she oversees the sending out of cards and gifts, the value of which is dictated by the employee's current level of sales and customer satisfaction. It makes me wonder if he's had clandestine meetings with Mandy on this trip after making up some lame excuse to Sara. I don't like thinking about Sara and the secret we all keep from her, and yet I continue to do it. When I started at BVT eighteen months ago, I'd heard the rumours of the unofficial motto: work hard, play hard, don't fail. Once I'd found my feet, something deep inside me just clicked. I belonged somewhere with firm, long-established roots, and despite the competitiveness and long hours I felt I had a family, of sorts. A flawed one, admittedly, but compelling and oddly welcoming too. As long as I stuck to the rules.

I try to come up with an intelligent or insightful comment but nothing springs to mind, and so we sit in silence, apart from the sound of coffee beans grinding at the bar area. We both stare straight ahead. I watch a plane being loaded with cargo, rectangular shapes covered in packing tape and suitcases in varying sizes and colours gliding along a conveyor belt and disappearing into the belly of the aircraft. In the distance, another plane lifts into the air and is slowly swallowed up into the clouds.

'It was a shame our meeting was interrupted the other day,' Hugo says eventually, still staring ahead. 'There was more to say, but it was an important call and I had to take it. It ruined the moment, though.'

'What moment?' I ask.

'I have something of grave importance to tell you and you need to know why you are here. Why you were picked and what you're really playing for.'

'OK,' I say. 'Sounds ominous.'

Although Hugo is prone to exaggeration, I don't like the use of the word 'grave'. Unease expands in the pit of my stomach. Is he going to expect me to stab a colleague in the back or do something borderline illegal for a client? Working at BVT has blurred the lines between the person I am and the person I could become, if I'm not careful. I've already sat too close to the fire. I've not questioned BVT's less than conventional business practices, like their tough hiring and firing methods and ludicrously high sales targets, out of loyalty and gratitude for my sense of belonging to the BVT family, but sometimes I wish I had spoken up.

I wait, yet still Hugo doesn't meet my eye. He looks as though he's trying to find the right words, which is very out of character. I focus on our ghostlike reflections in the glass.

When I can't bear the silence any longer, I look down at my phone to calm my nerves. A now familiar photo of Kilimanjaro – snow covering the summit – fills my feed. It takes a few seconds before I realise that it's not one of us who has posted it, but Ethical Getaways. I read on, disbelieving. Several of their employees are also on their way to climb Kilimanjaro. Admittedly on the other side of the mountain to us because they're planning on climbing the northern Rongai route. But still.

Proof that you can travel without destroying the planet . . .

It's hard to digest all the supposed good deeds they've crammed into the post. In short, they are trying to steal our thunder and, by the look of things, have already done a bloody good job of it.

'A word, please.'

I look up to see Jacob standing over Hugo, his phone clutched in his left hand. Clearly, he's just seen the same post.

'I've found out what Ethical Getaways is up to,' I say, holding up my phone, desperate to get the first word in.

'Yes,' says Jacob, glaring. 'So have I. It's not that difficult when you've got your eye on the ball.'

And then we both speak at once, like teachers' pets determined to get the gold star.

'We're happy to announce that the flight to Kilimanjaro International Airport is now ready to board. Please make your way to the boarding gate.'

Saved by the bell. More than ever now, I'm determined to win.

Hugo shrugs. 'You both know what to do.'

As I slide my phone into the side compartment of my carry-on bag, I notice that I've left the main section unzipped. It bothers me because I'm very safety conscious. If I'm slipping, it means the stress really is getting to me.

I climb the wobbly boarding stairs at the rear of the plane, clutching on to the handrail, the heels of my sandals clinking. A crew member says, 'Please wait,' and I lift my face to the sky and enjoy the gentle breeze.

I turn and watch Hugo and his third wife approach. Sara walks in terrifyingly high heels, swinging a Louis Vuitton vanity case. Her cream hat perfectly matches Hugo's Panama. A gust of wind blows her hat off her ash-blonde hair, sprayed into a tight bun, and we all watch as it rolls along the ground.

Casper, VIP client and old school friend of Jacob's, dashes after the hat, retrieves it and hands it to her. This trip may be a bit too incestuous; friends and business are a dangerous mix. For this reason, I persuaded Hugo to place Imogen in Jacob's team. She and I get on well enough, but I don't want to have to deal with her many food requirements. It makes me cringe when she passes on tips to the waiting staff for the chefs, and I feel as though I should apologise for her.

Sara gives a large, red-lipsticked smile of thanks as she puts on her hat, pinning it down with one hand. Ruby earrings dangle from her ears and the sun briefly catches the gold chain around her neck. Hugo and Sara reach the bottom of the steps and their footsteps clatter against the metal as they approach me.

Jonessa, Casper's fiancée, her face half-hidden by her outsize

Versace sunglasses, strides towards the aircraft alone while Casper hovers by the bags. It looks as though he and Jacob are having a disagreement, and I can guess it's because Casper's luggage didn't make it to Nairobi. His precious walking boots were in his checked-in luggage – what experienced traveller does that? – and he's blaming BVT. Naturally. Those two have an odd relationship if you ask me. They put on this 'old friends' act and yet they seem wary around each other.

'Excuse me, madam? You may board now.'

'Thank you.'

I locate my seat and push my cabin bag beneath the seat in front. It's a squash but I like to keep my things close by. I gaze out the window. The rest of our clients – Adrian, Russell, Lara, Imogen, Hettie and Shona – board as a group. They think they won this trip in a raffle at one of our legendary parties. Invitations are highly sought after. Fact is, they were hand-picked by Hugo, as is the norm. Certain clients make up twenty per cent of BVT's business. The 80/20 rule most definitely applies in our case.

Mr and Mrs Armstrong are bumping along the tarmac in a buggie. This isn't out of necessity; they're both perfectly fit and well. It's a status thing. They asked me if they could be helicoptered on to Kilimanjaro, rather than having to climb. For real. Fortunately, it's not advised, regardless of how much money is offered, due to the need to ascend slowly to avoid mountain sickness. There's no fast track to the mountain, which is good. It means the teams are as even as they can be.

There are at least ten empty seats, I reckon, as I look around. A harassed family with a baby and twin toddlers in matching mauve dresses board with multiple bags. Luke, who is walking behind them, helps stow away their paraphernalia. I switch off, forcing myself to focus on creating decent content to post ASAP. Jacob will be doing the same thing, for sure.

As I get to work on some short videos promoting the charities we're supporting, I emphasise the fact we're deter-mined to be travellers, not tourists, without ramming home the difference. This is something that has been eating away at my conscience and it gnaws again. I love what I do but I can't ignore the fact that so much of what I get involved in is OTT. Not everywhere we visit practises sustainable tourism. I feel that BVT should be doing even more to facilitate this, though I can't deny that now I've been immersed in luxury and privilege, it has gotten harder to stick to what I believe in, like gradually sinking in cashmere quicksand.

'Mind if I sit next to you?' Luke says when he's finished stowing baggage.

I'd prefer he didn't. But then, I catch a waft of Luke's aftershave and déjà vu hits. George, Luke's best work buddy, wore a similar one. For a moment, I expect to see him here boarding the aircraft with us too.

'You can hold my hand if you get scared,' Luke says, sitting down, mistaking my non-response for a yes.

'Ha, ha,' I reply and look out of the window.

The last straggle of passengers is boarding. Mainly tourists, by the looks of things.

'I think you're in my seat,' I hear Mandy say.

I turn my gaze away from the window and see Mandy clutching a printed boarding pass which she holds face out to show Luke that she's right.

'Sorry,' he says. 'Do you mind sitting in the row in front of us?' He points it out. 'The seats are free. It doesn't look as if there are many more to board. They've shut the rear door.'

Mandy looks unsure as she studies the vacant row, as if to check what he's saying is in fact correct. I notice she looks pale; it's obvious she's been quite ill.

'Are you all right to fly, Mandy?' I ask.

'Yes,' she says. 'Probably better if I'm sitting alone, though, just in case I need to use the sick bag.'

'I understand,' I reply, relieved, if I'm honest. 'But let me know if you feel unwell again.'

I met Mandy at a tennis club, and we hit it off. I was perfectly happy and successful in my position as head of a large team and had won the most awards out of any employee in the company's history. I was aware of BVT, naturally – who wasn't, in the industry? – but I was comfortable where I was. My tour-guide colleagues and I were a close-knit team. Mandy persuaded me that I'd be mad to turn down an opportunity to work under Hugo's tutelage. I could learn from one of the best, she said.

I take out the passenger safety card and study it. The plane is a twin jet, similar to the 737. Something I've learned since working at BVT is that you can't reach the secret, privately owned hidden places, the world-beyond-your-wildest-dreams kind of exclusive hideouts, if you fear flying. Tiny planes, helicopters, sea planes, planes I've had to skydive out of because a client didn't want to jump alone . . . These are just some of the transport options I've had to endure.

I've learned that it's best to embrace the fear, turn a blind eye, ignore the turbulence, the unfamiliar noises, and try to enjoy the magnificent views, because it makes life easier. And more fun. Usually. Prior to being invited on the Great Escape,

I've experienced hairy moments on normal work trips, like sitting in the back of a Mini, whizzing around hairpin bends in Italy, clutching an open bottle of Krug and two glasses by the stems because the clients wanted to celebrate when we arrived at their favourite viewpoint. They needed a sober driver (me) for the return. Needless to say, their favourite movie was *The Italian Job*. I've arrived at a castle in Switzerland in a Lamborghini, slept in a treehouse under the stars in Cairns, been driven in a sidecar in the south of France, gone dune-bashing in a 4x4 in Dubai, scuba-dived off mega yachts – the list goes on. Whatever the client wants, the client gets. That's our USP: specialised one-to-one service. For a price, we can accompany our clients on their trips rather than simply being on the end of a phone. To give it up and return to a life of being a head tour guide, or only booking holidays for other people, feels like giving up on life. Not many people get to climb Kilimanjaro for work. The world, almost literally, is my office.

Our danger money is paid under the guise of client satisfaction bonuses. The insurance bill for BVT is pretty hefty, according to Jacob. He likes to pepper conversations with hints at his inner knowledge to cement his place as The Future Leader. Like we need any reminders.

'Are you nervous?' asks Luke.

I don't know if he means the flight, the entire trip, or both.

'No,' I say, not turning to look at him.

Showing vulnerability is a weakness that will be sniffed out and taken advantage of at BVT. The thing about Luke, however, is that he's good to mull things over with. I've sometimes thought that he'd make a good therapist. Not that I'd ever tell him that.

The aisle-sitters don't know what they're missing, I think, as I watch the last-minute flurry of pre-flight fuelling and baggage loading. The aircraft doors close and the safety briefing commences. The engines start, sending a shudder through me. If I'm being honest, I would prefer a larger plane every time, even though I don't believe that size matters when it comes to safety. A lorry can crash just as easily as a Smart car.

Our plane pushes back and I feel a surge of excitement for the week ahead, despite everything. As we taxi towards the runway, a crew member asks Imogen behind me to fasten her seat belt; she responds by demanding a vodka. I peer through the gap in the seats and see Hettie (head of corporate travel arrangements for a global bank) fish around in a plastic bag and remove a bottle of duty-free Amarula. She offers it to Imogen, who studies the label first before unscrewing the cap and taking a swig. The vibrations intensify and we speed up, the Jomo Kenyatta International Airport sign and the unlit runway edge lights shooting past us.

As we lift into the air, my stomach drops. Below, life continues. A main road snakes through the dry countryside. Cars and trucks crowd the streets as the drivers go about their daily lives.

'Shall I order us a couple of glasses of champagne?' says Luke.

'No, thanks. Too early for me. I'll go for coffee – decaf – or herbal tea.'

'Are you sure?' he says. 'You know what they say about all work and no play?'

The thought of potential hardship ahead persuades me to grab at luxury while I still can.

'Go on, then. Just a small glass.'

Alcohol might take the edge off. And it is my birthday, after all.

'Champagne, please,' I hear Luke order from the drinks trolley. 'Two glasses.'

The champagne is chargeable, which will no doubt be put on his company card. To be fair, if you're successful, a couple of glasses of bubbly aren't going to be held against you. If you're not . . . woe betide.

Luke is currently single. He says his lifestyle isn't conducive to a long-term relationship, as much as he'd like one. I have my doubts, although I understand where he's coming from. I can't imagine telling Hugo that I couldn't work late to sort out an issue on the other side of the world because I have plans with my other half. Jacob seems to manage it all right, but Clarabelle is very accommodating.

Luke's hand touches mine as he hands me a glass of bubbles. The contact is oddly comforting.

We raise our glasses.

'Cheers.'

'Magic, isn't it?' he says. 'Beats working for a living.'

And that's the thing. Despite the drawbacks, the fact is, there are worse jobs. One of my friends is out of work at the moment and she's struggling to find another job within the travel industry that pays enough. I've suggested she move in with me if it helps her out for a while.

I get a sudden urge to stretch my legs. Curiosity from my unfinished conversation with Hugo lingers. Being trapped in a small aircraft seat isn't helping. I really need everything to go smoothly once we land at Kilimanjaro International Airport: the cars, the welcome drinks at the hotel, the rooms with the requested views of the mountain.

'Excuse me,' I say, placing my plastic glass down on the pull-down table.

A flash of annoyance crosses Luke's face as if he'd thought we were settled down for a good tête-à-tête. Still, he stands up, clutching his glass of champagne, and asks a crew member to move the trolley to let us out. I pick up my handbag, ease myself out of the narrow seats then make my way to the back, where, according to Hugo, 'the smokers used to hang out, back in the good old days'. I can't imagine it now. Hugo still smokes – although it's mainly the occasional cigar – and he claims that the smokers were always the most fun.

'I spent many a flight huddled at the back, cognac in hand, making friends and drumming up business,' he's told me more than once. 'Glorious.'

Right now, Hugo and Sara are sitting in the front row of seats. To their right are Mr and Mrs Armstrong. Behind them are Jacob and Clarabelle, then Casper and Jonessa. The four couples.

Russell, Adrian, Lara and Shona are taking up the old smokers' position, standing by the rear doors, drinking.

'Care to join us?' asks Shona. 'We're on rum and Coke.'

She is the most down-to-earth out of all our clients. As an executive for a big European pharmaceutical company, she's a frequent traveller, so her opinion counts for a lot in her firm. She's quick to put in a complaint to us if she's disappointed with any aspect of her travels but they're always fair, not petty. I like her.

Lara, Russell and Adrian smile their encouragement.

'Thanks,' I say, 'but I have a drink waiting at my seat and I think I'd better stick to the one.'

I smile, hoping I came across as professional and friendly,

rather than aloof. It's a fine balance. Adrian is a new client for BVT. He and his business partner, Lara, run a successful company specialising in memorable gifts . . . days out at the races, romantic lunches in Paris, theatre trips, dinner in posh hotels . . . They've confided in Luke that they feel the pressure to come up with bigger, better, more daring and unique experiences, hence their hefty travel budget while they explore potential options. Kilimanjaro has been on their bucket list and they were delighted to be contacted by Mandy about this trip.

Hugo has asked me to keep an eye on Adrian and Lara. Poachers come in many guises.

Jacob weaves his way up the aisle to join us. I'm not surprised. He won't like that I'm here mingling without him.

'Hi,' he says, with a big grin.

I smile at him. We're good at maintaining a united front whenever clients are around.

Russell takes a sip of his drink. I'm not sure what he does, exactly. Apparently, he was transferred to the UK by his Australian company. He's one of those mysterious 'works in IT' sort of people. I've only met him twice and both times were at BVT parties. Each new season, BVT hosts a lavish, invitation-only party for our VVIPs. This is the carrot to be dangled if clients ever use the words 'budget' or 'looking for ways to bring down travel expenses'. Our guests love the office's swish surroundings, the plunge pool and indoor mini-beach, the exotically named cocktails, the organic wines, the nibbles made by a top chef. They think they've #madeit.

'I reckon that the airplane toilet will be luxury compared to what we'll have halfway up Kili,' he says.

'True,' I agree.

We all laugh.

'I've been reading about the long-drop toilets which are essentially holes in the ground,' Russell adds.

'I reckon it will be easy enough to go behind a rock,' says Adrian.

'I've brought a trowel along with me,' says Shona.

'A trowel?' Adrian queries.

'Think about it,' Shona replies. 'I'm not spelling it out.'

'Oh!' says Adrian, then we all laugh awkwardly.

'We've arranged for two toilet tents per camp,' I say. 'It will be fine.'

Meanwhile, I wonder how I will manage. I like my privacy; I need a certain amount of downtime. Still, it's not like we're about to summit Everest.

'Speaking of toilets . . .' I say, excusing myself.

It's a relief to lock the door and hide away.

As I wash my hands, I catch sight of myself in the mirror. I appreciate that people complain about how they look in aircraft mirrors, almost as much as they do about the food, but I do look rough. It's not the image I want to portray so early in the trip, or ever. I pride myself on my professionally put-together image. This trip is different but still, the one thing I can control is my looks, good or bad. I unzip my bag and reach inside for my make-up pouch. But instead of soft canvas my hand touches something smooth and hard. A small box.

My mind jumps all over the place. Am I losing it so badly that I've forgotten what I packed in my own bag? Or has someone planted something on me as a prank? As I peer inside my bag, the plane jolts and I nearly fall over. I place my hand against the flimsy door and steady myself, fighting back the urge to be sick. The box is wrapped in crimson with a black ribbon.

My hands tremble so much that it's a struggle to untie the ribbon. Inside, a silver St Christopher on a pendant and a gift card written in Hugo's handwriting.

To Dearest Florence. Wishing you a wonderful birthday. Love, Dad.

Dad? My mind reels back over the past few hours and pauses on one thing. My unzipped bag in the terminal. Hugo's awkwardness. His words: 'grave importance'.

Oh my God.

It can't be true. But if it is, this means that for the past eighteen months I've been under an even bigger microscope than I could possibly have imagined. My father moved from out of the shadows and into my life and I never suspected a thing.

Oh. My. God.

I try and put the pieces together, but nothing quite matches. Dates, times, places, comments, the potted history provided by my mother, the distinctive wrapping paper for my birthday gifts . . .

Someone bashes on the door.

'Are you all right?' Luke's voice.

'Fine,' I call out. 'Just a bit travel sick.'

I close my eyes. Then, I really am sick.

The seat belt sign illuminating makes me jump. I rinse out my mouth, and as I do so a violent rage hits. Who the hell does Hugo think he is, playing games like this?

I emerge, keeping my expression neutral.

Jacob is looking at photos on Russell's phone with a politely interested expression. 'Cute kids.'

Everything looks normal. And yet, for me, everything has been turned upside down.

'Please can you sit down and put on your seat belt,' says a crew member, approaching us.

'Sure.' My response emerges automatically, and my voice doesn't even sound like my own. I can't bear to look ahead to the front of the plane, I can't bear to see him, I can't bear to give him the satisfaction of knowing he's got to me.

It's utter bollocks, I now realise, that he didn't have time to speak to me. He didn't have the guts. He must've known I'd most likely need something from my bag during the flight and by doing it while I'm trapped on a plane – on show, in front of clients – I can't make a fuss. What the actual fuck? Does he think that by the time we've landed I'll be calm? No, Hugo is clever and calculating, and if he wants me to find out now, in this way, there's a reason.

If Hugo wants games; I'll give him games.

I make my way to my seat, holding on to the head rests to steady myself as the plane rocks. I'm still the same person I was half an hour ago, but now any joy or relief at discovering my father's identity is tinged with rage and horror.

'Feeling better?' asks Luke, as I manoeuvre myself back into my seat.

I nod, downing the entire glass of champagne.

Happy fucking birthday to me. I crane my neck to spot Hugo through the gaps between the seats. How on earth am I supposed to *be* around Hugo, or Sara? She is so different from my mother – a hardworking, proud woman who gave me everything she could and more. Another wave of sickness hits at the thought of my whole life being a big lie. Fresh facts intermingle, tainting memories. I'd thought I was an only child. Hugo is the man my mother feared, not the warm, kind father I always dreamed would materialise out of the blue one day. He is also the man who denied me a proper father growing up. He is my boss.

A PA announcement from the pilot rings out. 'As we drop beneath the clouds, those of you on the left-hand side of the aircraft can catch sight of Kilimanjaro.'

Despite the illuminated seat belt signs, several passengers on the right climb out of their seats and crane their necks to catch a glimpse of the snow-capped mountain. Its dark brown ridges become clearer through wisps of cloud, hanging majestically. I study the view in awe, all the while becoming increasingly aware of my own insignificance. As we descend, buildings, trees and roads come into view among the green patchwork of land. The touch-down is smooth, an almost perfect landing. I swallow hard.

As we taxi, I spot several airlines plus a blue and white Air Tanzania plane with a giraffe painted on the tail. The sign for Kilimanjaro International Airport fills me with reassurance. I need to get off the plane and into my room as quickly as possible, to gather my thoughts and adjust my plans. I came here to win, to make my mark, to see for myself exactly what happens on these annual trips. I didn't realise I was going to find the answer to the biggest question mark that has been hanging over me my whole life. Hugo. My *father*. It still isn't sinking in.

Immigration is smooth and quick. Even so, my heart pounds as our passport pages are flicked through, half anticipating a problem with the visas. None, thank God. Among the waiting drivers, I spot three holding up signs: *Blackmore Vintage Travel*. Relief floods through me. I called twice from Nairobi to ensure we didn't have any more mishaps. Jacob should watch out. I fight fire with fire.

I fall into step with Hugo and Sara on the way out of the airport.

'Good flight?' I ask with a smile, determined not to give anything away.

'Excellent,' says Hugo.

I wonder if he's dying to ask if I've found the gift and the note. Still, he's doing a good job of hiding his emotions – as am I. Strange to think that less than an hour or so ago I was preoccupied with limousines, rooms with views and welcome drinks.

We pull away from the airport and leave the perimeter with its ornate green gardens and colourful hedges, heading on to a tree-lined main road leading to Moshi, the regional capital of Kilimanjaro.

As we approach the city, the road gets busier and motorbikes and tuk-tuks weave through the traffic. Pedestrians walk by on an adjacent well-worn path, many carrying heavy loads.

The sights are a welcome distraction. We crawl past market stalls selling fresh produce, green and yellow bananas hanging alongside trays of melons, limes and pineapples. I love travelling to places I haven't been before. Billboards advertise the usual worldwide: washing powder, Coke, beer, banking. I catch sight of a restaurant promoting black tea, cappuccino, roast chicken and meat bone soup, among a variety of juices and ice-cream. A small stall set up under an umbrella has a sign which reads *Shoe Shine*. A woman sits outside a shop feeding red fabric into her sewing machine.

I take out my phone and surreptitiously study pictures of my mother, Hugo and Jacob, looking for family resemblances.

It's hard to say. My hair is brown, Hugo's hair is darker and is flecked with grey. Jacob's eyes are green, like mine. Our noses are different. I googled Hugo's wider family before I joined the company. He has two more sons, Tom and Dan, with his second wife. They are two and four years younger than Jacob. He has a son and a daughter with Sara, aged eight and six. Sara doesn't like to share images of them online, so I don't really know what they look like. I've never really given it any thought, never cared. Why would I?

I've never particularly taken to Jacob, and now I find that I'm related to him it has sent my mind into a total spin. I will be forced to look at him differently. He's the sort of person who would hold his wedding abroad in a six-star hotel and make you feel guilty at the mere hint that you couldn't afford to fork out for it. He would then have the audacity to send a gift list where the minimum spend was five hundred quid for some kitchen gadget that he and Clarabelle (she's too nice for him) would toss in a drawer to be forgotten about.

I receive a message from Hugo.

Mandy requested welcome G & Ts. Double-checked this is set up? Mrs Armstrong is dying for one. It would be a shame to disappoint her.

I have a moment of panic. I consult Mandy's list. Confirmed by the hotel yesterday. Thank God.

Yes, I reply.

As I go through my many lists – croquet on the lawn with sundowners this evening, social media updates, chasing up Casper's still-missing suitcase – Luke's voice interrupts.

'Are you all right? You look a bit pale.'

'Fine,' I reply automatically.

Still, I take out the mirror from my make-up bag to check my face. I see Hugo looking back at me. Then I glance to my right and see Jacob tapping furiously on his phone and it properly dawns – no, smacks me in the face – that my rival is my own brother. Only I don't think he knows it yet.

FOUR

Jacob

Moshi

The view from their hotel balcony is pure heaven, clichéd as that may sound. Waking early to see the sun rise, Jacob stares at Mount Kilimanjaro, pleased that it looks exactly as it does in the pictures. Streaks of snow cover its crest. Bathed in early-morning light, it's majestic. It has its own unpredictable weather pattern, something Jacob read in a guidebook on the plane from London. Seeing it for real makes him keen to refresh his memory.

The approximate distances, heights and names of camps appear to differ slightly from book to book. But from what he's learned overall, Kilimanjaro is a dormant volcano, created by three volcanic cones, Kibo, Mawenzi and Shira, and is the highest free-standing mountain in the world and one of the seven summits. What's so incredible, however, is that you don't need any specialist equipment to climb it. No ropes, no ice picks, no specialist training. It's potentially accessible to old and young alike. Still, apparently nearly a third of all those who attempt it don't make it, mainly because of altitude sickness. He blanked it out the first time he read it, but reading it again, it's a sobering thought.

As much as it leaves a bitter taste in his mouth, Jacob caved in and agreed that both teams should visit the coffee plantation and schools and explore the local area instead of the awesome safari he'd booked. It was put to the vote on the croquet lawn and they all went with Flo's 'amazing idea'. Jacob reluctantly let Florence win the first battle because he means to win the annual challenge war. It may even work to his advantage if it lulls her into a false sense of security. He's seen it so many times on the football pitch when a team goes from being three goals up to eventually losing five–three. It's never wise to underestimate the underdog.

Even so, Hugo's criticism still hurts like a punch in the gut. Jacob can't get his words out of his head. *Success is about leadership and making the right decisions.* He keeps reliving the conversation, going over all the things he should have said in response.

It's the unfairness of Hugo's comments that really gets to him. He feels stifled. He wishes they hadn't booked so many days' rest to 'acclimatise' because he'd like to start the hike up the mountain today, get it over and done with. The Winner (him) will be whisked off with all the clients to a luxury resort in Dar es Salaam. The Loser (Florence) will fly back home and back to work (if she's lucky), tail well and truly between her legs. He wasn't going to smoke once they left Nairobi. In fact, he was going to use this trip as an opportunity to give up completely, but he can't resist one final one. He sinks down on to a sun lounger and relishes every single drag.

He takes one last look at the mountain and steps back into the room. Clarabelle is still asleep in pretty much the same position as last night, back facing him. It's one of the reasons he can't see a marriage between them working: the passion is already cooling. If he's honest, he felt under pressure to propose, his best effort was recorded for several reels of Insta. Clarabelle was thrilled. *The most likes ever! Maybe you should propose every day, Honey.* Jacob doesn't think she was joking. She's used to getting what she wants. Her family is wealthy but they're warm, loving, generous and not stingy like Hugo. Clarabelle's not expected to work for it, or even get out of bed early.

Irony is, she earns more than Jacob as an influencer. Her apartment doorbell buzzes frequently throughout the day as yet more mystery parcels arrive. Jacob hears her talking to the camera about 'this darling that' and 'that amazing value the other'. He shouldn't mock it. She's lent him money without the third degree. More than can be said for others. Clarabelle's a good person. He can't end things because he's trapped. Story of his life.

In the shower, he fantasises about winning the EuroMillions. He'd love to see Hugo's face when he tells him to stick his job. In one fortunate moment all his problems could be solved. He'd be generous and share his winnings. He'd do good. Things like paid internships at BVT and a support group to help people with unwieldy debt, gambling or otherwise. It's a total load of crap, he believes, when people imply that it isn't necessarily a blessing to win money. How can it not be? Throw enough money at any problem and it becomes the fictional equivalent of a magic wand.

He shrugs himself into the hotel's white waffle robe, then

picks up the phone on the desk and orders room service breakfast. A cheese and mushroom omelette with hash browns for him, and for Clarabelle, an egg white and spinach one, with hash browns – also for him.

He makes her a tea and places it on the bedside table.

'Morning,' he says.

She opens her eyes.

'I made you tea,' he says, pointing.

'Thanks.' She sits up. Her long blonde curls almost cover her peach pyjama top. She takes a sip. 'Honey,' she says, 'I'm not going to come today. I have a stomach ache and I want to go to the spa, hang by the pool and post fresh content. My followers are dying to see what I'm up to.'

'Sure,' he says, half-relieved but remembering to look disappointed. 'I've ordered you an omelette.'

'Thanks, but you can have mine too. I'm not that hungry,' she replies. 'I'll grab something by the pool later.'

She picks up her phone, starts scrolling and then telling Jacob about a celebrity he's never heard of who is pregnant.

There's a knock on the door. A hotel staff member stands clutching the most enormous tray laden with mini sauce bottles, including ketchup and mustard, a silver rack of toast and the omelettes. Jacob tips with US dollars; part of his trip preparation had been to help himself to various currencies from the BVT safe.

He switches on the TV, but the news is depressing and he doesn't fancy watching football or golf, the only things on offer, so he switches it off and eats in silence. He sends messages to several of his clients – Happy Birthdays, Good lucks and such-like. Jacob's got a good memory and it never harms to use the personal touch. That done, he scrolls through his feeds.

Shit, bloody Ethical Getaways are doing a giveaway, a long weekend camping trip in a yurt. Why didn't he think of that? Not the yurt, BVT can do way better than that, but a giveaway to encourage donations rather than merely appealing for charity funds.

He scrolls through his online efforts and feels embarrassed.

Then he looks at Flo's efforts, which, to his delight, aren't much better. Thinking about it, she hasn't been quite herself since the flight over. She picked at her food more than usual last night and didn't seem to be focusing on the conversations around the dinner table. Again, unusual. Florence is a good conversationalist, he must admit. Maybe she's caught the same bug as Mandy. Christ, he hopes there isn't something going round. Last thing he needs. Regardless, he needs to focus, come up with something bigger and better. And then it comes to him. He has access to someone on the inside of Ethical Getaways. A person who can, at times, be loose-tongued. He fires off a message, feeling better the moment he presses send. He stares at his phone for several seconds, half-expecting an immediate reply. Nothing happens and doubt begins to seep in.

Time to get moving, Jacob, he thinks. *What's done is done.*

He often talks to himself in this way.

Once dressed, in shorts, a T-shirt with a climate change slogan (he's wilier than he's given credit for) and his favourite burgundy baseball cap, he picks up his wallet, sunglasses, room key and backpack. He opens the door, then, out of a sense of guilt, he walks over to the bed where Clarabelle is dozing again and gives her a goodbye kiss on the cheek.

'Have a nice day,' she murmurs without opening her eyes.

Maybe she wants to call it a day too. Perhaps she'll do so without him having to look like the bad guy.

Jacob is one of the last to arrive. Hugo gives him a pointed look as he joins their assembled group in the crowded lobby. Near the reception desk, Sara is in deep conversation with the Armstrongs. A porter navigates through the hotel guests wheeling a brass luggage trolley, piled high with bags in varying colours and sizes. Casper and Jonessa are sitting on a leather sofa, Casper's arm around her shoulders. On the coffee table in front of them is a folded newspaper. Russell, Adrian and Luke are watching something on Adrian's phone. Every now and then, they all burst out laughing and one of them says, 'No way, man!' Jacob feels like the odd one out as he sinks into a chair near Casper and Jonessa.

'Any news on my delayed luggage?' Casper says. 'Will it turn up today?'

No *Good morning*. No *How are you?*

Sometimes, Jacob detests Casper.

'That's Flo's department,' he reminds him.

'Really? Where is she?' Casper looks around as if she is going to appear genie-like to smooth over his troubles.

For once, Jacob wishes Flo was here. He's about to message her, when he spots her speaking to the concierge before she strolls over to the main group, clutching four see-through plastic carrier bags, two in each hand, filled with children's books, notepads and colouring pencils.

Luke rushes over to help her but a doorman beats him to it. Jacob watches him load them into the boot of a 4x4.

'Cars are ready,' Florence announces. 'Mr and Mrs Armstrong, you're in the front one.'

Florence appears slightly off-key, her smile fake.

Jacob hopes that the pressure is getting to her. He rolls his eyes at Jonessa and Casper behind Flo's back. Jonessa grins.

Casper frowns. He's turning into a right stick-in-the-mud. Casper was the life and soul back at school. Too much so, but he's gone from one extreme to the other. Jonessa told Jacob in confidence that Casper's ultimate dream in the distant future is to become Prime Minister, so he's keen not to make any mistakes that could come back to haunt him. They were at the gym at the time and Jacob nearly fell off the exercise bike. Casper really is living in a dream world. He's no more prime minister material than Jacob is.

The morning flies by and OK, Jacob is forced to admit, the school visit was heart-warming. He learned the words for welcome (*karibu*), nice to meet you (*nafurahi kukuona*) and goodbye (*kwa heri*). He's glad Clarabelle didn't come. She's broody and there's no way he could deal with a baby right now when his own life is such a mess.

At the coffee plantation, they huddle in the shade of banana trees and watch as the dried coffee berries are crushed inside a large mortar with a long pestle. When they're given a turn, Jacob is surprised how heavy it is. During the following demonstrations which cover the manual processes of milling the beans, sieving, then roasting them, Mandy whispers in Jacob's ear.

'Makes you realise that we don't really work hard, doesn't it?' she says.

She has stuck to Jacob's side throughout the day because obviously it's awkward that Sara is on this trip. She wasn't supposed to be, brazen as Hugo can be. Maybe Sara has an inkling, which is why she was a fairly last-minute addition to the trip. According to Sara, her parents offered to babysit when their nanny was off-duty.

'Would you like to try the coffee?' the guide asks.

Mandy declines the offer, stating that she still doesn't feel one hundred per cent and can only drink water.

Jacob sips from his mug and then places an order for several bags of a deliciously strong coffee which will need to be shipped home. He loves coffee – he has cappuccinos and espressos delivered to the office at least twice a day.

'Right, everyone, it's time to head back into the cars, please,' says Flo in her bossy tour-guide voice. 'We've got a fifty-kilometre drive for our lunch at a safari lodge over-looking Lake Chala. Some of you may already have looked it up, but for those who haven't, it's a crater lake at the border between Tanzania and Kenya.'

The coolness of the air-conditioned 4x4s is welcoming. Jacob sits next to Jonessa and their thighs touch. They inch away from one another, but it's not their fault that they are being thrown together by force. Casper, sitting at the window opposite Jacob, looks lost in thought.

Jacob doesn't know if Casper is regretting hitting the bar again last night or if he's fretting about his boots. Casper had a lucky pen at school for exams, he still has lucky socks and wears certain aftershaves for particular events. The boots situation will seem like a bad omen, not that he'll admit it. If he's being generous-minded, perhaps he also appreciates what's at stake for Jacob. Casper has always believed in mutual back-scratching, so Jacob is counting on his best effort to ensure that their team comes out on top.

Jacob would support Casper too, if need be, and yet he can't stop thinking about Jonessa. They shouldn't have done what they did at BVT's New Year's Eve party. It was a mistake, of course, a total one-off. A fresh new year can be a lonely time of regret and self-analysis. They both agreed on that.

Compartmentalise and move on. Which they did, because here they are. Jonessa is still happy enough with Casper and Jacob is still happy enough with Clarabelle. It's all fine. Blank it out.

Except . . . Casper doesn't believe in forgiveness. Jacob saw with his own eyes at uni what he did to someone who merely commented on the appearance of his then-girlfriend. The poor bloke left soon afterwards; it was only his second year. His silence was bought by Casper's family money covering some pretty hefty private medical bills. Jacob felt strangely envious because he never knew if Hugo would bail him out of trouble. On the plus side, it kept him on some sort of straight and narrow path.

Jacob's spine jars as the car hits a pothole on the dusty road particularly viciously. Jonessa smirks as he sits upright, soldier-like. Jacob thinks she enjoys having a secret. Maybe he's not her only one. The thought makes him feel strangely betrayed, which is pretty fucked up, really. Sometimes he's not a good person. He struggles to stay within the moral maze which other people seem to navigate perfectly well.

He takes out his phone and shares pictures from this morning. #paradise #sofarsogood #TeamJacob to win. He devises a trip that BVT can offer up as a giveaway without making it look like they're copying Ethical Getaways. Or the worst outcome, in Jacob's view, looking like they had their feathers ruffled by their rival. Publicly, Jacob's going for the 'And so what if it comes off as imitation?' approach. There's plenty of room for them on the mountain – for now, at least.

He checks on Clarabelle. She has posted pictures from their balcony during her early-morning yoga session. #gratitude #kilimanjaro. (She doesn't practise yoga, apart from the few poses she has memorised.) He stares out the window as he waits for responses to his posts. A group of children wave at them, calling out something he can't quite catch. They wave back. A long-forgotten memory hits Jacob. As a child, he used to love standing by a railway fence near his mother's house, waiting for trains he could wave at.

They splash through a shallow ford, droplets lightly hitting the windows. He watches them slide down the glass. Ahead, he sees the other cars disappear around a bend. Out of the blue, he's reminded of the toy snakes he loved as a child. He'd hold one by the tail and wave it at his mum, the plastic rectangles curving awkwardly side to side. He doesn't ever remember doing that with Hugo. Even at an early age, he must've sensed that Hugo was bored by him.

They pass a campsite, a mound of yellow, red and navy tents, just before they arrive at Lake Chala – 'a caldera, or large volcanic crater', as Flo has informed them. A reminder that Kilimanjaro is a dormant volcano. Out of the three volcanic cones, Mawenzi and Shira are extinct, but Kibo is dormant. Apparently, the most recent activity was over two hundred years ago, which is reassuring. Or not.

Regardless, Jacob can't wait to get out of the vehicle and stretch, but no sooner have they alighted than Florence is back in full tour-guide mode, herding them along a path towards the lodge. She's as overbearing as Hugo at times. Ahead, Jacob notices a vast expanse of blue lake, surrounded by hills smothered in green vegetation.

Casper falls into step alongside him and clears his throat.

'I need a walk before I sit down again,' he says. 'Fancy joining me? Jonessa says she's wearing the wrong shoes.'

Jacob glances over at her feet. She's wearing gold strappy sandals, with only a small heel. They look fine for walking in.

'Sure,' he replies.

There's something in Casper's voice that makes him feel as though he can't say no. He wishes he hadn't sat next to Jonessa in the car.

Casper has a word with their driver, who points to the left, away from the lodge.

'Anyone else fancy stretching their legs?' Jacob calls out, making desperate eye contact with Mandy.

Mandy hesitates but then Casper grabs Jacob by the upper arm and steers him away from the rest of the group.

'Keep moving,' says Casper. 'I want to talk to you in private.'

No one ever wants to talk to someone in private about anything good.

'You're not going to go on about your boots again, are you?' Jacob jokes.

'Ha, ha,' Casper replies, but he doesn't smile.

They make their way down a steep, well-worn path with a sheer drop at the side. Casper is behind Jacob and it's making him uneasy. Twice, he stumbles over small rocks.

By the time they reach the bottom, Jacob is sweating. However, the walk was worth it because the water is a stunning turquoise shade now they are closer. Glints of sun sparkle off the gently lapping ripples. They sit on a small boulder and remove bottles of water from their daypacks and take much-needed gulps. Shouts of delight come from several metres further down. Swimmers, splashing water. Then, silence apart from the odd bird chirping.

Jacob mentally reels through realistic-sounding denials, convinced this is about Jonessa.

'There's something I've been meaning to bring up,' Casper says, staring ahead.

Jacob's insides twist. No matter what Casper accuses him of, he will deny it.

'Fire away.'

'That ten grand you owe me? I need it back.'

Shit.

'Yeah, sorry about the delay on that. You know how it is,' Jacob says.

Casper is wealthy beyond his comprehension. He does not need Jacob to pay the money back. He reminds him of Hugo, in some ways. There's a hidden agenda behind everything he does.

'I'll sort it as soon as I'm back,' Jacob adds.

'Cheers.'

'We should head back up for lunch or Florence will give us a lecture on punctuality,' Jacob says, standing up.

He holds back at the beginning of the path to ensure that Casper is walking in front of him this time.

'Did you win much at the casino in Nairobi?' Casper asks.

Jacob stares at his back. A vertical stripe of sweat on his beige T-shirt. Beige. That's Casper nowadays, all right.

He can fuck off, it's none of his business. It's not easy to ask someone to lend you money. It takes a great deal of courage. It's humiliating to be put in a position to ask. Casper has no right to make him feel like a piece of shit. No right at all.

'I only popped into the casino because I met a bloke on the flight and said I'd meet him in there for half an hour,' Jacob says. 'I was just being friendly. I'm not much into betting any more.'

Casper doesn't respond. They trek up the bloody hill, which feels so much longer than the way down. Casper is a miserable git. So, he's pissed off about money because Jacob popped into a casino for a quick dabble. Like Jacob tells him how to spend his free time. He's not his nanny.

When they arrive at the restaurant, Jacob's mood sours further as he discovers the others are all waiting out on the patio because Florence didn't confirm the booking. It wasn't even him this time who messed up the arrangements. It was Florence, being incompetent.

'Don't worry,' Hugo tells Florence when she apologises to the group for the second time. 'These things happen.'

Not when 'these things happen' to him, thinks Jacob.

Still, once they're finally seated at a table with a view over the lake, he orders some bread and olives and perks up a little, reminding himself that every time Florence messes up it simply makes him look better.

Lunch is a blur, despite the stunning vista. Jacob is fighting the urge to speak out across the table in front of everyone and demand to be treated with respect by Casper and Hugo. It strikes him briefly that he's missed out on enjoying so many experiences because his mind is clouded with worry about this or that or the bloody other. The only silver lining is that Florence looks like she's inwardly screaming as Mr Armstrong regales her with a tale of his top walking-boot tips.

Jacob sits beside Mandy on the return journey. No sooner has the Jeep pulled away from their venue than her face goes slightly pale as she stares at her phone.

'What?' Jacob mouths.

Mandy tilts the screen in his direction. Ethical Bloody Getaways are not content with merely doing the same trip as them, albeit on the north-eastern side of the mountain, the Rongai route. Now they're supporting a project which promotes the fair treatment of the hard-working Kilimanjaro porters. They seem to be garnering a lot of interest and donations, already worryingly more than Jacob's managed so far.

Just because we're paranoid, he thinks, *it doesn't mean they're not out to get us.*

FIVE

Florence

Day One: Moshi to Machame Gate

After a broken night's sleep, I lie still for a few seconds, shivering. The air conditioning in the hotel room is icy but I can't bring myself to get up and adjust it. Never mind the temperature, I intend to cling on to the last moments of five-star luxury. Then it hits me afresh that Hugo is my father.

It still doesn't feel real.

Instead, like some kind of twisted Groundhog Day, I sift through the mental fragments and examine them for clues. Random moments from my past life jostle for space. Cryptic things my mother said, the anonymous gifts – especially the photo of my mother, sent after her funeral. She looked happy, and yet she was adamant that my father was bad. So bad, in fact, that his identity was kept a secret from me. But at some point she was happy. Or so Hugo wants me to think.

I message my grandmother, but end up mistakenly sending it to her landline on my first attempt.

I'm fine so please don't worry. But my boss, Hugo Blackmore, has dropped a total bombshell. It seems he's my biological father???!!! PLEASE tell me if Mum said anything. Please, be honest.

She responds within minutes:

I'm sorry, my love. I'm as much in the dark as you. If I knew anything, I'd tell you. I always imagined he was a big shot because your mother had her head well and truly turned. You just concentrate on keeping yourself safe. Gran x

Before I can reply another message comes through.

One more thing, my love. He doesn't sound like a nice man. And how do you know he's telling the truth? There was a crime drama on telly yesterday afternoon and it made me think about the fronts people can put on. Just keep your wits about you. Gran. X

I type back:

It's fine, Gran. There are lots of people on the trip. Flo x

She has a point, though, I think as I make my way to the bathroom and look in the mirror for what feels like the hundredth time, turning my head left and right. Am I his daughter? I frown. I run a finger along the bridge of my nose.

I can't see anything of Hugo in me but I do see my mum's eyes, and the rush of grief is like a punch in the stomach.

It's exhausting. My fractured night's sleep hasn't helped. I don't feel hungry, and yet I must pull myself together and focus on the days ahead. Deep down, despite my mental confusion, I do believe that my survival in the BVT world is dependent on winning. While I'm in the process of doing so, I will try and get as much truth out of Hugo as I can.

What is blatantly clear is the fact that Hugo waited until my mother died before he coerced, bribed or conned Mandy into befriending me. Then she went headhunting – or luring – me to join BVT. This makes sense to me now when I think of how super-friendly she was to me from day one. Whatever the finer details, Hugo, it seems, wanted me suitably ensnared in the family business before he was brave enough to reveal his identity. God, if I'm not in therapy for the rest of my life after what's happened over the past couple of years, it will be a miracle.

It's sickening to imagine that he was behind it all, pulling secret strings. I'd thought Mandy and I had a connection, my judgement about her affair with the boss aside. Now I wish I could think of a way to get her off my team. I was played from the moment I met her. I remember how she used to send clients our way for guided tours at my previous company. Clearly she was buttering me up for my father.

'Don't take this the wrong way, but day trips are small fry to us,' she explained when she called my then-boss. 'However, we pride ourselves on offering a comprehensive and flexible service, so we have to show willing.'

My then-boss, Rosemary, didn't like dealing with Mandy, said she was too 'abrasive' and would pass her on to me to set up whatever it was she needed organising. Mandy mentioned one day that there was a vacancy at BVT. Knowing what I know now, it was all so fake and casual; I can even recall the tone of her voice and I'm furious with myself that I didn't pick up on the fact that something was off.

'It's a VIP client liaison role. I think you'd be perfect,' she said.

Flattery works. The money helped too, nearly triple what I was earning. I should've smelled the hugest of rats right there and then. I was good at my job, yes – but not almost triple the money good. I realise that now.

Outside, dawn is breaking. Shades of pale orange and pink seep across the skyline. The peak of Mount Kilimanjaro, however, is invisible because it's covered in cloud. I hope it's not an omen.

God, I wish I could speak to my mother. People sometimes ask me how my mum died. Pneumonia, I tell them. I see their expressions relax a little, assuming that it's unlikely to happen to them or their loved ones. I'm probably just as guilty of doing this to other people, albeit unintentionally. We'd all like to be aware of what potential life dangers lie ahead. I don't tell them the whole story. That I couldn't visit her in hospital. I had to say goodbye via video call. I sat in my car in the hospital car park and hoped that she sensed I was nearby. Until now, I've done my best to bury the anger and sorrow by putting everything into my job.

Desperate to try and stop *thinking*, I pack, separating my belongings into two piles: stuff to be left for safekeeping by the hotel and the rest, my essentials for the mountain climb. I consult my packing list, the only way I will be able to get anything done.

Sleeping bag
Boots
Snow socks
Hiking poles
Water bottle/bladder/thermos
Inflatable pillow (nice to have, not essential)
Wet wipes
Balaclava
Sunscreen/insect repellent/first aid kit & medications/water
purifying tablets
Head torch
Crocs (for camp)
Batteries/power bank/camera/solar charger
Sunglasses
Snacks – fruit bars and dried mango
Beanie/sun hat
Gloves
Thermal base layers
Dry bags

My heart's not in it. I find myself dialling Hugo's number, but it cuts off immediately. I try again, same result. How dare he? Desperate for answers, I pick up my key card and phone, along with the St Christopher (which I haven't removed from its box) and head for Hugo's suite, still dressed in the tracksuit I wore to bed last night.

I knock on his door, beyond caring about being polite. A few days ago I wouldn't have dared step out of line. As I'm about to rap again, the door opens. Hugo is dressed in a white hotel robe. His hair is wet, and he smells of luxury toiletries.

'Good morning, Florence. To what do we owe the pleasure? Nothing wrong, I hope?'

As he frowns, his bushy grey eyebrows crease. A burst of confidence hits me, and I hand him the gift box I found in my bag.

'This isn't mine,' I snap, 'but I do believe it's yours.'

'My dear,' he says after a painful few seconds' wait. 'I'm delighted you found it. I decided it was much easier than explaining it.'

I realise now that I was half-expecting him not to admit it. I stride down the corridor before I stop, turn around and add, 'You've not given any proper proof that it's true. It's cruel to play games.'

No response. No apology. No begging for forgiveness. Tears form and I don't fight them as I reach the lift, return to my room, then firmly shut the door behind me.

Trying to focus on my packing, I separate my mountain essentials once again. Night items go in my duffel bag, which will be carried up the mountain by porters, and in my daypack are the essentials I will carry with me. But something is missing.

My diary. I use a slim black diary instead of a digital calendar. I like physical back-ups. Digital anything can disappear without warning.

I rummage inside my handbag, then open all the hotel drawers (even though I never use them). I check beneath cushions, down the side of the sofa. All the while, I know that deep down, it's futile. The diary is always in my bag, so what has happened to it?

A sudden horrible thought. What if I didn't imagine an intruder in Nairobi? What if there was someone there, hiding in the shadows, all along? I notice that I'm shivering slightly and now that I've become aware of it, despite putting on a fleece, I can't warm up. I turn off the air conditioning.

A little voice in my head niggles.

You could quit, both the job and the challenge. Go back to a different life. But to what? You can't forget what you know. You're here for a reason, to find the truth. You can't lose sight of that.

Thing is, ever since I decided to embrace my ambition, I've had to accept that there's room for improvement at BVT. There's a site called Invisible Travel Ink, or something along those lines, where employees can post insider gossip anonymously on what it's really like to work for a particular travel company. Before I joined BVT I did some digging.

I didn't check it again until fairly recently. Since the opening of Ethical Getaways, the comments have become increasingly accusatory, hinting that the owner of a supposedly respected travel firm has blood on their hands. They also mention ill-treatment of staff in some travel resorts abroad and apparently unethical employment contracts. I appreciate it doesn't mean it's true – the negative comments about various companies outweigh the positive – but there's been enough to make me poke around. Maybe I shouldn't have done my snooping on my work computer. If someone wants to know what I'm up to, then it means there's a reason. Just as there's a reason why my mother kept Hugo out of our lives.

An assertive rap on my door makes me jump.

'May I come in, my dear?'

'Don't ever call me my dear again,' I tell Hugo, as I step back to allow him in. I then add a 'please', immediately hating myself for it.

'Look,' my apparent father says, ignoring my request and raising his right hand as though he's about to swear to tell the truth in court, 'the timing's not ideal, I'll give you that. But I ask you, when would have been the right time?'

'Are you serious? From the moment I was born,' I say.

'It wasn't an option.'

'Why not? My mother told me that you weren't to be trusted.'

'It's all about perspective,' he says. 'Fact of the matter is that the relationship between your mother and me soured.'

'My mother wouldn't have had an affair with a married man.'

'Well, I thought my marriage was over. Like I've said, it's complicated.'

'Why the gift secretly shoved in my bag at an airport? Why now?'

'The reason this particular trip is so important is because I may gradually start to hand over the reins.' He pauses. 'Not completely. BVT will always be my company, but the person who wins will become my right-hand advisor and take over the company should anything ever happen to me. Obviously, we're talking about the top job here.' He clears his throat. 'Now, my dear – sorry – I mean, Florence. This is a delicate situation and I appreciate your confusion. You'll get your answers when we have a chance to talk properly, a real heart-to-heart, but here's the thing. Jacob is good at what he does, yes. But he doesn't excel. And there's a big difference.'

'He doesn't know about me?'

'No, I'll tell him when the time is right. The important thing is that you know the truth and that you know why I so desperately need you to understand.'

'I don't think I do.'

'All will be revealed,' he says. 'Trust me.'

'But I don't. What about Sara? Does she know?'

'You're the first and only one,' he says. 'No one else knows.'

I'm not interested in keeping his secrets for him.

'Please accept the gift in the spirit in which it was intended,' he says, handing me back the St Christopher.

I'm still in shock, taking it from him.

'Look, Florence. Good people don't always come out on top, it's not how life works. I needed to inject a little extra fire in your belly to make sure we get the outcome that will work best for us all, Jacob included. I'll have a judicious word with him when the time is right,' he says. 'Scout's honour. No point in upsetting the applecart so close to the climb, I think you'll agree?'

When I don't reply immediately, he adds, 'It's a win–win. Let me make everything up to you.'

I can't believe him. But I think he believes himself. He holds up an A4 envelope and hands it to me.

'This definitely isn't the time or the place, and I suggest you don't open it until after the trip because there's certainly a lot to digest, but perhaps this will help convince you. I've debated whether to share it or not. I still don't know if I'm doing the right thing, but it feels to me like you need proof. I know you probably won't take my advice, but remember, Florence, I'm older than you, and sometimes curiosity really does kill the cat.'

My phone pings. I glance over to the desk and as I do so, Hugo gives me a wave and lets himself out. The door clicks gently behind him. I put the gift box on the bed, alongside the envelope, resisting the urge to rip it open only because I suspect the contents may paralyse me.

It's only eight-thirty in the morning and the clients are asking me the same questions about what to pack, what to leave at the hotel, sending panicked lists of the items they've forgotten.

I send out the itinerary with essential items yet again, with reassuring comments.

Don't worry! ☺ That's what this morning's briefing is for. You can speak to the guides, and we can hire anything that's still needed. It will all be OK. This is going to be so much fun! See you in the function room in half an hour. Breakfast will be available during the talk. And remember – there's a twenty-kilo absolute maximum limit, the porters aren't allowed to carry anything heavier than that and your bags will be weighed at the park entrance gate. Fifteen kilos is preferable. Florence

These privileged adults all had extensive pre-departure lists which I sent twice, with reminders. I feel like a teacher on a camping trip where half the children have turned up in flip flops instead of trainers. Despite being used to this type of behaviour, inside, I'm screaming.

Casper texts me for the third time this morning to see if his boots have turned up. The message is pretty much the same as the first two.

One hopeful last message regarding my missing boots? Pretty please.

FFS. Casper is one of those people who think they are the only client and that my sole purpose on this trip is to look after him and solely him. I spoke to a traveller in the bar last night who was drowning his sorrows with Kilimanjaro beer after a failed summit attempt due to acute mountain sickness, meaning he had to be carried down to a lower altitude by two guides. As luck would have it, he and Casper are the same size and this person was willing to give them to me to pass on to Casper, so they could save the day.

'They're no use to me any more,' he said. 'I'll be glad to hand them over to someone else. Hopefully they'll bring your client more luck than they did me.'

I bought him another couple of beers to show my gratitude.

I reply to Casper.

No, sorry. Anything wrong with the boots I gave you last night? If they're no good, we'll have to speak to the guides about the possibility of hiring some ASAP. Florence.

By 'we will' I mean 'he will'. Yes, he's a client, but he's been such a pain, plus I reckon he's Jacob's problem, not mine. Casper's belongings were supposed to arrive this morning. All his luggage, obviously, not just the boots, although the thought of a pair of boots flying solo does make me smile briefly.

With not much time left to get ready, I head for a quick shower. As welcome hot water hits my shoulders, I still feel horribly tense. My mind homes in on my missing diary. I reassure myself that, violating as it feels, fortunately my handwriting is practically illegible.

My hair still isn't fully dry by the time my phone alarm reminds me that it's time to go. I take one last look out of the window at the peak. It's hard to believe that in less than a week, I'll be at the top. Hopefully.

I take one last scan of the room, then open the door, one bag over my shoulder while I carry the other two. Luke comes out of the opposite door at the same time, looking equally laden. We both laugh.

'We're cutting it a bit fine, aren't we?' says Luke.

We are. He and I had arranged this morning's safety briefing for yesterday afternoon, as is apparently the norm. However, Hugo insisted we dazzle our guests with another full day's outing. So, we did. Well, most of us. Luke managed to wriggle out of it because he needed to visit the hire store to pick up bits and pieces of equipment for Mr Armstrong. So, it fell upon me to dazzle. We visited the Materuni Waterfalls and took a dip in some hot springs. I arranged for hotel robes and flip flops to await them as they stepped out, as well as virtually endless fresh towels. By the time we returned everyone was shattered. But, most importantly, they were happy. Or should I say, suitably dazzled.

I shrug in response to Luke's question. 'We're not late, yet. Plus, I've hardly stopped this morning.'

Luke and I are among the last to arrive. We take a seat near the back of the room after helping ourselves to breakfast.

'Is this what it was like on the Great Escape last year?' I say to Luke in a low voice. 'Did you have safety briefings?'

'Sure, of course we did. They're compulsory. Why?'

'Just wondering.'

Two men walk into the room and stand near the front. Hugo greets one of them like a long-lost friend and the other one gives Luke a friendly wave.

'Good morning, everyone,' they say.

The chattering dies down as everyone pays attention.

'My name is Samson, one of the lead guides, and this,' he

points to the man standing beside him who seemed to know Hugo, 'is Ben, another lead guide. We're here to answer all your questions and to make sure you have a safe and successful climb.'

There is a chorus of thank-yous.

'Samson is great,' says Luke. 'He was my guide during my first attempt to climb Kili. I'm glad he's going to be with us.'

'You've climbed Kilimanjaro before?' I whisper. 'I didn't know that.'

He shrugs. 'I don't tell everyone because as soon as you do, they ask if you've summited and it's painful to have to explain that no, I didn't. Especially when people then go on to relay a story about how their hundred-year-old granny or ninety-one-year-old neighbour made it with no issues whatsoever on their first attempt.'

'I can understand that. But, joking aside, I've read that the oldest person to climb was about eighty-nine.'

He makes a face as if to say: *See what I mean?* 'That's why I keep quiet. I climbed a different route before, the Marangu route. I've heard that there are loads of ways, though, and I'd love to try and find a secret one.'

'We're on one of the best routes,' I say. 'So I reckon we're all in for a pretty good chance of success.'

The briefing takes over an hour, during which time I realise how hungry I am, after not being able to stomach dinner the previous evening. I dig into a bowl of fruit – papaya, passion fruit and bananas – before devouring a bacon and fried egg sandwich. It seems the mountain air is already affecting my appetite.

Everything at BVT naturally must be bigger and better, so we have six guides, three for each of our groups of nine (mine) and Jacob's (eight). There are two to three porters per person to carry their bags and supplies as well as several chefs and a dedicated medic per group.

We are split into our separate teams, as previously decided by Hugo, for a more detailed briefing. During our planning meeting we decided that splitting up for the initial part of the climb would give each group more time to gel.

My team consists of: Luke, Mandy, Clarabelle, Mr and Mrs Armstrong, who have been included as one to even up the numbers, Adrian, Russell and Lara. We will be climbing via the Machame route, taking seven days to do so.

Climbing with Jacob on the Lemosho route, taking the same number of days, are: Hugo, Sara, Casper, Jonessa, Imogen, Hettie and Shona.

Jacob's team guides are Ben, Michael and Eric. Our teams will meet up on day three at Barranco Camp. Jacob's team have a slightly longer route than ours: theirs is around 72 kilometres of trekking, ours, around 65, depending on the exact route. It's not unfair because there are pros and cons to every route. For example, both routes have high success rates and are ranked as moderately difficult, but I've read that the Machame route is busier, meaning less chance of spotting wildlife. The Lemosho route is more secluded, the paths tend to be less busy and there's more chance of spotting wild antelope, buffalo or even elephants.

The guides for my team are Samson, John and Collins. They're in charge of our climb. Our route can be done in six days, but the longer it takes, Samson explains, the higher the chance we have of summiting. '*Climb high, sleep low.*' We'll spend one of these days on an acclimatisation climb, meaning we'll ascend then descend, returning to the same camp. We all listen intently as Samson (who is well over six foot) holds up a large white sheet of paper listing all our camp names, the height we will climb each day and the length of our walk.

'There are three main things that will help to ensure your success.

'*One*: drink lots of water. More than you think you will need and then some more. *Two*: walk slowly. There is nothing to be gained by trying to walk faster than your guide. We will lead the pace. Please be respectful and don't leave people behind. Please be patient. The two words you'll probably hear the most are: *Pole, pole*. This means slowly, slowly in Swahili. *Three*: Listen to your head guides. We are in charge, so please follow any instructions carefully. Any questions?'

Mrs Armstrong asks about the toilet tent to check that there will be more than one. The answer is yes. BVT has arranged two per group, which is above what a lot of other climbers will have. Adrian asks about the food and whether he's brought enough snacks. He lifts a carrier bag crammed with breakfast bars and sweets.

Samson laughs. 'That will be more than sufficient.'

'Hugo has attempted to summit too,' says Luke while we're waiting to have our items checked for their suitability for the climb by our guides. 'Apparently once, but I reckon it could even be twice. That's how he knows Ben so well. He wanted to climb with Ben again as he's the guide BVT use most often.'

The more I learn about Hugo, the more I realise that I don't know him at all.

Samson checks over our equipment, and one by one, we take the belongings we will leave behind to reception for safekeeping. We're advised to make a note of our passport numbers before they, along with our credit cards and other valuables, are placed into envelopes. We seal them and are asked to sign the back. Then they're all placed together and put into the hotel safe.

I hang around in the lobby, trying to see what things people put away for safekeeping, looking out for my diary. I want to find out who went poking around my room in the dark and scaring the life out of me. I want to confront them and discover what they were so desperate to find. When it's Jacob and Hugo's turn to hand in their things, I catch flashes of passports, blue and red covers, but nothing diary-like.

After the inevitable last-minute questions, toilet visits and good luck wishes – not just among us but other hotel guests, too – I take one last look around my luxurious surroundings, at the bright giraffe prints on the wall and the comfy sofas scattered with cushions. The lingering smell of breakfast hangs in the air: coffee and burnt toast. Then we leave the hotel and climb into a fleet of 4x4s.

This is it. I'm as ready as I'll ever be.

It's a relief to finally be on our way. Mandy appears much better as she reads out loud snippets from her latest favourite guidebook, insisting on re-telling us facts we already know, such as at 5,895 metres high, Kilimanjaro is the world's tallest free-standing mountain, and that Ernest Hemingway wrote a collection of short stories called *The Snows of Kilimanjaro*.

'Yes, but what does the book say about the average success rate of climbers?' asks Clarabelle. 'That's the important information. We don't want the others to win. God, Jacob will be *unbearable.*'

True enough.

'It backs up that we are definitely on one of the more

popular routes,' says Mandy. 'And it's not the longest. Although . . . it is one of the busiest.'

Still feeling angry towards Mandy and the manner in which she befriended me, I stare out the window at the acacia trees, pedestrians, clusters of houses. As we pass a church, I see a smartly dressed family head for the entrance. I used to crave that sort of togetherness when I was growing up. I most likely still do, however much I try and suppress it to focus on my career and embrace the reality of my situation, not the fantasy of a large family. There is genuinely a lot to be grateful for in my life: health, my grandmother, good friends, a well-paid job, the centrally located flat I rent in Surbiton. I can walk, jog or cycle to work along a path by the Thames which takes me into the centre of Kingston. I have a generous expense account and often don't have to pay for lunch and/or dinner. And now . . . here I am, in Tanzania, about to go on an adventure a lot of people can only dream of.

Our car hits a pothole, and we all jolt. I hit the side of my head against the window and feel slightly dazed for a few seconds as I rub it. Looking out at the lush, vibrant vegetation, we pass by farming villages cultivating maize, beans and coffee, avocados, mangoes and bananas to name a few, according to one of my guidebooks.

'I can't believe that this is Jacob's life,' says Clarabelle, her clear voice butting into my thoughts. 'I knew it was glamorous, but this . . .' She gestures out the window, 'It's another level. My Insta is going to be bursting to full of genuinely motivational content. How cool is it to climb an actual mountain rather than metaphorically?'

I smile because she's making me realise that I've become somewhat spoilt. I've come to expect the absolute best, just like our clients. Sometimes, I admit, the lines can become a bit blurred. I forget who I am or think that I'm one of them.

'How did you get into this line of work?' Clarabelle asks.

I hesitate. I thought I'd got here through hard work and talent, and now I've made the horrible discovery that I'm not too dissimilar to Jacob. My father handed me a job on a silver platter.

'I travelled a lot with my mother when I was young,' I say. 'When we arrived in a new place, she'd learn some fun facts and turn it into a game, exploring the area. I could tell you an awful lot about seaside towns.' I pause, memories trickling back. 'Apparently, there are some long-lost tunnels beneath the Royal Pavilion and Dome in Brighton.'

'Your mother sounds fun.'

'She was,' I say. 'She adored kids and would've loved to have loads but only had me.' I pause. 'I wasn't aware of it until I was older,' I admit. 'Now . . .'

I can't bear to share the truth. I feel disloyal to my mother's memory now that my perspective has changed, especially when it comes to those birthday gifts. One memory particularly stands out: my thirteenth. My annual gift was a Burberry handbag. I took it everywhere with me, proudly showing it off. My friends thought it was awesome to have a mystery, rich dad, and sometimes, it was. Briefly. And yet I'd have given anything to have my dad come to watch my hockey and football matches, or go out for a family dinner at a pizza restaurant. I'd love to have been one of those families who gather round their child in a restaurant, ordering a dessert with a candle fizzing like a firework and singing 'Happy birthday' so that the rest of the diners look around, smile and join in.

Our driver calls out that we are approaching the Machame

Gate. I peer ahead at the gates. *Kilimanjaro National Park.* We drive through the entranceway, beneath the A-shaped roof, and pull up near a wooden building.

It's a relief to escape the car and stretch.

'Right, photo time!' announces Clarabelle. 'Stand by that sign.' She points.

MACHAME GATE
ELEVATION: 1800M AMSL

'One thousand eight hundred metres above sea level,' Adrian reads out loud as we all congregate in front of the sign obediently and pose and grin before swapping phones and cameras to repeat the poses.

The wooden board lists the distances to all the camps en route. Uhuru Peak is 40KM (32HRS) and the distance to our first camp – Machame Camp – is 11KM, which should apparently take us approximately five hours.

The excitement lights like a spark. Every single one of us – even the Armstrongs – share photos while we still can. Who knows when we'll have the chance to do that again?

Beneath my pictures, I type: #challenge #dogood #bethe-bestversionofyourself #charity #climatechange #sustain-abletourism.

We've been worried about the fact that Ethical Getaways are climbing too, but then I pointed out to Jacob that we must be doing something right if they are copying us. Besides, two can play their 'look at us, we're doing so much better' game. They're not so different from us. They flew here by plane (which presumably used as much fuel as ours) and got cars from the airport. Though I do have to admit, they're staying in privately owned guest houses which support the local communities and projects. On Ethical Getaways' website they state that they wish to be climate positive within the next ten years.

We sit on wooden benches in an open-sided hut, waiting. Our guides are in conversation with a group of porters who are also waiting around. I watch as our duffel bags are unloaded from the vehicles and placed in a pile beside a set of weighing scales. I check Jacob's Insta. He hasn't updated it this morning.

'What's the wait for?' I ask Samson discreetly. 'There's not a delay or anything wrong, is there?'

'No, this is normal,' he says with a reassuring smile. 'We're just sorting out which porters will be going with which group. Enjoy this time.'

Mrs Armstrong takes out a fan decorated with peacocks and flamingos and waves it in front of her face rather theatrically.

I take the hint. I approach the hotel staff member who has accompanied us for this part of the journey.

'Is it possible, please, to settle in a shady spot with a snack?' I ask her.

Within moments, a table and a set of chairs are set up beneath a tree, a red and white checked tablecloth laid neatly on top. A basket is unpacked, and we're served egg mayonnaise and cucumber sandwiches, tea and coffee, fruit cake, crisps and slices of watermelon. I add my own little touch – a packet of digestive biscuits – as I know Mr and Mrs Armstrong enjoy these little reminders from home.

I'm aware as we all tuck in after a chorus of thank-yous that other groups of tourists are staring at us. Most are sitting on the wooden benches, leaning against walls or sitting on their jackets on the ground, sipping from water bottles and tucking into packed lunches wrapped in foil or greaseproof paper. I blank out their stares even though it's embarrassing. It's impossible not to stand out when you're a BVT ambassador. Here, it's not like a lot of hotels, resorts or private islands and mansions where there are secret rooms, entrances, tunnels, doorways and secluded beaches to hide away the opulent displays of wealth and privilege.

Maybe I'm changing inside already now that I know who I really am. Perhaps some inherent desire to turn against my background is bubbling up to the surface. Until Hugo's bombshell revelation I thought I was different and therefore superior because I hadn't come from money. I worked hard, earned my living and paid my own way. Now I'm afraid that I'm the same as Jacob.

'The coffee's a bit strong,' says Mrs Armstrong. She looks at me. 'Is it possible to add some hot water?'

'Sure,' I lie, taking her mug.

I walk away, behind a hut, stand for a minute, then return and replace the cup in front of her.

She takes a sip. 'Oooh, much better, thank you.'

Luke catches my eye and grins.

'You're very welcome,' I say, suppressing a smile.

The client's wish is still my command, even if it is all in her head.

Samson walks over.

'We're ready to go.'

We all stand up and heave our day bags on to our backs. No one attempts to put away our feast or tidy up apart from me and Mandy, who place everything in as neat a pile as we can manage.

Samson organises us expertly into a line to sign the visitor book. It's a relief to have Samson, John and Collins in overall charge, leaving me with a few moments to myself. While I wait for everyone else to sign, I rearrange the weight in my backpack, and as I spot the envelope Hugo brought to my hotel room earlier, the overwhelming urge to open it takes hold. It's a mistake, of course, because the first thing I see is a DNA result and the second, a private detective's report.

Goosebumps cover my arms as I attempt to digest the sheer creepiness of what I'm seeing with my own eyes. Not only that, but I'm about to go off-grid with Hugo, the man who paid a fortune to have my entire life recorded and monitored in horrifying detail.

SIX

Jacob

J acob's team leave Moshi in a fleet of people carriers, heading in the direction of one of the entrances to Kilimanjaro Park, Londorosi Gate. Casper and Jonessa are in the car behind with Hugo and Sara, which is good because Casper is still sulking about his bloody boots.

Jacob stares ahead as they leave behind the city houses. It's finally happening. He can't wait to start climbing. Their journey is longer than Flo's team's by well over an hour because they're beginning their climb at a different gate. It's cloudy outside so he can't see as much as he'd hoped. Not that anyone else seems particularly interested in looking out the window anyway. Everyone is on their phones, trying to get in a final fix, just in case. Every now and then they are overtaken by other cars.

'Is it possible to stop for a break?' asks Imogen after less than half a bloody hour.

'I suspect not,' Jacob says, 'unless it's urgent?'

'It's not *urgent*,' she replies in an icy tone. 'I just wasn't expecting the drive to be quite this long.'

Christ. Jacob plugs in some headphones and listens to a book about how best to ensure success on Kilimanjaro. Their head guide's words are repeated often: walk slowly. *Pole, pole.* Stay hydrated. Listen to your guides who are the experts. He stares out at the landscape, at the passing maize farms, pine trees and lush grass. The narrator mentions keeping belongings dry at all costs, communicating with team members, avoiding alcohol. The latter is easier said than done, because Jacob's going to have to pull a few tricks out of the bag to make things special. After nearly two hours on the road, they bump along a dirt track.

'We're here!' announces their driver with a happy smile.

Jacob sees a signpost listing the distances to various camps. He focuses on two: the beginning and the end.

LONDOROSI GATE
ELEVATION: 2250M
UHURU PEAK: 47KM (26HRS)

Thank Christ. His body aches after sitting for so long and already there's a knot of apprehension deep in his gut. He hopes he's up to this. The rest of his team slide out of their seats and step out into the humidity, a stark contrast to the overly efficient air conditioning inside the people carrier. He stretches his arms, reaching up to the blue, almost cloudless sky.

Jacob sees Hugo step out of his own car looking as cool as the proverbial cucumber. He reapplies his insect repellent because he's a magnet for bugs of all kinds. After cleaning his hands with a wet wipe, he checks his messages. One from Clarabelle.

Good Luck! X

Jacob doesn't know why, but it feels like a taunt.

We're off to a good start! he replies.

In fact, they have a team budget which Jacob's already blown at the casino, so he feels at a disadvantage already. He can conceal some charges and, if he's particularly creative, can even cast blame for some of them on Florence. Their clients do have expensive tastes, after all. But still . . . what makes him mad is that Hugo wouldn't be able to arrange the type of trips they do and stay in budget, even though one of his favourite subjects is 'the bottom line'.

There is excited chatter amongst the team as their bags are unloaded and Jacob liaises with the guides and porters. It's busy, way busier than he imagined. Minibuses, Land Rovers and other 4x4s crowd the car park and climbers hang about in various sized groups, with different climbing company logos written on T-shirts, jackets and bags. According to Ben, a typical season sees around thirty thousand climbers.

Jacob and his team hang out in an open-air hut, sitting on green plastic chairs, eating snacks provided by the hotel. Jacob downs a lemonade. If he's going to pretty much be drinking chemically treated water only from now on, he may as well treat himself.

Sitting down, sipping his drink, he looks around at the various shades of green. This rainforest doesn't resemble any he's visited in places like Peru or Ecuador. In fact, it's not dissimilar to woods he's explored in Wales. It certainly doesn't feel – at least not right now – like they're about to climb a dormant volcano, the highest free-standing mountain in the world. Jacob has snowboarded, trekked and survived white-water rafting in *supposedly* shark-infested waters (regardless, it's not a nice thought if you capsize) so this will hopefully be a lot more manageable than they've been led to believe.

'Photos!' Jonessa gestures to the entrance sign.

They all gather and put their arms around one another. They all grin, then grin some more.

While they wait for their baggage to be weighed by their guides to ensure that they haven't exceeded the weight limit, he posts one of the pictures on both his personal and the BVT official pages. He selects one where his face is half-hidden by his sunglasses. He looks rough in the rest. #climbingkilimanjaro #BlackmoreVintageTravel #charity #savetheenvironment #climatechange.

The last one he shared was just after the school and coffee plantation visit. He 'warned' their followers that they may be off grid for a while. He didn't bother posting any of the selfies they had snapped in the bar because he didn't want any 'helpful' comments about not getting hangovers or not taking things seriously enough. It's a perpetual tightrope, the balance between persuading people to dig deep into their pockets to support their charitable cause while simultaneously not putting them off by thinking they're funding a jolly.

He announces a #giveaway #allexpensespaidcruise #competition #win #loyaltypays, noting with relief and pleasure the immediate traction before he signs the Kilimanjaro National Park Registration Book.

There are jokes about the luxury of the toilets – 'it will all be in the great outdoors from now on' – as they hang around waiting for Ben to tell them when everything is ready.

A group climbing with a different company burst into song next to them. Jonessa tries to grab Jacob and Casper by the arms and pull them over to join in.

'No,' says Jacob. 'Count me out. I can't sing.'

'Go on,' she laughs. 'Don't be boring.'

Jacob holds up his phone. 'Last-minute work stuff,' he says. 'Sorry.'

Instead, he checks out what Ethical Getaways are up to. Among the various comments, he sees a reference to the Anonymous Traveller mentioned recently. Curiosity takes hold as he sees there's a new post.

At the time of writing, the annual challenge for a well-known travel company is to climb a mountain. I hear from insiders that it is supposedly to test the fittest of their workforce. And where better to do so than halfway into the stratosphere. Stripping them to their bones. Figuratively, of course. It's considered the best way to ensure that the backbone of the company is stronger than any potential rivals. The trouble is that you don't get anywhere without attracting the evil eye. It's something they should watch out for.

Jacob skims to the bottom of the page and reads the last paragraph.

People reveal themselves under pressure. Reality TV works for that very reason, every action is logged and recorded. If someone has puffed up their achievements and abilities during the recruitment process, they'll crumble. Some of these employees have a tough road ahead of them.

He looks up from his phone and sees Ben heading their way.

'All formalities have been completed,' says Ben. 'And I'm pleased to say that none of your bags have exceeded the maximum weight limit the porters are allowed to carry. It's a short drive to the trailhead now.'

The time has come.

As the porters set off ahead of them, carrying their bags, some on their backs, some on their heads, Jacob is already in awe of them. He had seen them pack provisions – bread, fruit and bags of jam and honey jars. Even with just his own daypack full of essentials, he knows this is going to get harder.

Ben organises their team into a crocodile line. Hugo is placed directly behind Ben. Casper and Jonessa have been split up. Sara is behind Jacob, Imogen in front. Jacob reads some of the park rules listed on a wooden sign: It's prohibited to enter without a valid permit, damage anything, litter, enter or leave the park other than at the designated entrances and exits. All campers must sleep in tents in designated campsites.

'Time to go,' says Ben, with a smile.

This is it. They pass another sign. *Have a nice climb!* Jacob feels sticky and hot.

They meander along a dirt track, weaving through the welcome shade of the forest. Coolness brushes Jacob's bare arms. The forest is alive; the sounds of birds and insects dominate. A bird with shimmering blue wings swoops past and disappears into the foliage.

'A turaco,' says Hugo.

'If you listen, you can hear the howls of the blue monkeys,' Ben calls back to them. 'And if we're lucky, we should spot them.'

They all automatically gaze upwards into the trees, cedars and other evergreens, their branches covered in thick carpets of dark green moss, but apart from the sudden movement of the odd branch or two, Jacob doesn't see any monkeys. Bearded lichens drape the branches above, dangling in pale green wisps. A butterfly, rich in shades of brown and yellow, hovers above a red flower shaped like a teardrop. The sound of birdsong and cawing reveals the hidden depths of this new and magical world.

'A monkey!' Sara cries, pointing upwards.

Jacob sees a flash of a white, fluffy tail scampering up a tree trunk. He's disappointed that he didn't even have time to snap a picture on the lightweight camera he bought especially for the trip. A friend who'd climbed Kilimanjaro several years ago warned him not to rely on his phone battery.

'This walk is like being in a fairy tale,' Sara says, beaming.

They stop for water and light snacks, mainly popcorn. Jacob licks the saltiness from the surface before he chews and swallows. According to Ben, today will be the easiest day as their camp is only seven kilometres away. There's no sign of the porters who are already way ahead.

Jacob studies the others. Casper and Jonessa are sitting on the ground, side by side, both looking at their phones. Hugo and Shona are in deep conversation, sitting slightly apart from the group. Jacob can tell by the way Sara glances in their direction every few seconds that she is watching them. Hugo has put them all in a difficult position – him, especially – because Mandy confided in Jacob when they were working late recently that she's fed up with being silenced like a sordid secret. Her words, not Jacob's. He knows what it feels like, when resentment builds. At some point, it needs an outlet.

He stands up and approaches Shona and Hugo. She stops laughing as she spots Jacob.

Hugo says, 'Yes?' impatiently, and Jacob's transported back in time, a young child vying for attention.

He changes his mind about interrupting them.

Hugo sent him off to boarding school, supposedly because it would give Jacob opportunities, when it was obvious that, in truth, he wasn't keen on having Jacob around. Every time he sees him with Sara's children, his half-siblings, however cute and innocent they are, it stings.

Sara has put her foot down over boarding school because, unlike Jacob's mother, she stands up to him. Jacob likes her. She's not stupid, either. This time round, he hopes Hugo has bitten off more than he can chew. It's hard to fight his father alone.

He sits beside Sara.

'How are the kids?' he asks.

'I Facetimed them before we left the hotel,' she says. 'I really miss them. I'm starting to wonder if I've done the right thing by coming away. They're happy with my parents and Amy, their nanny, but what if one of them gets ill?'

'They'll be fine,' Jacob reassures her. 'Once you get into climbing properly, you'll be too tired to worry about them. You'll be reunited before you know it.'

'Thanks, Jacob.' She pauses. 'I feel torn,' she adds.

'In what way?'

'I wanted to come, because why should Hugo get to do all the fun things while I put in all the hard work at home?

I thought that by immersing myself in part of his world, maybe I'd understand him better.'

She knows about Mandy, Jacob thinks. *Or at the very least, suspects.* He wonders if he should say something cryptic, that he's always happy to be a shoulder to cry on. When it comes to the secrets he could spill . . . He looks over at Hugo giving Shona his full attention. He had bragged to Jacob once, after a brandy or two, that he could give someone his undivided attention while listening in to other conversations around the room.

'It's early days,' Jacob says. 'I've read loads of blogs, and everyone describes this as being a life-changing experience, regardless of whether you summit or not. From what I understand, there's something magical about the mountain. It helps you to see things more clearly when it comes to important decisions. Your children will be proud of you when they're old enough to understand. Meanwhile, Sara, just go wild in Duty Free before you go home. All kids love a homecoming gift.'

Jacob pauses as he remembers winning the annual trophy for player's player for his excellent goal-keeping skills when he was ten. Hugo had made a throwaway comment about the strikers doing the hard work. Jacob remembers feeling winded; he'd been so sure that Hugo would be impressed. Even when he changed positions and became a relatively good striker, his father never expressed admiration. This time it will be different, he's determined: Hugo will finally respect him. He knows what needs to be done.

Sara laughs. Hugo glances over.

'Thanks, Jacob. I needed that. You're a good person,' she adds.

'Time to get moving,' announces Ben.

They all obediently stand up, gather their belongings and follow him. As they climb up the widely spaced steps cut in the path, he's stunned to realise that he's already feeling a little out of breath. He stares down at his feet and counts his footsteps as a distraction. Ferns line the side of the walkway, their curved leaves brushing against his calves.

'What animal dung is this?' asks Casper, pointing at the ground just ahead.

'Probably buffalo,' replies Ben.

'Is it safe?' asks Imogen, looking around.

'Yes, we're unlikely to see elephant or buffalo.'

'But it's still possible,' says Imogen.

It hadn't crossed Jacob's mind that they would get too close, but he spends the next few hours staring into the dense forest, on the lookout. What he does spot are wildflowers, violets and red impatiens covering parts of the jungle floor.

The team arrive at Big Tree Camp after over four hours of slow trekking, which involved one or two slightly steeper parts where they had to grip tree branches for balance. Jacob is delighted to see that the porters have already set up camp for them. Sweat has made the back of his T-shirt stick to him and he'd love a shower. Tents in various shades are set up among the trees. *Blackmore Vintage Travel – Welcome* is written on a sign by their cluster, obvious by the company logo on the canvas. Jacob's group have been allocated slightly more space (that is, a metre or two) away from the many other climbing groups. Welcome juices – small cartons of mango and passion fruit – are served moments after they arrive. In each of their tents is a welcome bag: wet wipes, a motivational quote and boiled sweets.

Another BVT haven has been created in yet another part of the world. Jacob feels the sense of pride he always does when he's pulled off an incredible experience.

KILIMANJARO NATIONAL PARK
TANZANIA
MTI MKUBWA CAMP
ELEVATION: 2650M

As well as Big Tree and Mti Mkubwa Camp, Jacob's also heard this called Forest Camp. He's learned that Big Tree is the English name and in Swahili it is Mti Mkubwa. Indeed, they are among tall trees providing welcome shade.

After they've signed into the camp and been shown around – toilet tent, mess tent and their own tents – he seeks out a rock beneath a nearby tree. He closes his eyes, inhaling the fresh air and for the first time in as long as he can remember there is no familiar pull drawing him towards a casino. It was an ex who introduced him to the thrill of gambling. She booked a long weekend in Vegas as a birthday gift and from the moment they landed, it was as if he'd come home. He'd never felt so alive as he did then, surrounded by the slot machines and poker tables.

Darkness is swift and the temperature drops noticeably at the same time.

With nothing artificial to distract him, Jacob makes himself at home in his single tent, unpacking his essentials – torch, sleeping bag, inflatable pillow – before he visits the infamous toilet tent. When they were shown how to use it, he noticed it smells strongly of chemicals. The tent, although tied to the ground with four ropes and with rocks at the base for extra security, feels a touch flimsy, as though it could potentially blow away with Jacob in it. God, the horror if it happened while he was in it.

When he emerges, he discovers that everyone has gathered around a table in the mess tent. No sooner has Jacob sat down than he's served a starter of steaming hot vegetable soup with bread.

'I'm so pleased that we're finally on our way,' says Jonessa. 'I was starting to get really nervous. I'm surprised I don't feel more tired.'

'I think today eased us in gently, babe,' says Casper. 'I don't feel tired either, but I know that as soon as my head hits that pillow, I'll be out like a light.'

'As usual,' replies Jonessa.

'Is everything gluten-free?' asks Imogen.

Jacob reassures her that the chefs are aware of her dietary requirements.

The same question comes again when they're served the main course of chicken curry and rice.

'Is the rice gluten-free?'

'Isn't all rice?' asks Casper.

Seems she's irritating him too. It pleases Jacob, makes him feel better about himself.

'There's no harm in double-checking,' she replies. 'I'm very in tune with my body and I know what I can and can't eat to ensure maximum health and fitness for the climb.'

'The chefs have a chart with our names and dietary preferences,' says Hettie, in a soothing voice. 'I've seen it.'

'It's all very professional and organised,' Jacob adds. 'The whole point of coming away on these trips is to switch off and not have to worry about the day-to-day things. Try and relax.'

Imogen gives Jacob a tight smile.

He manages to switch the conversation by talking about how much money they've raised so far and how quickly the donations are pouring in.

'I checked before we started climbing. It's nice to feel like we're doing some good,' Jacob says. 'Especially while enjoying an experience such as this.'

'An impressive amount,' says Jonessa.

She smiles at Jacob and he feels ridiculously happy, like being awarded a gold star by the teacher.

'So, what did everyone think of our first day?' asks Hugo.

'Easier than I imagined,' Jacob replies.

'So far, so good,' says Casper, sitting back in his chair and sighing.

'It wasn't too arduous, but my calves ache after all those steps,' says Jonessa. 'I hope I can sleep well tonight.'

It feels like the right moment to do something out of the ordinary. From Jacob's daypack, he pulls out two bottles of rosé champagne from Fortnum & Mason wrapped in bottle chillers. Of course, alcohol is pretty much a total no-no if they want to succeed, but everyone will love the chance to photograph themselves toasting the high life. It's exactly the sort of thing Jonessa will adore.

'Oh, wow!' says Imogen as Jacob produces the bottles. 'What a treat! You're a total star, Jacob.'

She's not allergic to anything in alcohol, it seems.

He pours champagne into mugs he's borrowed from the dining tent.

'Sorry there aren't more bottles of champagne,' he says. 'But the weight restrictions meant that I did the best I could. I couldn't let the beginning of such a momentous trip pass us by without marking it in some special way. Cheers!' He raises his mug. 'Here's to success and friendship.'

'Cheers!' everyone choruses.

'Rosé?' says Casper, taking a delicate sip and screwing up his nose. 'I prefer regular champagne.'

Ignoring Casper's remark, Jacob tries to catch Hugo's eye to see if he's impressed, but his father doesn't look at him. For once, Jacob doesn't care. Everyone is in great spirits, wishing each other luck for the days ahead. The bubbles have offset the dullness of their earlier dinner conversation. It's so often the tried and tested simple things which work the best, but with a twist. A luxury picnic in the desert made by top chefs, served by waiting staff wearing black tie and clutching silver trays. A midnight beach campfire with a barbecue and cocktails from a fully stocked bar. A platter of seafood and ice-chilled champagne after a scuba dive in a remote coral reef. Anything served out of context is a real pleasure. Plus, Jacob *knows* these people. The thought of completing a challenge without any immediate rewards is unthinkable. They need to be drip-fed golden breadcrumbs along the track to their success at the peak.

Although Jacob has arranged all these things and more, right here, right now, he feels proud to have pulled off something small and simple, yet with such impact.

After dinner, the medic, James, tests and records their oxygen levels with a pulse oximeter.

'I've got bloody blisters already,' moans Casper.

'I brought plasters,' says Jonessa.

'Plasters aren't going to solve it,' he says. 'If we lose because of my boots, I'm suing the airline.'

Yeah, yeah, thinks Jacob. As long as no one cuts themselves

– Jacob hates the sight of blood – Casper can moan about his blisters as much as he likes.

Jonessa whispers something in Casper's ear, and mercifully he quits going on about it. She throws Jacob a guilt-ridden look. He glances away.

Bellies stuffed, the group navigate their way to the tents by torchlight. It's only now that the magic truly hits Jacob and excitement sets in. A slight breeze brushes his cheeks as he inhales the coolness of the night air. He shines his small handheld torch up and into the branches of a tree to see if he can spot the glowing eyes of any wildlife. Nothing, but the sound of sudden movement in the branches prompts Jacob to head for the safety of his tent. Hugo and Sara's tent is next to his.

'Night,' Hugo calls out, as he unzips his tent.

'Good night,' Sara calls out too as she crawls in ahead of Hugo.

'Night,' Jacob replies.

Hugo pauses outside his tent. For a brief, mad moment Jacob thinks that he's going to congratulate him on a job well done so far.

'Get some rest. Don't let the team down.'

Jacob waits but Hugo doesn't add anything else. Jacob stares up at the clear sky, marvelling at the stars. He feels clean. Maybe he could get used to a simpler way of life. But no, he reckons, he'd miss the buzz of decision-making and the adrenalin rush. Who is he trying to kid? He climbs into his own tent, feeling the welcome draw of his sleeping bag.

Yet sleep doesn't come. Above the magical sounds of the rainforest – the whispering wind, the calls and howls, the distant chatter of the porters, guests and guides, the banging of pots and pans being washed and cleared away – he hears the zip of his tent opening.

He jolts up to see Jonessa, her hair in two neat plaits, crawling through the entrance. She puts her fingers to her lips before she turns around and zips the opening shut before unzipping his sleeping bag.

He smiles, feeling as though he's winning at Baccarat.

'Well, this is a nice surprise,' he whispers.

It is such a bad idea. But playing with fire is addictive.

SEVEN

Florence

*Day Two: Machame Camp. 3,000 metres
or 9,900 feet (approx.)*

The report Hugo gave me is the first thing I think about
as I remove my sleeping mask and my eyes slowly focus
on the inside of my tent. It details how he had me
followed over a period of a year before I joined BVT.

When I went for my morning run, I was watched: 6.36
a.m. on the 2nd of November is listed as one such example.
The report from Hugo's private detective goes on.

When I went to the gym, I was watched.

When I went on dates, I was watched.

When I went out with friends and gossiped carelessly in
bars and pubs, I was being listened to.

And those are only the ones Hugo deemed suitable to
share with me. It's sick. I don't know how he got my DNA,
or even if the test is a fake, but however he did it's a horrible
thought to have my father as an omnipresent puppeteer. I'm
in my own personal *Truman Show*.

I lie in my sleeping bag, trying to block out the smell of bacon and the unfamiliar sounds of people walking past my tent. If I was at home, I'd use an app to time my breaths while listening to classical music, but I can't risk wasting any phone or tablet battery. It was my idea that we arrange to carry lightweight power banks and spare batteries for the clients, but I annoyingly forgot about mine, even though they were on my list. Maybe it's a good thing, this break from our collective reliance on technology. It also means I can't continue my recent obsessive googling: *How accurate are DNA tests? Is it legal to spy on someone?*

I think back to my mum's funeral last year. It was a large affair; she was well loved by the local community and the families she'd looked after as a nanny, then a childminder. I was born in Italy, hence the name Florence. We moved in with my grandmother when I was three, living first in a seaside town near Newcastle, then Suffolk, then another one in Kent. We moved around the coast, clockwise. As I grew older, I could virtually plot our next move. I assumed we'd go to Wales, then Scotland, and finally end up back on the east coast where we'd started. However, we stopped once we reached Brighton.

'The only place I've ever felt at home since Italy,' my mother said once we'd settled into our new home.

I never knew what she meant, not really. She said that the reason why some places make you feel at home is impossible to articulate. Now, I think I understand. I feel at home in my job. Blackmore Vintage Travel has become a part of me. Let's face it, it's in my blood. If I ignore the one giant, Hugo-shaped fly in the ointment. If Hugo waited until my mother had died to lure me into his life, then it can only mean one thing: he must've suspected that my mother would talk me out of it.

I locate a rock on the outskirts of camp to sit on, a cup of tea made for me by one of the chefs in one hand, my phone in the other. The sky is clear and my life and routines back home feel far away. As I sip, I re-read the challenges set by Hugo, aware that once the climb is over I won't care to ever see the list again, like textbooks after an exam. Find out what Ethical Getaways are up to – tick. Wow the clients from day one in Tanzania – tick. One draw, one win. Arrange a unique activity while in camp – in hand. Raise a minimum of twenty-five thousand pounds. When I last checked it was at fifteen grand, up an impressive thousand, but the donations are dying off after the initial flurry of enthusiasm and generosity. I must update the blog for the BVT website. I take a pen and notepad from my bag and write a paragraph: *life-changing experience, panoramic views,* blah blah. Dull. Unimaginative. My mind drifts as I put down my pen and shut the notebook.

Attention to detail is something Hugo drums into us at every meeting. One of the problems with making everything super-competitive is that it creates desperation, and the dirty tricks played on rival colleagues get more creative – that is, increasingly irresponsible or downright dangerous – every year. Hence my missing diary.

Hugo sends me a text message to 'make me aware' that Jacob has done a holiday giveaway, which, to my mind, makes us look desperate if we've had to resort to copying Ethical Getaways. Closing my eyes, I remind myself what makes customers feel special and valued: taking their complaints and concerns seriously, apologising for any wrongdoing, perceived or real, making them think that they're right. Most of our followers are clients or potential clients dreaming of the day they can afford to be whisked off to a land of make-believe perfection. What would capture my attention if I was scrolling online? Something interactive, maybe, with the chance to win something at the end. I'm a sucker for a quiz.

I mull over the possibilities and decide on a photo where I can hide an item of mine. Then, the first person who correctly locates the hidden mascot each day could win a free holiday-planning consultation with a senior member of the BVT team because, as a rule, we only deal with VIP clients. Attached to my daypack is a keyring which my fiancé bought me on our first city mini-break together: a silver camera, plane and mini globe is attached. I decide to use that.

George loved that we worked in the same industry: 'We'll always understand the pressures and anti-social hours.' He was a loyal partner; he'd have probably given Hugo a piece of his mind after how he's treated me, had he been able to come on this trip too.

Photographing the keyring then working up a witty caption on my iPad momentarily takes my mind off George – and Hugo. I wait for the online reaction to my post, but the signal has disappeared.

I glance at my mountaineering watch, finish my tea and set up my lightweight travel mat for my yoga stretches. I sit cross-legged; inhale, exhale. In one of my regular work appraisals I was told that I can come across as standoffish, so I'm working on becoming more relaxed. When I open my eyes, I see the view afresh beyond the camp and the trees: seemingly endless land stretching into a vast nothingness.

I hear footsteps and swing round. It's Mandy. Her freshly highlighted blonde hair is tied up in a neat bun and she visited her favourite salon before she left for eyelash extensions. When she first fell ill, I mentally prepared to be one person down. Now I wish we were. How am I supposed to trust her? Whether or not she knew why Hugo wanted me to join BVT, it seems she played her role in the deception. The moment I found out about her relationship with Hugo, I should've realised that she was blatantly able to compartmentalise and deceive.

'Why?' I asked Mandy when I found out about their affair.

'I love him and he, me,' she said, 'it's complicated,' and that's all she'd say on the subject.

And yet . . . Possibly Mandy is in the same situation as my own mother was. It's messing with my head.

Regardless, I suspect that Mandy is sending frequent reports back to Hugo. I'm going to put on a show if it kills me. There is nothing I won't do to win, especially now. It's not just because I want to show Hugo that I'm capable of running BVT someday – although there is an element of that – it's because I want to show him that I'm better than him. That I'm not just in this position because I'm his daughter and he tricked me into being here. He's too secretive, personally and in business. I must dig deeper to figure out how it's all interwoven.

'I can't believe we're finally on our way,' Mandy interrupts my thoughts.

'Incredible, isn't it?'

We're surrounded by shrubs and trees. As I look at our camp in the clearing, I see the neat rows of tents are being dismantled by the porters. A chef emerges from their tent and places a red and white striped tea-towel on a rock, smoothing it out flat to dry.

'We need to make more of an effort with the clients.' Mandy is like this, cuts straight to the point. 'I'm concerned that we don't have enough surprises or added extras to pull out of the bag.'

I push my feelings about her to one side and reply in my work voice, sharing my 'Find the Mascot' idea.

'It might work well,' she says, mulling it over. 'It's simple, but then, as we all know, quite often those are the things which surprisingly take off.'

'Fingers crossed,' I reply. 'I've also organised via our guides a surprise afternoon tea when we reach camp. I reckon it will go down a treat.'

'Well, that's positive,' she says. 'I got the impression from Adrian yesterday that he'd rather be with Jacob and Hugo. I don't want anyone to feel that they're in the second-best team. That's totally not the point of this. We need to up the rivalry. I managed to get a few minutes online this morning and Jacob's team look on top form on Insta this morning.'

'I'm on it,' I reply. 'Ignore Adrian. He's a whinger.'

I stand up, shake the dirt off my mat and roll it up.

'What about the eye masks?' I ask. 'I bet everyone loved them?'

I placed silk eye masks, monogrammed with our clients' initials, on their pillows as a surprise.

'You forgot to put the personalised sweets out. That's not like you,' she adds.

'They were all a bit sticky,' I lie.

I've no idea what state they're in because I did forget them.

'I've a brilliant idea!' Mandy claps her hands together. 'How about you do an early-morning yoga and meditation class every morning for all of us? It will be a great way to start the day and it shouldn't be too much extra work for you.'

'Maybe,' I say, trying to hide my irritation. I'm already

giving one hundred per cent. 'It must be time for breakfast,' I say, glancing down at my watch.

In the mess tent, we are served a feast of porridge, fried eggs, bread and oranges sliced into quarters. Adrian pulls together an egg sandwich and the yolk drips down his chin as he bites into it. Imogen picks at the food as though she's struggling. I take out a small jar of Marmite from my bag and spread it on to a slice of bread.

'You brought your own Marmite?' says Mandy.

'It's my favourite comfort food,' I admit.

'May I have some?'

Reluctantly, I slide the jar across the table. As I watch her stick her buttery knife into it, it strikes me how little I know about her. I can't help but look back on all our interactions in a different light. Did she really enjoy my company or was she spying and prying into my life only to feed back to Hugo? I hate that I was taken in by her.

She doesn't bother putting the lid back on the Marmite. I make a point of screwing it on, extra tight. Petty, I know.

'Any chance you could arrange to get some apricot jam instead of strawberry, Flora, dear?' asks Mrs Armstrong.

'It's Florence, Mrs Armstrong, and yes, I'll see what I can do,' I lie.

'I did put it on my list of essential foods,' she says. 'It's Mr Armstrong's favourite.'

After breakfast, I swallow an altitude sickness pill because it's supposed to help prevent acute mountain sickness, but the downside is that it makes me wee more. What I would love is a Valium if it wasn't such a bad idea at altitude. I pull on some gaiters over the bottom of my trousers to keep out the dust, a top tip from one of my clients.

'The dust!' she exclaimed. 'You do not want it in your boots, trust me on that. And expect rain, plenty of it. I hope it doesn't, but be prepared. You *do not* want to get your belongings wet – they'll never dry and you'll be the most miserable you've ever been in your life.'

I wander over to other tents on the off chance anyone has any apricot jam to spare. I'm met with head-shakes and looks of bewilderment each time I ask. I lie and tell Mrs Armstrong some is on the way.

'Delightful. Well done,' she says.

I bet they wouldn't even eat it, if I did manage to get my hands on some.

Samson arranges the order in which we will walk today, in single file. I like Clarabelle – behind me – despite her dubious choice in men. I remain conflicted about Jacob. Sometimes I think he's not too bad, other times he gives me the creeps. I get the sense that I've only ever seen a fraction of his true self. When he's around Casper, he pretends to love that he went to boarding school from a young age. Yet however much the two of them witter on about the 'fun and larks' they had, there is a wistfulness about Jacob and his bull-in-a-china-shop approach to life. I catch him looking at Hugo sometimes for approval, and it's sad. Maybe it's this vulnerability that Clarabelle latches on to.

'Today,' says Samson, 'will be steep and short as we climb through the moorland zone. We're not expecting any rain; it will remain dry and sunny.'

As I take in the rocky terrain, covered in vegetation, moss, shrubs and pink, red and yellow spikey-looking flowers, I hear Mrs Armstrong ask one of our guides, John, what the names of the various plants are. I overhear 'alpine sugarbush and red-hot poker'. I'm aware that Edward Armstrong calls Mrs Armstrong 'sugar' when he thinks no one can hear. Her first name is Madelaine, but I try to forget that because I'm scared that I'll accidentally call her by her first name one day and she won't approve.

We step over rippling waterfalls as we navigate the mountainous rocks. We stop frequently, not just for refreshments, but to stare at the vast landscape. I draw as much air as I can into my lungs. The air smells sweet and fresh. I mentally write my blog describing how this trip has reminded me that it's so important to spend time in nature. While that's certainly true to a degree, online I'm far more upbeat and positive than I am in real life. I'm going to suggest a monthly 'spend time in the outdoors day' for everyone in the office. Hugo will try and veto it, but if I sell it by telling him it will look progressive, he'll be forced to give in.

I love the long moments of silence because there's a strange bliss in having nothing to focus on but my steps – *pole, pole,* slowly, slowly – as our guides keep reminding us. We navigate the rocks, my calves brushing against twigs which scratch against my hiking trousers.

Mandy is on fine form on one of our many water breaks. She makes everyone laugh as she regales us with a story about her carefully navigated night-time visits to the toilet tent. I pretend to laugh but I can't stop staring at Mandy. Before I accepted the position at BVT I did plenty of online digging, as you do. Sara and Hugo had a whirlwind romance, and their first son was born three months after their wedding which was plastered all over magazine covers. An apparent fairy-tale beginning that's clearly already been shattered, as I realised when I joined the firm and became privy to the juiciest in-house gossip. Mandy isn't just my colleague any more; she's my father's *mistress*. It's amazing how quickly your opinion of people can change.

'I can't believe we are finally doing this,' says Clarabelle. 'It's mad.'

Everything is mad to Clarabelle.

She and I are members of the same gym. When we occasionally bump into one another, she is always dressed in matching everything and hanging around the café with her personal trainer. The plum sofa in the centre of the café is unofficially 'their' seat. They tend to order sickly looking smoothies made of blueberry and spinach, vegan chocolate peanut butter or strawberries and banana, which they slowly sip, exuding an air of health and importance.

'Yeah, it's mad,' I say. 'Don't you wish you were with Jacob, though?'

'No. He's too competitive.'

I don't reply and the silence hangs there.

'Don't you think?' she pushes. 'What's he like at work?'

I notice she twists her diamond and ruby encrusted engagement ring around her finger. It's too loose. She should be careful. I automatically reach up and touch my engagement ring on the chain around my neck, resting alongside the St Christopher. I never wore mine at work – too many questions. I don't even know why I'm wearing the St Christopher, but for some reason, I didn't want to leave it behind at the hotel.

'I don't have much to do with Jacob,' I say.

'Really?' she says, as though he's told her the opposite.

I don't bite.

'You're lucky to have each other,' I say. 'When Jacob and

I are working late, he never talks much about his family set-up.'
I'm keen to know more about my half-brother. 'He doesn't
mention many friends, outside his childhood ones.'

'He likes to visit his mother in Capri, though it's the norm
for him to stay at Hugo and Sara's for Easter, Christmas and
such-like. I invited him to spend it with my family last year
but he said he wouldn't be able to relax.'

I get it, because I feel the same. Hotel rooms are different
because they're my own space, but other people's houses are
a minefield of unknown rules.

'That's understandable,' I say.

'He and I need some honest conversations when we're
back,' Clarabelle confides. 'I'm ready for children. Since I
brought up the subject, he's distanced himself. I even thought
he might be seeing someone else behind my back but he
assures me this isn't the case. He doesn't have a good role
model in his father, but it doesn't seem fair to judge Jacob
based on his father's actions.'

'It can't harm to talk to him about your concerns,' I reply
inanely. After all, I'm hardly a relationship expert.

'Anyone special in your life?' she asks.

I hesitate because my relationship is complicated.

'Yes and no.'

She doesn't push.

'I think he loves gambling more than me,' she says quietly.
'Maybe that's his other woman.'

I can't think of a good enough response.

When Clarabelle finds out who I am, she may feel a similar
way to how I do about Mandy now. She'll look back at my
prodding for information and see it in a different light. I take
a sip of water.

'Jacob says you used to be a tour guide,' Clarabelle says. 'That must've been fun.'

'It was.'

Clarabelle waits for me to say more but I know she's being polite and is not particularly interested in tour guiding. Fresh paranoia hits. How many 'tourists' on my guided tours were fake, paid to report to Hugo? Unsettled, I stare at the horizon, trying to remember if anyone stands out from those trips. There was the man who stood in a shop door, staring at me while the rest of the group were swallowed up in the London crowds on Oxford Street. A woman who recorded me on her phone because 'I was so interesting and knowledgeable'. God, there are hundreds of suspects. I took a self-defence course after I'd been mugged but I hadn't realised that there were other dangers.

Luke is sitting with Mr and Mrs Armstrong during our break. He smiles at me and I smile back. He can be intuitive, and it makes me wonder if he's concerned about me after my distracted behaviour on the flight over. I can't help but like it that someone cares.

'I think Luke likes you,' says Clarabelle in a low voice. 'How do you feel about him?'

'I don't know much about him.'

'He seems really nice.'

'He's very friendly, always the life and soul of every BVT party.'

'There's phone signal!' someone calls out.

'I need to check my messages,' I say, relieved. I'm not comfortable dissecting how I feel about him.

Clarabelle takes the hint and wanders off to talk to Luke. I glance over. I hope she's not meddling. I unzip one of the multiple backpack compartments to get my phone. Before I can slide my hand in, something scuttles out. I cry out.

'Oh my God! There's some sort of spider in my bag!'

As it scuttles across the ground towards the bushes, Adrian stamps on it before I can object.

'That's not a spider,' he says, poking it with a stick.

Samson comes over. We all peer. It looks like a beetle, in vicious shades of black and red. But then I see the stinger.

'That's a scorpion. A red-clawed one. I've never seen one up here before,' Samson says.

As everyone stares down at the ground, a horrible thought hits, and fear unfurls in the pit of my belly. Last year, when Luke and George were the team leaders for the annual trip, there was an accident – an almost fatal one. I remember disconnecting the call, sitting down and staring into space. I couldn't believe it. It was the kind of thing you see written. '*A tragic accident.*' Thing is, until then, I was the sort who believed accidents happened to other people.

In the lead-up to the trip, Hugo had sent the team several stern memos. George showed a couple to me. The pressure he felt under to perform and achieve was huge.

It has made me wonder if Hugo had already heard rumours about Ethical Getaways. George and Luke had to stick to a staff budget but not skimp on the luxury for the clients. He pushed the team leaders on the Great Escape much further than usual. George was panicking, and clearly unable to think straight when it came to their choice of climbing company. He assured me that the firm was reputable, that he wouldn't take any unnecessary risks and yet . . . apparently he did take a risk which didn't pay off.

There's a section in my missing diary where I wrote down

my suspicions after George's accident. His blog detailed the prank-playing as harmless, but most of the things he described didn't strike me as particularly amusing. Extra hot chillies hidden in their breakfast, missing shoes or trainers left outside in the rain, lost phone chargers . . . Ridiculously childish pranks, yet with an edge of something darker.

I realise my legs are shaking. Bloody hell, a *scorpion*. I like to think that I'm not easily spooked by creepy crawlies . . . but come on! Someone had to have put it in my backpack. Scorpions didn't go around unzipping compartments and then closing them up after them, not in my experience.

'Do you think it could've hurt me?' I ask, because I need to know.

Luke puts his arm around me.

'The main thing is that you're safe,' he says.

The human contact is comforting. I'm desperate for someone to properly confide in. I smell his deodorant and it's momentarily disorientating, at odds with the freshness of the mountain.

'Why my bag?'

'I don't think the scorpion meant it personally,' Luke says.

'Mountain life isn't for everyone,' says Mr Armstrong. 'A few discomforts and little surprises are part and parcel.'

Oh, fuck off! I want to scream.

'I can take over as team leader for a day or so, if it helps,' says Luke.

I shrug away from his embrace.

'There's nothing wrong with me,' I say, aware that my tone is a little harsh. 'I've had a fright, but I'm fine.'

I don't like the way the rest of my team is looking at me.

'Come on, guys,' I say, with a smile. 'How many of you

would like a creepy friend like that in one of your backpacks? Or worse, your sleeping bag?'

'No one, dearie,' says Mrs Armstrong. 'But as Luke said, the scorpion didn't choose you specially.'

She needn't think she's getting a good night treat on her pillow tonight.

'I remember when your colleague, George, got a little overly concerned before his accident on last year's Great Escape,' continues Mrs Armstrong. 'At the time, he also insisted nothing was wrong with him and yet he was clearly stressed. Look what happened.'

'The strange thing is,' Mandy jumps in, 'I did a ton of research before I came here and poisonous creepy crawlies weren't mentioned.'

I think about what Samson said: he's never seen one on the mountain before.

We're all aware some accidents are caused by a series of events or circumstances eventually leading up to the catastrophe. Mrs Armstrong is right. George was stressed. He had a terrible fall and almost died from his injuries. He's still in a coma, after a catalogue of so-called mistakes on last year's trip. All because Hugo pushed them too hard and made them feel like winning was a life-or-death situation. I don't intend to end up with a similar fate. I mustn't let the Hugo situation overshadow what's really important. Yes, I want to win and yes, I want answers, but not at the cost of my own life. Otherwise, how will Hugo learn his lesson?

EIGHT

Jacob

Day Two: Mti Mkubwa Camp. 2,800 metres
or 9,200 feet (approx.)

Rainforest Zone to Heath and Moorland Zones

Jacob's woken by a cheery *'Hello!'* He opens his eyes and looks for Jonessa, even though she slipped away before midnight. He unzips his tent and accepts a cup of coffee from a porter.

'Thanks very much.'

He's grateful. It tastes better than any flat white with extra smooth ground beans an experienced barista has ever served him.

'There is a bowl of warm water. For washing,' the porter adds, pointing.

'Thank you. *Asante sana.*'

Florence taught them how to say please and thank you the other night, among a few other words.

He's grateful for the water. He stinks already, which doesn't bode well for the next week. He's neat and tidy by nature and missing the routine of his morning shower and evening bath. Jacob inhales the sweet scent of the fresh morning air and listens to the birdsong. Patches of sunlight dot the ground. Above, a gentle gust of wind rustles the trees.

There are so many things he didn't think about before he began this climb, water being just one of them. They are encouraged to drink a lot and are provided with limitless cups of tea or coffee, and yet the water needs to be collected and carried to camp.

Last night with Jonessa felt like a dream. He should've said no, he should've talked some sense into them both. Regret hits, like the morning after an all-nighter at the casino. A few hours of high for a much longer period of self-flagellation. All to be repeated over and over in a vicious circle of pleasure and shame. He tries not to think about Clarabelle. And here, there's nothing he can do to block it out of his mind, except put one foot in front of the other.

Christ. He must write a blog and make it sound perky, interesting and full of the joys of their success so far. Exactly like some work reports he writes: mostly fiction. If Hugo sacks him maybe he could write a bestselling novel about a company that crumbles after the shock departure of its star executive.

Jacob crawls out of the tent and stretches. He observes other campers as they shake out their boots or shrug themselves into their jackets before heading for the dining tents. For a few seconds, contentment hits and the guilt and shame get shoved to the back of his mind where he prefers to keep them. If he could stay like this, bottle this feeling, he would pay anything. He has been living in fight or flight for too bloody long.

Casper emerges from the toilet tent, his hair sticking up all over the place, and gives him a wave. Jacob's stomach tightens but he waves back as if nothing is wrong. 'Smile and wave,' Mandy says when they've had to show difficult clients to the door. 'Smile and wave.'

My life is a mess, Jacob thinks.

It's all going to implode if he can't sort things out. He looks over at the green of the forest and fantasises about living cocooned in a treehouse.

He heads for the mess tent, but suddenly Hugo blocks his way, holding up two empty champagne bottles.

'These were chucked into some shrubs last night,' he says.

'Oh. My. God,' Jacob says. 'I don't know who would do that?'

It's true, he doesn't. Littering appals Hugo.

'I assume you safely disposed of the bottles. Where was that?' asks Hugo.

Jacob didn't. He left them on the table among the ketchup and mustard bottles, fully expecting that they would be cleared away. That was his error. He carried them up the mountain, he should've been prepared to carry the empties back down.

'I'll deal with it,' he says, taking the bottles from his boss. 'I'll put them back in my tent.'

'I don't think alcohol was the right call, Jacob. In fact, far from it.'

'Why didn't you say something at the time, then?'

'It wasn't the right moment, in front of our clients. You should have consulted me or the guides. It most certainly wasn't what I had in mind when I dreamt up the challenges.'

'Have you an example of what you did have in mind, then?'

Hugo taps the side of his nose before disappearing into

the mess tent. Cheeks flaming with humiliation, Jacob takes the empties back to his tent and stuffs them in his daypack. He didn't think it through. Now he'll have to carry them all the way to the top of the mountain.

When Jacob enters the dining tent, he finds Hugo and Sara are already there, eating porridge. Hugo wolfs it down, while his wife eats more delicately. It strikes Jacob that he has always hated the sound of Hugo eating. He sits at the other end of the table to them, near the back of the tent. Not that it will make much difference as it's very cosy inside the tent. Once the others arrive they will all be quite close to one another.

'Morning!' they chorus.

'How are you?' Sara asks.

'Fine, thanks. You?'

'Great,' she says. 'I'm feeling good about today.'

'Top of the world,' says Hugo, then laughs at his own joke. 'Although . . .' he continues.

Jacob's stomach drops. What now?

'I was concerned to hear from Casper last night that he, and indeed, several of our other clients on this trip have been offered quotes by Ethical Getaways.'

News to me, thinks Jacob.

'It's all under control,' he lies.

'I hope so. To lose any big client would be a disaster, but to lose Casper, a friend, well, that would be beyond careless.'

'Which is why I'm moving BVT along with the times,' Jacob says.

A sore point. Hugo says he expects them to compete in a competitive world, meanwhile he's living in the past.

'Tried and tested works,' Hugo insists. 'Loyalty creates traps. Make sure they can't escape.'

Every improvement Jacob makes is an uphill battle. He dreams of the day when Hugo lets go of the reins and he can run the show.

When Jacob turned thirty, Hugo cut his allowance.

'You earn more than enough,' he said at the time. 'I shouldn't have allowed it to continue for this long. It was an error of judgement on my part.'

Ashamed as Jacob is to remember, he begged. Hugo threatened to fire him if Jacob didn't remove himself from his office at once.

The tent flaps open and everyone else files in, Jonessa last of all. Jacob concentrates on his porridge, as if he's ravenous.

'Sleep well, Jacob?' she asks, in a smooth voice.

Reluctantly, he glances up. 'So, so. You?'

'Eventually.'

She smiles at him and he reaches for a slice of bread, focusing on buttering it without poking holes in it. He avoids Casper's eyes. God, just imagine if he ever found out. The repercussions wouldn't just have an impact on Jacob; Casper would pull his business from BVT, placing the blame on Jacob's shoulders, and it would be yet another stick for Hugo to beat him with. He slathers on a dollop of marmalade.

The conversation revolves around sleep, the number of times people needed the toilet in the night and talk about how much harder it's apparently going to get as the air becomes thinner, the higher they climb. Jacob smiles and nods at the appropriate times, as though he doesn't have a care in the world.

They're interrupted by Hugo swallowing his vitamins and

pills. One gets stuck at the back of his throat, and he gags. Everyone stares before Jonessa gives him a whack on the back.

'I'm fine,' Hugo repeats, clearly mortified at the attention. 'Fine.'

Jacob turns his attention to Imogen, sitting to his left.

'Looking forward to today?'

'Of course!' she says. 'I've been reading all about it and the slopes won't be too steep today. It will be more of a manageable incline.'

'Good to hear.'

'Actually, I've been meaning to ask you,' she says. 'Could you have a word about the food? There simply isn't enough of my preferred options.'

Jacob looks at her, incredulous. Does she think there's a supermarket nearby? Their chefs have been working hard to provide them with feasts, and in Jacob's opinion, they have gone out of their way to cater for Imogen. And he would know. He has been on many trips like this one and the service here is among the best he's ever encountered.

'Sure,' he says. 'I'll do my best. What is it that you'd like?'

'I'll write you a list,' she says, whipping a small notebook and pen from her back pocket.

Hugo glances over as she scribbles away and Jacob half-wonders if he has put her up to this, a mini challenge to see how Jacob handles it. He can't complain, it's his job to ensure that their clients are more than happy. If Imogen isn't happy, Jacob must be seen to fix it.

Ill at ease, he takes the list itemising such things as apricots and chia seeds to Ben and asks if there's any way they can accommodate Imogen's requests. Jacob pulls an apologetic face to show that he's embarrassed to even ask.

'I'll see what can be arranged,' he says.

'Forget it,' Jacob says, taking the list back as he realises that of course one of the hard-working porters will need to go back down the mountain to get the supplies. 'I'll explain to her that she'll have to make do with the food we have.'

He means it. For once he feels good about his choices. There have been many times when he's felt under pressure to ask staff members at various places around the world to go more than above and beyond. Up until now, he's managed to blank it out, focus on the job in hand, think about what makes the client happiest. This trip is already beginning to help him shift his perspective and realise where changes need to be made. Sometimes people need to hear that enough is enough.

'I'm sorry, Imogen. It's not going to be possible,' he tells her upon his return.

A message pops up on his phone from Clarabelle.

Morning, Jelly Tot. I have news!

Jacob detests Clarabelle calling him that ridiculous name. She knows it full well, yet unfortunately it has stuck. He glances over and sees Casper and Jonessa posing for loved-up couple selfies. He can't even manage to have a relationship with the woman he really loves. Every area of his life is twisted. He reads the rest of the message.

There was a scorpion in Flo's day bag! ☹ Thank God it wasn't me. Florence is antsy because they aren't usually found up here.

Curious. But Flo is the paranoid type. She's a dark horse. The information she puts online and shares with everyone is minimal. He wants to know where she really came from and how she managed to weasel her way in to his business. Her CV is very basic. Mandy did, however, check out her references, which is one thing. At least she has worked where she claimed she did. It's surprising how many candidates' CVs are almost entire works of fiction.

He asks Clarabelle if there's anything else.

I'm not one hundred per cent certain but she and Luke seem to be getting very pally.

In what way? he asks.

In the way that people do when they fancy each other.

Please, no. *Pillow talk*, thinks Jacob. It can be lethal. Christ, the things he's told Jonessa. Even Hugo's not immune. Jacob knows for a fact that Mandy is privy to information she shouldn't be.

Must go! Love you! xx

He doesn't reply. He's asked Clarabelle to become Flo's confidante. It sounds as though they've barely covered the basics. Jacob has learned more about giggly Imogen and her endless dietary requirements than Clarabelle knows about Flo.

One thing Jacob has been mulling over is the fact that Florence visited George way more times than the rest of them. She was devastated after his accident, lost loads of weight.

Maybe that's what enticed her to BVT: love. If they were an item, he can understand why they kept it quiet. Hugo would've sacked her. Or George. But more likely, Florence, based on experience.

George was good friends with an ex-BVT manager named Simon who did not go quietly. He refused to leave the offices until Hugo threatened him with the police.

'I'm supporting my in-laws as they both need full-time care,' he said. 'I'm a couple of years from retirement.'

Like others before him, Simon struggled to find a job post-BVT after his bubble was horribly burst. Jacob suspects that some of the particularly vicious ex-employee comments he's read online were written by him. They used to joke that Simon spoke like he'd swallowed a dictionary and Jacob remembers some of the language on the forum, such as *noisome* and *exceptionable*.

The last time Jacob looked online, however, Simon was running a garden centre. Jacob does that from time to time, checks on the 'past people', as he thinks of them, to cement his hope that things work out all right for them in the end. Jacob visited the garden centre where Simon worked one bank holiday weekend. Simon was carrying a large watering can in the outdoor plant section wearing a work apron, a biro behind his ear. He'd aged enormously. The visit did nothing to alleviate Jacob's residual guilt about the particularly vicious annual restructuring that had led to Simon's departure. Annual cull, more like. He feels momentarily sorry for Florence. Christ, if he wins, she'll be fired too. Jacob shakes himself, shoving the pity from his mind. Survival of the fittest.

Still, he thinks, if Florence loves George maybe loyalty will stop her getting attached to Luke. She probably has better morals than Jacob, Jonessa and Hugo combined. And yet . . . loneliness does things to a person. He should know. Jacob often feels alone, apart from when he's in a casino, among kindred spirits. Another thing bothering him is that he's read that Kilimanjaro changes people and makes them reassess what's important in their lives. Luke doesn't seem the type for introspection, but honestly, who knows. Ever since he and Luke fell out, Jacob's had this horrible feeling that their antipathy will have repercussions.

Back in his tent, he packs his daypack, sliding out one of the empty champagne bottles and putting it in his larger backpack. He doesn't feel comfortable handing them over in his litter bag along with the rest of his rubbish. The garbage is collected and weighed to ensure it's taken back down the mountain to prevent litter. He feels like a kid hiding cigarettes at the bottom of a school bag. Which reminds him, maybe he should slap on some nicotine patches. It might give him a bit more of an edge.

After the morning preparations, they all gather beneath a sycamore tree as requested by Ben, to await their walking order for the day. Jacob watches his tent being packed away efficiently.

'Where's Hugo?' he asks, looking around.

'Toilet tent,' Sara says, in a low voice.

There's little point in being coy or discreet, up on the mountain. Everyone knows everyone's business. There's no hiding anything. Well, Jacob thinks that, but look what Jonessa and he have already gotten away with. An unpleasant thought hits . . . what if there are other secrets being concealed in plain sight?

While the group waits, Jonessa comes to stand beside him. She smells of her favourite perfume.

'I never really thought about it until now, but why *do* you call your dad Hugo?'

'It sounds better at work and it's stuck.'

'Do you call your mother by her name too?'

'No, I call her Mum. Her name is Ivy,' he adds, unnecessarily. 'What about your parents? Are you close?'

'We are,' she says. 'They love Casper.'

'Everyone loves Casper,' Jacob says, lowering his voice slightly.

'I'm not sure that's true,' she says.

She's right.

'They'd love you too,' she says.

Jacob doesn't bite. He can't. He owes Clarabelle too much.

'Do you like being called Joey?' he says. 'Florence goes mad when I call her Flo.'

Jonessa laughs. 'I know, I've heard her give you a right earful. I quite like being called Joey. Jonessa is a bit of a mouthful.'

'I like Joey,' he says.

She looks as though she needs more from Jacob, but he can't give it. Clichéd it might be, but it's complicated. Despite their betrayal of Casper and Clarabelle, he does feel a strong sense of twisted loyalty towards his old friend. Yet history has a way of sneaking into the present. Casper stole one of his first girlfriends. Maybe all this is some subconscious payback. Their friendship has been years of like and hate, support and competitiveness, respect and envy. Sometimes he envies Clarabelle and her many friendships without hidden agendas and resentments.

'Sorry to keep you all waiting!' Hugo appears, brandishing a hiking pole.

An apology. Wow.

'We're going to hike through the moorland zone today, leaving behind the rainforest. Remember, I will set the pace,' says Ben.

Led by Ben, they begin today's walk. It's surprisingly hard and monotonous to walk slowly.

'Don't forget to drink water,' he calls back to them from time to time.

The trees start to decrease in size, shrubs scatter the land as they enter the moorland zone. Jacob spots flowers, no idea what they are – he can only recognise the common ones, like roses, sunflowers and orchids – but they appear to be a much hardier version of daisies. The mountain is described in guidebooks as having many seasons and landscapes and his experience so far is that this is true. The steady, at times uneven, ascent is already beginning to feel more arduous. He is seriously regretting all the alcohol and cigarettes he didn't give up.

On they trek, *pole, pole*. His breathing becomes more laboured. They take frequent breaks and during one, Hugo comes to stand beside him.

'Managed a conversation with Casper yet?'

Give me a bloody chance, thinks Jacob.

'I will do, later, in camp. When it's appropriate.'

'Look what Mandy's sent me,' Hugo says, handing Jacob his phone so he can read the text.

Ethical Getaways is a new company doing exactly as their name suggests by encouraging mindful and respectful tourism. As part of a climb on Kilimanjaro's Rongai route, on the north-eastern side of the mountain, they are raising money for a project which supports the fair treatment of staff. For every mile flown, Ethical Getaways have paid a pound to promote sustainable tourism.

'Why in heaven's name don't we have this sort of coverage?' Hugo continues. 'They're stealing our ideas and making them look like their own. It's blatant plagiarism!'

It's because of Hugo and his dinosaur ways. He thinks social media is something you 'do' in five spare minutes and all that's needed is a random photo with a relatively witty caption.

A rage. An urge to push him over the side of the mountain and really hurt him swamps Jacob. After all he's done for him. All the bad stuff he's buried for him, all the people he's calmed down and smoothed things over with. And yet . . . he's helped Jacob too. He paid off a huge gambling debt last year, despite warning him that it was the first and last time. Maybe he just needs to trust Jacob again.

'We have got decent coverage,' Jacob says. 'I think it's a bit inflammatory of Mandy to send this through. She should be working with us, not comparing us to Ethical Getaways.'

If this is Mandy's attempt to stay in contact with Hugo, then he's not impressed. She knows what he's like. She knows he'll give Jacob a hard time.

'Have you heard from Tom or Dan lately?' Jacob asks.

His half-brothers tend to keep their distance. Jacob is making the point that he's here, that he's the one who deserves Hugo's respect.

'Not much,' says Hugo. 'They don't need me for money.'

Touché. God, the old man can be a bastard.

Jacob walks away and leaves Hugo standing there alone. The ascent is getting steeper and as they climb the steps cut into the ground, Jacob's chest pounds. Everyone turns quiet. They navigate their way along the well-worn paths, which widen at some stages, meaning that occasionally Joey can walk alongside him.

'Look!' she calls out.

He looks to where she's pointing. A lizard stares at them from a rock before disappearing. Silver, feathery leaves dangle off branches, and white strands stick to his jacket. Bulbous flowers, shades of red, orange and purple, pepper the greenery. They step along a plank placed between two rocks as they cross a waterfall.

Imogen says, 'Oh my God,' repeatedly as she makes her way across. As if it's Niagara Falls rather than a gentle, smooth flow of water she could easily leap across.

The shrub-like trees of the Moorland Zone become dominant as they leave behind the lush greens.

'It's not going to get too steep, is it?' Jonessa asks Ben. 'Strange as it may sound given what we're doing, heights aren't my favourite.'

'It's fine,' he says. 'The route isn't treacherous, but one thing to watch out for is stinging nettles.'

His half-brothers all automatically look to the ground.

It's news to Jacob that Joey's scared of heights.

When they pass a big wooden building, Ben explains that it's the headquarters for the mountain rangers, especially when a rescue becomes necessary.

'I hope I don't need to be rescued,' says Jonessa. 'I went for hypnosis before we came away to try and overcome my fear of heights. Are there many people who need assistance?'

Ben shrugs. 'Maybe several hundred a year.'

Jonessa looks horrified.

'You'll be OK,' Jacob reassures her. 'I'll look out for you. We won't need rescuing if we're all sensible.'

She smiles.

There are questions Jacob would like to ask him but Ben announces that it's time for a rest. Jacob has heard that some climbers think they know better than the guides, making stupid statements like their GPS can guide them more accurately. Jacob hopes his team won't do anything so disrespectful. And then he remembers the champagne.

Ben points to a small clearing with views of the plains below in a patchwork of greens and browns. Blue sky arcs above them, scattered with clouds. Jacob sinks down on to a rock and slides out his phone – a habit that, even up here, is so automatic and instinctive that he can't break it. He decides not to look at it and slides it back into his jacket pocket.

Shona, sitting to Jacob's right, laughs at something Hugo says. She's the sort of person who is easy to overlook. She blends in, doesn't say much, yet Jacob always gets the feeling that she's *watching* them through her glasses. He gets a sense that she can see straight through him and she doesn't like or approve of him.

Jacob's phone vibrates. He takes it out of his pocket. Mandy's name pops up in a text.

This is what I didn't send to Hugo:

The name Blackmore Vintage Travel comes up enough times for it to be more than a coincidence that their clients don't always make it back from their sports and once-in-a-lifetime experience holidays. Safety doesn't appear to be a

*key element in their made-to-measure, no request too big
or too small packages. Even one of their own staff members
almost didn't return from a trip to New Zealand last year.
But obviously, this isn't in the brochures. It wouldn't be,
would it? But let this be a lesson to you to check more than
the small print. You're welcome. I wouldn't work there again
if they quadrupled my salary. Not that they would – wages
are well below industry standard. You're supposed to be
grateful just to be allowed to work there, like they're doing
you a favour. I digress. The guy from New Zealand is still
alive, still has a fighting chance. Unlike someone else who
was ditched during their annual cull.*

Although the post is partly fiction – yes, there has been
the odd accident over the years, they can't control the decisions
their clients make while they're white-water rafting or driving
at speed – if Jacob doesn't bury this, Hugo will kill him.
Because if Miss Marple Florence sees it she'll open her mouth.
She'll grind and gnaw her way at that particular bone, and
raking over the past won't help George's situation. Florence
is a newbie; she won't understand that you don't achieve what
BVT has without cutting the odd corner or two. It's normal.
But something niggles . . . He scrolls back to some of last
year's comments.

Ask Hugo Blackmore about Bridgetown.

Jacob's phone signal cuts out but he remembers reading
some of the comments on this post the first time he saw it.
People suggested that the poster should either spit out what
they had to say, or do something constructive about it. The

author of the post never commented again. Jacob asked Hugo what he thought the author meant and he shrugged. But now . . . Jacob recalls something, many years ago. There was an incident. He remembers a senior manager talking about it one night after a drink too many. He scrolls back in his mind. He's pretty sure it was on a Caribbean trip. Barbados. Someone died after a drinking game. But then the autopsy discovered an underlying health condition that the client hadn't declared. BVT was cleared of any responsibility for the tragic death.

Suddenly, relief hits. His breathing returns to normal and his legs stop shaking. Thank Christ. *Of course*, the truth is staring him in the face. Florence has been brought along on this trip so that Hugo can get rid of her, not him. She's always asked too many questions.

It all ties in. If she and George were an item, Florence could be extremely inconvenient. Hugo must know all this and has set her up to fail on this trip. She'll think it's her own decision to leave the company, and everyone will be happy. Well, not Florence and obviously not George – but certainly everyone left at BVT. Including Jacob. His dad doesn't want him to fail, after all – any digs are just a cover. The truth is, he's after Florence. That has to be it. He's on Jacob's team to make sure he wins.

The first thing Jacob notices as they arrive at their next camp is the sheer number of tents in varying shades and sizes, so bright in contrast to the ground. Tufts of grass scatter the vast horizon and beyond. He stands at the camp entrance, relieved, and reads the sign:

SHIRA 1 CAMP
ELEVATION: 3610M
VEGETATION ZONE: MOORLAND

It lists all the distances to the camps they must still reach but as usual, Jacob focuses on the final line:

UHURU PEAK: 33KM (25HRS)

That's it. Thirty-three kilometres between him and hopeful victory.

They sign in at the rangers' hut, writing their signatures and the country they've travelled from, then Sara and Joey head straight for the toilet tent. They've both said that they feel uncomfortable going behind rocks or bushes, like the rest of them.

'Dinner will be in an hour,' says Ben.

After they're shown around, past the small wooden shacks with the pit latrines and on to their tents, Jacob relishes climbing into his own space. It's a relief to have some privacy, to not have to fake interest in every single word that comes out of the clients' mouths. He takes out his sleeping bag, unrolls it and lies down for a few minutes. Bliss. The next thing he hears is his name being called.

'Jacob! Time for medical checks first, then food.'

Hungry as he is, it's a struggle to force himself up. Outside, he stands still, taking deep breaths, trying to wake himself up. He focuses on the ground, and the multiple footprints of the porters who have put up his tent. The guylines are attached to small rocks. He yawns, feeling like he's been hit by a huge truck. His eyes are gritty, he feels dizzy with nausea . . . but it is a nice feeling to be in the middle of nowhere surrounded by these remote moorland meadows.

Once Jacob feels more awake, he's pleased to see a table set up for dinner, just outside the dining tent. The weather is pleasant enough, though Ben has warned them that rain is forecast. They're just ahead of the next rainy season, but as Ben keeps reminding them, mountain climates are unpredictable.

'Be prepared for anything.'

In the mess tent, Jacob reports for his daily medical check and waits while his pulse oximeter reading is recorded on the daily chart. He's pleased to be given a relatively clean bill of health, once again.

The mood at the table is energetic, despite the full day's trek.

'I wonder how the other group are doing?' says Imogen as they tuck into a vegetable soup.

'Well, from the little I've heard,' says Hugo, 'they're doing very well.'

'Who did you hear this from?' asks Sara.

'Mandy's been in touch about a few work bits and pieces via text,' says Hugo.

Sara puts down her spoon without finishing her starter.

For their main course, they are served a beef curry with rice, banana and green salad. Jacob could do with a beer to help him relax and get into the swing of the conversation. Hettie and Shona are 'buzzing'. Hugo is 'humbled by the experience so far'. Hard to believe. Imogen is giggling. Again. Jacob can't bear it.

Darkness falls fast and they finish up with dessert, a pineapple flambé, in the dining tent.

'Are we keeping you up?' says Hugo, as Jacob stifles a yawn. He spots Hugo and Casper smirking. 'What are the plans for the evening's entertainment?'

'Charades,' Jacob says, off the top of his head. 'Winning team gets breakfast in bed tomorrow, brought personally by me.'

Everyone laughs.

'Now this I've got to see,' says Casper.

Joey and Casper exchange an affectionate look.

'Excuse me,' Jacob says, 'I've some things to organise ahead of tomorrow. Enjoy the charades! Make sure someone lets me know who wins.'

'Please stay,' says Joey.

'I'd love to,' Jacob lies. 'But work has to come before play.'

Is she trying to get Casper to lose his shit on the side of a mountain? If so, she's going the right way about it.

'Are you bringing us breakfast in bed tomorrow, Jacob?'

'Ha, ha,' Jacob replies. 'Sure I am.'

In his tent, he can hear laughter coming from outside. He's glad to be missing the charades. He plays them all bloody day long as it is.

He's desperate for some rest but has one more task to complete. He pulls out a bag of natural sleep aids, including some lavender mini roll-ons, and delivers them to each tent, placing them on their pillows along with a personalised card wishing them a good night's rest.

As he slides and wriggles his way into his sleeping bag, desperate for the oblivion of sleep, something sharp rips at his hand.

'What the—' he says out loud.

He switches on his head torch and looks down. At first,

he doesn't notice that he's bleeding until he feels warm blood drip down his wrist. Shit. As much as he doesn't want to, he licks it, but it keeps dribbling out and on to his top. He directs the beam inside his sleeping bag. There's a shard of broken glass, a green champagne bottle, smashed and jagged. Some of the pink Fortnum & Mason label is still attached: *Brut Rosé*. Christ. This is deliberate.

After applying a plaster, he wastes a good twenty minutes of precious rest time shaking out his sleeping bag, checking and re-checking for any nastier surprises or the remainder of the bottle. It's not in his bag. It's not anywhere.

Jacob remains quiet, hidden inside the darkness of his tent. He's not giving the prankster the satisfaction of a public reaction. No, not prankster – perpetrator of a crime.

Another word floats through his mind. Karma.

It's one of Flo's favourites.

NINE

Florence

*Day Two Evening: Shira II Camp. 3,900 metres
or 12,800 feet (approx.)*

Distance to Uhuru Peak: 25 km

Samson and I walk slightly ahead of the team and the
other two guides as we head into our second camp. I've
achieved this by taking one less break because I need
time to set up the surprise I've arranged so that our fellow
climbers will be 'wowed'. The breeze we've experienced all
day has dropped and sunset is still an hour away, so there's
plenty of time to prepare. Yet my optimism is tinged with fear
and paranoia. The scorpion incident is still giving me the creeps.

Inside the tent porch, I carefully remove everything from
my daypack, just in case there are any further nasty surprises.
I place every item on the ground sheet after giving them a
shake. Nothing. Already, at this altitude everything feels like
much more of an effort due to the thinning air. It's exhausting
just unpacking my bag, so I'm relieved that there are no nasty
surprises.

I crawl inside the tent, unravel my sleeping bag, and sit cross-legged on top of it. I re-tie my hair into what is hopefully a neater ponytail, and with the help of a handbag mirror, I apply mascara. If I'm going to plaster myself all over the socials to show off what I've managed to pull off on the side of a mountain, I want to look the best I can manage. I frown. Worry and stress is plastered all over my face. I untie the ponytail and weave two plaits. It doesn't make me look any better, but it will be lower maintenance.

Back outside, as arranged, a table has been set up with a checked red and white tablecloth, held down by small rocks. On it, cardboard place names rest neatly in front of the plates. They wobble slightly in the wind but miraculously stay put. Luke's name is in between Mr and Mrs Armstrong who have small pearls (not real) placed by their names as a nod to their thirtieth wedding anniversary next month. My name is placed between Adrian and Russell. Mandy is between Clarabelle and Lara.

I look back, and over my shoulder I see my team as they trek down towards camp. I rush over.

'I have a surprise, very special afternoon tea for you all!' I say with a smile.

I feel full of energy and ridiculously excited.

Everyone picks up on my mood and perks up despite their tiredness at the end of a day's trekking. It only takes a few minutes for everyone to dump their bags in their tents, queue for the toilet tents, sign in to camp, then head over.

We are served Earl Grey tea with cucumber and fish pâté sandwiches, mini chocolate cakes, strawberries, slices of melon and cheese scones. Joy travels around the table. It seems we are all starting to learn the meaning of true gratitude. Mrs Armstrong doesn't even try to ask for a different filling for her sandwiches. We all take photos and most of us post them because the backdrop is so Instagrammable, it's social media perfection. Afternoon tea on a mountain, the snowy Kibo peak in the distance and the magnificent slopes below, dotted green shrubs amongst dusty brown earth. Our world feels limitless. We couldn't be in a better place. #gratitude #bemindful #appreciatetheenvironment #travel #explore #teamflorencetowin.

'Here's to a successful climb,' I say, raising my teacup. Then I turn to the Armstrongs. 'And here's to your pearl wedding anniversary.'

'Thank you,' they both chorus. 'This is wonderful!'

A fond gaze passes between them, and it makes my heart ache for a moment. Will I ever have that?

As the sun sets, I excuse myself and seek out Samson and the team.

'Thank you for fulfilling my request with such professionalism,' I say. 'You've made it truly beautiful.'

'My pleasure,' Samson replies with a smile.

Despite our feast, it's astonishing that we still manage to eat a reasonable dinner under cover of the mess tent when night falls. Every day so far, the moment the sun drops, the cold sets in almost immediately. After our nightly health checks – all fine apart from Mandy's stomach still not being one hundred per cent – I would describe our overall mood as buoyant. I have a good feeling about winning.

A good feeling which disappears when I'm alone with my thoughts. I can't understand why it's so difficult to fall asleep, given all the physical activity.

It's much colder than the first night. I can hear people coughing, something Samson and John had warned us was quite common as we reach higher altitudes. My tent companion, Clarabelle, snores softly beside me and I envy her ability to drop off without a care. At some point, I decide she was the one who planted the scorpion, probably on Jacob's orders, and I risk briefly shining a torch at her, lighting up her face in a ghostly fashion. I shiver, feeling scared of what lies ahead although it's hard to put my finger on exactly what I'm afraid of. My fears expand and I can't switch off. I came here to find out what really happened to George. Hugo's revelation that he is my father temporarily threw me off course, but I'm determined not to let it do so any more. This could be my last chance. If his accident was an attempted murder, what if I'm next on the list? Distraction could cost me dearly.

George was the person who alerted me to a report he'd found in a box by the office shredder.

'I went to destroy some of my own figures and noticed that there was a bundle of papers marked *Sensitive* and *Extremely Private and Confidential*. It was the word "extremely" that caught my eye. I mean, how many levels of "confidential" are there and who would draw attention to something so sensitive by writing such a thing?' George had a point. He'd taken photos of the papers which detailed the number of deaths or accidents on trips booked with BVT. I still have the copy he sent me on my phone.

Before this trip, I googled how many deaths occurred on the mountain each year. It was hard to find an exact number, but it seems that it's fewer than ten out of the average 30,000 people who climb it each year. I'd found those figures reassuring at the time, educating myself on the signs and symptoms of high-altitude pulmonary edema (HAPE) and high-altitude cerebral edema

(HACE) to reduce my chances of falling victim to mountain sickness. I bought the best boots I could afford, hoping to avoid falling and injuring myself, also thermal everything I could lay my hands on, to avoid hypothermia. I paid for a thorough medical to ensure that I didn't have any underlying health conditions. I ignored the online articles about appendicitis, heart attacks, frost-bite and bleeding at the back of the eyes because they didn't seem relevant or likely. At least, I hoped not.

But deaths do happen. This trip is not risk-free. And what if someone assumes that George and I knew more than we'd let on? What if they think I'm behind the malicious online comments? Hugo wouldn't try and get rid of his own flesh and blood, would he? *He doesn't care about you*, the voice at the back of my head reminds me.

As I try to drift off, George's last message to me – also written in my diary – flits through my brain. *I think there may be more to it than we thought*. At the time, I assumed he meant the trip itself, that the competition was tougher, that the prize was something bigger. But I never had the chance to discuss any of this with George. We'd never speak again. When I woke up there were no phone messages from George, but plenty from his sister and mother. Messages I don't want to remember.

I hear footsteps walk past the tent. I listen to them fade away before I drift off.

Thank God, when awareness next hits, it's light. I lie there, unable to face getting out of my sleeping bag. I daydream, trying to make sense of my previous night's thoughts.

'*Good morning!*' says a cheerful voice.

I sit up, my eyes feeling gritty and sore, and unzip the tent, gratefully accepting two cups of ginger tea. One for me, one for Clarabelle. She sits up and removes her eye mask.

'*Asante sana,*' we both say.

I take a sip of the hot water, inhaling the soothing smell of ginger.

'God, I could do with at least another few hours' sleep,' I say to Clarabelle.

'Me too.'

My neck and back ache and I don't know how I'm going to get through the trek today. It's going to be a long one. On top of that, tonight is the night the two groups will merge at Barranco Camp. I'm not sure I'm ready. I've loved being in a small bubble with fewer people. This could be the calm before the storm.

We've all fallen into our routines and against the backdrop of birdsong and the clatter of breakfast dishes, I prepare myself for today's hike. We will climb for approximately nine hours, heading east and cover a distance of roughly ten kilometres.

Mandy and I are the first to arrive for breakfast in the mess tent. I decide to make an effort with her. Companionably, we place mini chocolates decorated with the BVT logo beside each plate. Some little visual reminders for our clients as to why they are here.

'Not hungry?' I say, when Mandy picks at a slice of dry bread.

'No. I still don't feel one hundred per cent. I can't believe I was unlucky enough to get food poisoning before we even left for the trip.'

'It happens,' I say. 'Just don't push yourself.'

'That will look great, won't it?' she says. 'Hugo would love it if I showed weakness and pulled out. Not.'

'It's not up to him,' I say. 'Besides, who even knows if he will make it?'

'Good point.'

'It's none of my business,' I say gently. 'But it must be hard, Sara being on the trip too?'

'I reckon she suspects something's up.'

'And if she does confront him?' I push.

I half-wish I could tell her that he had an affair with my mother. It may help both of us.

'He and I have been together a lot longer than people realise,' she says. 'Even before he met Sara.'

'That must've been a real kick in the teeth.'

'He wanted more children. Lots of heirs and lots of spares.' She pauses. 'I can't have children. Hugo was honest with me from the start when I told him.'

'I'm sorry.'

I am sorry, but I can't resist probing.

'Why did Hugo ask you to recruit me?'

She looks at me as if deciding whether to speak or not.

'He said he'd heard you were good. He wanted Jacob to have some decent competition.'

'But there was George and Luke. They were here way before me.'

'They were all too friendly for Hugo's liking, I imagine. Perhaps he knew you wouldn't put up with Jacob's entitled bullshit. He made George and Luke heads of the previous year's team, knowing that it would drive a wedge between them professionally and friendship wise. It's what he does. Divide and conquer. Perhaps with you and Jacob he feels that he doesn't need to worry quite so much.'

'And yet, here we are . . .' I say. 'Do you think it's because he wants to get rid of me?'

'No, I think it's because he wants to get rid of Jacob.' She looks at me. 'I've been an idiot, haven't I? My friends and family have been telling me for years, but it's hard, you know. When you invest so much time, energy and love into a relationship, you believe what they tell you, don't you?'

'I guess, yes.'

It's hard to concentrate because I'm trying to work out exactly what game Hugo is playing and, more importantly, who is involved in the game and what the rules are.

'I did something stupid when I was angry,' she says. 'And now . . . I don't know how to undo what I've done.'

'What was it?'

'I wanted to get back at Hugo, you know? Hit him where it hurt.'

'I can understand that.'

Obviously, I really can.

'Yeah, but if he finds out, he'll kill me.'

'Find out what?'

'I opened my mouth when I shouldn't have.'

We're interrupted by our clients entering the tent, one by one, led by Adrian.

'Morning! Hi! How did you sleep?'

'So, so,' says Lara. 'Those bloody pills make me get up all night to pee. It's exhausting. I'm wondering if I should've bothered. I hope they're doing the trick and sparing me from altitude sickness.'

Everyone agrees with her.

'What did you say?' I mouth to Mandy.

'Tell you another time,' she whispers back.

Lara interrupts with another tale of going to the toilet.

I'm half-relieved, half-disappointed that we can't continue our conversation, but I'm glad Mandy's pushed back in some way. Hugo deserves consequences for all his bad actions.

It's horrible, keeping the secret of Hugo's true identity to myself. I guess that's why he chose that moment to deliver the news, when I'm cut off from friends and family, with no one to reinforce my belief that he's behaved abominably. And not just to me.

I glance over at Luke and he smiles.

'Love the chocolates!' he says, holding his up. 'Chocolate for breakfast, what more could we all want? We truly are in paradise.'

Luke's confidence warms my cheeks. If he believes I'm in with a good chance of winning, then it feels like he has more faith in me than Jacob.

I smile back and he turns his attention to Lara and Mrs Armstrong. They both listen intently to his story about his friend who climbed Kilimanjaro and said it was the best, although hardest thing he'd ever done.

'No gain without pain is the moral of that story, I'm assuming?' says Mrs Armstrong with a smile. 'Don't worry, young man, you don't get where I am in life without a struggle or two.'

She laughs at her own words.

I don't know much about Luke's personal life. It's a long-standing joke in the office that instead of someone in every port, he has a special someone in every country he's visited.

After breakfast, we prepare for the day. I find it hard to fully concentrate on what I need as I pack up my daypack, fill my water bottle, swallow an altitude sickness pill. Even the simplest tasks really do feel like climbing a mountain. Not only that, my head feels so crammed full that it's almost like there's no room left for anything else. I leave the larger bag outside my tent to be brought to our next camp. Not for the first time, I wonder what the success or failure rate would be for our travellers, if people had to carry their own supplies and fetch their own water. A surge of gratitude fills me. Whatever real-life crap is going on, I can choose to enjoy these precious moments. If I've learned anything from what happened to George, I should appreciate them. He'd give anything to be able to walk and talk again, let alone be climbing Kilimanjaro.

Samson organises us in our walking order for the day. I feel smug because I've figured out that the lead guide puts those who are coping the best near the back. While we're waiting to be given the go-ahead to set off, Luke moves next to me.

'I know what it feels like, you know,' he says. 'To want to win. It's only natural. For what it's worth, I think you've the best chance. Jacob is a hothead.'

'I thought the two of you got on?'

'We did . . .'

He doesn't elaborate.

'You have to tell me now.'

'I've lent him money on several occasions. I've always received it back, but there's something that bugs me about him. He's so privileged, and yet where's it got him?'

'Look at Hugo,' I say. 'The apple not falling far from the tree and all that.'

'Yes, but no matter what we think of Hugo, he's made his own success. My parents struggled financially and told me *never a borrower nor a lender be*. Jacob's got this way of making me feel like I owe him.'

He's right, I think, as we set off. We are only a few minutes into the trek when my breathing becomes more laboured. There is no conversation, only the sound of our footsteps falling into rhythm. It's soothing. We ascend a path scattered with small boulders and shrubs. Ghost-like clouds hover and a light mist descends, obscuring everything but our immediate surroundings.

I look down and focus on Lara's blue boots ahead of me. When we stop for a break after an hour, Clarabelle makes her way to my side.

'I've a bit of a headache,' she says, rubbing her forehead.

'Make sure you drink plenty,' I remind her.

Our guides keep very good, careful watch over us and constantly remind us of the importance of drinking enough. She takes several sips.

'God, I'm going to need to go and hide behind another rock to send an email,' she says. 'I didn't think that one of the hardest parts of the climb would be finding the perfect Wi-Fi spot all the time.' I laugh, because the toilet tent is now referred to as the Internet Café and going for a wee is sending an email.

'Shame we won't be roomies any more after tonight,' she continues. 'I'll be with Jacob.'

Wonderful news.

'Of course,' I say.

'Jacob let it slip while we were in Moshi about Mandy and Hugo,' she says. 'I wonder if someone should tell Sara? Jacob won't, out of warped loyalty to Hugo, but if it were me I'd want to know. I feel uncomfortable, especially as we're seeing Sara tonight. Jacob said that this type of thing has been going on his whole life. It's hard to imagine having a father like that.'

'I wouldn't know,' I say. 'My father wasn't around when I was growing up.'

I've got used to saying that over the years, but now, in this moment, the thought of who Hugo really is hits me again.

'I'm sorry,' she says, sounding genuine.

I don't know how to reply, so I don't. But someone should tell Sara, she's right.

'It does make me feel very uncomfortable,' I admit.

'Or maybe she knows? I do hope that Jacob wouldn't dare expect me to turn a blind eye to anything he does.'

Is she asking me if I know anything about Jacob? I decide to put her mind at rest.

'Seriously, Jacob is pretty much all work and no play,' I say. 'Well, no, that's not true. He does play but it's still work to him. He networks and wheels and deals. I've never seen him pay much attention to his colleagues unless he thinks he can get them to work harder, or they're withholding information from him which could be useful.'

'He got on well with George, though,' Clarabelle says. 'And Luke. But now they've fallen out. Luke seems quite chill, but I think the divide-and-conquer atmosphere at work can bring out the worst in some.'

'It *is* a toxic work environment,' I say. 'If I were in charge, things would be very different.'

I mean it. They would be.

'Jacob comes across as tough, but he's not quite as hard as he likes to make out. I sometimes wish he didn't work for his father's firm,' Clarabelle says.

I didn't even know *I* was working in my father's firm until a few days ago.

Samson picks up his backpack, indicating that we're ready to set off again. I shove my water bottle into the side of my rucksack, pleased to be ending this conversation. The clouds surround us, and the mist thickens. I concentrate on my footsteps and listen to my breathing. Breathe, step. Step, breathe.

I navigate the yellow lichen-covered rocks and tufts of grass, keeping my eye on the trail. As we approach the Lava Tower, the mist dissipates. As far as I can see, the landscape is rocky yet flat beyond. The sky is filled with a scattering of altostratus clouds, hopefully a harbinger of the weather to come. It looks like the sky has been raked, just like the sand at some of our luxury resorts. We all take out our cameras.

Adrian, Russell and Lara record a video with Adrian's camera.

'And here we are on day two of our incredible, once-in-a-lifetime journey . . .' I hear Lara say in a news presenter's voice. 'Behind me you can see the moon-like craters of the landscape in the shadow of Kibo. Right in front of me is the Lava Tower, a volcanic plug ninety metres tall.'

While they're busy recording their video, it reminds me to do my daily 'Where is the mascot now?' post. I'm pleased with how popular it has been so far.

As we approach our lunch stop, I notice some metal debris in the near distance.

'What's that?' I ask. 'It looks like the remains of a plane.'

'A helicopter,' says Samson. 'It happened a few months ago, it's very sad. Sometimes people go off on their own or they need to be rescued.'

'That's awful,' says Luke. 'Carelessness costs lives when people go rogue. I guess that's the reason BVT have so many safety rules in place when we get involved in extreme sports.'

'It didn't save George, did it?'

The words fly out of my mouth. I miss George more than ever on this trip.

'Oh God, I'm sorry. That was so careless of me,' he says. 'And very judgemental.'

I lower my voice. 'He and I are an item,' I blurt. 'But I

don't know if he's even aware of me when I visit him in hospital.'

It feels nice to say the words out loud after keeping it a secret at work for so long.

'Oh,' he says, matching my quiet tone. 'Oh,' he repeats. 'I see. I think.' He pauses as if digesting my revelation. 'Oh God, I had no idea. I'm sorry again,' he says. 'I feel so guilty about what happened. We all did. We all felt as though there was something more we should've done.'

'What do you mean? Do you think there was more to the accident than meets the eye?'

Luke sighs, as though giving my question careful consideration.

'No, that's not what I'm saying. I mean, *George* – climber extraordinaire. Of all the people for this to happen to . . . But it was thoroughly investigated and I can't see how it could be anything else.'

Luke sighs again before he continues. 'I think it was human error,' he says. 'His. I really do. Nothing else makes sense, and believe me, I've gone over and over the horror of that day. It took a while for it all to sink in. But he's alive, so there's hope, isn't there?'

There isn't. Honestly, short of a miracle, but I don't say this out loud. We've been warned by the medical staff that George is in a vegetative state and they are unable to offer much hope for the future. The longer he spends in this state, the less likely recovery is. People like believing there is hope. 'Perhaps,' I say, wondering whether to confide in Luke a little more.

'Every time I visit him, I get a fresh bout of survivor's guilt,' Luke admits.

'What do you think led up to it?' I say, staring ahead.

'We've been through this before,' he says. 'But if it makes you feel better . . .'

'It would,' I push.

'It was an incredibly intense trip,' says Luke. 'It felt like one of our heads would definitely be on the chopping block. Hugo was insufferable. More so than usual. Edward and Madelaine Armstrong were particularly demanding. The change in them on this trip is day and night. They used to be much worse. I think what happened to George shocked them as much as it did all of us.' He looks around and lowers his voice. 'It was Edward Armstrong who insisted we go caving. He told us all at the start of the trip that it was on his bucket list. He has some sort of hold over Hugo because of the death of their daughter.'

Luke stops.

'That reminds me of something. Have you read those comments by someone called the Anonymous Traveller on that work travel website?'

'No. What are they saying?'

'Someone is writing about BVT online anonymously. Thing is, the pressure we're put under on these trips is real.' He stops to take out his phone. 'Look,' he hands it to me. 'I've got some screenshots.'

Hopeful candidates are asked at their interview about their fears. An example: one of the first managers of this company was terrified of water after a near-drowning accident as a child. He was persuaded on to a team-building weekend coasteering: an exhilarating eco-adventure, with a blend of swell-diving, cliff jumping and rock-hopping. The outcome of the trip was interesting to say the least, so I've heard.

The point of this process is clear for anyone to see. It doesn't matter what anyone's individual fears are: snakes, spiders, heights, enclosed spaces . . . the details become irrelevant. Sooner or later, any fear will paralyse. And that's when this company flushes out a traitor or weak link. I predict things will get tough for this year's mountain climbers before they know it, because they no doubt will have divulged their fears. Every last one. It's too late.

'God, that sounds creepy,' I say. 'Do you reckon it's someone at Ethical Getaways?'

'It's likely.'

Before I can ask Luke if he thinks it could be linked to last year's disaster, we're interrupted by the sound of someone crying out in pain. We look back. Mandy is doubled over, clutching her stomach. Everyone rushes around her but the medic waves them away.

'Give her air. I'm dealing with it.'

'God, it feels like the food poisoning has hit again,' she cries, before she is violently sick.

A horrible thought hits. What if this isn't food poisoning? What if it's simply . . . poison?

Everything is happening around us so fast, it's hard to take in. Mandy is being held up by two of the guides. The three of them disappear into the distant mist without saying where they are going.

An eerie silence settles over the group.

'We will continue,' says Samson. 'She's in safe hands. An air ambulance has been summoned.'

We automatically line up in the same order, but Mandy's absence is stark.

Subdued doesn't even begin to cover it. The mist clears again, but there's no sign of anyone else until we hear the shuddering of a helicopter approaching. Not so long afterwards I spot it taking off – a disappearing speck – all the while knowing that it's whisking Mandy away into the unknown. All my anger towards her has gone.

Still, I can't stop myself looking ahead every now and then, expecting to see Mandy's sky-blue jacket. I feel a renewed pang of guilt each time I remember how ill and scared she looked and I can't stop shivering. *Pole, pole*, I repeat over in my mind like a mantra that will keep me safe. *Slow and steady wins the race*, no matter Hugo's opinions on the subject. I spend the rest of the walk beating myself up because it self-ishly crosses my mind that I'm a team member down now that Mandy has left us. That's already one of Hugo's challenges at risk. How many will make it up the mountain in good health? Or, more importantly, how many will make it back down?

'One of us should've gone with her,' says Lara.

She's right. And it should've been me, not a client. Not just out of concern for Mandy's welfare – it might have been my only chance to escape.

TEN

Jacob

Day Three: Hike to Barranco Camp

J acob wakes up and, for a moment, wonders where the hell he is as he watches his breath cloud in front of his face. Then he remembers. He can't be in actual hell because it's freezing. He moves on to his other side. It's no good, his bladder won't let him get comfortable. He hates that he can't make it through one night without this ritual of inconvenience. It was Flo's crap idea that they all take altitude sickness tablets and he wonders if she recommended it to their team as a sick joke. If he finds out that her team hasn't been taking them, he will lose it. He lies there, drifting in and out of sleep, trying to delay the inevitable. When he feels he's about to explode, he switches on his head torch, scrambles out of his bag and picks up the bottle, unzips his trousers and waits . . .

Nothing happens.

Christ, this is miserable, Jacob thinks. He lies back down. The same sensations of cold and pain reappear.

'Fuck this,' he mutters.

He pulls on a jacket, slides his feet into his boots without tying the bloody laces and shuffles to the toilet tent. Everyone else seems to have gotten the memo about bringing along a pair of flip flops, sliders or Crocs. Sitting on the toilet, despite the stench of chemicals, turns out to be a blessing in disguise as he has the runs as well. Seriously? He has forgotten bog roll, so he – thank God – manages to shuffle back, fish around in his bag, locate some and repeat his steps. He'll be lucky if he gets any more sleep at all. He immediately feels better. Until he realises just how exhausted he is from the effort. He'll never take en suite for granted again.

He sits there for a few more seconds, uncomfortable and cold, to ensure he doesn't have to traipse back a third time. He hears the thud of approaching footsteps. The zip starts to open.

'I'm in here!' he calls out.

Usually people call out, asking if it's free.

The unzipping stops but the gap remains. An extra blast of icy air comes rushing through. Whoever is out there doesn't speak or attempt to re-do the zip.

'Hello?'

Nothing. Jacob hears the footsteps receding. They don't even try the adjacent toilet tent. Perhaps it's a sleepwalker, but it's still odd as it takes monumental effort and desperation to leave the tent. Jacob navigates his way back, shining his torch around to see if he can spot anyone, but it's as if he's alone in the world. There's a calm silence, and if he wasn't feeling so ill at ease, he'd enjoy this moment of peace. It's a different kind of tiring having to be on duty all the time for their clients.

He looks around, still spooked. There are no tell-tale beams of light shining through the canvas from any of the other tents. He pauses when he passes Casper and Joey's tent. Nothing, not even the sound of snoring. All he can hear is the odd cough every now and then from the tents further away. Maybe it was someone from a different tour company who got lost and was too embarrassed to identify themselves. An unpleasant thought hits. Maybe the culprit of the glass-in-his-sleeping-bag jape isn't in their camp. It could have been a stranger climbing with a different tour company. The mountain is busy, there are endless suspects.

He stands still, despite the cold and wind. Above, the clear, starlit sky is mesmerising. But soon, the temperature gets to him, so he bends down to his tent. The zip is slightly open. Jacob knows he did it up properly because he remembers thinking that any protection against the cold night air was better than none. His stomach lurches. More broken glass? Is it his turn for a scorpion? Or worse, a snake – his biggest phobia. He pokes his head in and twists around so that the beam from his head torch rotates around the tent in a circular motion, checking out the entire space. Nothing untoward. Exhausted, he crawls inside. He shakes out his sleeping bag, just in case. Still, nothing. No amount of lavender oil is going to help him sleep, he thinks, wishing, for the first time, that he was sharing a tent.

It's light when he rouses and immediately checks his phone. There's a message from Clarabelle.

Can't wait to see you later! I reckon Florence will be glad to get rid of me as it means she can share with Luke without being rumbled! Love you, Jelly Tot. xxx

This does not put Jacob in the greatest mood to start the day. The smell of bacon and sausages wafts over. He hears the chefs chatting and laughing. The sounds and smells of camp life are becoming comfortingly familiar.

He cleans his teeth after adding an iodine tablet to the water. BVT paid for a large water purifier system but he's been advised that it can't harm to treat water a second time to prevent potential illness. At first, he struggled with the taste, but he's become used to it. From his brief chats with climbers from other groups, no one else has their own water purifier. Jacob wouldn't say they have an unfair advantage, but it would be wrong to think that everyone is attempting this climb from the same position.

One thing that has been bothering him is the occasional chocolate bar wrappers or such-like that he spots scattered across the mountain, no doubt dropped by careless tourists. He's seen the hard-working team pick up bits and pieces and it strikes him that he could do it too to make up for the champagne incident. Hugo may even be impressed if he sets up a litter-picking scheme. 'See it, pick it up, do good while having fun' type of thing.

Dipping his fingers in a mug, he wets the parts of his hair which are sticking up, patting them down. He applies sunscreen and insect repellent. He's desperate for a decent shower, not least because the layers of chemicals and cream feel sticky and uncomfortable. Having done the best job he can to freshen up by using wet wipes and deodorant, he wanders over to the dining tent.

He is the last person to arrive in the dining tent and is forced to squeeze on to a bench between Imogen and Joey. He tunes them out and digs into porridge, followed by eggs, sausages and bread. If he's going to suffer from lack of sleep today, he's certainly not going to suffer from lack of food.

'I hate eggs,' says Imogen. 'They don't agree with me. Honestly, I get the runs just looking at them!' She giggles.

Jacob grips his knife and fork just a little tighter.

As he's mopping up the yolk with a huge slice of crusty bread, he spots Casper and Hugo knocking back coffee, asking for more and chatting away like best friends. Paranoia hits. What if Hugo has decided that Casper would be a better bet than him? If Casper does know about him and Joey, it's exactly the kind of way he'd take revenge. An eye for an eye.

Jacob loses his appetite. He picks up his phone as though he's very busy and important, even though he currently doesn't have any signal and it's getting harder to work. In a way, it's good. He'd struggle to post anything positive right now, especially after bloody Florence posted last night about her sunset afternoon tea. Hashtag bloody Florence and her ridiculous ideas, like the keyring mascot. Pathetic, and yet people seem to love it.

Still, it's better than in previous years. Like last year, when George and Luke were the leaders. They had to be the first to complete what Hugo referred to as an exhilarating challenge. Both opted for bungee jumps. Irony is that it was safer than the so-called easier caving option they completed just two days later.

The year before that was a guy called Gareth Snow and a woman named Jen Howard. Jen won and Gareth had his contract terminated. Jacob suspects that it wasn't because he'd lost but because Gareth was, in Hugo's words, 'becoming a liability'. Jen left soon afterwards anyway. She said that the challenges they'd been set, one being a version of hide and seek in a Norwegian forest while cross-country skiing, were OTT when the whole point of their job – surely – was to keep the clients happy.

'If I wanted to be in a reality show where the aim was to get rid of my opponent at all costs, then that's what I'd do,' she said. 'But I'm a travel visionary and experienced agent who doesn't need any extra crap in my life. This company sucks.'

Hugo said if he'd known she referred to herself as a travel visionary he'd have spared Gareth and gotten rid of Jen on that basis alone. She runs an online travel company now and by all accounts is doing well.

Around them, porters pack up camp in readiness to leave. Someone walks past Jacob with his duffel bag which has been wrapped in canvas. He's also clutching a carrier bag filled to the brim with bread. Jacob half-wonders if they're Imogen's gluten-free loaves, packaged separately from the others because she's been such a pain in the arse. The thought, for some reason, makes him want to laugh out loud. Casper and his boots, Imogen and her bread. Jacob and his debts and paranoia. Not quite so funny.

Ben organises the group in their walking order. Hugo is always positioned at the front behind the lead guide. Not because of who he is – it doesn't count for anything here – but because he is the least fit and the weakest. Hugo has various ailments for which he takes specialist medication, despite trying to give the impression that he's immortal. Jacob's usually near the back. He likes being able to keep an eye on

165

the others. Today will be tough because they're going to aim for Barranco Camp to merge with the other group, rather than spending the night in a closer camp.

'We are going to head towards the east,' says Ben. 'Remember, *pole, pole.*'

Their initial ascent is gentle, and Jacob finds it frustrating walking so slowly. If he could run, it would help block out all the dark thoughts. He wonders how the hell he's going to pay Casper back. Clarabelle has already lent Jacob more than he owes Casper. It's one problem on top of another. It's not that Jacob likes borrowing money, far from it. He never thought that Hugo would cut his allowance, it's criminal really. Companies wouldn't be allowed to slash their employee's salaries down to nothing without warning. The same courtesy should've applied to Jacob with regards to his allowance, he feels.

He looks at Joey who is several people ahead in line. It's her he should be with. Clarabelle deserves better than Jacob and Casper doesn't deserve someone like Joey. He doesn't get her like Jacob does. He's always talking down to her, and Jacob hates the way she doesn't pull him up on it. The trouble with being in debt – one of the many problems – is that it takes away free choice. Clarabelle wants them to live together. The very thought of it is suffocating. If she owed Jacob money and not the other way round, he wouldn't be beholden. Fact of the matter is that he doesn't want to traipse around viewing houses and discussing wall colours. He simply doesn't care enough about the boring details. Jacob hired a respected interior designer to create his haven – an apartment with a riverside view over the Thames. He finds it calming. He loves the silence at the end of a long working day or the privacy to lick his wounds without having to pretend he's OK.

He exhales. He's only one big win away from solving all his problems. He must remind himself of that.

The vast, barren landscape takes over. Step, step. Step, step. Stop for water and popcorn. Repeat. Jacob slides a packet of nicotine gum from his pocket and chews on it. He's resisted up until now but the craving for a real cigarette is getting stronger. He barely has time to remove it from the wrapper before Ben asks them to set off again.

'Keep going,' Ben says. 'We're heading to the east and the plan is to have lunch near a volcanic rock formation called the Lava Tower. No doubt you've all read about it. There's an incredible view from there. By then, you will have climbed to fifteen thousand feet or four thousand six hundred metres.'

'Wow. That's feels like some achievement,' says Sara. 'I've never really done any climbing.'

Fifteen thousand feet is good, but Jacob mustn't take his eyes off the ultimate prize: winning. He and his teammates must summit. He's panting slightly, despite the slowness of his steps. The sky is a brilliant, fresh blue and there's barely any wind. It's so much warmer than last night. Their guides remind them how fortunate they all are because apparently there are times at this point when temperatures can be bitter.

Jacob runs through their itinerary again to stave off the boredom.

Tonight: Barranco Camp, two nights. Reunite with Flo's team.

Tomorrow: Acclimatisation walk. (Designed to give us maximum chance of summit success, according to Florence.)

The day after: Hike for approx. six hours. Climb the Barranco Wall, created from volcanic rock. Spend the night in Karanga Camp.

The day after that: Hike approx. six hours to 4,600 metres. Night in Barafu Camp, last camp before the summit attempt.

Set off for summit around midnight.

Final night to be in Mweka Camp on the descent.

Beers and a smoke. Chill on a beach in Dar es Salaam, celebrating winning the challenges.

Jacob loses track of time. As they are weaving up a scree path, Jacob's spirits are raised when he hears someone – he doesn't catch who – cry out.

'I can see the Lava Tower!'

A tall stone tower comes into view. It's surrounded by smaller rocks which look as if they are precariously balancing on top of one another.

'Unbelievable,' says Jacob, staring up at the volcanic structure. 'Worth the walk.'

'I agree,' says Casper.

'This will be the highest we climb today,' says Ben.

Jacob is relieved. He can tell that the altitude is getting to him because this is the hardest he's found it to breathe so far. After lunch, they'll descend and head for their next camp. Their trip is bespoke, as in, designed by Florence, determined to prove her organisational skills. Apparently, some organised tours spend an extra night at Shira II camp before setting off for Barranco Camp and it crosses Jacob's mind that Flo planned it on bloody purpose to try and make his hike harder. Too late to worry about it now.

While they are sitting among the smaller rocks near the

base of the three-hundred-foot tower, Hugo strolls over and sits beside Jacob while he's staring at his phone, willing it to send him some good news. There's no signal.

'Any updates?' Hugo asks.

He's wheezing slightly. His face is red and he coughs.

Jacob doesn't ask him if he's all right because Hugo doesn't like to draw attention to anything he perceives as weakness. As usual, Jacob tells him what he wants to hear.

'Ethical Getaways are doing well enough, to be honest, but I've come up with a scheme to show that we're not just climbing to raise money for charity but also to do our bit. I may persuade everyone to get involved in a couple of minutes of daily litter-picking to highlight our commitment to the environment too.'

Hugo looks at Jacob as if he's lost it.

'You want our valued VIPs to try and help you win?'

'No. I think they'd enjoy being a part of something which helps, in however small a way.'

'I haven't seen any litter, myself,' Hugo says. 'Apart from your champagne bottles.'

'I think it's a good idea,' Jacob pushes. 'I'm not saying there's loads. We can make a small difference. I thought you'd approve.'

'There is no litter. The camps are clean and well maintained. Why don't you speak to other climbers in our camps to get new business if you have excess energy? They're the perfect targets. They've already shown themselves to be willing and open to travel by being here. Flo's managed to bring in a considerable amount by using her own initiative. She's wandered around the campsites, networking amongst travellers, listening to stories, learning things of value. Mandy says she barely sits down, she's always on the go.'

Familiar rage festers. The thought of Simon, the fired ex-BVT manager, pops into Jacob's head. If this is how angry Simon had felt at times, it was no wonder if he'd taken to posting angry messages online.

'I'm not trying to knock you down for the sake of it,' Hugo continues. 'I'm just saying that you can't try and force our group to hunt for litter which doesn't exist.'

'I'm not saying it's a huge problem. I'm saying . . .' Jacob gives up.

Sara looks over at them. Hugo blows her a kiss.

'It would be a shame if Sara were to find out about Mandy,' Jacob blurts out.

From the look on Hugo's face, it suddenly feels as though the mountain temperature has plummeted.

'And how would that happen?'

'I'm just saying . . .' Jacob stops. He doesn't want to be the one to hurt Sara.

'You're just saying that if you can't win fair and square, you'll blackmail me? How do you think that's going to work out?'

The knot in Jacob's stomach suddenly disappears. He feels as if he's watching himself from afar. He's not prepared to accept his father's treatment of him a moment longer. After all, he's done more for Hugo than anyone else in his life.

'I'm not blackmailing you. I'm telling you that I'm going to win.'

And he is. One way or another.

Jacob stands up. Time to give Hugo food for thought as he slowly, slowly tackles the mountain. Hugo's getting weaker, Jacob can see it. This is his perfect time to strike while the iron feels nicely hot. It's not fair the way Hugo treats him.

He's done everything in his power to get Hugo to respect him. Jacob takes his camera out of its case and leaves Hugo looking after his backpack. He takes his time snapping photos until he notices Ben gathering everyone together. He strides over to Hugo, then picks up his hiking poles in preparation. Hugo jolts back slightly as he does so, as if he's afraid that Jacob's going to strike him. He recovers himself quickly, clearly ashamed, and picks up his own poles. Jacob notices that his father's hands shake slightly.

'Are you feeling all right?' Jacob asks, putting a hand on his shoulder. 'You look a bit unsteady.'

Hugo shrugs him off. 'I'm fine. Don't fuss.'

And just like that, any sense of affection or concern for his father tears apart and disappears on the mountain breeze.

They begin their descent towards camp along a path of loose rocks and pebbles, treacherous underfoot. They pass beneath the distinctive giant groundsel trees, found only on Kilimanjaro. They look like woody cacti and it highlights to him what a different landscape they're in.

They're just a few minutes along the path when he feels a splash of rain hit his cheek. It's the first rain they've had, Jacob thinks, as everyone yanks up their hoods and double-checks that their bags are fully protected with covers. They've been warned several times that soggy clothes for the rest of the trip could be the end of their climb. They push on, only now Jacob's senses are muffled by his hood. He feels cut off from everyone and everything.

Jacob looks up and sees Blackmore Vintage Travel written in silver across the back of nearly everyone's daypacks. BVT's shiny company logo – pearls in an oyster, surrounded by a map of the world – glistens in the rain. It increases in intensity, hard and fast. Then, as quickly as it began, the rainstorm dies down. There's a new freshness in the air. Jacob would even go so far as to say it's joyful. Clients, friends and a couple of cousins who have climbed Kilimanjaro all told him that it was life-changing and that he'd never feel the same. Every day, he understands their words more.

As they descend into the valley, one of the volcanic cones looms beyond it. They navigate the moon-like surface, and one of the guides points out landmarks and areas of interest.

'. . . a unique, micro-climate area . . .'

Above the guide's voice he suddenly hears what sounds like a helicopter in the distance. They all look up when the vibrations get louder as it passes over them, the different shades of silver and grey visible, before it moves away and lands out of sight.

'Does that mean that someone is being rescued?' asks Joey.

'Perhaps,' says Ben, appearing unconcerned. But on their next break, Jacob spots him urgently typing a message into his phone.

'Is everything OK?' Jacob asks, drawing near.

'Fine,' replies Ben. He looks at his watch. 'We must get going.'

Upon arrival into camp, Jacob's knees ache and he's shattered as they line up to sign in.

He'll miss having his own space because even though they'll remain in their separate teams, Jacob knows Clarabelle will want to share his tent. He can't think of a good enough reason to talk her out of it. According to Ben, who keeps in touch with the other team via handheld radio, Florence's team are half an hour behind them. They should've made it to camp first, so Jacob assumes they left later than anticipated.

He unpacks his torch, e-reader and water bottle, and places them in easy reach of his sleeping mat. Since the broken-glass incident, he no longer unrolls his bag until he's ready to wriggle inside. Shit. His spare phone battery is missing. Jacob checks the contents of his daypack, but he already knows, deep down, that it's futile. Someone has stolen it to put him at a disadvantage. He scrolls back through his mind, trying to think who would've been close enough to him during the breaks. Hugo is the prime suspect.

He clambers out of the tent, trying to draw as much air into his lungs as possible. He'll wait until Hugo and Sara have gone for dinner then he'll search their tent. Hugo's not getting away with this.

He sees a fresh group of arrivals and at first he doesn't recognise anyone, but then he spots Flo and Clarabelle. He walks over to greet them, secretly glad that they look so rough.

And then he feels like a total shit because the reason they're so glum is because the helicopter was for Mandy.

'She was in so much pain, it was just awful,' says Clarabelle.

'I guess she shouldn't have climbed after her food poisoning,' Jacob says. 'I had a bad bout once after some minestrone soup and it does come and go in waves.'

Flo goes off to talk to Samson, and Clarabelle murmurs, 'I overheard Flo say to Luke that she wondered if Mandy had been poisoned. Why would she think that? She looked embarrassed when I asked her.'

'Why would anyone deliberately poison Mandy?'

And yet, he thinks privately, although it sounds far-fetched, when Jacob adds all the little things together, the glass, the mystery person creeping around camp, his missing phone battery, it all makes him wonder . . . what if someone found out the truth about what really happened on last year's trip?

ELEVEN

Florence

Day Three Evening: Barranco Camp. 3,960 metres or 13,000 feet (approx.)

The backs of my calves feel tight. But as soon as we descend into the valley, I take in the view of the camp and the incredible sight of the groundsel trees. My eyes seek the blue, orange and yellow tents with *Blackmore Vintage Travel* boldly splashed across the sides along with our logo. As soon as I do so, I speed up towards familiarity, desperate to rest.

The first person I see is Sara. Her hair is tied back in a crimson scarf. She's wearing mirrored sunglasses and sits alone, sipping from a mug. As I get closer, I see steam rising from it.

The sight of her throws me because according to the itinerary I devised, our group should have arrived first.

My heart rate picks up at the thought of seeing Hugo. Authentic interaction between us feels impossible until I have all the answers I need.

Despite my desire to sink down to the ground and process what's happened to Mandy, I hesitate by the welcome sign, to delay seeing Hugo for as long as possible. I take my camera out of my side pocket as the rest of the group file past me.

KILIMANJARO NATIONAL PARK
TANZANIA
BARRANCO CAMP
ELEVATION: 3900M
VEGETATION ZONE: MOORLAND
UHURU PEAK 15KM (15HRS)

Fifteen hours . . . Sounds so easy. Sara looks over in my direction, so I approach her.

'Florence, hi. Hugo got a message about Mandy. Sorry to hear the sad news.'

Sara doesn't quite look me in the eyes as she says it.

She knows about Hugo and Mandy, flashes through my mind.

'It was awful,' I say. 'One moment she was fine, the next she was in great pain.' I look around. 'Where's everyone else?'

She shrugs, as though she has no idea. But just at that moment, Hugo appears from behind a tent.

'Hello, hello, my dear!' he says, giving me an awkward pat on the shoulder.

I stiffen. 'Hello. I'm worried about Mandy. It's awful.'

'Yes, it is awful,' he says, hastily changing his expression into one of concern. 'Good thing is, we have the best money can buy private healthcare available to us at BVT, so I can guarantee that she'll have tip-top care.'

'Just like George, then,' I say.

He gives an awkward smile. 'Exactly. Just like George.'

'And George is far from fine,' I remind him, walking away.

I've just been waylaid by Clarabelle when I spot Jacob emerging from his tent. He looks cheerful – no doubt delighted to have arrived at camp before us – but his expression changes when we tell him about Mandy. Feeling suddenly exhausted, I give some excuse about needing to talk to Samson and slip away.

I zip myself into my tent, remove my boots, brush the soil off my socks and unroll my sleeping bag. Then I sit cross-legged. I close my eyes and relish the feeling of being off-duty for a few blissful seconds.

'Flora, Flora, dear . . .' I hear Mrs Armstrong outside my tent.

For fuck's sake. How many times do I have to tell her it's Florence?

'Yes, Mrs Armstrong?' I call out, after taking a calming breath.

'Can you come to our tent, please, and sort out an issue? It's urgent.'

Another deep breath. 'Of course.'

It turns out that the issue is a broken zip on Mr Armstrong's sleeping bag.

'I have an emergency sewing kit,' I say. 'I'll do my best, but if not we can swap sleeping bags.'

'Thank you, that's very kind,' says Mrs Armstrong, without hesitation.

I reach down to pick up the sleeping bag, roll it up and take it back to my tent for a closer look. The zip has clearly been yanked hard, so no wonder it broke. I fold mine up, put it neatly in its bag and deliver it to Mr and Mrs Armstrong's tent.

'We're very grateful,' says Mr Armstrong.

Our group reunion is a strange affair and not how I imagined it would unfold.

Imogen gives me a big hug as I approach the mess tent.

'I missed you,' she said before whispering in my ear, 'Jacob can be a right old grump.'

I laugh.

Casper, Jonessa and even Jacob appear on edge, unsure what to do once we've gone through what happened to Mandy in detail. In dribs and drabs, we hang out in our mess tent, sipping tea, largely ignoring the plate of digestive biscuits on offer. The inevitable comparisons about our past few days surface and we swap tales of relative hardship and our collective determination to summit. I find it hard to care as much as I did at the beginning. What seemed like fun and healthy competition when we planned this trip now feels sinister and unsettling.

'Did you see any birds?' asks Mr Armstrong during a silence. 'I'm sure I spotted a green sunbird when we arrived in camp. I'm annoyed that I wasn't quick enough to get a photo.'

As Adrian and Russell respond, claiming that they are keen to spot as many birds as they can, Luke puts his arm around me and gives me a tight squeeze.

'Mandy'll be all right,' he says.

Jacob looks over at us, his face stricken. He and Mandy have always seemed fond of one another.

'Samson has a satellite phone,' Luke continues. 'He's sure to keep in touch if we aren't able to, and pass on any relevant information. We can make decisions on a need-to-make basis. Mandy will feel guilty if we all give up then it turns out she's right as rain tomorrow.'

'Maybe,' I say, releasing myself from Luke's grip. 'She did look awful, though.'

'She's in good hands,' says Luke. 'I'm sure of it.' He pauses. 'I've an idea,' he continues in an authoritative voice. 'Why don't we put it to the vote? Stay or continue?'

We exchange glances across the table, gauging reactions.

'Definitely stay,' says Jacob. 'I know that's what Mandy would want, and no news is good news, surely?'

The Armstrongs raise their hands. 'We agree,' they say.

Everyone present votes unanimously to continue the trip.

'Even with heavy hearts,' says Luke. 'If anyone wants to talk about any concerns, I'm happy to be a listening ear.'

'As am I,' I quickly add, before Jacob or Hugo can accuse me of not taking the lead.

It's way too cold and windy to eat outside this evening, so we eat dinner in separate mess tents in our usual teams, as there isn't one big enough for us all to eat together. It's a relief, because to act normally in front of Jacob and Hugo is an effort.

Our feast this evening is a potato and leek soup with brown bread and butter, followed by spicy fried chicken and rice.

After dinner, as we're awaiting a promised dessert of chocolate cookies, and flasks of tea, there's a tickling sensation across my wrist as something scuttles over it. I yelp, half-expecting it to be a scorpion.

'Did anyone else see a spider?' I say, standing up and brushing down my arms, despite no sign of any creepy crawlies.

'No,' comes a chorus of replies.

Still, everyone humours me by shining torches beneath the table and lifting their feet, searching for an insect or a spider, but no, there's nothing.

'Who's up for a game of Scrabble or cards?' Luke asks after

we've eaten our cookies, thanked the chefs and are sipping our hot chocolates.

Everyone, it seems by the enthusiastic show of hands. Both groups crowd into our tent, carrying extra canvas camping chairs, and although it's a squeeze, we play Uno as if our lives depend on it.

Jacob chucks down a card half-heartedly into the central pile. It's not even the right number or colour to match with the top card.

'Oi, that's cheating,' says Adrian.

'A mistake,' says Jacob. 'Anyway, it's to your advantage. You know what one of my cards is now.'

'Big deal,' Luke mutters, as everyone else laughs.

'Do you like cheating, Jacob?' asks Jonessa.

He appears not to hear.

'Shame no one brought Travel Monopoly,' says Casper. 'Jacob could be the banker.'

'I quit,' says Jacob, throwing his cards down on the table.

He stands up and Clarabelle does too, concern etched across her face.

'No,' he says to her. 'You stay. I just need some fresh air.' He laughs to himself. It goes quiet for a few seconds before Hettie suggests a game of gin rummy.

'I'll sit this one out,' I say. 'I'm getting tired. I'll just watch.'

'You sure?' says Luke. 'Do you want me to walk you back to your tent?'

'Nice idea, thanks. But I've not been sleeping very well and I'm going to give it another half-hour or so. Maybe I'll even take a leaf out of Jacob's book.'

I slip out while everyone is engrossed, arguing over different interpretations of the rules.

Immediately, I aim for Jacob's tent.

He's not there.

I check the internet café – aka the toilet tent. No sign.

From inside a cluster of tents I can hear chatter, laughter, some eighties music.

Torchlight hovers on the far side of the camp. I follow the light and discover Jacob – my *half-brother* – standing beside a large green tent, staring ahead into the dark. The logo on the tent is the name of a competitor's adventure travel company. I hadn't expected the mountain to be so populated. It seems that each time I look, I spot company names I've never heard of, and we're surrounded by different languages. My world has become a bubble and I've lost track of what's going on beyond it.

Jacob swings round. 'Who's there?'

He sounds frightened.

'It's me. Florence.'

'Oh.' A pause. 'What do you want?'

Good point. What do I want?

'The scorpion,' I say. 'It was a prank too far.'

'Ditto.'

'Now you've lost me.'

'The glass in my sleeping bag?'

'No idea what you're talking about,' I say. 'I was never into that ridiculous pranks crap. I just want to do my job, do it well and succeed in summiting.'

'Strange, don't you think? That neither one of us knows what the other is talking about? Especially as Hugo believes in divide and conquer. If you think about it, Flo, how on earth do you think I smuggled a scorpion through two sets of customs, and then, what the hell do you think I fed it in my hotel room? I don't even know what they eat, for Christ's sake, let alone where to find them. I barely remember to feed the fish in my aquarium. A company comes round to my flat twice a week to clean and do whatever it is fish need doing, like maybe give them extra seaweed. Who knows? I don't know and I don't care.'

Put like that . . .

'Or do you think in Moshi I nipped out for a spot of scorpion hunting between looking after our clients?'

'You seem on edge,' I say.

'Of course I'm on bloody edge,' he says. 'I'm stuck halfway up a mountain with a bunch of mismatched people for a team, I haven't had a cigarette in three days and Imogen never shuts up about her food likes and dislikes. It's enough to send anyone hurtling towards the edge. And on top of that, I'm concerned for Mandy. I know she'll be OK but I'd rather she was here than—'

'Me,' I finish for him.

'I didn't say that,' he says.

I mull over how best to word what I want to ask him. I've grilled him before but now he seems less on guard, vulnerable, even.

'Mandy's situation has dredged up the memories of last year . . .' I begin.

Jacob crosses his arms and glares.

'I still don't understand how it happened . . .'

'Neither do I,' he says. 'It was all so fast.'

'Can you talk me through it again? It was vertical caving . . .' I prompt.

'I can't remember much,' he says. 'I try so hard not to think about it.'

'You abseiled into the caves,' I push. 'Were all of you there?'

'Initially, yes. Me, Luke, Hugo, Mandy, George, the Armstrongs, all the VIP clients, including Casper.'

'Casper?'

'Yes, he comes on all the trips. He's a permanent tag-along, just like the Armstrongs. It seems once our guests have had a taste of what's offered on the Great Escape, they can't resist coming along every year.' Jacob shrugs.

I didn't know that about Casper. Why didn't I know that? I thought it was only the Armstrongs who attended each year, in memory of their daughter. I remember at the time when they announced the names for the trip feeling so annoyed that I hadn't been picked to accompany the team. Instead, I was part of the skeleton staff left to man the office, and it had rankled. And then afterwards, it had been such a horrific shock. Once George had been cleared to fly home with medical assistance, I waited at Heathrow for hours. I knew I was too early for George's flight, but I hadn't known what else to do to distract myself. George's parents arrived early too. We sat in a chain café, drinking bottomless coffees.

'I don't remember seeing Casper in any of the photos.'

'He joined us late. He flew in from LA because he was at some conference in New York the previous week.'

'What happened on the way out of the caves?' I ask. 'Were you all there?'

'Yes. We were all gathered, waiting. George was the last climber. It was pretty simple. Scratch that, it should have been simple. All we had to do was jumar out of the cave. It was our last challenge. We were going to have a celebration meal at a local restaurant that evening.'

Caving is one of the few things I haven't experienced at

BVT yet. I recall George explaining to me that a jumar is a clamp attached to a fixed rope which automatically tightens when weight is applied and relaxes when it's removed. What they were doing wouldn't have been difficult for him. Not at all.

'And then . . .' He stops. 'I really don't want to talk about this, Florence. We've got enough to worry about, getting ourselves to the summit and back. Going back over old times won't magically fix him. Poor guy.'

We stand in silence.

'Do you think Mandy was poisoned?' He breaks the silence.

The hairs rise on the nape of my neck. 'What makes you say that?'

'Do you, or don't you?'

I try to imagine what it would've been like if we'd been brought up together and developed an authentic brother and sister relationship. I can't help but wonder who'd have won the arguments. Me, I reckon, although Jacob would've given as good as he got. I wonder if he'd have been protective of me. Although I can imagine him, with a group of friends, sneaking into my room or taking the piss. Thing is, we'll never know. It's something else Hugo denied me – a huge chunk of my childhood.

I feel a sudden rush of affection towards Jacob. He looks vulnerable. I should tell him that we're related. But I'm too tired to deal with any drama, and if I start battles, I'll lose. Brother or no brother, I can't afford that.

'It did cross my mind that she may have been poisoned deliberately,' I admit.

'Why?'

'Someone stole my diary while we were in Nairobi,' I say,

watching his reaction closely. 'Someone who knows that I'm determined to get to the bottom of what happened to George. I think they broke into my room while I was asleep.'

'You're losing me,' he says. 'I can't keep track of poison, stolen diaries and whatever else is going on with you.'

He's quite convincing. Maybe he didn't have anything to do with it after all.

'I think we should head back,' I say.

'Yes,' he agrees. 'We're enemies. We shouldn't be out here, having this conversation.'

'Enemies sounds harsh. I prefer the term rivals.'

He shrugs, switches off his torch and disappears into the darkness.

As I navigate my way back to the mess tent, more diary entries flood my mind.

George said that all the team-building exercises he arranged while in New Zealand were cancelled prior to their arrival and any further ideas were dismissed as unworthy of consideration. Only the activities arranged by Hugo or Jacob were allowed, which was odd, given that George and Luke were the leaders. In fact, the whole trip felt like a farce, George said. 'It's all a load of shit. Team building is supposed to strengthen bonds and commitment, and yet every year it seems to have the opposite effect.'

A façade for something else, perhaps? But what?

I recall writing *BUT WHAT?* in capital letters and underlining those two words.

I've looked back at past itineraries. They were all pretty formulaic, give or take the extreme team-building exercises or challenge details. The winners are whisked off for a long weekend of luxury. Butlers, massages, five-star cuisine, limousine transfers . . .

The losers are expected back in the office. They appear at their desks early, despite the inevitable jet lag, keep their heads down and tap away furiously on their keyboards as though it will save them from their fates.

A gust of wind hits my face and sends shivers down me. I realise that I left my inner jacket in the mess tent. I retrace my steps and poke my head through the opening.

Empty.

The camping lights are extinguished. I shine my torch around. It's hard to see, and when the light flickers and dies, I realise that the batteries have run out. I switch on my head torch and I'm pleased to spot my jacket hanging on the back of a chair, but it's not the same one I sat on. Odd.

I catch sight of something shiny on the table. A Scrabble board and a carving knife. Weird. The chefs are meticulous at clearing up. Annoyed that the last players didn't tidy away these items, I decide to ignore them. Probably Mr and Mrs Armstrong, expecting someone else to do it for them. As I pick up my jacket, I catch sight of some words on the board.

Failure. Florence. Quit before it's too late. The *f* in *before* is represented by a blank tile. The tip of the knife is pointing at the word *late*. I hear boots stomping on the ground outside, but when I open the tent's flap there's no torchlight, no sign of anyone. Shivering, I take a photo of the scene as evidence that I'm not imagining it. Then I place the knife to one side and fold away the Scrabble board, tipping the tiles into the box.

I came here to win and to find out what happened to George, but Hugo's bombshell confession has thrown me off course. Someone is trying to push me over the edge, someone who doesn't want me to win. Jacob. Or maybe I'm wrong. Perhaps someone doesn't like the thought of me looking too closely at George's accident. And if not, why?

Someone steps inside. Before I can help myself I let out a yell and pick up the knife.

'What the hell?' says Jacob.

I look down at my hand gripping the handle, the tip facing Jacob. 'Oh God, I'm sorry! There was a strange threatening message here,' I say, lowering my arm to my side, still clutching the knife.

'Can you put that knife down, please,' he says, looking down at the Scrabble box.

I slowly place the knife down on the far side of the table.

'I took a photo, look,' I say, showing him the image.

He glances down briefly but then stares at me as though I'm mad. I remember how Luke looked at me the same way when I shared my poisoning theory about Mandy. I hate these types of glances.

'I don't think it means anything,' he says.

I can't think of a suitable reply.

TWELVE

Jacob

*Day Four: Barranco Camp. 3,960 metres or
13,000 feet (approx.). Acclimatisation Hike*

T his morning's acclimatisation hike feels like a slight
hindrance to proper progress. Jacob gets that it increases
their chances of summiting, but most companies don't
add in acclimatisation days and they still make it. Admittedly,
he doesn't have figures of the exact success rates and the
breakdown of the health and fitness of their clients. Clarabelle
sleeps silently beside him. Last night, she wanted to sleep in
the same bag, squashed so tight neither of them could turn
round. Eventually, she had to admit it was a crap idea but not
until she'd taken a selfie of them for Insta.

According to his watch, it's 6 a.m. They're not expected to
be up and about for another hour and a half. *Peace and quiet*,
thinks Jacob. He crawls into the outer part of their tent and
puts on his walking boots without doing up the laces. As he
steps out, the cold hits. A piece of paper skitters across the
ground. He finds himself rushing over to pick it up, pleased

it proves his litter point while at the same time aware that this is what his life has come to: his being pleased to see rubbish. The piece of paper is, in fact, a Blackmore Vintage Travel leaflet. Hugo's mouth grins at Jacob like a toothpaste advert. Freshly enraged at so many things – this bloody leaflet almost summarising everything that is wrong with his life – he unzips Hugo and Sara's tent slightly and posts it through the hole, finding it childishly and deeply satisfying. He doesn't bother to zip the tent back up.

In his day-to-day life, Jacob would go to the gym for a half-hearted run on the treadmill while watching bad news unfold across the world on the giant, unavoidable TV monitors. Or he'd have a coffee, smoke a cigarette or scroll through other people's lives to measure his achievements and failures. Here, he's stuck with people he mostly doesn't like, stuck with the wrong woman, stuck without cigarettes or alcohol, stuck with his fears and thoughts. Stuck. Even the word sounds ugly.

Ben walks towards him.

'Good news!' he says. 'My colleagues at base have informed me that Mandy has made a full recovery.'

'That is good news. What was wrong with her?' Jacob asks.

'I don't think she'd gotten over her food poisoning.'

As Jacob composes a message to Mandy, he receives one from an unknown number. The words make him feel like he'll be the next one to throw up.

See you've enough to pay for a holiday. Enjoy your time!
Me and my mates will be waiting at Heathrow.

The next message names the right airline and the two possible dates for a return. There are two because the winner and loser will be returning separately. The winner will be whisked off to Dar es Salaam for a few days of luxury and the loser will be expected to fly back to the office.

Christ. This feels like they have insider bloody knowledge.

Six weeks ago, Jacob borrowed money from a bloke, 'Billy', he met in a pub. He's fully aware of how stupid he has been.

The pub was down the road from one of his favourite casinos. And yes, he knows that it was hardly likely to be a coincidence that he just happened to encounter a loan shark in such a location. In his defence, Jacob thought he was a good judge of character. Clearly not. It had been a particularly bad night and the offer of a short-term loan seemed the temporary end to all his immediate problems. Now, reading this latest threatening message, it's as though Jacob threw the final ingredient of a bad spell into a stinking cauldron. And now, he's even more screwed.

Someone from the BVT office has been indiscreet. Billy had to have gotten Jacob's flight information from a colleague. Jacob composes a terse email to 'All Staff' reminding them of the importance of confidentiality and data protection. It reads more like a rant than a request or a reminder, but he's too shaken up to care.

He goes through the morning routine. Washes himself with the hot water provided and wet wipes, hovers by the toilets awaiting his turn, eats breakfast, prepares himself for the day by layering up, filling up his water bladder, packing snacks and applying sunscreen. Four days in and these little routines are helping him hold things together.

Florence isn't her usual fake chirpy self, either. She walks around camp, holding up her phone to the sky at various points and waving it around.

Jacob walks up behind her.

'Mandy's all right,' he says. 'Ben said so.'

She looks at him, momentarily puzzled. 'Yes, I know.' She appears to gather her thoughts. 'It's not just that, it's . . . Oh, it doesn't matter. I just don't like being out of touch. It's a horrible feeling. If something goes wrong, we're all trapped.'

It's in his best interests if she's distracted. It was her idea for the two groups to merge, not Jacob's. Luke, Hugo and Mandy backed her up. Jacob said that it would muddy the waters, that it would be better to climb completely different routes – there are several to choose from after all – but he was outvoted. And these are the consequences. He's sharing a tent with a competitor, for Christ's sake.

'I'm sure you don't need any reminding,' Ben says as the groups line up for the acclimatisation hike, 'but we're going to tackle this slowly, as always. Although it may feel like we're not making progress because it's an acclimatisation walk, you're very wise and fortunate to do this. Slow but steady wins, remember.'

Samson nods his agreement.

'Please, stick to your groups. We may take some slight detours and it's still Samson's and my responsibility to look after you all in each group.'

They navigate the rocks and shrubs, weaving in and out. When they reach a small waterfall, the sound of the rushing water is so soothing that Jacob crouches down, removes his gloves and trails his fingers in the freezing water. He feels temporarily calm enough to run through his options rationally.

Realistically, he owes way more than he can ever raise for

charity on this trip, but the money raised will at least make a dent. He can pay back some of the debt to Fake Billy – there's no way that Billy is his real name – which will buy him time to get Casper off his back.

If that's not enough, the winner of each year's challenge is awarded a bonus. This isn't explicitly divulged to the team leaders because Hugo likes to see if they are hungry enough to win because of the kudos. But Jacob's aware, thanks to his close enough friendship with a woman high up in the accounting team, that these bonuses are substantial. But only if you're the winner.

'Jacob?' Ben's voice cuts into his plotting. 'We need to keep going.'

Jacob looks up, surprised to see that everyone else has carried on. His fingers are numb as he shakes off the water and replaces his gloves.

'Are you all right?' Ben asks.

'Sure,' Jacob replies automatically.

They fall into silence, their rhythmic footsteps hitting the ground as they walk slightly faster than usual to catch up with the others. One step, then another. Repeat.

Ben asks Jacob again if he's OK.

Physically yes, he thinks; *mentally, not really.* 'I'm fine,' he says. 'Just a bit tired.'

Ben nods.

'How many times have you climbed Kilimanjaro?' Jacob asks.

'Over two hundred times,' his companion says. 'Maybe more.'

'Wow. Do you just do this route?'

'No, I've done them all.'

'Do you have a favourite?'

Ben pauses to mull it over. 'Yes and no.' He doesn't elaborate.

'Do you like this one?'

'Yes, it's one of my favourites, but it's getting busier. However, it's good to see the wildlife in the forest at the beginning.'

'It was amazing. What's the hardest part of the job?'

'Sometimes people don't listen,' Ben says. 'They think because they have GPS they know better than us. And I miss my family.'

'Do you have children?'

'Two,' he says with a big smile. 'A boy and a girl.' He points ahead. 'We're nearly with the others,' he says. 'It's lunchtime.'

Their packed lunches are served in a clearing with Flo's group. Jacob sits beside Sara as they take the lids off the plastic containers containing biscuits, a chicken leg, a tuna sandwich, mango slices and an apple. He suddenly feels famished after his moment by the water and his chat with Ben. Summiting and winning feels way more likely.

As they eat, Jacob notices that Sara seems overly preoccupied with Hugo, who's taken off his jacket and keeps wiping sweat from his forehead with one of his favourite red striped handkerchiefs, lined with a black edging, with Hugo and Blackmore Vintage Travel's initials interwoven in the corner – a Christmas gift from Dan.

'Are you OK?' Jacob asks Sara.

Hugo is talking to Imogen. Is that what she's worried about?

'I wouldn't worry about Imogen,' Jacob says. 'She's probably regaling him with how many times she's visited the internet café. That, or how many things she can't stomach in her lunch box. If I were one of the chefs, I'd have pushed her off the mountain by now.'

Sara laughs weakly. 'No, it's not that.' She takes a deep breath. 'He'll kill me if he knows I've said anything, but he's not well.'

'Not well . . . as in?' Interesting, thinks Jacob.

'He's been having bad headaches. He's also feeling more tired than he's letting on. It's not like him.'

'Everyone's shattered. Surely it's the nature of the beast?'

'Mm. Maybe. Excuse me.' Sara stands up, puts her lunch box down on a rock and heads over to Hugo.

Jacob receives a message from Mandy.

How's it going? Gutted I'm not on the climb. I'm fine now.

You're missed, he replies. *Glad you're OK.*

I'm flying back home soon.

Safe trip.

They're back at Barranco Camp by early afternoon. It's a pleasant change not to have to unpack as usual and Jacob feels the urge to celebrate his achievements so far. He knows just the way to do it as he brought along three hip flasks containing brandy. He was going to use them to celebrate summiting but this feels like as good a moment as any. And the person he wants to celebrate with is Joey.

He makes his way over to the BVT tent she shares with Casper.

'Knock, knock,' he calls out before sticking his head in without waiting for a response.

Joey is lying on her sleeping bag, headphones on. She removes them when she sees him.

'No Casper?' Jacob checks.

'He said he had something to do.'

'What, like climb a mountain?'

They both laugh as he climbs in, and this is why Jacob should be with her, not Clarabelle. Joey gets him. It's effortless. Jacob's about to zip down the opening to the tent to give them some privacy when he hears Imogen's voice. 'Cooey!'

Christ. He zips up the flap extra quickly.

'Cooey!' she repeats. 'Jonessa, are you there?'

'Let her in,' Joey mouths.

Jacob pulls a face and unzips the tent.

'Oh, hi, Imogen.'

'Hello, Jacob. What are you doing in here?'

'Chatting. What are you doing here?'

'I'm in need of some company,' she says. 'Hettie and Shona are taking a nap.'

Jacob would put all the money he doesn't have left in the world on the fact that Hettie and Shona have feigned tiredness to have a break from Imogen.

'I want lots of bambini,' she's said, over and over. 'I come from a large family and I've always known that I'd like to recreate that happiness.'

'Good for her,' Clarabelle has said. 'It's useful to know what you want and aim for it. I like the sound of a large family too, don't you? Of course, I'd be happy and grateful for any kids, but it would be lovely to have two of each, wouldn't it? Think of the outfits! I'd love to splash matching mum and baby clothes all over my Insta. Sometimes, it's a struggle to be original and keep things fresh, you know?'

'We can't have children just for Instagram,' Jacob had snapped.

Clarabelle looked deeply wounded and he felt like a shit all over again. He pushes Clarabelle out of his thoughts.

'Please, join us,' says Joey now.

'Yes, do,' Jacob echoes. He doesn't need 'Immy call me Ginny' reporting back to Casper that she found him and Joey unchaperoned in their tent.

'What are you lot doing in here?' says Casper, appearing at the entrance and climbing in. 'There's hardly any space.'

Jacob's suddenly very grateful to Imogen for giving him an alibi. He removes two hip flasks from his bag. 'Thought we could have an early celebration?'

Casper's face lights up.

'Good man. What a legend!' He grins. 'I'll buy you a beer back in Moshi. Hell, I'll buy you two!'

They laugh at their private shared joke. It's a silly ritual from their first illegal visits to pubs (sneaking out from school with fake IDs supplied by some boys in the year above) that whoever bought the first round got away with one drink. The next person had to buy two, then three and so on. Jacob can't remember why it started, but it stuck for many years. It's an excellent reminder of their shared history and it feels comforting. They were friends long before Joey arrived on the scene. It feels good to do something right, for once.

Jacob hands one of the hip flasks to his friend. Casper twists open the lid and takes a swig. Jacob does the same, relishing the burn at the back of his throat. It's like welcoming home an old friend. He wipes the top with the sleeve of his fleece and offers it to Joey.

She takes a large swig and hands it to Imogen.

'I'm not sure,' she says.

Good. More for the rest of us.

'We're not supposed to,' she adds. 'Isn't alcohol forbidden?'

'We had a few drops of champagne the other evening,' Joey reminds her. 'Nothing bad happened then.'

'Yes, but we were lower down . . .'

Jacob takes the flask and downs a large gulp. His eyes water.

'Oh, go on then,' says Imogen and takes a small sip.

Both hip flasks are empty within moments. Disappointing.

Casper rummages around in his daypack and produces another two hip flasks. Seems that great minds do think alike. Jacob recognises one of them – a twenty-first birthday gift from Casper's parents. A strong rush of nostalgia hits along with the alcohol. Suddenly, he feels hot, wants to remove his top layers. They sit and laugh like teenagers and Jacob feels the happiest and most relaxed he has in a long time. Casper seems to have mellowed towards him. Jacob hopes that maybe he'll even write off the money. Jacob shouldn't have worried so much about everything. It usually works out one way or another in the end.

When they've exhausted Casper's brandy, Imogen and Jacob leave for their tents to take a rest.

'Where have you been?' asks Clarabelle, wiping angrily under her arms with a wet wipe. 'Oh my God, you're drunk! You stink!'

'I'm not,' says Jacob. 'Just one or two sips to calm my nerves.'

She looks at him with disgust. Ignoring her, Jacob lies down and it's bliss to feel himself falling asleep without the gnawing worries needling. It doesn't last long because his dreams turn into a nightmare. One where Casper tells Hugo about Jacob's betrayal with Joey and he's banished from BVT before Billy and a gang of masked men with machetes apprehend him upon landing at home.

'Jacob! Jacob! Wake up! It's Imogen!'

Clarabelle's voice cuts into his certain death.

'What?' he says, sitting up, disorientated.

'Imogen has tripped over a tent rope and she's hurt herself badly. Everyone's furious because they've realised she's been drinking.'

Crap. Trust it to be Imogen who ruins the vibe.

In a daze, Jacob pulls on his jacket and laces up his boots properly because it's now dark. He's no idea how long he's been asleep, it feels like all afternoon. He picks up his hand torch and steps outside. He zips up his jacket as far as it will go and pulls down his woolly hat, then yanks up his neck warmer so that it covers his mouth and nose, just in case he smells of brandy.

He doesn't need to ask where Imogen is because a cluster of lights hovers by the mess tent.

A body lies at everyone's feet.

THIRTEEN

Florence

Day Five: Barranco Camp. 3,960 metres
or 13,000 feet (approx.)

It's funny, the details my mind fixates on.

Imogen hasn't done up the zip on her fluorescent yellow jacket.

'The best thing everyone can do is to stay in their own tents and keep away,' a medic says, as I approach. 'Let us do our jobs.'

I hang around until I see her helped to her feet and taken to her tent, flanked by two guides.

'Pissed. Can you believe it?' says Adrian who has sidled up to me.

'Pissed?'

'Jacob thought he'd throw a tent party, rumour around camp has it.' Adrian sounds bitter about not being invited. 'I thought we weren't supposed to bring alcohol on to the mountain?'

'Well, it's certainly not advisable,' I say.

'It just seems like it's one rule for you and another for us. Probably you have champagne and caviar stashed away.'

'It's best if you take it up with Jacob,' I say. And I mean it. It's not up to me to answer for him.

I struggle to remain present in the moment. Every time something happens to someone it makes me think of George, and in my mind, all suspicious roads seem to lead to his accident. And if someone doesn't want me to dig a little deeper – I mean, wouldn't they all want to know how their friend and colleague ended up in a coma? – then it suggests to me that there's a huge rat to sniff out.

Despite the terrible memories it dragged up for them because of their daughter's horrific accident, Mr and Mrs Armstrong agreed to speak to me via video call a few months after the fatal trip.

'Awful, just awful,' they kept repeating when I pressed them for details. 'One minute he was halfway up, the next, well . . . He wasn't.'

Apparently, Luke was first on the scene.

'I thought he was dead,' Luke told me when we had a debrief in Hugo's office. It was unusual to be invited into Hugo's domain. 'The relief when the ambulance staff said he wasn't . . .'

'Where exactly was Hugo when it happened?' I asked Luke after the meeting.

'Not sure,' said Luke. 'It's all a blur.'

'Who called the air ambulance?'

'I don't know. Everyone seemed to be talking frantically into their phones.'

I will quiz him again. He's never keen to talk to me about it, perhaps understandably, but if I keep pushing, maybe he'll finally give in.

★

At the evening meal, Mrs Armstrong has several complaints. First her tea is too cold, then it's like dishwater. She's fed up with ginger biscuits, she'd prefer a nice digestive. She's like the princess and the bloody pea.

Desperate to escape, I feign a stomach ache, batting away the sympathy that follows.

Outside, I stand still. I slowly inhale cold air, relishing the peace after the claustrophobia of the dining tent. I shine my torch in the direction of my tent and as I do so, I notice a cluster of mustard-yellow tents on the right of the camp. A feather flag rests outside the first one, maroon lettering spelling *Ethical Getaways*.

I can't help it, I walk over. The tent is zipped closed.

'Excuse me,' I call out. No response. 'Excuse me,' I say a bit louder.

'Who are you looking for?' A voice from behind me makes me jump.

I turn round and see a woman wearing a pink jacket and matching hat. She is wearing a head torch and holding a camping lantern. I feel drawn to her clear blue eyes.

'Hello, my name is Florence,' I say. 'When I saw your company name, I thought I'd come over and introduce myself.'

'Hello,' she says, not bothering to hide a yawn.

'I work for BVT,' I add. 'Excuse me, but I heard your firm were climbing on the northern side, the Rongai route?'

'My firm?' she says, looking puzzled. 'One of our guides did say something about Gareth Snow, the CEO of the company, who is climbing that particular route. As are one or two others who work for Ethical Getaways. But I wanted to do this one.'

'I see,' I say. 'Is it just you on this route?'

201

The woman stares at me. 'No. I'm with a friend. I'm sorry, but I'm shattered,' she says. 'I'm not really up for a long conversation – I need to conserve my energy. Good luck.'

She unzips her tent and crawls in. I read the words *Be Mindful* across the back of her jacket before she zips the opening firmly closed behind her. It's large enough for more than one person, so I stand for a few moments, listening for voices. Nothing.

I take a circular route back, mulling over her brusqueness and the appearance of Ethical Getaways in the same camp, at the same time. I meander around the desert-like camp, navigating rocks, torchlight illuminating tufts of long grasses and shrubs, past the drop toilet area and the rangers' hut on the northern side. As I pass the group of tents before mine, I hear them speaking in French.

Unzipping the opening, I crawl in. At first, I don't spot the pink envelope on my sleeping bag. It's only as I sit on it while I neaten my plaits that I notice it. A spark of delight – has someone left me a turndown gift for a change? – is swiftly quashed.

Private and Confidential. Florence

My stomach flips. What now?

I rip open the envelope and during the first read, it's impossible to take it all in.

Mid-climb Appraisal

Is this a sick joke?

Effort – 8/10

Customer Satisfaction 5/10 – Anonymous client complaints attached for reference.
Chances of winning – fifty per cent.
Challenges completed satisfactorily – two.

Hands shaking with pure rage, I skim-read the alleged complaints.

We're not Florence's priority, she's distracted and doesn't appear to be taking things seriously.
Florence's team isn't gelling. Good team spirit starts from the top.
The food is pretty much a variation on the same theme every day. More variety, please!

I rip up the pages and shove them in my litter bag.

FFS! I start to type a message to Jacob to ask if he's received one too, but then delete it. If he hasn't then I don't want to give him the satisfaction of knowing I have.

I go through my night-time routine, exhausted. I wake up at least four times in the night, feeling wrung out. I'm so cold that even two hats don't keep me warm enough for when I trudge to the toilet. It's an effort to pull out the plastic handle at the bottom of the toilet which we're supposed to do after each visit, then replace it, because my hands are numb. Twice, I feel as if I'm going to fall asleep while sitting there and I wobble, feeling like I'm going to tip over.

Come daybreak, I feel so sick with tiredness I could vomit. I wonder how Imogen is feeling. I reckon she'll be advised not to continue, which makes it one less team member for Jacob. I feel bad for her, but it's Jacob's fault as he supplied the alcohol, according to camp rumour.

After cleaning myself with wipes and drinking a coffee, I note with satisfaction that my rubbish bag has been collected early today, taking away the shreds of the so-called appraisal.

I write a piece on my iPad for the blog I'm supposed to be composing, but my brain struggles:

Beautiful and stunning are the main words I think of when trying to describe the mountain. So far our trip has been a huge success, thanks to the wonderful guides, porters and chefs. Without them, we wouldn't even have a chance of making this climb. Every time I look up, I find it hard to believe that I'm here, that I'm doing this. If anyone ever gets the chance, I suggest that they jump at it.

I can't resist looking to see if Ethical Getaways have posted an update. They haven't. Strange. They've seemed quite keen on their promotion. Curious, I look up the Anonymous Traveller Luke mentioned the other day. There's a fresh comment.

Divide and Conquer is the latest title.
    A little bird has told me that the teams are becoming increasingly fractured. Feedback is a powerful tool. Instead of mystery shoppers, for example, there could even be a mystery climber, in this case. Perhaps the team leaders may realise that the only person they can rely upon is themselves. Now halfway through the climb, they'll be beginning to feel even more pressure.

Odd, I think. But rumours and gossip are nothing new. 'Breakfast is ready,' says Luke, poking his head through the tent.

'Thanks,' I call out, shutting down my iPad, pushing all thoughts of gossip from my mind.

It's a subdued breakfast, only partly due to three members of Jacob's group having hangovers. I, on the other hand, can't help scanning everyone's faces, looking for tell-tale signs that they were the ones who shared treacherous words with Hugo.

Speaking of whom, he announces – sitting bolt upright, back straight – that he has something for me and Jacob after breakfast.

'What?' says Jacob, sounding uncharacteristically impatient with Hugo. 'Just spit it out. It's hard to keep secrets on the mountain. Talk about exposure.' He chuckles. 'Or is it another *appraisal* made up by you to demotivate us?'

A flood of relief. It wasn't just me.

An awkward silence lingers until – thank God – the atmosphere is broken by Samson and Ben who gather us round for the morning's itinerary and briefing.

'Today we will climb the Barranco Wall,' Samson says.

'I'm terrified of heights,' says Jonessa. 'This is the part I've been dreading the most.'

'It's not as bad as it looks to climb,' says Samson. 'There's a very good, well-worn path which zigzags to the top.'

'How high is it?'

'Two hundred and fifty-seven metres.'

'I can't see the wall properly at the moment because of the mist,' Jonessa says, her face pale. 'But when I looked over yesterday afternoon, I couldn't see a path. The advice was that we didn't need any specialist experience. I don't have any. I've never climbed before.'

Jacob puts his hand on her arm. 'It will be fine,' he says.

Casper jerks his head up from his phone.

'He's right,' says Samson. 'Most people are fine as there are places for you to grip with your hands and feet in the rocks. Even though the path isn't visible, I promise you it's there. I've done it many times with hundreds of climbers and we're there to help you every step of the way.'

'Does anyone ever turn back?'

Samson hesitates. 'They do, occasionally. But there's no need. Once people are at the top, they're always very pleased that they did it. I've never had anyone say otherwise.'

'But I could go back if I want to?' Jonessa says.

'We would never force anyone to do anything they aren't comfortable with,' he says. 'But I must warn you, the way down from here, the Umbwe route, is very steep. Whichever guide accompanies you will make sure you're safe, so there's nothing to worry about, but it's certainly something to keep in mind.'

'Thanks,' says Jonessa, staring into the mist. 'Thank you. *Asante sana.*' She heads off to her tent.

Casper follows her. 'What do you mean?' I hear him ask. 'Are you thinking of not doing it?'

Jacob looks like he wants to follow her too but is holding himself back.

'Not so fast,' says Hugo when the rest of us start to make tracks to go and pack. 'We need an employees-only meeting. Back into the dining tent.'

'We need to get going,' says Jacob.

'We've forty-five minutes or so,' says Hugo. 'And I now have an opportunity to speak in some privacy.'

Once the four of us have sat down, Luke opposite me, Jacob and Hugo side by side, he begins his rant, only in a much quieter voice than usual, conscious of being overheard.

'So irresponsible,' Hugo says again and again. He focuses

on Jacob. 'What kind of impression are you giving about the company? We came here to show that we are better than Ethical Getaways, and instead you've made us look like amateurs. No, in fact you've made a laughing stock of us over the getting Imogen drunk incident!'

'You're making a mountain out of a big, bloody molehill,' says Jacob, refusing to back down. 'Loads of tourists drink.'

'Not according to Ben and Samson,' says Hugo. 'I feel ashamed.'

'Well, that's your prerogative,' says Jacob. 'We were discreet, we weren't harming anyone. If bloody Imogen knew how to behave, none of this would've happened.'

'Bloody Imogen is lying in her tent, unable to complete the rest of the climb,' says Hugo. 'James has checked her over, but that means we're a team member down.'

I decide to step in.

'Without Mandy,' I say, 'it does even it up.'

Hugo glares at me. 'That's not the point.'

'I'm out of here,' says Jacob, standing up. He leaves the tent flap open, allowing the wind to rush in.

'I'll go after him,' Luke says. 'Calm him down.'

'Yes, do,' says Hugo. 'It's a tough day physically and I want everyone on tip-top form.'

Luke closes the tent flap behind him. While it doesn't warm up, it's instantly less chilly. Which is more than can be said about the atmosphere. I bite the bullet. I've waited long enough, he owes me.

'I want you to tell me as much as you can in the time that we've got,' I say. 'I'm not going to take no for an answer. It's not fair to put me in this position. I've made up my mind, if you don't at least start telling me a bit about my background, I'm going to Jacob.'

Hugo must sense that I truly mean it because he looks like he's going to acquiesce. My heart rate speeds up.

Truth time. Maybe. If he's capable of telling the truth. It's just the two of us. A nice, cosy, father–daughter chat. Outside, the wind has really picked up. I shiver and even though my mind is bursting with questions, I can't seem to sort them into any kind of order. Hugo doesn't help. He sits silently, as though it's all down to me.

He's aged on this trip. He looks utterly shattered. I've only ever known him to be cool and in control, smartly dressed, with an air of confidence which he seems to wear like body armour. It's a nice feeling to see this diminished version of him. Less of a monster, maybe.

'Jacob should be here with us,' I say.

'You're right, of course you are. Perhaps I haven't handled this quite as well as I should have.' He pauses. 'I thought that if you knew what you were competing with and why, it would give you a lead. I couldn't have Jacob winning through some random stroke of luck. I don't take risks, I act. I'm not as young as I was, and the tiredness is starting to get to me. Retirement certainly isn't a word I've ever associated with myself and I still hope I won't have to for a long while yet. I don't want to see all my decades of hard work flushed down the pan because there's no one trustworthy enough to take over. Jacob will ruin the company within weeks. It will be in liquidation before I've even retired, let alone met my maker.'

'The deceit doesn't make me feel good,' I say. 'He's going to feel even more betrayed when he finds out I knew I'm his half-sister before he did.'

'There's no need for him to know that. I won't lie, but I'll let him assume that you both found out at roughly the same time. I'll take him away on a golfing weekend when we're back home. Jacob's keen to improve and I owe him a late birthday trip to Gleneagles. It will be just the two of us and I'll give him plenty of opportunity to digest the news over a port or two. Please don't worry. I'll fix it.'

I'm still not convinced but I don't want to say anything because I'm so desperate to hear him speak, to finally hear the truth. If indeed the truth is what I'm about to hear.

'What you need to bear in mind, my dear, is that if I'm to speak freely to you, it's best that he doesn't hear all the nitty-gritty details. We are talking about a situation involving his mother. They're close. She's always spoiled him.'

'Go on . . .'

'Your mother, Anna, was a stunner,' he says. 'There was a chemistry between us the moment Ivy – Jacob's mother – introduced us. Ivy struggled to cope after a difficult birth and I admit that I didn't do anything constructive to help, other than hire a maternity nurse and then various au pairs. I was preoccupied with the business and I didn't want to be up in the night with a crying baby who seemed to hate me. I'm pretty sure Jacob sensed how useless I was because he only had to look at me before he'd screw up his face and scream.'

He looks a little – only a little – sheepish before he continues, a faraway expression on his face. The wind smacks against the side of the tent but he doesn't seem to notice.

'After a nightmare year, we decided to move to Italy and I suggested we find a full-time nanny. It seemed like a win–win for everyone. I could pour my energy into my work. What Ivy never appreciated was that her father had lent me a great deal of money to set up Blackmore Vintage Travel. He was a fair man but harsh, and to admit any sort of failure to him would've been unthinkable. He'd given me a chance. Who, in their right mind, looks that sort of gift horse in the mouth?'

'Couldn't you have got a loan from a bank?'

He throws me a disappointed look. It stirs up a strange fear inside, a panic almost, that I mustn't disappoint him if he's to hand over the company to me. But I deserve it after living all those years in doubt. Jacob may not have had the father he wanted, but he did have one, and that's more than I had. And yet . . . this man, in one way or another, is behind my fiancé's accident. I should be destroying his company, not saving it. The paths leading to right or wrong have never felt so confusing.

'Your mother seemed to understand me,' he says. 'One day, I saw her kneeling on the floor with Jacob, playing with a train set. I'd assumed I didn't have a paternal bone in my whole body, but in that moment, I felt a lightning bolt of love for Jacob. I was so grateful to Anna for that. I'd been concerned that I was some sort of unfeeling monster.'

'My mother did have an amazing gift with children. Why Italy if your work was primarily in the UK?'

'My grandfather was half-Italian. I had very happy memories of visiting him as a child and I thought Ivy would enjoy the gorgeous villa, surrounded by vineyards. The place was a steal. I couldn't have afforded similar elsewhere at the time. We agreed that it would be an incredible place to raise children. We had this fantasy of being surrounded by our children and grand-children in our golden years.'

My mind is racing, but Hugo's finally opening up and I'm

scared that if I don't push now, this moment may never come again.

'Who chose my name?'

'Your mother, but I loved it when I found out. Absolutely perfect.'

'So, what happened with her that made you risk all this dream life with Ivy?'

'We didn't mean for it to happen. Your mother was a good listener. I opened up to her in a way I was never able to with anyone else. I told her that Ivy and I had discussed divorce, that we'd married too young and hadn't been getting on, but Ivy said her father would never accept it. He would have demanded payback of his loan in full immediately and he'd never forgive her if she got divorced. She told me that it wasn't an option and she'd fight me any way she could. She even threatened that I'd never see Jacob again. I couldn't let that happen – I'd always dreamt that one day my firstborn would take over the company that I'd built. Call me old-fashioned – which, by the way, I know you all do behind my back – but dreams are dreams.'

'I still don't understand how Anna fits in to all this,' I say. 'My mother would never have had an affair with a married man. She always said she was against it. Any boyfriends she had were most definitely single, and the slightest hint that they hadn't quite moved on from a previous relationship meant that they were out the door.'

Now it dawns on me: maybe this was why? She'd been burned – by the man sitting in front of me.

'It happened so fast and in the heat of the moment that I may have made promises that I wasn't able to fulfil,' Hugo says stiffly.

'Why did you abandon us?'

What I don't say out loud is, why didn't my mother force him to acknowledge me?

'I've explained,' he says. 'My hands were tied. I ensured that your mother received a fair allowance, and in return she agreed to sign an NDA. She was never to disclose anything about our relationship, or you, to anyone.'

Oh. My. God.

I think back to all those ridiculously expensive birthday gifts, my joyous reaction. I must look aghast because Hugo leaps in to defend himself.

'You must understand, my dear, I mean, Florence, that in business, you have to do things properly. There was someone who used to work for us, Simon, that was his name. He was determined to spread rumours. And that's just one example. You simply can't have loose ends. They will come back to haunt you. Believe me, I've had more than my fair share of skeletons reappearing out of the closet because I hadn't dotted the "i"s or crossed the "t"s.'

'But you had a relationship with my mother. Plus, you had plenty of time – years – to acknowledge me. You got divorced. Surely you could've become a part of our family then.'

He laughs. 'Do you honestly think your mother would have had me back after all that happened? She told me to keep away. I wanted to see you, I really did, but she said that you were better off without me. Maybe she was right. I insisted on the gifts, though. I wanted something concrete to prove that you meant something.'

'And now you need me because you don't trust Jacob. Your latest children are still little and your other sons aren't interested. Did you abandon them too when they were young?'

'No, that's equally complicated. There's no one-size-fits-all to sort out problems. In business, you have to put your thinking cap on.'

'Oh, stop making excuses and going on about business!'

I need space. I don't want to breathe the same air as him any more.

'I'm going to get ready for the hike,' I say, looking at my watch. 'You should, too. I need to clear out my tent. I don't want to hold the porters up.'

'Florence!' He grabs hold of my arm as I stand up to leave.

'Please let go of me.'

He does.

'Before you go, I want to promise you one thing. I will look out for you now. I can't change the past, but I do need someone to take over BVT, at some point. I know you may find it insulting if I say that you're a chip off the old block – so I won't. But so far, I like what I've seen of you. These trips are hugely illuminating. They highlight what people are like under pressure and in business. *Everything* rides on how you handle pressure. Well done.'

'And what about Jacob?'

'I can deal with Jacob.'

The higher I climb the ladder and the closer I am to Hugo, the more chance I have of exposing how he put too much pressure on George during the last getaway. But, like it or not, Jacob is my flesh and blood.

Back in my tent, rolling up my sleeping bag takes huge effort as I stuff everything into my daypack. I force down some water.

When I emerge, I see Imogen standing alone, tapping her phone furiously.

I walk over to her.

'I'm sorry that the climb is over for you,' I say.

'Thanks,' she says. 'I'm disappointed, but to be honest, I've been kidding myself. This isn't really my thing.'

She gives me a hug.

'I hate heights too,' she laughs. 'Silly of me to agree to come, really. I hate messing around with my diet because I suffer so much, but I thought it would be a case of facing my fears.'

'You've done well,' I say.

'Stupid of me to drink, too. I got caught up in the moment. Sometimes, I don't want to be the boring one.' She laughs again. 'At my age, too. You'd think I'd have grown out of this.'

'We all have our concerns,' I say. 'See you in Moshi. We'll definitely have a few drinks then to celebrate.'

'Maybe,' she says. 'I might fly home early. I've a headache that I can't shift, and I want my own bed.'

She gives everyone a wave as Samson and Ben arrange our walking order for today's climb. John is staying behind to accompany her back down.

'Wait a minute,' Hugo calls out. 'I have an important announcement.'

We all stare at him.

'I'm switching sides,' he says. 'I'm walking with Flo's team from now on.'

'Oh, great,' says Jacob. 'You do that. You're a traitor just like Luke.'

He glares over at us all as though I've put him up to this.

'Darling,' says Sara, reaching out and putting her hand on Hugo's arm.

He pulls it away.

'It's decided,' he announces, walking over to Ben and Samson. They speak quietly and it looks like they're trying to dissuade him, but everyone already knows that there's no way that Hugo will give in. Sara stands, arms folded, avoiding eye contact with everyone.

Adrian is beckoned over by Hugo.

'Right, it's been agreed,' Hugo says. 'Adrian and I are swapping places.'

'It's like a hostage swap,' Jacob mutters. Then, raising his voice: 'Cheers, Adrian. Good man. I've wanted you on my team from the start. By the way, we've lost Imogen too.'

'Do I get a say?' I call out. 'We've also lost Mandy.'

And gained a liability, I think.

'We need to get going,' says Samson, putting an end to our bickering.

Hugo doesn't respond so I have my answer. No, I don't have a say.

The mist begins to dissipate as we leave camp, naturally giving me better vision of my surroundings. I catch sight of Jacob looking at me. His expression is pure hatred. I don't blame him, and when he discovers who I am he's going to hate me even more. I don't want him to find out while we're up here. That's one thing I agree with Hugo on. In fact, I'm not sure I want him to find out at all. Ever.

FOURTEEN

Jacob

Day Five: The Barranco Wall to Karanga Camp
Alpine Desert Zone

Screw Hugo, Jacob thinks as he tucks his hiking poles into the side of his daypack. He can go to hell. He doesn't need him on his team, anyway. He was one of the weaker members. Hugo probably realises that he'll lose less face in front of Florence.

They walk downhill into a valley and cross a small stream on stepping-stones. The sound of running water is instantly calming and it makes Jacob wish he could spend some time sitting there, alone, hidden in the mist.

As the two groups walk up towards the Barranco Wall, Jacob tries to focus on his footsteps instead. One, two. Slowly, slowly. *Pole, pole.* When they stop and gather at the foot of the wall, Samson reminds them what to be mindful of.

'You will need to keep your hands free for scrambling up the wall,' he explains. 'Please keep your distance so that you don't accidentally poke other people with your poles.'

'I can't see the top,' says Jonessa.

'Probably a good thing,' says Casper. 'The mist is doing us a favour, but it's lifting fast. By the time we get to the top, I'm sure we'll have a much wider view.'

It strikes Jacob that he's been climbing a mountain his whole life. One where he'll never reach the peak. He can't play Mr Nice Guy any longer, there's too much at stake. If Hugo thinks that he's switched sides to back the winning horse, he's seriously underestimated Jacob. He gave Jacob this opportunity to prove himself and that's exactly what he's going to do. Whatever Hugo's game is, if he is setting him up to fail, or if he's using Jacob to get rid of Florence, the intent doesn't matter. As long as Jacob wins.

Jacob hangs back as Flo's group climbs the wall ahead of his team. Mr and Mrs Armstrong then Luke are the last ones in their team to climb. As Luke grips the rock and pulls himself up, a stone falls, echoing as it thuds on the ground below.

'What's that?' Joey says, pointing to something lying on the ground, close to where Flo's team had huddled.

Joey picks up something small and black. A diary with the year written in gold lettering on the top right corner. Jacob recognises it.

'Someone must've just dropped this,' she says, handing it over to Ben.

'Oh, that's mine,' says Jacob before Ben takes it from her. 'I don't know how it fell out of my pocket. Thanks, Joey.'

Jacob takes it from her and slides it into his backpack.

Joey looks a little confused.

'Odd thing to bring with you?' she says.

'It's a working trip for me,' Jacob says, with a smile.

'Remember? Plus, I had no idea how reliable the internet connection would be.'

'Fair enough.'

'I'll go last, if that's OK with you,' Jacob says to Ben.

'Are you worried about the height too?' he asks.

'No,' Jacob says, the urge too overwhelming to stop himself. 'To tell you the truth, I'm pissed at my father and want as much physical distance between us as possible while I calm down.'

Ben looks as though he understands. It's comforting. They wait as the rest of their team climbs, until it's just Jacob and Joey left.

She takes a deep breath. 'Right, I can do this. I didn't want to climb near Casper as he gets impatient with me. He keeps telling me that there's nothing to worry about, which is all well and good, but fears are fears, aren't they? We're all different.'

We are, Jacob thinks.

Joey climbs ahead of him accompanied by Michael.

'I've seen many people who think they can't do this right up to the moment they reach the top,' Michael says.

She smiles and looks like she believes him. Jacob watches her navy jacket disappear into the mist. He can't see anyone else either. Right now, it's just him and Ben and he'd happily keep it this way.

Further ahead, Joey comes into view again. She is trying to hug a rock as she inches her way round, very slowly.

'I can't do it,' she's saying. She sounds close to tears.

'You can,' Jacob calls out to her. 'You're nearly there.'

'What if I fall?'

'You won't!'

It appears she kisses the rock she's been hugging before she tentatively takes baby steps on to the next ridge.

Jacob follows in her footsteps. The mist clears above and he sees the others further ahead, all slowly inching their way to the top.

'The views will be worth it,' says Ben.

Jacob is barely out of breath and yet his breathing is loud. He sips from his straw, taking in as much water as he can. He leans back against a rock and snaps a selfie, then a picture of the others, coloured dots in the distance. Shit. He barely has any battery left. Fresh anger at whoever stole his spare phone battery hits.

Tufts of dry grass poke out between the lichen-covered, jagged rocks. Twice he almost slips on stones scattered across the path. Up and up, slowly, slowly.

Once he makes the final few steps and reaches the top, he sees that Ben is right. The views are worth it. They sit on a flat rock, eating biscuits and mangoes. In the distance, he catches sight of Mount Meru across the steep-sided valley. It makes Jacob feel alive. Another group is gathered a few metres away. He can't read the company name on their jackets, but as they laugh and look at ease with each other, he wonders what it would feel like to do this climb with people you really care about. Incredible as it is, it highlights how alone Jacob feels.

Clarabelle looks over at him and smiles.

Jacob smiles back.

He wonders if she's feeling lonely too or if this is a positive experience for her. Clarabelle has her thousands of followers, and she says they can feel like family at times. Jacob glances over at Joey. He inhales as deeply as he can and wonders if his lifestyle has spoiled things for him because he takes them so much for granted. He expects every experience to be top-notch. He's like his clients in a lot of ways, bank balances aside.

He looks at his watch, surprised to see that it took nearly two hours to climb the wall. Their hike for the rest of the morning will be ascending into Karanga Camp, their last full night in a camp before they attempt the summit. He looks down at the clouds skimming below and hears a bird caw. He raises his face to the sky and enjoys the warmth of the sun. It feels odd to experience it while looking at the snow-capped peak.

As they meander through the valley, the track widens but still they step, step, slowly, slowly, as always. There is dust as far as Jacob can see. His mind drifts. Someone is playing an Oasis track without headphones up ahead: 'Don't Look Back in Anger'.

When they stop for one of their breaks, Jacob nearly pulls the black diary from out of his pocket by mistake as he reaches for his phone. There's a message waiting for him from Mandy. He can't bear to read it; the guilt at what he's going to do tonight is overpowering. What seemed like an amazing idea when he was planning it now seems somewhat ridiculous. But he's gone this far.

Fearful anticipation heightens as they approach Karanga Camp. A large red and white tent, quite obviously larger than any other, has arrived, just as Jacob arranged. Splashed across every side is *Blackmore Vintage Travel* with their logo peppered in between the wording. Also written are the words: *Unity, Save our Planet* and *Mindful Travel*.

'What the hell is that monstrosity?' he hears Hugo say to Sara.

Jacob wants to laugh. Suddenly, no matter the outcome, in

this moment, it feels worth it. Unbeknown to him, Hugo has paid thousands for that monstrosity: for the design, shipping, workforce to transport and erect it. No expense spared. Hayley in Accounts has managed to divide the costs so they aren't obvious when it comes to the thousands already spent on this trip. Hugo told Jacob he needed to think big, after all. Well, he has. The tent is large enough to hold all of them so that they no longer need to stay in their separate mess tents for dinner. They're all going to be one big happy family, and Jacob will have a captive audience for his announcement this evening. He couldn't have timed it better even if he'd already known that Hugo would defect to the other side.

'It's our new base when we're in camp,' Jacob says.

'You have to be kidding me!' says Hugo, shaking his head.

If Florence had come up with a plan like this to 'wow' the clients, he'd be complimenting her and going on about what an amazing idea it was.

'I think it looks pretty cool,' says Casper.

'Thank you,' Jacob says as they approach, peeking inside.

The large plastic windows are perfect for admiring the view from the warmth within. There are enough chairs for all of them, neatly arranged around two rectangular tables. In the corner, as requested, is a poster mounted on a portable stand of Hugo and Jacob. In the picture, Hugo has his arm around Jacob and they're both grinning like they're the closest father and son ever. The photo was taken after a travel awards ceremony. Jacob wrote Hugo's winner's speech and Hugo loved it. He never thanked Jacob, but he clearly relished reading out every word. The night had been a success.

Hugo had no choice but to call Jacob up on stage when he was asked if Blackmore Vintage Travel was a family business.

Being Hugo's son is Jacob's trump. Hugo will never be able to replace Jacob or cut him off. Dan and Tom even rarely visit the premises.

They held a celebratory party afterwards at the office. The theme was 'Beach Ice Bar' and cocktails were served from a wooden bar on their makeshift beach by the small plunge pool. A few metres away was an ice room. Fake fur coats and hats hung by the ice seats so guests could swap their holiday beach cocktails for an iced vodka or an espresso Martini. Encased in blocks of ice were replicas of some of the awards won over the years. Roses, black and crimson, Hugo's favourite colours, were dotted around the bar area.

'Amazing.'

'Incredible.'

'Unbelievable.'

And these compliments were from people who'd seen it all.

Videos were projected on to the office walls of them white-water rafting, at the Rio carnival, in a hired submarine taking them to a private island retreat, on top of the Statue of Liberty and the Eiffel Tower, the Taj Mahal, Luxor, the Sydney Opera House, the bullet train from Beijing to Shanghai, the Great Wall of China, Machu Picchu, cruising the Amazon, flying in a helicopter over the Grand Canyon and Niagara Falls, party after party, scene after scene.

As a result, their bookings went up by ten per cent the following week. Hugo likes to think that he understands business, that he's made money by spending a pittance and serving cheap wine after the initial good bottles because he thinks guests won't notice, but they do. Everyone likes to be treated as if they matter, as if they're most important, and that's what Jacob understands so well. It's Hugo's inadvertent gift to him.

'Ta da,' Jacob says. 'Our home away from home.'

He throws out an arm as though he's welcoming guests into his mansion.

On every seat is a T-shirt, made locally from organic cotton. On top of each is a leaflet. The person with the most likes on Insta wearing these T-shirts, standing in front of the tent and showing the stunning backdrop, will win ten per cent off their next trip with Blackmore Vintage Travel if booked within a fortnight of returning home.

'Wow, this is so cool,' says Jonessa.

Jacob cannot stop a large grin spreading over his face. He's glad Hugo is in earshot to hear, maybe a bit too glad. This puts Florence's attempt at a picnic right down at the bottom of the list of memorable events. There are even two beanbags in the corner for the chill-out zone. Jacob knew that come this stage of the trip, everyone would be ready for a bit of the luxury they're so used to. Plus, getting their clients to do the promotion for them – both for their business and the good they're doing – it's more than just win–win, it's a total slam dunk!

Joey looks over at him and grins. 'Amazing!'

'Well done, mate,' says Adrian. 'Any chance of a corner telly to watch the footie game later?'

Jacob has no idea what match he's referring to but grins good-naturedly. He loves seeing all their reactions.

'Well done, Florence,' says Mrs Armstrong, looking around and nodding her approval.

To give Florence her due, she corrects Mrs Armstrong immediately. 'Oh, this is nothing to do with me. This was Jacob's idea.' She turns to him. 'You've gone all out.'

There's something slightly patronising about her tone that,

momentarily, takes the edge off his glee. He decides to take control.

'So, everyone, if you could listen, please . . .'

Everyone looks at Jacob. Casper sucks at his water bottle straw. Flo clutches her phone as if she's dying to stare at the screen. Joey looks at Jacob with pride. Clarabelle looks miffed that he's kept this a secret from her, but he didn't see the point in spoiling the surprise.

'If we could all meet back here in half an hour. Any longer and I'm concerned that some of you may drop off before you hear my special announcement,' Jacob says.

'Any clues?' asks Hugo with a look which is equal parts concern, admiration and curiosity.

Let him wonder, Jacob thinks, tapping the side of his nose like his father always does. 'All will be revealed.'

'We're supposed to rest this afternoon,' says Hettie. 'I'm feeling out of it, to be honest. My calves ache and I didn't sleep at all well last night. I've got a cracking headache. I need to talk to James about it.'

'I didn't sleep well either,' says Russell. 'My head's felt better too.'

'You do all need to rest,' says Flo. 'Samson and Ben said so.'

'It won't take long,' Jacob says. 'I'm not taking no for an answer. It's a compulsory meeting. Besides, you can chill in here too if you like. Have a little snooze on a beanbag.'

Then he strides off in the direction of his tent, feeling like a minor celebrity. No sooner is he inside, than Clarabelle climbs in behind him.

'What's all this about?'

'It's a surprise,' Jacob says. 'One of the challenges.'

'You're a dark horse,' she says.

'You're on the opposing team.'

'Not by choice,' she says. 'I'd never divulge anything to Flo that you tell me in confidence.'

'I know, babe,' he says, feeling a bit bad. 'But so much is riding on this trip and I can't afford to slip up. It was easier to keep it to myself. Also, I wanted to surprise you.'

'OK,' she says, suddenly concentrating on unpacking, pointedly turning her back on him.

Her frostiness is useful. With her gaze averted, he can hide the diary inside his sleeping bag. Thank God he had his wits about him when Joey discovered it. He won't be letting that happen again.

Everyone is waiting by the time Jacob makes it to their new dining tent, sitting on chairs, their phones on the table. No matter where they are or where they go, no one can ever seem to leave their phones alone for long. Jacob stands by the poster and thanks them all for coming.

'Before I continue,' he says, 'I would firstly like to thank everyone who has worked so hard to make this possible. This is one of the pinch-me moments of my career and I hope you're all getting a lot out of this amazing adventure.'

'It is amazing,' agrees Mr Armstrong. 'I thought I'd been everywhere and done everything, but I have to admit, this is next level. Top notch, Jacob. Top notch.'

'Thank you.' Jacob pauses to savour the moment.

His breath feels a little laboured but he's into the swing of things now and he's not going to let the thin air get in the way of his big moment. He needs these wins along the way. By the end of this trip, Hugo will be forced to listen to him. One way or another.

'If you'd all like to take up your leaflets,' he says, 'you'll see that they have individual numbers on. The winning number which I will pull from a hat – literally – will ensure that one lucky individual will receive an early copy of BVT's book, before it's even officially published.' Jacob pauses for dramatic effect. 'Yes, you heard it here first. Not only are we a number-one travel company – we are also branching out into the book world.'

Hugo goes bright red and looks like he might explode.

'A book?' Hugo says, with a forced smile.

Jacob raises his hand in a Hugo-style gesture signifying *All in good time.*

'Well, this is exciting!' says Mrs Armstrong. 'I love travel books.'

'This one won't disappoint,' Jacob says. 'Although, rather than a travel book, I'd call it a behind-the-scenes memoir.'

He hands a sheet of paper to Hugo.

'I thought my father could read out an extract. Words of wisdom spoken by the author himself.'

Hugo peers through his glasses to read the extract. From the way his face reddens even more, it's clear that he recognises it immediately. They're from his comments as the Anonymous Traveller. But they're not all his words. Hugo's poker face is impressive but Jacob can tell by the way his knuckles are turning pale that his father is not just angry – he's absolutely furious.

'A word, please, Jacob?' Hugo says, pointing to the exit flap.

'I can hand out a copy to everyone if you'd prefer not to read it out loud?' Jacob says.

The copy Jacob has handed Hugo is from an older post entitled *Winners and Losers*, detailing real examples lifted from social media, written by ex-employees. Hugo has used – or stolen – other people's stories at varying points. Some of the case studies are brutally honest, detailing the fallout after being sacked.

Jacob knows all this because Mandy told him, in confidence, that she is Hugo's ghost-writer. There are even comments lifted from a closed group which Mandy managed to infiltrate, discussing what it's like to feel so powerless after forcibly leaving BVT.

'I don't want to do it any more, I'm sick of it,' she told Jacob. 'He said it was just a bit of harmless cajoling, meant to motivate you all. But it went too far, and I didn't want to scare you – or Florence. Nevertheless, Hugo insisted that the Anonymous Traveller posts need to keep coming until after the climb. He's a firm believer in stick over carrots, as you well know.'

He did.

Outside, the late-afternoon sun is dropping. Hugo marches Jacob away from the tent, out of earshot.

'What the hell do you think you're playing at? And why did you announce I'd written a book? I've done no such thing! On top of all that, how did you know those posts were anything to do with me?'

Jacob taps the side of his nose. 'What on earth did you think you would gain by posting them?' he asks.

'I thought they'd motivate you,' Hugo says. 'I hoped that if you suspected members of your team were closely monitoring you, maybe you'd dazzle me by pulling something spectacular out of the hat.'

'Bullshit. You wanted to scare us into thinking that we were being spied on 24/7. Although you could say that your ridiculous idea sort of worked,' says Jacob. 'I did pull off something spectacular and, as a result, everyone knows what you're really like.'

Hugo grabs Jacob by the shoulders and shoves his face into his son's.

'What the hell is your game?'

Jacob doesn't reply. He's been told often enough that silence is a powerful weapon.

Hugo lets go and pushes Jacob back so that he stumbles.

'Ah, I see. Blackmail.'

Jacob can't resist twisting the knife, even if that means throwing Mandy under the bus.

'This is all thanks to Mandy,' he says. 'That's the trouble with loyalty. If you treat someone badly enough for long enough, eventually any loyalty vanishes. Loyalty is earned, it isn't a given. Perhaps you could write about that?'

Hugo rips up the sheet of paper Jacob handed to him and for a moment Jacob thinks Hugo's going to shower him with the pieces, confetti-like. Instead, he shoves them into his jacket pocket. Hugo then takes out his phone and starts jabbing at it with his forefinger.

'Even without Mandy doing the right thing, I would've guessed it was you,' says Jacob. 'Especially when you mentioned the evil eye.' He walks back in the direction of his tent. 'By the way,' he adds over his shoulder. 'You should be thanking me. It could have ruined our reputation if anyone took the time to dig into how true those comments were. Anonymity is basically impossible nowadays.'

Their dinner en masse is a huge success. Despite the tiredness, headaches from the thinning air and aching limbs, they're all on a high after today's success in climbing the wall. Jacob ignores Hugo's glares as they tuck into their chicken casserole.

Afterwards, sipping hot chocolates and nibbling on melon for dessert, they play board games and cards, and even manage a hilarious attempt at charades. Jacob's on fire. He can't help but glance at Florence several times. Sadly, she doesn't give anything away, but inside, she must realise now that she's ultimately going to lose the challenge. It's almost a given.

Jacob takes his time, miming actions to *The Exorcist*.

After several wrong guesses, Luke shouts, 'Hurry up, mate. We've got a mountain to climb.'

'Ha, ha,' Jacob replies, taking even longer.

Hugo is the first to leave. 'That's me done.'

'Shall I come with you?' asks Sara.

'No, no. I'm fine,' he says. 'Just very tired.'

'You don't look well,' Jacob overhears her say.

'I'm fine, don't fuss.'

Sara shrugs.

Hugo waves as he steps out into the darkness. 'Good night!' They then hear him call out again in Swahili: '*Lala salama.*'

'Good night,' they all chorus.

Good riddance, Jacob thinks. Hugo's footsteps disappear into the distance. Within seconds, Mr Armstrong tells a slightly risqué joke. Everyone laughs.

'Right,' Jacob says. 'I'm going to call it a night, too.'

Even though he's on a roll, he wants to leave on a high.

'I'll join you in five, babe,' says Clarabelle. 'I'm going to ask for a hot chocolate to help me drop off.'

Once outside, Jacob pauses. The Milky Way is visible, and the stars feel so low, it's as though he can reach out and touch them. He's reminded of a school Planetarium visit. He smiles.

He and Casper (and probably the rest of the class) both wanted to be astronauts for weeks after that trip.

Behind him, he hears footsteps then he's blinded by the light of a head torch.

'Jacob?' Joey's voice.

'What are you doing?' he says, glancing over at the lights coming from inside the tent. 'Casper's sure to follow you. Or Clarabelle.'

'I just wanted to say well done. I know how much it means to you to win.'

'Thanks.'

She gets him completely.

'I'd better go,' she says. 'I'm exhausted.'

'Night.'

As she walks away, Jacob hears more footsteps and the sound of laughter coming from a tent to his right. Then silence.

He's so close to winning, he can almost taste it. Just like he feels he can reach the stars. He lifts up his hand and grasps at thin air before looking around, embarrassed, hoping that no one is watching before he returns to his tent. No Clarabelle yet. *Good*, Jacob thinks. He slides out the diary, which he must not be caught with. As he points his torch at the pages, he tells himself that he'll dispose of it somehow, just as soon as he's read it.

FIFTEEN

Florence

The Day Leading up to the Summit Climb

Karanga Camp 4,000 metres, 13,200 feet to Barafu Camp 4,600 metres, 15,200 feet (approx.)

The next twenty-four hours are crucial. However tired or sick we may get, if we succumb to illness or exhaustion, that's it for this climb. No winning. No answers. No second chances. I open my eyes, then go through my morning routine of cleaning my teeth in the water brought to my tent and doing the best I can with baby wipes. I'd love to wash my hair, but instead I have to make do with tucking it away in my hat.

Jacob annoyingly pulled it out of the bag with his tent ploy. He's going to raise a lot and I need to think of something quickly to match it. It was OTT, though, and not necessarily the best way to handle things. Hugo looked appalled that Jacob had stolen his thunder with the book announcement. I half-wonder if Hugo will do something unpleasant in retaliation.

As much as I'm still desperate to win, a part of me is glad that Jacob managed to pull something off. It stops me feeling sorry for him, thus enabling me to persevere with my own ambitions.

In less than seventy-two hours we'll be at the bottom of the mountain. *Just keep going*, I tell myself. For now, I must remain focused. I'd love to know what was on the piece of paper Jacob handed to Hugo. Whatever it was, it discombobulated him, and it was cruelly satisfying to witness.

I asked him discreetly over dinner what he had over Hugo.

'Maybe we could join forces,' I joked.

'Worried you're going to lose?' Jacob replied.

'No,' I said. 'Wait until you see what I have planned.'

He looked concerned but brushed it off. 'Well, that will be interesting to see, now that the bar has been raised.'

I bit back a joke about sibling rivalry. Plus, I don't actually have any other plans up my sleeve.

We eat breakfast in our individual group mess tents because Jacob's tent (as I think of it) has already been taken down, ready to be transported away. Our stay at Barafu Camp is our final chance to rest and gather up our mental and physical strength. From there, we will make our summit attempt at midnight.

'It's hard to believe that after all the preparation and anticipation, this will all be over soon,' says Lara. 'I hope I can make it today. I've a headache and I can't stop shivering.'

'Have you been to see James?' I ask.

'No. I will do though,' she says. 'I can't handle eating my bacon and eggs.'

She stands up.

'Would you like me to come with you?' I ask.

'No, I'm fine,' she replies, to my relief.

She leaves the tent in a gust of cold air.

I spoon porridge into my mouth and nibble on a bitter apple as Samson comes in to tell us about the day ahead.

'Today, we will climb to Barafu Camp,' he says. 'It's not far, about three miles or five kilometres, and as always, we will take it *pole, pole*. You must save as much strength as you can for the summit climb later tonight. We will be leaving at midnight.'

We are divided into our two groups. Hugo doesn't look well. I feel a twinge of concern. He's quiet, as in he's not trying to take over, and his face is flushed, but he pushes away any questions about how he's feeling.

We pace ourselves as we start with the initial uphill hike heading in the direction of Barafu Camp. Slow and steady, I remind myself.

Lara looks brighter and says she's feeling much better after a couple of paracetamols.

'Although,' she confides in me, 'I'll be glad when it's all over. I'm starting to feel a bit anxious. I'm not exactly feeling as fresh as a daisy.'

'I don't think anyone is, to be honest,' I say. 'But I'm certain we'll all be fine,' I add, remembering that I'm supposed to keep everyone motivated to win. 'Samson has faith in all of us.'

An hour into our gradual hike, I feel dizzy. I stop, lean against a rock and close my eyes. The ground stops moving as the wind, which has been steadily picking up, brushes past my face.

'Are you OK?'

I open my eyes. Hugo is staring intently at me. His whole

face looks wind-stung. My lips hurt and I remove some lip balm from the side of my bag and reapply it. The relief is instant.

'Fine,' I say.

Silence. The wind scatters sand across the rocks.

'This is the furthest I've ever got,' Hugo says. 'The last time I tried this, I only made it as far as the second camp on the Rongai route.'

'The route that Ethical Getaways are on?'

'Yes. I made it to the Kikelelwa Camp at three thousand six hundred metres but then suffered badly from altitude sickness. It was such a blow. I'm glad that this time is different. Samson assured me it would be, but I'm determined not to fail again. This trip was as much for me as it is about . . .'

He stops. Silence again. I decide not to tell him about the woman I saw in Barranco Camp. Instead, I can't help blurting out, 'I don't feel comfortable about Jacob. The fact that we're related is such a huge secret, and an even bigger burden, especially now.'

He pats me awkwardly on the shoulder.

'The burden is all mine.'

'Why did you join my group?' I ask. 'It will make things worse in the long run.'

He looks genuinely astonished. 'I don't see how. I wanted to be fair. Half the time with my son, the other half with my daughter.'

'You should've just told both of us the truth. A long time ago.'

'If I thought Jacob would take it well, I would have.'

'That's not strictly true,' I say, taking a gulp of water. 'Had Jacob been the son you're trying to mould him to be, you wouldn't have bothered with me, your daughter.'

'Maybe,' he says. 'Maybe not. But the outcome is that I did and I'm happy. I've enjoyed getting to know you on this trip.'

'Time to go,' Samson calls out.

'How much longer?' I ask.

'A few hours.'

My heart sinks. Today seems harder than any other so far despite the relatively gentle hike. It feels like we've somehow walked to a different planet.

My fingers are numb, despite my thermal gloves with extra lining, and it makes it tricky when we stop for lunch. I sit slightly away from everyone else, needing a break from Hugo.

'I can't wait until we can chill by the pool and have cocktails and beers,' Luke says, sitting beside me. 'I'm feeling really positive about us winning, despite Jacob and his publicity stunt with the giant tent and the leaflets.'

I laugh.

'It was big,' I say.

'That's Jacob for you,' he says. 'Full of hot air. And lies.'

'Why did you two fall out, exactly? Surely it wasn't just because you're on my team.'

'He broke a promise,' Luke says. 'And it had bad consequences for me. Not that he cared. He just carried on being Jacob.'

Despite the messed-up situation, I feel disloyal. Both to Jacob and to Luke. When Luke finds out that he wasn't joking about a mutual colleague, but my brother, he'll feel differently too.

I feel nauseous. I stuff my chicken sandwich back in my lunch box and hide it beneath the tinfoil to disguise how little I've eaten. I avoid eye contact with everyone as I don't feel like making small talk. Please, God, let me make it back to camp if I'm going to be sick. I close my eyes and try to block everything out. When I open them, Luke must've got the hint because he's busy, scrabbling around in his bag.

Feeling a little less queasy, I take out my camera, intending to snap some photos for 'Where's the Mascot?' for my Insta update of the day, when I get the chance to post it. We've made it this far! Thank you for all the support! #gratitude #dogood #dreambig.

'Shit,' Luke's voice interrupts my thoughts. 'I think I've left something behind in the other camp.'

'Oh, that's annoying. Is it valuable? I'm sure it will be found and handed in somewhere.'

'It's not valuable, as such . . .' he says, still shoving his hands down the various sections of his rucksack.

'What is it? Do you want me to help you look?'

'No,' he says. 'Thanks. It's fine, really. I'm sure it's here somewhere.'

'Fair enough,' I say, searching for my phone to see if it's possible to post anything online.

I have several missed calls. How very odd – all my friends and clients know I'm away. My heart rate picks up because, as a general rule, phone calls mean bad news. The first few numbers I don't recognise. The next three, I do. George's sister. My heart plummets. The voicemail symbol illuminates ominously. No one I know leaves a voicemail unless it's something serious. I check my texts. Nothing. I can't connect to voicemail. I'm struggling to breathe. I stand up, my lunch box falling to the ground, and hold my phone up higher.

'What's up?' asks Luke.

'I think something's happened to George.'

He frowns.

'What do you mean?'

'There are several missed calls from his sister. She never calls me,' I add.

'Oh my God,' Luke says. 'Do you think he's woken up?'

'Maybe . . .'

I can't shake off the feeling that it's bad, though. I appreciate that miracles happen, but the hospital have repeatedly told us that there's practically no hope.

'No, it can't be good news,' I say. 'She knows I'm halfway up Kilimanjaro. She knew I'd be out of contact. She wouldn't get in touch unless it was urgent. It's early morning in the UK.'

Luke glances at his phone. 'No missed calls or messages here. Hugo,' he shouts over to him. 'Do you have any phone signal?'

Hugo checks. 'No,' he shouts back.

Everyone is looking at me. I don't care.

'Does anyone have a phone signal?' I call out. 'It's urgent.'

I see most people take out their phones to check. Some hold them up towards the sky and frown, shaking their heads.

'It's George,' I say. 'Something's happened. I can't access my messages, so I don't know what the problem is.'

'Send a text,' says Luke. 'It might get through.'

My hands are shaking so much that I struggle to type the words.

Is everything OK? I'm halfway up the mountain! I can't hear my messages. Please respond ASAP. Fx

It doesn't send. I stand up and survey the valley. I'm cut off, helpless and frantic. Guilt swamps me. Perhaps I shouldn't have come away. Maybe he sensed that I'd gone abroad, perhaps he thought I'd moved on. I wish I could just talk to him and hear his reassuring voice.

'I'll mention to the others how close you were to George,' says Luke. 'They'll want to support you.'

I nod. I can't think who I've told, who knows, who doesn't. It seemed like such a big secret because we were colleagues, but that's so unimportant now. I feel my engagement ring around my neck. We chose it together on a weekend to Rome. We had so many plans. Safaris, the Blue Train from Cape Town to Pretoria, the Orient Express, a trip to see the cherry blossom in Japan and visit the Victoria Falls, exploring the Grand Canyon together. Our dreams are all gone now, and more than ever, I need to understand why. But first, I have to make contact with George's sister and find out what's going on.

'We should move on,' Samson announces.

'I'm going to ask Samson if I can use his satellite phone,' I say to Luke.

He looks uncertain.

'I think it's for rescue emergencies only,' he says. 'It will be OK. We'll get better signal soon and I'm sure it will be fine.'

'You should tell your face that,' I say. 'You look as worried as me.'

It's painful to walk so slowly. Despite the cold in my fingers, I keep checking my phone. Finally, the message sends. No reply. When we stop, I send another text begging for news. Nothing. It's torture. Luke seems to sense my impatience and anguish because twice I hear him telling other people to hurry up, first Jacob, then Casper, even though they can't. Casper's response is way more polite than Jacob's.

By the time we arrive at Barafu Camp, all the magic I'd felt about arriving this close to the peak seems to have disappeared. The land is barren and feels desolate. The wind is bitter.

Jacob and Luke keep checking their own phones as we stand in front of a sign welcoming us to Barafu Camp, above a warning about potential breathing problems.

We queue up to sign in at the rangers' hut. Still, my phone stays silent despite sending yet another message. I pace, trying desperately to get a signal. Nothing. I try calling but it keeps cutting off. No messages. Because there are so many tour companies, the camp goes further up the ridge than I imagined. Behind the green-roofed rangers' hut, over to the east, is a view of Mawenzi. I hear Samson explaining, 'It's one of Kilimanjaro's three volcanic cones, and the third highest peak in Africa.'

I hear myself join in automatically with the group thank-you's when Samson finishes checking us in.

Our camp this evening is situated behind a large rock for shelter, near the edge of camp, higher up the ridge.

Jacob's giant tent isn't set up because he arranged it as a one-off, so we eat in our separate mess tents. Everyone but me picks at a chilli con carne, eating in silence. I want to get off the mountain. I can't just sit here, waiting. I can't bear the scraping of the knives and forks, the slurping of the tea. Luke isn't eating either; he's pushing his food around his plate. Halfway through the meal, he gets up suddenly. When he returns, he looks like death.

'Are you all right?' I ask.

'Think the altitude is getting to me,' he says.

This is the first time I've noticed any sign of Luke being affected.

'Everything will be all right,' Hugo repeats twice. 'Try not to let your imagination run wild. Focus on your physical challenges.'

'You don't know that everything will be all right,' I snap.

'You're right, actually, Florence. I don't.'

As we are waiting for Samson's summit briefing, a message finally appears on my phone. Thank God.

But then I open it.

The shock is so numbing that my brain refuses to take it in. I have to reread it more than once.

George died at 3 o'clock this morning.

We're three hours ahead. I was fast asleep, in a different continent, just when he needed me the most. Like my mum, I wasn't there for George. And I'm no nearer to finding out what happened to him. It's all been for nothing.

I realise I'm shivering. Someone – I don't know who – puts a blanket around my shoulders.

'What a shock,' everyone repeats.

'I'm sorry,' says Luke, taking hold of my hand. 'I really am.' I notice he's shaking, too.

I expect there to be tears, but none come. There's merely numbness. Knowing that this day would come, doesn't make it any easier.

'Does anyone have something for shock?' Sara asks.

'We're all shocked,' says Hugo. 'It's terrible news, but it was a tragic, tragic accident and knowing George, he'd want us to carry on. He'd hate it if we all gave up at the eleventh hour because of him.'

Despite the fact that Hugo cannot appreciate my love for George, he's right. And I'm going to use the pain and rage I feel to push me through the final hurdles. I know now, without any doubt, that I'm going to win. I'm going to do it for George, for his family, for my mum and for my younger self growing up wondering who my father was. I'm going to show Hugo that I'm strong, that he can't manipulate or control me any longer.

I shut out the noise by typing a response to George's family.

I'm so, so sorry I wasn't there. All my love and I'll see you as soon as this climb is over. Much love.

Decision made. I ask everyone not to mention anything to Samson.

'I'm fine to walk,' I say. 'I don't want any sympathy or special treatment. I want to win fair and square.'

'That's my girl,' says Hugo. 'Fighting spirit. That's what you need to be a winner. Block out the bad. Move forwards. You're doing the right thing. It really is the only way.'

I focus on Samson's words about the summit climb. In fact, it's easier to concentrate than it ever has been because it numbs the pain of thinking about George. Being on the other side of the world helps me to distance myself from the reality of home. Still, a part of me feels guilty.

'Have you eaten and drunk enough water?' he asks.

We all nod.

'James will come in shortly and do the nightly checks,' he says. 'You must try and get some sleep between now and midnight. Even if you can only doze, it will help. We have a long night and day ahead of us, but it will be worth it. You have nearly completed your challenge, and come sunrise, you will be on the roof of Africa!'

We all look at one another and even I manage a smile. I

do want this. No matter what. I came here with the intention of summiting, and I will.

'You have already completed most of the hiking.'

Lara puts her hand up as though we're in school.

'I don't feel well,' she says. 'I'm not sure that I'm up to it.'

'In what way?' asks Samson.

'Nauseous,' she says. 'But maybe it's just tiredness.'

'We will get you checked out and you can also share your concerns with James. It is just nerves, I'm sure.' Samson turns to me. 'Are you feeling all right, Florence?'

A hush falls on the group as I struggle to answer. I opt for the truth.

'Not really, but physically I'm fine to climb. I had some bad news from home. I'll speak up if necessary.'

As we leave the tent to try – somehow – to get some sleep before midnight, Luke falls into step with me.

'Do you want to sleep in my tent? Just so you're not alone?' he says. 'I don't think I'm going to get much rest.'

'Good idea, thanks.' The thought of going to my tent alone fills me with dread. 'I'll just go and get my stuff.'

Jacob and Clarabelle make their way over to me.

'Are you really all right?' asks Clarabelle. 'I mean, as all right as you can be, given the circumstances. Jacob's in total shock. Aren't you, babe?'

He nods.

'I'm going to rest in Luke's tent,' I say. 'So I'm not alone.'

'Luke's tent?' Jacob looks unimpressed.

'He offered,' I say. 'I think being near someone else may help.'

'Can't you go in with one of the women? Sweetie,' he turns to Clarabelle, 'I could take Flo's tent and she could come in with you?'

'Honestly, it's fine,' I say. 'Thanks for the offer, though.'

'If you're sure . . .' says Jacob, looking unconvinced.

'I am.'

I don't waste much time packing, just the essentials. Sleeping bag rolled up under one arm, inflatable mat under the other with my bag on my back, I head for Luke's tent. Jacob is crawling out.

'What were you doing in there?' I ask.

'Just had to ask Luke something quickly,' he says. 'See you at midnight.'

'Sure.'

Luke is already cocooned in his sleeping bag, his BVT eye mask primed on his forehead.

'You OK?'

'Yes,' I say. 'Let's try and get some sleep.'

'I'll try, but I'm worried about you, Florence. I'm so sorry about George, I really am.'

'Thank you.'

My head aches from the effort of holding back the tears. I'd forgotten how physically painful grief is since the death of my mother. It's like something is pressing hard on my chest, pushing me into the dirt.

'Wake me if you need me,' Luke says, putting in earplugs and pulling down his mask.

I unroll my mat, put down my sleeping bag and scramble in. I can't get comfortable, there's something hard digging into my back, but I don't want to move around too much in case it disturbs Luke.

I shuffle around as quietly as I can, but it's no good. There's something beneath the thin ground mattress. I twist around awkwardly and feel beneath. Something small, slim and hard. I slide it out and shine my torch.

It's my missing diary! I open it and flick through the pages, wondering why Luke, of all people, would have taken it.

And then I see lines and lines of my own words highlighted in yellow. And right in the moment when I need to sleep and get maximum rest, the mystery clicks into place, and I'm wider awake than I've ever been. I rummage through Luke's bag and am surprised to find a shiny blue A4 plastic wallet. Inside, are several sheets of typed reports. Comments in Luke's handwriting are scrawled on the edges. Oh. My. God. Now I get it. This is what I came here for.

Finally, my answers.

SIXTEEN

Jacob

Barafu Camp. 4,600 metres or 15,200 feet (approx).
The Hours Before the Summit Attempt

Thank Christ, Jacob still has a secret stash of cognac. His mind is all over the place.

George. Is. Dead.

The two of them were almost the same age. Jacob gulps a swig of brandy from the engraved pewter hip flask that Hugo gave him for his twenty-first. He was holding back, planning on saving its contents for a mini celebration at the summit to toast his success with his dad, but fuck it.

The alcohol is an instant pick-up. After several swigs, clarity hits. Jacob knows exactly what must happen. It's something that he and Luke should have done a long time ago. They need to have it out instead of pussyfooting around each other. In Nairobi, they had the perfect opportunity to finish what they started – the childish dodging of blame – so that it was no longer bottled up before they faced one of their biggest physical challenges ever. Luke's not going to fuck this up for him. *Luke* went too far, not him. Jacob cannot be held responsible for the decisions of others.

He wishes he hadn't sent Luke a message last year insinuating that he could be his deputy when Hugo is eventually persuaded to step down. He doesn't like the thought of anything that could be used as evidence against him, but he realises it won't achieve anything of use, because during their latest argument, Luke was too determined to blame Jacob for his own mistakes.

Beside him, Clarabelle sleeps, unaware that he's in utter turmoil. Jacob feels an overwhelming urge to wake her up, tell her everything, so that he can hear her say out loud that he's not a bad person, that they can sort this out. But then, what if she can't see things from his point of view? What if he can't make her understand that he's not a killer? No, he's alone in this. Only one person can save him.

Himself.

Jacob sits up. Every bone in his body aches and he feels stiff with cold. He adds on another layer, then his jacket, wishing he was anywhere but on the mountain. He picks up his phone. Ten per cent battery. It would take ages to charge with his back-up charging pack. He slides his hand beneath Clarabelle's inflatable pillow to take her phone, just in case. Clarabelle's code is still her birth date – thankfully she's rubbish at remembering passwords.

But he can't find her phone. Clarabelle stirs. He removes his hand and sits, waiting. She rolls over on to the other side, coughs, but mercifully she's still asleep. He shines his torch into the various compartments of her daypack and pulls out a spare phone battery. *His* spare phone battery.

Jacob feels sick. The cognac has made his head feel fuzzy

and his thoughts collide. Why would Clarabelle have his spare phone battery? Is she working with Luke too? Are they all working with Hugo behind his back, on some elaborate scheme to get rid of him? The useless son Hugo has never respected. Jacob needs air. He can't breathe.

As he tugs the zip opening, Clarabelle coughs again.

'Babe, where are you going?'

He freezes.

'Toilet. Go back to sleep.'

She turns silent.

Jacob replaces his phone battery with the spare one, willing it to work. He's heard of gadgets freezing, making them useless. But then, his phone lights up, as if grateful to be given a new lease of life.

Thank God for technology.

As he stands up, he realises that he really does need the toilet. *Christ, I'm pissed.* Not good.

The camp is quiet. He sees the occasional light on in random tents, but it does seem everyone is trying their best to rest before the summit attempt. He removes his hand torch from his pocket and shines it around. Rows of tents, no sign of life. The wind whistles and a loose strap flaps furiously against the opening of the toilet tent. The *thud, thud* is punctuated by brief moments of acute silence. Why is he the only fuck-up? The only person who isn't sleeping soundly in anticipation of one of the hardest nights and days of his life? Usually, when this realisation happens, he's able to block it out, visit a casino, quash the overwhelming fear that he's not normal, whatever that is.

The stench inside the toilet tent hits him more than usual.

He doesn't have to climb the summit. He could invent a sprained ankle. Hell, he could even deliberately twist an ankle. Hugo wouldn't be able to pronounce Jacob the loser because of an accident and it may well be the best way to save him from losing face. If he's going to try and summit half-cut and utterly miserable then he's reducing his chances of managing the physical challenge before he's even tried.

Leaving the tent, he can't spot any guides, porters or rangers. The wind brushes something soft past his ankles and he leaps aside. He shines his beam at the ground. Nothing. Jacob switches off his torch and lets his eyes adjust to the eerie surroundings. A crescent moon shines from above, suspended in a sky full of stars.

A calmness descends and he imagines that perhaps this is what it feels like before going into battle, acceptance of the inevitable. But what is his inevitable? Failure? No, he mustn't think like that. Jacob makes his way in the semi-darkness to Luke's tent then hesitates outside. He needs to talk to him, sort everything out. Which one is his? He's pretty sure it's orange, like his. Yes, he's certain this is the right one.

Jacob slowly unzips Luke's tent. It's too loud, even above the wind. Jacob fears someone's going to poke their nosey, unwelcome head out of one of their tents. Wind whistles past his ears and he pulls his beanie down lower.

'Luke!' Jacob says in a loud whisper. 'Luke! I need to talk to you, it's urgent. Florence? I need to speak to you, too.'

Silence. He shines his light in. The tent is empty. Odd. He didn't hear anyone else in the other toilet tent. Dread hits. He must be in Flo's tent. Perhaps Florence and Luke have been working together the whole time behind his back. Rage surges – at Luke, at Hugo, Florence, Casper and at everyone who's ever crossed his path.

Jacob shines his torch left and right, up and down. He spots loo roll with minimal toilet paper remaining, a roll-on deodorant, a compass. Outside, he hears something. He remains alert for any sign of Luke's return, a torch light, a silhouette, footsteps, anything. But there's only the wind.

He takes off his gloves and slides his hand beneath Luke's sleeping bag. There's some cash in a clear plastic wallet – local currency and sterling and a slim guidebook. On the other sleeping bag lies Flo's diary, spread open, face down. Good, she's found it. Florence nearly caught him when he planted it.

Jacob wishes he hadn't drunk that brandy because although he doesn't feel as woozy as he did earlier, he's having trouble adding all the pieces together. But he can't shake off the horrible feeling that Flo is in danger. Luke must be in her tent, there's no way he's taking this long in the toilet. He switches off his torch, allowing a few moments for his eyes to adjust, and creeps to Flo's tent, only a few metres away. Feeling a little stupid, he consoles himself with the fact that he would never forgive himself if another person got hurt. Because Jacob knows exactly what Luke is capable of.

Outside the tent Jacob hesitates. He thinks he hears snoring but it's difficult to tell because of the wind. He's sick of the wind, it's relentless.

'Flo,' he calls out as loud as he dares.

No reply. He undoes the zips and pokes his head in.

'Florence? Luke?'

He shines his torch inside.

Her tent is empty.

SEVENTEEN

Florence

Barafu Camp. The Hours Leading up to the Summit Attempt

I draw cold air into my lungs. There aren't enough layers to warm me up. Even my bones feel frozen. From where we are standing on the edge of the camp, the light of the crescent moon gives the entire area a ghostly, shimmering atmosphere.

'It's beautiful,' I say to Luke, beside me. 'Shall we walk further away and take a photo? You can point out the route you said you wanted to take if you hadn't been stuck with us.'

'I think we should maximise our rest time,' he says. 'We're going to need all our energy. Plus, we won't be able to see or photograph much in the dark.'

'Just a few more minutes,' I say. 'I don't want to go alone.'

'Sure,' he says.

Luke's a good guy like that.

Our footsteps sound ridiculously loud, though we're all

used to tuning out the sounds of camp life by now. Utterly
shattered, desperation is the only thing fuelling me. As I nearly
trip over a stone, Luke grabs hold of my arm. I shudder and
try to stop myself from pulling away. I keep walking, one foot
in front of the other, as I've learned to do over the past few
days.

'Stop,' says Luke, breathless.

I turn around so that the light from my head torch shines
right in his face. He raises his hand over his eyes.

'Ouch!' he says. 'You nearly blinded me.'

'Sorry.'

I take out my phone and pretend to snap some photos of
the night sky, then zip it away safely. But the cold takes over,
and my whole body starts to shiver violently.

I switch off my torch and stand in the gloom. I look down
at the camp and see a beam of light snaking its way through
the tents. It stops near the area where the toilet tents are
situated. There's no way to make out who it is. Luke puts his
arm around me and draws me close to him. He's freezing too,
his teeth are chattering.

'This view, this moment . . . it's magical,' he says.

'How does it compare to other trips?'

Confusion crosses his expression as though he needs to
think about it, but then a torrent of words pours out.

'This is the best so far. I've enjoyed my time with everyone,
but especially you. I am sorry about George,' he continues. 'I
never guessed. I even thought that maybe you and I had a
chance. This romantic moonlit walk makes me wonder if I
had it right.' He gives an awkward laugh. 'But I realise it
would be terrible timing. Then again, sometimes an experience
of death makes you realise how much you need to seize the

moment. Otherwise, life is in danger of feeling meaningless. But what's happened to George has changed me.'

'George and I,' I say. 'We weren't just *together*. We were engaged.'

Luke frowns, as though he's been handed a puzzle.

'I see.'

I'm about to reply when there's an abrupt crack behind us, like a rock hitting the ground. At the same time, we both swing round.

'Hello?' Luke calls out.

There's nothing but darkness.

The wind has frozen my ears so badly they feel like they're burning. I wonder if it's possible to get frostbite just standing here. I can't lose my opportunity. Time really is of the essence.

It comes out without me even realising.

'You're a killer,' I say.

I didn't mean to say it so brutally, but I let the words land.

Luke turns round and stares at me. 'Have you been drinking? Or is it the altitude?'

'You killed George,' I say. 'It's your fault.'

'No. No,' he repeats in a firmer voice. 'It was an accident.'

'What happened? Tell me the truth, for once.'

'I've told you multiple times. I'd do anything to go back to that cave in New Zealand, but I couldn't save him. It was so dark, apart from flashes of his head torch. I remember wondering if it was the glow worms.'

'You told me before that you weren't near him. He was the last climber, the rest of you were waiting, so what could you have done?' I hesitate. 'Unless you were mistaken. Or . . . lying.'

Luke looks like he's having a panic attack. Suddenly, his breathing sounds like Darth Vader, emerging in clouds.

'Are you all right?' I ask.

'No! It's fucking cold and I'm tired!' he snaps. 'I'm only here because I felt sorry for you, so upset about George, but this is stupid. I need to sleep. We're going to ruin our chances of success. I'm sorry about George, I really am. I had no idea at the time that you and he . . .' He takes a long, ragged breath. 'I don't appreciate being called a killer.'

'But that's what you are,' I say. 'I *know* what you did,' I add, praying that he doesn't see through my minor bluff.

'It wasn't me,' says Luke. 'If you want answers, talk to Jacob.'

'I have,' I lie.

Luke looks pale. His fists clench. 'What did he say?'

'That it was your idea to mess with George's ropes. That you were responsible for his accident. And his death.'

'Shut up! You don't know what you're talking about. It wasn't like that.'

'How was it, then? Was it because he was competition? Was that it?' I push when he doesn't reply.

'No. It wasn't like that. Jacob said—'

'Jacob said what?'

'Nothing.' He gathers himself and smiles. 'Nothing. Let's talk when we're at the hotel in Dar es Salaam. We're going to *win*, Florence. I just know we are. Let's not screw it up by wasting our time out here, freezing to death. We can talk everything through . . .'

'Someone has highlighted sentences in my stolen diary,' I interrupt. 'I wrote down things I remembered George saying. "*Luke reckons that it doesn't matter what the outcome is, he's going to win anyway. He thinks it's a given. Insider knowledge, that's what it is."* George texted those words to me after you and he had been at the bar one night. He said that you felt bad for him because you knew that no matter how hard he tried, he didn't stand a chance.'

Just like I know that Jacob doesn't have a chance in hell.

'Look,' I say, 'I just want to understand. I want to sleep, too. I want to win, but I can't because George is dead and all I can think about is what would've happened if the roles were reversed. Had I been in George's situation, he would've insisted on the truth. I can't sleep, can't eat, can't move, can't stop thinking about him, and I believe you know more than you're letting on. If you didn't, why did you take my diary?'

'This is crazy,' says Luke. He looks at his watch. 'We've three hours before one of the biggest nights of our lives. I get that you're grieving, of course you are. And so you should. But not here, not now, in freezing temperatures on the side of a mountain. We'll talk back at the hotel – we can get Jacob and Hugo involved too. I barely have the energy to speak any more. Honestly.'

'I know you're just trying to buy time. So, we're staying here until I have proper answers. Did you break into my hotel room in Nairobi?'

'I didn't break in. I asked for a key to the interconnecting room because I knew Jacob and Clarabelle had turned down the room. I was going to take it, but my original room was nicer in the end. I overheard Jacob calling you Miss Marple and he said that you were on to something, that you kept writing notes in your diary at the office whenever George came up in conversation, like a detective on the case.'

'But why would you be so concerned? I mean, we're talking breaking, entering and theft. Who does that? You scared the life out of me and then made me think I was imagining things.'

'I'd been drinking. It seemed like a good idea at the time. I thought that if I took the diary, Jacob and I might be able to figure out your line of thought, if you were planning any further investigation, we could talk to you and . . .'

'And what?'

'Let's just get this over with,' he says. 'Jacob promised me that I could be his second-in-command. All I had to do was slow George down a bit so that he didn't win. Jacob and I go back a long way.' He struggles for breath. 'Hugo had spent some time in hospital. Even though it was a straightforward operation, his health wasn't looking great. Jacob thought his moment had finally come and it was only George who stood in the way. His team were winning all the challenges up until that point. We knew George would likely win – he had that killer instinct – so we came up with a plan. It wasn't a bad plan, it was . . .'

'Was what?'

'Look, it wasn't my idea.'

'To do what?'

'Because George and I were the team leaders, it had to be me. I had to win.'

'And how did you do that?'

Luke takes a breath then coughs as though the cold air is stinging his lungs. 'With just a small tamper of the ropes. He wasn't supposed to fall, we just wanted to give him a fright, slow him down.' He closes his eyes and sighs as he opens them again. 'Just for a little while. That's all. A bit of healthy competition, a prank. It wasn't anything George wouldn't have done to me or Jacob. I mean, what would the world be if we all took it so bloody seriously?'

'Well, George wouldn't be dead, for starters.'

Luke grabs me by the shoulders.

'You must believe me. It was an accident, and that's what the investigation found. George was hung-over. I know it sounds bad, but I'm trying to tell you the truth. George must've made a mistake. I've let myself feel awful for it, thinking that it was my tampering, but I know deep down that I shouldn't feel guilty because it wasn't my fault.'

'You're lying to yourself,' I say. I want to kill Luke myself. Instead, I add in as clear and icy a voice as I can manage, 'Between you and Jacob, you killed him.'

'No! You've got it all wrong. Shit. I haven't explained it properly.'

'You've explained it well enough. And maybe I'd have believed you if you hadn't taken my diary, but it's obvious that you have a guilty conscience. You and Jacob have blood on your hands.'

'No, we don't. If you're looking for someone to blame, blame Hugo. He was insufferable in the lead-up to that trip. All those bloody emails about targets, all those threats and late-night calls. George and I were under immense pressure, as was Jacob. Jacob and I decided that if we could persuade Hugo to leave, or force him to somehow, we could make it better for everyone. George included. You, too. We can still do it, Florence. You can join us. Jacob is pissed off because I chose your team over his, but he'll get over it. There's huge amounts of money involved, more than all of us put together have ever dreamed of. BVT is worth a fortune.'

Luke takes some deep breaths before he continues. 'The other thing is that the diary went missing. It disappeared from my daypack, or maybe I dropped it somehow, and then it magically reappeared in my tent. I don't know how you found it in my tent because I didn't have it. Strange, but true.'

He's clutching at the proverbial straws, trying to buy time. We don't have time because we'll freeze to death.

'What's the real reason you and Jacob have fallen out?'

'Because he's a prick,' says Luke. 'Because he blames me to ease his own conscience over the incident and he tried to make me feel like a killer. Jacob is the sort of person who needs other people to blame. It stops him having to look too closely in the mirror.'

'It's so much to take in,' I say.

It's true. But what I do now know is that Luke, Jacob and Hugo are all responsible.

I turn to walk away, and Luke grabs my arm.

'You can't say anything, Florence,' he says. 'You must keep this to yourself until we can talk properly. God, it's freezing. What are we even doing out here? Let's go back to the tent and warm up. We can try and get some sleep and talk again.'

'Let go of me,' I say.

'It was awful, Flo. Just awful. Every time I visited George in hospital, I told him how sorry I was. Because I am. Desperately sorry. If I could turn back time, I would.'

'But you can't turn back time, can you? And I have to suffer, not you.'

Instead of letting go, he grips my arm tighter. Grief, rage and exhaustion surge through me and I push him as hard as I can against the chest. He finally releases the grip on my arm.

'Calm down, Flo,' he says. 'This isn't getting us anywhere. I understand you need an outlet, but you're ruining your chances of winning and achieving something amazing. How many people do you know get to climb Kilimanjaro? George wouldn't have wanted this. He was a good guy.'

Surely everyone knows that the worst thing to say to someone who is angry is to tell them to calm down.

'A good guy you killed with your actions.'

'Look,' he says. 'What I will confess is that I planted the scorpion and wrote on the Scrabble board. I hid your jacket so that you'd have to come back to the tent. All I was doing was entering into the spirit of things by playing a few pranks, and I didn't mean to frighten you. I was afraid that—'

'Afraid that you'd get found out,' I finish for him. 'What about the knife planted next to the message? Are you suggesting that was part of a harmless prank as well? You're so full of shit, Luke.'

'Florence. Please. If there was anything I could do to make a difference, I would.'

'Except tell the truth.'

I start coughing. I take several breaths, struggling to draw the freezing air into my lungs.

'You'd do the same if you were in my position,' he says. 'I guarantee anyone would.'

I walk away and Luke grabs hold of my wrist. Muscle memory from my self-defence course kicks in. I push against the weak part of his grip to break free, then stride off in the direction of camp.

'Florence!'

He grabs me from behind. 'Stop, just listen. You need to understand.'

He sends me tumbling to the ground, pinning me down, hands around my neck. I kick as hard as I can. It's almost a relief to cause him pain. I lash out again and this time, he grabs my leg, dragging me along the frozen ground. I reach out for something – anything – and I feel helpless, until my fingers grasp a heavy stone. I throw.

There's a dull thud and then . . . silence.

EIGHTEEN

Jacob

Barafu Camp. Summit Attempt
Arctic Zone

'Hello! It's time. Thirty minutes until we leave.'

The voice from outside Jacob's tent filters into his brain. He can't believe he dropped off. He hasn't slept properly at all. His eyes feel gritty, his mouth is dry, his back is killing him, and he'd rather be anywhere else in the world but here.

'Hello?' Ben's voice prompts, and Jacob realises he hasn't responded.

'Hello. *Jambo.* I'm awake, thank you. *Asante sana.*'

This is worse than any jet lag or hangover he's ever experienced. He wants to curl up and stay put, desperate to keep warm.

He forces himself to sit up. He leans over, unzips the tent flap and pokes his head out into the cold.

'Thank you,' he says to Ben, who hands him a steaming mug of coffee.

Blessed warmth.

The moon is low in the western sky, the light has dimmed and plunged the camp into near darkness. To his right, he sees their group huddled outside the mess tent, a mass of head torches. Have their groups merged? Jacob thought climbing in groups larger than ten wasn't allowed. Everyone seems to be ahead of him in the getting-ready game.

It's only now that he realises there's no sign of Clarabelle. Where is she?

Her daypack sits neatly on top of her sleeping bag.

With great effort, he puts on sunscreen, which feels an extremely odd thing to be doing in the dark and cold, and re-checks he has everything he'll need, including his mirrored sunglasses and hand warmers. His energy sapped, he clambers out, wishing tonight was over. He aims for their mess tent. Nearly everyone is inside, including Clarabelle – who looks peaky – Hugo, Sara, Hettie, Lara, Adrian, Mr and Mrs Armstrong, Casper and Jonessa. Beside Joey is Florence. Her beanie hat is pulled down lower than usual and she's shivering.

'I've a final challenge,' says Hugo. 'I'll make it as quick and painless as possible, seeing as we all need to conserve our energy. Florence, Jacob. As quick as you can, you need to pick a team member who you believe won't make it. Make the decision whether or not they need to be dropped for the sake of the team.'

Florence puts down her spoon and stares. First at Hugo, then at Jacob.

'Babe, I think it should be me,' says Clarabelle. 'I can't eat, I feel sick. I don't want it enough to put myself through this.'

'Whatever. Your choice,' Jacob says. 'Are you all right?' he adds when he realises everyone has clocked his harsh response.

He didn't mean it, he's just too tired and wired to care about anything other than his immediate survival. Still, he can't help responding to Hugo.

'What if Florence picks you?' he says.

Hugo shrugs. 'Am I your weakest team member?' he asks her.

'I just don't want to do it,' Clarabelle cuts in. 'I'm not the only one,' she quickly adds, seemingly unable to bear any tension within the group. 'Russell and Shona aren't going, either. They've gone back to their tents to rest. We're all relying on you guys to take lots of photos for us.'

Jacob can't resist throwing Hugo a look as if to say, 'Well, that's the end of your final challenge, then.'

Florence doesn't look as if she even heard what Hugo said.

'Does anyone know where Luke is?' Samson pokes his head through the opening. 'He's not in his tent.'

Everyone shakes their head.

'I haven't seen him since dinner,' says Hugo.

'Same,' says Sara.

Florence looks like she hasn't the energy to speak.

'So, no one has seen him since dinner?' asks Samson.

'I feel disloyal saying this . . .' Florence begins. They all look at her. 'But he told me that he'd heard about some secret paths. He thought it would be good to shake things up a little and do something he hasn't done before. Luke's a bit of a daredevil. He's climbed Kilimanjaro before and he was tempted to do something different this time. He was toying with the idea of going alone.'

'He's climbed here before?' says Sara. 'He never mentioned it.'

'You cannot be serious!' says Casper to Flo. 'How selfish can one person be?'

'Are you sure?' asks Ben.

He and Samson exchange words out of earshot.

'There's a reason not to wander off. It's just too dangerous. The guides are going to have to send out a search party,' Casper continues. 'Do you really think he might have gone alone?' He looks at Florence.

She shrugs. 'It looks that way. I'll text him. See if that does anything.'

Florence removes her right-hand glove and does so, hands shaking as she taps the screen.

'Un-be-liev-able!' Casper exclaims. 'So selfish. It may put the rescue party at risk, as well as Luke. Did he not say anything more specific about where he was heading or when he would set off?'

The group all wait for Florence to reply. She's closest to Luke. She looks utterly stricken, as though hoping someone else will answer for her.

'I . . .' she says. 'I think he said he was friends with one of the guides.' She's not behaving like herself. She and Luke always seemed close. Ben seems to have picked up on this too.

'Which guide?' asks Ben. 'No one we know would do that in the middle of a trip.'

Florence shrugs. 'Sorry, I wasn't listening properly. I didn't think he was serious.'

She's shaking and looks like she might burst into tears at any moment.

'I remember now overhearing Luke say something similar,' Jacob chips in. 'He said that he felt he should challenge himself more.'

'Maybe we should call this all off,' says Flo. 'It feels cursed, this trip. First Mandy, then Imogen, now Luke.'

'Call it off?' says Hugo. He glares at her. 'Why? Because of the selfish actions of one person?'

'No. Because we're now one team instead of two. Because there isn't going to be one winner. Because things simply aren't working out as they are supposed to. Because of George,' she says. 'He and I were closer than we let on at work. He was my fiancé.' This last bit all comes out in a rush, as though she's forcing herself on.

Jacob understands how she feels about the trip. It's so tempting just to think, *fuck it*. They could go back down, settle into a comfy hotel, regroup, forget this ever happened and go back to their lives. Win–win.

'Well, there's a turn-up for the books,' says Hugo. 'I'm sorry to hear that. However, I can say with confidence that George wouldn't have wanted you to give up. He had a killer determination. Now, you need to summit or you'll be disqualified. Don't let the fact that you've lost some people in your group get to you. If you want to succeed in life you have to push on despite the setbacks. They are inevitable. When tough things happen, the tough get going.' He pauses. 'Or, at least, something like that.'

Florence sits, staring straight ahead.

Setbacks are inevitable is pretty much the same sentence Hugo has repeated to Jacob his entire life.

He can't deny it feels good that Hugo is seeing Florence for who she is. An imposter. He always makes Jacob feel like he's the only one who doesn't have what it takes.

'We must go,' says Ben.

It takes a bucketful of inner strength for Jacob to stand up and step outside. As they all gather, getting colder by the second, Hugo looks as though he's struggling for breath. His speech seems to have taken everything out of him. The wind whips past Jacob's ears, the whistling getting louder.

'There's no time to waste,' says Ben. 'Michael and Eric will try to figure out what route he took and look for Luke so they can lead him back to camp. There's every likelihood he will be lost and regretting his stupid decision.'

'It's now or never,' Casper says, as if the rest of us don't get the urgency. 'I've read that come daylight, the ground can become too soft to walk on.'

'Like you're the lead guide all of a sudden,' Jacob hears Joey say to him.

Jacob looks up and sees the tell-tale head-torch lights of the other groups who've already left camp. His hands are already numb and he rubs his gloves together for warmth. He can barely feel his feet.

Ben organises them into what's left of their two groups:

Jacob, Casper, Joey, Sara, Adrian and Hettie.

Flo, Hugo, Lara, Mr and Mrs Armstrong.

The order in which they are selected to climb no longer feels as important as it did a few days ago. Jacob's ego is too frozen to care where he's placed in this particular pecking order. He can still do some basic maths, however. They're six down from when they started: Mandy, Imogen, Luke, Clarabelle, Russell and Shona. Maybe Flo was telling the truth about one thing. This trip really is cursed. On the plus side he is currently in the lead with the number of climbers, he's also winning with the most amount of money raised, at the last count.

'I've still got blisters,' Casper mutters to Jonessa.

That man never quits when it comes to making a point. They're never going to hear the last of his boots. Ever.

Jacob waves his hand in front of his head torch to switch it on. It flickers and for a horrible moment he thinks it's going to conk out, but it eventually illuminates. Jacob feels disproportionate gratitude.

He takes a sip of water from his flask before stepping into the darkness, concentrating on Ben's steps. He can see why Hugo insisted that Ben should be their guide. Calm under pressure, knows instinctively when they need his expertise.

And now they really need it.

NINETEEN

Florence

The Final Push to the Summit

One foot in front of the other. That's how I've got through this so far and it's how I'm going to get through what is already the longest night of my life. I'm wired. I haven't slept. I want to be anywhere else but on this mountain. So many things are painfully clear to me now, such as how fragile life is. Also, how I've never fully understood the phrase, *It feels like a bad dream*. I keep hoping, over and over, that this is a nightmare. That I will wake up to discover that I'm in bed, at my mother's house, the only person who could ever make all the bad stuff go away.

My mother told me to grab hold of happiness and not let it slip through my fingers if I was ever lucky enough to meet the love of my life. George offered me a chance at the kind of life I craved – in-jokes, traditions, banter, brutal honesty, favourite meals, security. A family history without any gaps or missing fathers. His parents have told me that I'm always welcome in their home, even after his accident. But that's all gone now. I am the outsider again.

It wasn't my fault. It was an accident. It was self-defence. Oh God, I'm going to have to do it, I'm going to have to walk past the literal scene of the crime. I barely know what's real any more and what isn't, but what I do know is that Luke's body is prone on the ground. It didn't take a medical degree for me to know that he died instantly. I stood there willing it not to be true, my teeth chattering in the freezing night air.

When we walk within metres of where the body of George's killer lies, I don't know what to do. If there was any chance that he was alive, any at all, I'd have summoned help. I am a killer, just like he is – or was. The difference is, I didn't plan it. This time two years ago, George and Luke were alive. No, two *days* ago they were both still alive. I'm frozen with indecision and self-preservation. Everything feels surreal. My breathing is shallow and I can't stop shivering. And yet I must go up to make it back down. The best thing I can do right now is act as normally as possible even though the thirty-miles-an-hour wind is relentless.

I don't want to think of Luke's family. It makes me feel sick. I've done the same thing to them that he did to George's. My rage at his involvement in George's death might have diminished, but now it's replaced with a new emotion – terror. Terror at being found out. On we walk, single file, into the darkness, leaving Luke behind. *Pole, pole.* I repeat the words over and over like a mantra. Step, step. Left foot, right foot. I distract myself from the mental and physical discomfort by counting my steps. Each time I give up at around twenty and start again. No one speaks. An eerie silence simmers beneath the shrieking of the wind. Oh. My. God. What have I done?

Why didn't I get help? I froze and switched on to auto pilot. I look at my watch. It feels like I last checked it an hour ago but only a mere seven minutes have passed. My beam catches sight of the boots Casper hates so much. A few short days ago, it seemed so vitally important to replace his missing boots, that my ability to sort any problem was a matter of life or death. Ridiculous. Now, I really know the difference between life and death.

I nearly scream out loud – probably would have, if I had enough breath – when I think I see him, staring at me, ghost-like, from behind a rock. His expression is blank, empty, questioning. I can't make any sense of this whole catastrophic situation. Luke said it wasn't his fault. Could he have been telling the truth? Was it Jacob's fault, and therefore both of their faults?

I look up and see a trail of lights – another group – ahead of us. From somewhere, deep within, I get a surge of strength and defiance. I have a right to be here. I have a right to do this. More than ever, I want to win.

The mind-numbing walk in the dark and sub-zero temperatures continues. In the moments I can bear to look up, I can't see any stars. The sky must be blanketed with cloud. Because of what I've done, the world has turned dark. Step, breathe. Breathe, step.

A shout. Adrian stumbles and falls ahead of me. He's on the ground and yet we all stand frozen as Samson helps him up.

'How are you doing?'

'Fine, fine,' he says. He looks anything but.

Step, breathe. On we plod. Time really does seem to stand still, as if we'll never make any progress.

269

We stop for water which I don't feel like drinking. The same words go round in a loop in my brain with each heavy step. Paranoia and clarity interweave, and I no longer know which part of my brain to trust. What if Luke wasn't dead? What if by not raising the alarm I did actually kill him? No. No. His eyes. I could tell from his eyes. Fresh nausea hits and I feel a fresh pool of sweat forming on my back. Maybe I have a fever.

The group gets going again, and from somewhere deep within sheer determination emerges. I grit my teeth to stop them chattering. I can do this. Step, breathe. Breathe, step. The wind stings my eyes and I have moments when I wonder if I should just give up. I could just sit down, go to sleep and never wake up.

My head torch starts to flicker, then without further warning, dies. Blackness.

'Wait!' I shout out above the wind. 'I can't see where I'm going.'

Hugo bumps into me.

Ben appears at my side. 'Do you have a spare?'

'Yes, but my hands are too cold,' I say. 'I don't think I can get it out of my bag.'

'You can try,' he says. 'I'll help you.'

I struggle to take off my backpack, place it on the ground and then rummage around with the help of Ben's torch. I feel like I've lost my fingers. I can't see it.

'It's not in there,' I say. 'It's gone.'

Now paranoia really hits. Someone is out to get me. Luke's ghost. Someone who knows what I did.

'It's gone!' I repeat, close to tears. 'My spare torch is gone. I packed two. I know I did.'

'It's all right,' says Ben. 'I have a spare one you can use.'

'Thank you,' I say. 'Thank you.'

By the time I've fitted the head strap and Ben has helped me adjust it, I'm so frozen, I feel dead. I desperately want to return to camp, but I can't because what's waiting for me down there is worse than continuing. I have no choice, none at all. I'm truly between a rock and a hard place. I keep walking, plodding higher and higher, into the unknown and the darkness.

We stop for more water and a nibble of dried mango. We huddle. Breathe in, breathe out. No one speaks until Jacob breaks the silence.

'You were right,' says Jacob. 'This trip is cursed. Everything feels off.'

'That's encouraging talk,' says Casper. 'Speak for yourself.'

'It's just the altitude,' says Joey. 'It's playing tricks. Just keep putting one foot in front of the other and we'll get there.'

'I feel the same,' I say. 'I don't think I can go on.'

I wish I could slip away quietly without anyone noticing. I feel hot again, which is such an alien feeling after the vicious cold. I unzip my jacket. Ben looks over to me and beckons to James who is carrying the portable oxygen.

'I'm fine,' I say. 'I'm not ill.'

Ben doesn't look convinced and starts asking me a load of questions. At his insistence, I do up my jacket.

'You've done one of the hardest parts,' he says. 'It will be sunrise soon and then it'll get easier. Trust me. We must push on.'

As I try to step forward a rush of nausea knocks me back. I bend down, lean over and am violently, horribly sick. I wipe my mouth with the back of my gloves – beyond caring how disgusting it may be – and then I'm sick again.

'Is she going to be all right?' I overhear Jonessa saying.

No, I think. *I'm never going to be all right ever again.*

'Lots of people get sick.' Samson's voice.

As I stand up, I feel better than I have since the whole, horrible situation with Luke. I catch sight of Hugo, staring at me, hands on hips, his hiking poles sticking out behind him, breathing heavily, observing everything, yet not uttering a word. It's intensely creepy because it's like he's judging, God-like, the strong and the weak. My reactions are helter-skelter. They don't match with the emotions I should feel. I'm partly disgusted but there's still that sliver of defiance worming its way through. I get an urge to push myself harder, prove that I really am a winner in his eyes, and yet, deep down, I also know that I must pull myself together. Focus on what's really important here: survival.

I throw Hugo a look of grim defiance. In return, he turns away from me, but not before I catch something in his eyes, some sort of taunting look which seems to say that even up here, on top of a mountain, far away from all that is familiar, he has the power to command and control. I can no longer tell if I'm shivering from fear, sickness or cold. I pinned so much hope on this trip. It was supposed to be life-changing, a fresh chapter so I could focus on what's important. I suck in more breaths of the thin mountain air.

I hear George's voice in my ear, as loud and clear as if he was walking alongside me.

'Get a grip,' he says. 'You did the right thing. It was an accident and there was nothing you could've done. Keep walking. You've got this.'

I have got this. I've easily raised thousands of pounds for charity. I have proved myself trustworthy and capable in Hugo's eyes. The prize must be within reach if I can just summon up enough strength. Keep going. Loads of people have been successful. You can do it too. Just. Keep. Going.

Samson points into the darkness, indicating that we should all start walking again along an unseen path.

'*Pole, pole,*' someone calls out from the blackness and gloom.

I don't have the energy to do anything but walk slowly. My mind drifts as I concentrate on Samson's boots ahead of me. Step, step. I always wanted a father who would comfort me, protect me from life's evils. Then I found out my father was Hugo.

We stop again. This time, Jacob is staring at me.

'What?' I say.

'I'm curious,' he says, 'how do you do it? How do you pretend that everything is all right?'

What does he mean? Has Hugo told him who I really am?

'I'm not sure what you mean,' I say. 'I'm too exhausted to talk.'

That is true.

'None of this is real,' Jacob calls out.

'What's he on about?' says Sara to Jonessa.

Jonessa just shakes her head slightly as though it's too much effort to reply properly.

'It's all an illusion,' he says.

'I wish Jacob would shut up,' says Sara. 'He's unsettling everyone. Maybe he should be taken back down?' She looks over at Samson.

'He's having hallucinations,' says Jonessa.

'How do you know?' Casper asks.

Jonessa looks at him. 'It's obvious.'

Jacob leans forward, hands on his knees with his head down.

'I'm fine,' he mumbles.

'I'm so over this,' says Sara. 'It's bloody exhausting and we're all frozen stiff. We need to keep moving and get this whole experience over and done with. I miss my children. What was I thinking?' She bursts into tears. 'I didn't mean to make Mandy so ill. I just wanted her to be sick enough so that she changed her mind about the trip. I saw on Hugo's iPad that she'd messaged Hugo over fifty times over the past few weeks. She said she loved him and then when he ignored her, Mandy said she was going to break her silence over that poor man, Simon.' She struggles for breath before continuing. 'Mandy wasn't supposed to make it on the plane. I've been feeling so bad. I even managed to change some of her medical chart readings on the first night in the hope she'd get sent back.'

'Who the fuck is Simon?' I want to ask but can't speak. My mouth feels frozen shut.

'This is absurd,' says Hugo. 'Why didn't you talk to me? What did you do to her?'

I notice the lack of an apology.

We all stare at Sara as her confession spills out of her. On the day before the trip, we were invited to Hugo's for lunch. Sara, it seems, served Mandy a different seafood salad to the rest of us.

Dear Lord, I hope I don't get whacked with the confessional urge stick. That really would be fatal. Any chance I had of proving Luke's death was an accident disappeared the moment I made the traumatic decision to leave him lying there, alone. Survival instinct kicked in. After the horrific incident, I forced myself to go to his tent, resisting the overwhelming urge to sink into a sleeping bag and sleep forever. Instead, I picked up his daypack, packed it and with huge effort, walked back to the scene of the accident and left it near his body.

When I told everyone that he might have gone rogue I partly believed my version of events because it wasn't a lie. Luke *was* interested in other routes. I couldn't believe my luck when Jacob backed me up.

'Hugo claimed it wasn't his fault what happened to Simon,' Sara continues.

I can sense the rage emanating from Hugo. The word *thunderous* comes to mind. His fists are clenched, and he looks like he wants to put his hands over her mouth.

'It's in the past,' says Hugo. 'We can't talk about it now. Let's wait till we're at the hotel. For God's sake, I can barely breathe, let alone deal with this.'

It's hard to properly assess reactions, as all our faces are covered up past our noses with neck warmers.

'What happened to Simon?' asks Jacob.

'Nothing,' says Hugo.

Silence follows. Jacob just stands there, looking stricken.

'If we don't move,' says Hugo, 'we're all going to freeze on the spot.'

He's right. So, on we plod, enveloped in the endless, relentless darkness. A white mist seems to hover immediately above my head but it's too dark to see exactly what it is. Maybe it's George's ghost urging me to keep moving. Or my mother has come down to earth to apologise for dying before she could tell me the truth.

'You deserve to win,' George's voice whispers above the wind. 'I believe in you. You haven't done anything wrong. It was an accident.'

The word *accident* echoes around me like someone really did say it out loud.

'How much longer?' I ask Ben.

Even he sounds like he's breathing a little heavier than usual. I don't know how he manages to do this, time and time again, all the while working so hard. All I've had to do is eat, walk and sleep. And kill someone. Fresh shock hits in a wave of fear. I still can't believe what I did. I pray that it's all a hallucination and that by the time I get back down, he will appear fit and well, really having disappeared to take a different route.

'Not too long until sunrise,' Ben replies. 'We will reach Stella Point at the crater rim in a couple of hours.'

'There's still two more hours to go?'

He doesn't reply.

I know why he doesn't reply, because when we reach the crater rim, the nightmare won't be over. We'll still need to reach Uhuru Peak. And then, there's the return journey. We're all aware that there is no option to stay up there and chill for a few days while we recover.

Step, step. Step, step. Zigzagging backwards, forwards, up, down. It's utterly disorientating and relentless. I feel like I'm being watched by ghouls who have come to punish me for my evil deed. Their invisible presence is both foreboding and oddly comforting. I check my watch. Only four minutes since the last time, and yet it feels like I've been walking for at least another half-hour.

The bitter wind is relentless. My face stings. Our goal feels unattainable. But I can't stop, can't stand still, can't embrace the oblivion I so desperately crave, can't collapse on to the snow and ice. I must fight through the physical and mental pain. I didn't expect the climb to be so brutal on the body and mind. Surrounded by darkness, I force myself to take more steps with my heavy, aching legs, left, then right, repeat.

Shadowy figures ahead blur in and out of focus. My head throbs. Fingers of ice claw and knead my brain. It's not an ordinary headache, it's an all-consuming one which makes thinking almost impossible. But, even through all this, I can see clear images of Luke's twisted neck, his horrible, vacant, staring eyes on bloodied rocks.

Someone cries out from behind me. I'm too tired and too cold to even turn round to see who it is. I don't care about anyone else. We all grind to a halt. Reluctantly, I look back. Sara is on her knees, sobbing in between moments of being violently sick. Hugo pats her awkwardly on her backpack every couple of seconds. What is shocking is that Hugo still looks fine, as though all this is a real walk in the park for him.

'I can't do it. I can't take another step,' says Sara.

She sounds as though she is struggling to breathe.

Samson goes over to speak to her and then he consults with Ben. They only have a brief chat before it's decided that Sara will return to camp with Collins. Ben administers oxygen. She grasps at the mask desperately.

It's tempting, so incredibly tempting, to say that I will go with them. Jacob stares at me as though he's willing me to cave in.

'Do you think you're going to make it?' Jacob asks me.

'I am,' I say. 'I'm not giving in unless I collapse.'

'Me neither,' he says in a grim tone, like he's throwing down the gauntlet.

'I haven't seen anyone from any of the other groups head back, have you?' says Casper.

'So what?' says Jonessa. 'If people don't feel up to it, then they don't feel up to it.'

'I can't do it either,' says Mrs Armstrong. 'I'll go back with Sara.'

'It's not too much further,' says Ben. 'If you make it to Stella Point, it's still a huge achievement. You'll get a certificate.'

'A certificate?' she says. 'I think I'm dying. If I was going to push through the pain, it would have to be for . . .' She stops. 'For what, I don't know. I can't think any more. My brain is too cold. I'm sorry.'

'The rest of us need to keep going,' says Ben.

Sara and Mrs Armstrong turn round and trek slowly down with Collins. Their lights are quickly swallowed up into the darkness. Our trek up continues. Overwhelming nausea hits again and I bend over and puke.

'Are you OK?' Jonessa's voice.

'Yes.'

No.

After another bout of nausea, I feel strangely better despite the weakness in my legs. I continue, gripped by bitter determination, all dignity and care about what I look or smell like, gone.

After what really does feel like forever, a welcome, glorious haze of pale orange and blue-grey light appears on the horizon and, along with it, much-needed hope. The darkness slowly disappears. Thank God. Daybreak. I experience a moment of pure and utter bliss as the blue expands then turns golden. Oh my God, this is it. I'm here, nearly at the top of Kilimanjaro. I'm alive. I'm going to make it. I feel as sure of it as I ever have of anything. A true miracle. I start sobbing.

The dawn of light seems to have gifted everyone with fresh energy. Our steps don't get any faster but they do seem less laboured. Please, God, let there still be a chance that I can win, despite Jacob raising more money than me. I count who is left in my team: Mr Armstrong, Lara, Hugo and me. Samson smiles at me. But then, I catch Jacob's expression. It feels like he's silently challenging me to a fight to the death. My brief moment of euphoria vanishes. Unless Jacob loses more team members, he's in the lead.

I reach up to touch my St Christopher, because now feels like the perfect moment to embrace faith. As I burrow my fingers below my neck warmer, I feel the naked smoothness of my throat. No ring, no St Christopher. I feel around my neck for the chain. Nothing. My legs feel like they will give way as a horrible thought hits. Please God, no. The last time I remember wearing it was when I was with Luke.

TWENTY

Jacob

Climb to Uhuru Peak

As they reach Stella Point, the southern crater rim of Kibo, it feels like a momentous milestone. Jacob knows that it's the point where most of the trails meet. He feels like the king of the world with the blue sky above, pale hues of gold and pink casting a glow on the snow. One of the other volcanic cones, Mawenzi, juts out majestically. Jacob feels like he could reach out and touch it. For a split second he fears that it's another hallucination. But no: while surreal, the beauty and sense of space is real.

They're so bloody, wonderfully, incredibly close to the summit. Right now, it's all that matters in his life. He feels that if he can do this, he really can do anything. To his right, Flo looks utterly exhausted and a little demonic. Her mask is slipping. She's not as confident and capable as she likes to make out. Jacob finally gets why Hugo sets up these challenges this way. It really does sort out the strong from the weak. Flo places her hands on her thighs and bends over.

Jacob glances at his brand-new mountaineering watch. They haven't made good time after all the delays caused by people needing to stop. They were supposed to summit not too long after daybreak and yet sunlight floods as far as he can see. Regardless, it's a relief to be out of the gloom and up here. There is a surreal peace, a sense of nothing in his life having had much meaning until now.

He even has enough energy to read the sign:

CONGRATULATIONS. YOU ARE NOW AT STELLA POINT. 5756M/18885 Ft.

He forces down a fruit bar, even though he doesn't feel hungry. Scattered on the ground are discarded hand warmers and strands of toilet paper. Jacob retrieves a couple of the hand warmers but it's way too much effort to bend down more than once. He looks down into the crater and then across the glaciers of ice fields. It's mesmerising. If he wasn't so exhausted, Jacob almost feels as though he could fly.

'I don't want anything to eat or drink,' Casper mutters before he lies down awkwardly on the ground, despite the snow and still wearing his backpack. Ben walks over to him and helps Casper up by the arm.

'You mustn't lie down. You must get up, eat, drink and keep moving.'

Casper shakes his head.

Ben and Samson confer.

Jacob overhears snippets but can't make anything out. He assumes they are assessing who is fit enough to continue. Jacob knows they have another hour to circle the rim and reach Uhuru Peak. Fresh determination ignites. It will not be him who is told to give up. Not at this point.

Casper stands up, his legs wobbly, his face as pale as death. Then he sits back down and pukes to his side. It's satisfying to see that this isn't a walk in the park for him. Seeing him vulnerable, so undignified, makes Jacob feel like he's got some of his power back. Casper's money affords him an illusion of protection and sense of superiority, and yet here he is, mortal like the rest of them. His wealth certainly isn't helping him now.

Joey walks over and rubs the back of his head. She's as awkward with him as Hugo was with Sara. Her face is still hidden beneath her neck warmer, but Jacob likes to think that she's feeling disgust.

The sugar from the fruit bar must've done the trick because he feels well enough to take some photos while they're all distracted. He wants to capture the raw essence of this entire trip, not that he expects anyone will thank him for some of the reminders. Casper has regained some strength as he's standing upright, supported by his poles.

'We must continue,' says Ben.

Following their guide, they negotiate the flat, winding trail covered in a thin layer of snow around the crater rim. Jacob feels filthy, itchy, dirty, cold and hot at the same time. Yet they're so close.

He mentally starts spending some of the charity money they've raised. He will return it as soon as he can; he's not a thief. He's only going to borrow it. Thing is, he really doesn't think people care. Most people donate money because they want to feel better about themselves. The moment they send it, their aim is achieved. Jacob has personally never come across anyone who donates to charity and follows it through to ensure the intended recipients receive it. Jacob sighs out loud. A large part of his adulthood has been robbing Peter to pay Paul. Story of his life. He gets a real urge to laugh out loud, then to tell Casper that he's never getting his money back, just so he can see his expression. Within seconds, Jacob comes crashing back down to earth, feeling like death all over again. Maybe nothing he's seen or experienced since setting foot on the mountain is real. Somewhere deep inside, he is aware that he's suffering because of the thinning air and freezing temperatures, but everything feels so vivid nonetheless.

His feet ache, and it seems he's joining Casper in the blister department. Still, they persevere. No one speaks as he focuses on the sound of boots hitting the ground in front and behind him. Brown, flat plains stretch out in the distance as far as he can see, along with the odd scattering of snow. He checks his watch for what feels like the millionth time. Surely, please God, not much longer? It's beginning to feel like the ultimate mirage. He doesn't dare ask Ben if they're nearly there as he doesn't want to hear the answer.

He looks back. Flo and her group are several metres behind and seem to be slowing down. It gives Jacob fresh impetus to keep going.

'Come on,' he says to Casper and Joey. 'We're winning.'

They both look at him like they couldn't care less.

They pass a group of climbers on their descent. Jacob has no energy to flag them down and ask what it was like. They don't look elated, in fact they seem exhausted. A woman near the front of the pack looks grim in her determination as she jabs her hiking poles into the ground, one after the other.

Still, they are luckier than he is because they're on their way back, having at least summited. He sees one man being held up by a guide and practically being dragged along. Just ahead, he spots another person being pulled up the incline by a guide with his hiking pole.

'How much longer?' he hears Casper ask Ben.

'Nearly there,' he says.

Please let that be true. He's starting to give up hope that it will ever happen. His footsteps crunch on the snow. Step, step. One, two. One, two. A glacier dazzles in the sunlight.

And then . . .

Jacob can barely believe his eyes. The wooden signposts with yellow lettering he's seen in nearly every guidebook or blog are just ahead of them. A crowd of people gather round, posing for photos, and there's a cluster of other climbers queueing to get their pictures taken in front of the iconic signs.

MOUNT KILIMANJARO
CONGRATULATIONS
YOU ARE NOW AT UHURU PEAK,
TANZANIA, 5985M/19341 Ft. AMSL

Jacob concentrates on the lower signs.

AFRICA'S HIGHEST POINT
WORLD'S HIGHEST FREE-STANDING
MOUNTAIN

The words start to blur, and it takes a moment to realise that his eyes are filling with tears. He turns away from the group even though they all look seriously shattered and emotional too. They're on the roof of Africa!

This isn't what he thought winning would be like. To be a winner has always felt intangible, like the ultimate prize that would finally make him feel worthy. And yet, physical exhaustion aside, it feels hollow. He wants to throw down his hiking poles and sink to the ground. He feels like he should punch the air, shout out loud, but all he can think of is how quickly they can take the pictures, prove they made it and get back down.

Florence and her team appear behind him. His team have won and yet she looks like she either hasn't realised or doesn't care. Yet it's obvious to Jacob that there is one extra person in his team. Apart from himself, his team consists of: Jonessa, Casper, Adrian and Hettie. Florence only has four in total.

'No hard feelings,' Jacob says to her.

She shrugs. 'We'll see.'

Jacob joins the queue of climbers patiently waiting their turn, a kind of summit rush hour. It's not how he imagined. There's no camaraderie among the different groups, no mutual exclamations of congratulation. Ben and Samson don't look as tired as their clients, but still . . . Fresh awe swamps him at the fact they can do this time and time again.

'Are you all right?' he asks Flo.

She keeps tugging at her scarf and her face is flushed. Jacob hopes she isn't going to collapse at his feet.

'I've lost something valuable,' she says.

'What?'

'Nothing. Maybe I haven't lost it. Maybe it's in my tent,' she mumbles.

Jacob stares at her. She seems to be making a huge effort to pull herself together because she closes her eyes and takes several deep breaths.

'Thank you,' a breathless Flo says over and over to the guides, like nothing bad has happened. 'Thank you for all your hard work and making my dream come true.'

It sounds like it's something she's rehearsed rather than a heartfelt thank-you. And anyway, it's not just her bloody dream. Trust Florence to try and make it all about her again. Jacob adds his profuse thanks too.

Jacob sees Casper and Jonessa high-five one another and everyone takes turns hugging.

When it's their teams' turn to stand in front of the signs, they pose and smile enthusiastically, quite an achievement, given that they all look half-dead. Although they manage a happy grin, Jacob notices that none of them hang around for 'one more photo'. They're all beyond caring – posting on social media with an amazing picture at the summit is a distant dream right now. They've made it. He's made it. That's all that matters.

'Wait a minute,' Flo calls out. 'I'd like to say a quick prayer for George. It doesn't seem right, otherwise.'

Awkwardly, they gather around in a circle. At first no one speaks, but then Flo leads them all in the Lord's Prayer.

'Our Father . . .'

They all join in, some louder than others, most mumbling self-consciously. When it comes to the part about forgiving our sins, Jacob sneaks a look at Flo and Hugo, but both have their eyes closed. He'd love to read their thoughts.

As they're gathered together in preparation for the descent, Jacob wishes he had the energy or inclination to draw the moment out. It feels too brief, given that summiting has been their aim for so long.

'You made it to the top of Kilimanjaro,' Jacob says to Joey. 'Despite fearing heights. You must feel very proud of yourself.'

She gives a weak smile. 'I'm glad I did it.'

'Are *you* glad you did it?' Hugo asks Jacob.

'Very.'

It's true. Hugo almost looks impressed, and it feels like the closest thing to a father–son moment that they've ever had. Maybe he's hallucinating, too. It strikes Jacob that, like most things in life, the anticipation feels more significant than the actual event.

'I won,' Jacob says. 'I bloody won.'

Yet Hugo's reaction is not what Jacob expects. His father shakes his head inexplicably. Before he can ask why, Jacob sees a tall man approaching them wearing a flame-orange jacket emblazoned with the Ethical Getaways logo. Although his face is covered by mirrored sunglasses, it is unmistakeably Gareth Snow.

'We just about beat them,' Jacob says to Hugo.

'You knew they were also planning to summit this morning?' Hugo says.

'I've kept one step ahead of the game,' Jacob continues, ignoring this question. 'I told you I was going to win.'

Hugo doesn't look pleased. No, that's an understatement. The word that springs to Jacob's exhausted, exhilarated mind is more sinister. Because in that moment his father looks like he is capable of murder.

'I would shake your hand,' says Gareth, as he approaches Hugo, 'but I don't want to get blood on mine.'

'What nonsense is this?' asks Hugo.

'Simon.'

'What about him?' asks Jacob.

Strange that it's the second time his name has been brought up in one night.

'Ask your father,' says Gareth.

Something crosses Hugo's face. He looks like a deer in headlights. Suddenly it clicks.

TWENTY-ONE

Florence

Descent to Mweka Camp

J acob looks how I feel as we start our descent. I fear I may collapse at any moment because daylight will literally shine a light on what I did. My knees feel under the most enormous pressure and the ground slides beneath my feet, like sand. Despite my gaiters, there's grit inside my boots. I try to ignore the discomfort, but it's no good.

'I have to stop,' I announce, sinking down on a rock.

It's the most laborious, exhausting thing to unlace my boots, shake them out and put them back on again. The group hangs around watching me and I can sense them willing me to hurry the fuck up. Everywhere I look, there is dust. It's impossible to think that this was the same spooky walk we did last night.

Jacob won. I can't quite believe it; we were so close. And I don't know where that's going to leave me, daughter of Hugo or not, because his rules are always clear. The winner wins; the loser loses. I didn't deserve to win after what I did. I keep hoping that if I can blank it out enough then I can erase what happened. That somehow, magically, everything will be all right.

Every now and then I try to catch sight of Hugo, to see if I can decipher what he's thinking or feeling, but his expression is completely neutral. He doesn't give anything away.

I keep expecting Ben or Samson to receive a call or message to tell them about Luke, but there is nothing about the demeanour of either one of them which indicates that anything is amiss. I keep descending because there's nothing else that I can do. I'm still violently cold, and it's no relief that the sun is now up. My toes feel like I've got frostbite and the endless dust is getting to me.

I wish I could remember if the chain was still around my neck after Luke's accident. But I can't. It's a blur, it all happened so fast. I do recall him putting his hands around my neck. If my necklace is anywhere near his body – especially if it's broken – I will be the number one suspect. It won't take a genius to figure it out. Oh God. I think of my poor grandmother visiting me in prison, sitting awkwardly on a nailed-down plastic chair. I'm going to have to ask Hugo for help. I'll have to ask him not to say that he gave the necklace to me. But then the answer to my problems comes to me. If I make myself the one to discover the body and raise the alarm – assuming I'm not already too late – then it won't matter. Damnit. I should have stayed behind at camp. How stupid of me.

I walk faster than I have in days and the whole time all that's on my mind is that I want a button to reverse time, so that I can reset this whole mess. The others are equally lost in thought. No one speaks as we slip and slide down. Occasionally, we pass climbers still on their ascent. We exchange brief greetings, but other than that they keep going up and we keep moving down. Already the air feels thicker and it's nice to be able to breathe normally again. Although, despite the relentless exercise, my toes still feel frozen.

'It's going to rain by the looks of things,' says Jonessa, glancing up at the sky.

'I thought it wasn't the rainy season yet,' says Casper, sounding annoyed, as if the weather is something that can be controlled.

'How much longer?' I ask Ben.

'Nearly there.'

I've noticed that he doesn't usually give exact answers. Perhaps he's discovered that if he tells the truth, it will be disheartening.

I push him for an answer because I really need to know.

'How long is nearly there?'

He points downwards.

'You can see the camp.'

I squint. I can just about make it out. Oh God. Fear shoots through my body like a lightning bolt. I peer down, expecting to see Luke's body, his red jacket highlighted like a beacon. But it's like it never happened.

'So, once we're back in camp, we can officially announce the winner,' says Jacob.

'Maybe,' says Hugo noncommittally.

'What do you mean, "maybe"? I won. Everyone will want to celebrate. Well, nearly everyone.'

'There are some things we need to smooth out first.'

'Like?'

'Logistics.'

Jacob clenches his fists and looks like he'd quite happily punch Hugo. I don't blame him.

A few minutes later, Ben's phone rings.

My stomach plummets. I've never heard his phone ring. It can only mean one thing.

I see him frowning before he says something I can't make out. When he cuts the call, his expression is grave.

'We must wait here before going into camp. There's been an accident. Someone has been badly hurt.'

I hold my breath, waiting to hear more, focusing on the word 'accident'. It's too late. I'm too late.

'Who is it?' asks Hugo. 'Is Sara all right?'

'It's not a woman,' says Ben. 'Right, everyone, we will wait here a while longer until we're given permission by the authorities to continue into camp.'

'Is it someone from our group?' asks Casper. 'Did anyone find Luke?'

Jacob gives me a strange look.

'Do you know if Luke is OK?' I ask Ben. 'Is everyone from our group all right?'

I must act normally, and if I can't do that, I must at least act like an innocent person is supposed to. I think I'm doing OK so far, if only Jacob would quit staring at me.

Ben's phone rings again after a painful twenty-minute wait. All the while I imagine how degrading it would be to be handcuffed in front of everyone.

'We can go into camp now,' says Ben. 'But we are to let the medical team and experts do their job when we pass the person who is injured. As planned, we are not staying in Barafu Camp. We will meet up with the others and all make our way down to Mweka Camp. If you try and rest here, you will never feel like getting up again. It's better to keep going because we have another thirteen kilometres – which is about eight miles – left to go.'

The mental and physical torture is never-ending, but I'm relieved that escape is in sight. Relief is short-lived, however, when I realise we are going to pass his body. The mere thought of it lying there while I try to act normally sends my head spiralling.

The brightly coloured tents of the camp come into closer view. But that's not what I focus on. As we get nearer, it's impossible to miss a group of people, some uniformed, huddled near the bottom of the track. Right where I left Luke. As we get closer, we are waved past. A makeshift screen has been erected to hide Luke's body. The urge to be sick is engulfing, but somehow my legs keep moving. Step, step. Down. If my knees didn't feel like they were on fire, I'd have the urge to run. As we walk past, my eyes feel drawn inexorably to the scene of my crime.

'What happened?' I ask one of the park rangers guarding the scene.

'Please, move on,' he says.

'Do you think it's Luke?' says Casper. 'Poor bastard.'

'No,' says Jonessa. 'It can't be. We must be positive.'

I hate when people say, 'be positive'.

'Move on, please,' the park ranger repeats.

I realise that I'm standing, frozen to the spot. Someone pushes me gently in the back.

'You need to keep moving.' It's Jonessa's voice, I realise.

As I walk down, I see that Jacob's ridiculous tent has been erected, but it's a welcome sight because once we're inside it, the familiar faces of the others come into focus. It turns out that Sara and Mrs Armstrong recovered well once they'd descended to a lower altitude. My eyes scan the enclosed space, half-expecting to see Luke. I still can't take it in – this time yesterday he was alive.

Shit, shit, shit. Where is my necklace? Please God, let me have lost it anywhere other than near his body. I hope it's packed away in my tent.

We're handed cups of steaming tea and biscuits, followed by cheese sandwiches. I nurse the tea, gripping the cup as if my life depends on it. Which it does, in a way. Everything now rests on me behaving as normally as possible. I'm vaguely aware of various people from our group entering and exiting the tent, and I feel hungry, which is odd as I know that I couldn't handle anything in my stomach right now. Those who do manage to eat, do so as if they feel guilty. They nibble half-heartedly and leave crusts on their plates.

'Has anyone seen Luke?' I ask.

My voice sounds strained, like I'm fighting a terrible cold.

'No,' says Sara, gently. 'Have a seat, Florence. Drink your tea.'

'Is it him?' I push.

'Everyone thinks so from what I've managed to gather,' says Clarabelle. 'He's wearing a BVT jacket.'

'Is he OK?'

'I don't think so,' says Clarabelle again. 'He's been out there too long.'

'Oh God,' I say. 'What a horrible thought. First George, then Luke. I can't believe this is happening again.'

How sickeningly true those words are.

'We don't know for certain that it is, nothing's been confirmed,' says Clarabelle.

But she's unable to hide the break in her voice, and I know she's putting on a brave front. It's her kindness that breaks me. Tears fall, and I can't stop them. I cry for George, for Luke and for myself, because I know that there's no good way of moving on from this. I'm going to hell, the hell I didn't think I believed in until now.

I'm offered more tea, patted on the shoulder, told it will be all right. They're nothing more than voices: Lara, Hettie, Adrian, Hugo, Sara, Jonessa. I half-listen to various conversations but all the speculation is unbearable when I know the truth.

Ben calls through the tent flap.

'We're moving down to the next camp,' he announces. 'Please can you meet me outside in ten minutes? We're expecting some rain, so make sure your waterproof covers are securely tightened around your bags.'

'What about Luke?' I ask.

'Don't worry, I'll give you any news as I get it,' he says.

'What about his family?' I say, thinking of George's mum, dad and sister, and all the messages I haven't replied to, couldn't reply to, because of what I've done to Luke and his family. I'm a hypocrite. 'We shouldn't just leave him. One of us should stay with him.'

I can't believe the words are coming out of my mouth. Does part of me really believe that I'm innocent? That I didn't cause this devastation?

'There are plenty of experienced people who are dealing with the situation,' says Hugo. 'Ben is right, we need to head down to the next camp as instructed. It's my duty to keep his family informed, but right now, I don't have any concrete information, and there's no point in worrying them until I have details.'

'Someone should at least warn them,' says Jacob.

'And say what?' Hugo asks.

'That Luke went off on his own and efforts are being made to locate him?' Jacob suggests.

'Right,' says Hugo. 'Yes, you're right.'

Jacob starts tapping into his phone.

'Wait,' I say. Jacob looks at me. 'You'll word it sensitively, won't you?'

He looks back down at his phone, ignoring me.

Jonessa pulls a sympathetic face.

Casper picks up his phone.

'Did anyone actually try contacting him last night?'

'I did,' I say. 'When we all gathered for the summit walk, I managed to type out several messages.'

It's a small relief to have had the presence of mind to work on my tech alibi.

'I'll try again,' says Casper.

We watch him, all fully aware that it's most likely futile.

'Who found him?' I ask.

I need to know.

'Michael and Eric. Apparently they spotted his jacket,' says Clarabelle.

'We must've walked right past him in the dark,' says Casper. 'We all just left him there. What the hell was he doing, going out on his own?'

'Maybe he didn't go out on his own,' says Jacob.

My heart skips a beat.

'What do you mean?' asks Casper.

'Nothing. I'm just saying it's odd, isn't it?'

'Perhaps he wasn't trying to go a different route, maybe he just wanted a head start,' Casper says.

'Still doesn't make sense,' says Jacob.

I feel like taking a mug from the table and throwing it at him.

'I think we should all get going,' says Hugo.

'Hear, hear,' says Mr Armstrong. 'I'm glad I climbed Kilimanjaro, but it's time to head down. Let's leave the authorities to do their job.'

'I thought we were going to get a longer break here,' says Lara.

'Samson has explained that it's probably better to keep moving, exhausting as it is,' I say.

I want to put as much distance between me and my crime – no, my accident fuelled by rage and self-defence and fear – as possible.

We all stand up, ensuring that the zips on our backpacks are properly done up and that the protective rain covers are snugly fitted. It's a relief to have a job to focus on, something physical. My calves, knees and neck ache like never before. I do some stretches and Clarabelle copies me. It's surreal that we're all carrying on as if nothing has happened, our brains latching on to the mundane to keep us going.

'My knees are killing me,' says Mr Armstrong.

'Mine too,' Casper agrees.

'I need a massage,' says Clarabelle. 'I wish I'd had the foresight to book into a spa before I left. I'll be gutted if they're too busy when we get down.'

I look at her and she has the grace to look embarrassed, as though suddenly realising how it must come across after the terrible things that have happened. I'm a hypocrite of the worst kind. I will never be able to look at myself in the mirror again. And still, a voice deep inside me whispers, there's no benefit to speaking up. It wouldn't change anything. Luke is dead. And it wasn't my fault. He killed George and it set off a horrible chain of consequences.

'Let's go,' says Hugo.

As we step outside, I hear Jacob call out to his father. 'Hold back a minute. I've something important to say.'

I turn away, and Jacob throws me a look of defiance that I can't interpret. I stand near the entrance, trying to eavesdrop, but he's speaking too quietly.

I look up at the mountainside and see more groups returning. Soon, they too will be walking past Luke's body on the mountain.

Clarabelle comes over and puts her arm around me, leading me over to the others.

'Don't walk alone,' she says. 'I'm here for you. I can't imagine what it's like to lose two colleagues. I had no idea that you and George were close. I'm very sorry for your loss – both of them.'

'It's horrible,' I say, as tears, both crocodile and real, well up. 'What's Jacob talking to Hugo about?' I add, curiosity getting the better of me.

She shrugs. 'He seems to think he can shed light on what happened to Luke.'

And then, with startling clarity, I remember that cracking sound nearby when I assumed Luke and I were alone among the rocks. I had forgotten it in my panic. But it could easily have been a person hiding in the shadows.

TWENTY-TWO

Jacob

Descent to Mweka Camp

Hugo has been avoiding Jacob since their encounter with Gareth, but now he's forced to listen to whatever it is Jacob has to say.

'What did Gareth mean about Simon?' he asks as they follow the others, weaving between the rocks.

'Simon passed away, sadly.'

'Oh my God. When?'

'Recently. Suicide. The family are trying to pin the blame on us.'

Jacob doesn't blame them.

'I had to pay them off,' Hugo continues.

'Hush money,' Jacob suggests.

Hugo doesn't deny it.

The sky darkens and unleashes the rain, the path quickly turning into a mud pit, which slows them down. Jacob's utterly exhausted, but at the same time he's never felt more awake. He's half-alive, half-dead.

'Why did you pay them?' he asks.

'Simon had set up a so-called survivors' group of ex-employees.'

'And?'

'And they were planning to bring a case against us. His sister got in touch and told me that him losing his job in such a brutal fashion was the beginning of the end.' Hugo pauses. 'He felt that the group he set up was a safe place, but someone used his story anonymously online. I took it down,' says Hugo. 'I didn't realise the impact it would have. I didn't know the online story I read was based in truth.'

Christ. It gets worse, thinks Jacob.

'It sounds as if Gareth is going to continue where Simon left off,' he says. 'You're not the only person posting anonymously. There are plenty of people who want you to pay for how you've treated them.'

Hugo doesn't reply. His silence is more unsettling than anything he could say. But then another question appears in Jacob's mind. Has Hugo been planning to throw *him* under the bus? He mentally shuffles through all the online comments and threats over the past months. Hugo doesn't have just one skeleton in his closet; it's so full that it's fit to burst. Christ, he can't wait to get off the mountain. They have about 1,500 metres to descend until they reach Mweka Camp.

'Seeing as we're having such a heart-to-heart,' says Hugo, 'you may as well know a few more things. It will do us good to clear the air.'

'Go on,' says Jacob.

'Luke helped me arrange the scorpion. On the day I insisted

you dazzle our clients by taking them to the Materuni Falls and the hot springs, Luke didn't join you because I sent him to meet a friend of mine and collect the creature. The glass in your sleeping bag was also down to me because, in all honesty, I was so furious after the champagne incident.' He pauses for breath. 'What? Don't look at me like that. It's all about putting the right amount of pressure on your people – even the spare battery and Flo's missing back-up torch. It's character building.'

'Unbelievable.' Jacob wants to laugh but can't summon up the energy. Instead, he hears himself replying, 'I guess none of it really matters now, in comparison.'

'Quite.'

Silence falls.

It's surprising how quickly the landscape changes. From the rocky surface, shrubs appear and Jacob even spots a lone flower growing between two rocks against all odds. He looks at his watch and reckons there's at least a couple more hours left. He starts to actually believe that they will reach the end of this descent, thank Christ, as they approach the heather zone. Tufts of yellowing shrubs dot the ground, which reminds him of a mangrove swamp. If he manages to get to the next camp without twisting his ankle it will be a bloody miracle.

He considers what he's going to say to Hugo. It's obvious he's the winner, and Hugo needs to understand that Jacob has finally more than proved himself. Jacob doesn't need a grand announcement – yet. He just wants Hugo to verbally acknowledge it.

The rain continues to pelt his hood, now dripping down his face. It's hard to believe that he's still upright after the longest day of his life. To their side, a mini waterfall has formed between the rocks. Jacob dodges the puddles forming along their route. The last thing he needs is soggy feet.

On the way up there was a goal, a destination to aim for. Now escape feels elusive, and he feels stuck. Jacob must sort it out. He can't live with the uncertainty of half or empty promises that 'everything will get sorted.' Not with debts to pay and creditors to satisfy.

Although when you compare those problems with death, they seem trivial. His conscience is pricking him as he thinks about Luke and how he let Flo leave him there, lying cold on the ground.

Jacob had the decency to check after she'd left his body. He's not evil. There's no doubt Luke was dead. Jacob stood there mulling over the options before deciding that Florence had made the right decision, for once. The ground was frozen, so he wasn't concerned about leaving a trace, and when they left camp for the summit, he made a point of standing close to the spot where Luke lay to 'sort something out' in his bag. Flo waited by his side too and Jacob knew she was thinking along the same lines, in case of DNA or other giveaways. But she had no idea what he was up to, he's sure of it. Jacob had gone looking for Florence. And find her he did.

A horrible part of him is relieved that the guy has been silenced. Whatever they were arguing about, Florence did Jacob a favour. Even if she now knows what happened to George, presuming Luke told her, it's Jacob's word against his. When Jacob found her diary after Luke had dropped it as they prepared to climb the Barranco Wall, it was like the universe had handed him a gift. He recognised it as Flo's. She'd already accused Jacob of stealing it, and yet Luke was the culprit. No doubt Luke had been feeling increasingly paranoid that Flo might suspect more than she'd let on about his and Jacob's mistake. Flo wasn't going to let it drop. And it was Luke's mistake. Jacob never meant for George to get badly hurt, of course he didn't. He just needed slowing down a little, so that Luke could win. Luke is – was – amenable. And Jacob hadn't lied. Luke *would've* made the perfect deputy, once Jacob had found a way to take over the reins from his father.

Jacob concentrates on not slipping as he walks. Every now and then he feels inside his pocket for Flo's St Christopher. The proof of what she did. Proof that she's a murderer.

Clarabelle cries out just in front of him. 'My ankle!'

They stop in the relentless downpour, water running off their hoods, while James investigates.

'I think it'll be OK to walk on,' he decides, much to their collective relief. He reminds the rest of them to be careful.

Like they have any choice.

The rain eases, then stops abruptly. Jacob removes his hood and looks up at the sky, barely believing it. And yet, just like that, it really has stopped. They continue down the muddy path.

Mweka Camp is surrounded by lush green trees, a welcome sight. Jacob searches the horizon, half-expecting to see a rainbow. The ground is soaked. Jackets and covers hang from branches everywhere he looks. A pile of duffel bags sits in the middle of camp on top of a large waterproof sheet, awaiting collection.

Jacob removes his soggy outerwear and hangs his jacket and hat on a forked branch. He watches drips fall to the ground, momentarily mesmerised. He bides his time, watching

Hugo's every move, waiting to pounce. He appreciates the thickness in the air as he inhales the fresh scent of the rain-washed atmosphere. It's the only thing that seems capable of calming him down right now.

Despite the exhaustion, they're encouraged to wait until after dinner to get a proper sleep.

'This is your last evening together, you should try and make the most of it,' says Ben. Despite there being no further update on Luke, he's right.

'Excuse me, Sara,' Jacob says after he 'knocks' on the entrance to their tent. 'I need to borrow Hugo for a few minutes.'

'Can't it wait?' she says. 'He's shattered.'

'No.'

Hugo clambers out of the tent. Jacob steers him to the edge of the crowded camp, virtually overflowing with tents from the multiple companies who have already set up for the night.

'Look, I won, fair and square. I got to the summit first, with the highest number of people, plus I've just checked the amounts and I've raised the most by more than a thousand pounds. One thousand, two hundred and twenty-three, to be exact. I've proved I'm a winner. I'm ready to take over BVT. You'll still have a say in all the important matters, I won't exclude you. But meanwhile, you can enjoy your achievements. Take Sara and the kids on a cruise. Or sit at home for once and think about perhaps turning your words of wisdom into an actual book. Enjoy life. There comes a point when there really is no point in all work and no play. You can't take it with you.'

Jacob's pleased with his speech. All the mental rehearsing during that endless descent has paid off.

Hugo looks at Jacob, a cross between pity and frustration.

'You didn't win, overall,' he says. 'The contest waters were most certainly muddied. If anything, it was pretty much a draw. You couldn't run the company alone if you tried, Jacob. You'd grind it to the ground within a year. And that's being generous. You've always been a disappointment to me, business-wise. I want a son who I can trust and be proud of to carry the Blackmore name into the future. I'm sorry, but Florence is the best bet. She's cool-headed with an eye for detail, both of which are crucial in business, and neither of which you possess, I'm afraid.'

Jacob has never wanted to smash someone in the face as badly as he does now.

'What was the past week for, in that case? It doesn't make any sense. You can't just change the rules because you don't like the outcome.'

Hugo continues, as though he has no idea how cruel his words are.

'I certainly can. These annual competitions are about identifying future leaders as well as winners,' he says. 'It's only by watching these team-building exercises that you can see what people are truly made of. Florence is more than capable of taking over BVT – eventually – and ensuring its success. Admittedly, she still has a lot to learn, but that's normal. We'll do everything properly and ensure that we maintain a position for you which is suitable for your skill set and talents. And, don't get me wrong, you have many. But we can't all be leaders in this world.'

'Let me tell you what the saintly Florence has done . . .' Jacob says, 'and then we'll see.'

Hugo holds up his hand.

'I don't want to hear it. There's something you should know. Something I should have told you a long time ago.'

'And I don't want to hear whatever it is, either.'

'She's your half-sister,' Hugo says.

At first, Jacob doesn't think he's heard properly. But then the ground starts to move and little things − then big things − start clicking into place. The St Christopher, for one. He should have guessed. Hugo gave him one too, for Christ's sake.

Jacob stares at his father but Hugo's breathing becomes more laboured, as if the energy it took to release such a big secret has finished him off after everything they've been through since last night.

'I don't understand,' says Jacob.

But he does. And as the memories start to crowd his brain it seems so fucking obvious.

'A story for tomorrow,' Hugo says. 'I promise.'

Rooted to the spot, Jacob watches him weave his way back to his tent as if he's drunk. He's not letting Hugo get away with half a story.

'Hugo!' he calls out. 'Dad!'

Hugo disappears inside his tent.

'Do not walk away from me!'

Jacob doesn't care who hears him.

When Jacob pokes his head through the opening, he does not expect to see Hugo already lying down on top of his sleeping bag, his eyes closed. Sara is bending over him, her hair hanging loose.

'Hugo! Darling! Answer me, please!' Twisting to face Jacob, she says: 'What did you do?'

'Nothing! He just walked away from me.'

'Pass me that bag!' She points to a leather washbag in the corner of their tent.

Jacob picks it up. 'His pills,' she begs.

'What are they for?' he asks, fishing around then lifting the lid of one of the plastic containers: *Monday*. Wait – is it Monday? He mentally works back to the day they arrived in Tanzania. Yes. He tips the contents into the palm of his hand before handing them over to Sara. 'There are a lot of different pills.'

'He's on medication for various things. There's the ones to help prevent altitude sickness, plus ones for high blood pressure, diabetes . . .'

'He has diabetes?'

'He doesn't want anyone to know. Damn! His water bottle is empty. Do you have any spare?'

Jacob pulls his from his backpack and hands it over, twisting off the lid.

'Here,' he says.

'Sit up, darling,' she says.

Hugo opens his eyes and props himself up on his elbow.

Sara feeds him his pills, which he swallows obediently, one by one.

'How much longer are we going to be here?' he says, appearing disorientated and confused. 'I thought I'd already taken my pills.'

'Just one more night,' she says. 'You need to get up and have something to eat. Ben and Samson have been very clear on that. And then you can sleep. We'll all feel better in the morning.'

Jacob can't see himself ever feeling better again. Too much has shifted his vision of life. He sits with Sara as Hugo forces himself to sit up. Jacob hands over the washbag in case she needs it again.

'Thank you. Go and have dinner,' she says. 'There's no point in both of us staying here.'

Laughter emanates nearby as he heads towards the mess tent, a reminder that he too should be celebrating his achievement. But it doesn't feel like the time or place, not least because he's just learned that his nemesis is his own flesh and blood, and further, this secret has been kept from him for his entire life. He can't imagine that anyone else was left in the dark. Florence must've known, she's sneaky like that. It's probably the reason she joined the company in the first place. How could he not have seen that something was amiss? And yet, as he takes his seat, he can sense something of Hugo in her now, like the way she laughs, or rubs her neck when she's stressed. Just like him. What does this all mean for Jacob? What does he do with the knowledge that she's a murderer? It matters. George died of his injuries. Luke died as a direct result of Flo's actions. He has to find a way to turn it to his advantage.

Jacob jabs his fork into the fish on his plate and bites into a bone. He picks it out from between his teeth, suddenly no longer hungry.

After a dessert of pineapple and mangoes, the tiredness swamps him like a hammer blow to the head. He feels so numb, he can barely summon up the energy to crawl into the tent.

'Jelly Tot, what's wrong?' says Clarabelle.

'I've told you not to call me that. I'm sick of everyone ignoring what I say.'

'You're tired,' she says. 'We all are. It's been a really tough day.'

That's putting it far too lightly. Jacob pulls his hood over his head and paces outside. Every time he passes the rangers who guard the camp, fresh paranoia hits that maybe they're being kept here because they've realised that Luke's death wasn't an accident. They're all going to be suspects and Jacob will end up taking the blame for Florence, because everyone will likely believe her when she says she didn't do it. He obsesses over every little detail he can remember, anything he might have overlooked or missed. He returns to his tent and slips into his sleeping bag.

Jacob lies there, suspended in an eerie sense of timelessness. It's suffocating, like slowly running out of oxygen after diving deep below the surface, knowing that he doesn't have enough air to last. It's like they've all checked into a haunted hotel that they're never going to be allowed to check out of. The rain falls again, hitting the roof of the tent like bullets. It strikes him, like the clearest of premonitions. They're not going to be able to climb down to the base of the mountain in the morning. They're stuck.

TWENTY-THREE

Florence

Mweka Camp. 3,050 metres or 9,900 feet (approx).

A scream wakes me from the sleep I half-hoped I'd never rise from.

It's animalistic, yet human. Then silence, apart from the sound of rain hitting the tent canvas. I must've dreamt the noise.

Sara's voice shocks me out of my daze. I'm still more asleep than awake.

'He's stone cold. Hugo's not well. Someone, help!'

I sit up, pain shooting through my head. I'm desperately thirsty and fumble for my water bottle, but there's no time as Sara cries out again. Quickly, I pick up my torch, then crawl out of my tent, the rain beating down on me as I stand upright, but in my haste trip over something. A tree root the most likely culprit. The ground is hard, it stings my knees . . .

I push my gloveless hands against the freezing earth and stand up, straightening my knees and hobbling over in the direction of Hugo and Sara's tent. There are multiple people already crowding around the tent flaps. Clarabelle, Jacob, James, Samson, Ben, Casper, Mr Armstrong, whose hair is sticking up all over his head.

'Stay back,' says Samson. 'James needs space to make an assessment. It would be better if you all went back to your tents and let us deal with the situation.'

'Is he OK?' asks Jacob. 'He wasn't feeling great last night, what's going on? He's my father.'

It seems like an unnecessary detail, but as he says it, he looks at me and I know for absolute certain now that he knows. I give a weak smile of apology – why, I don't know – but he stares right through me, eyes burning, as if he's about to do something truly terrifying.

'He's very sick,' Jacob persists, suddenly ignoring me. 'We have to get him off this mountain, to a lower altitude. He needs a hospital.'

Sara's shivering.

'Can I get something to warm you up?' I ask.

'No, thanks,' she says.

'How much longer until it gets light?' I ask Samson.

He looks at his watch. 'Six hours.'

Bloody hell.

'Let's go to the mess tent,' I say. 'We can ask for some tea if anyone's awake. Or we can just sit and keep together for warmth. There's no point in us all standing outside getting soaked.'

'She's right,' says Clarabelle.

Jacob hesitates. Clearly, he can't bear to be anywhere near me, but then he relents and comes with us. Nevertheless, he refuses to make eye contact with me. I don't blame him. I've no idea how I'd feel in his shoes – probably the same – and also how I'd have felt had I known that Jacob found out first. Damn Hugo.

We all sit, exhausted, until some flasks of fresh tea appear as if by magic. I feel bad, because someone has most likely been woken up after a tough working day to make it. I should've perhaps offered, but I've become so accustomed to not doing anything for myself that it didn't occur to me.

Sara sits, sipping the tea, staring straight ahead.

'It's all my fault,' she says eventually.

'No, it's not,' I say. 'How can it be?'

'It was my idea to climb Kilimanjaro. I suggested it to Hugo when he was pondering where to set this year's Great Escape. A friend of mine said that it was one of the hardest things she'd ever done. It sounded a good option for the annual challenge.'

'Then I honestly can't see how it's your fault,' I say. 'Mandy, Jacob, Luke, Hugo and I, we were all involved in the agreement and planning of the trip in various ways. You mustn't beat yourself up. And we all know that Hugo would *never* agree to anything he didn't want to.'

'She's right,' says Jacob.

'But it's all gone so spectacularly wrong,' she says. 'It wasn't supposed to be like this. None of it was, not even Mandy. Despite the fact I detest her.'

'It'll be OK,' I say. 'We'll all be back down by this afternoon. Hugo is a fighter. He'll recover, for sure. He'd hate it if we were all moping about, assuming the worst. And Mandy's apparently back at home and feeling fine. No lasting damage.'

'You didn't see Hugo, though, Florence. He looked deathly pale, and I do mean that literally.'

'Has anyone got any decent signal?' asks Casper, glaring down at his phone on the table.

'Who are you trying to get hold of?' asks Jonessa. 'It's the middle of the bloody night.'

I can't sit here. I feel helpless, like I'm sitting around simply waiting for bad news.

'I'm going to the toilet,' I lie.

Outside, I take a welcome breath. I don't think I'll ever take for granted again the joy of being able to breathe in an almost full lungful of air. I walk past the rangers' hut and over to Hugo's tent. Apart from the torchlight shining on the canvas, all seems quiet. But then, I'm pretty sure I hear a groan.

I hover. It goes quiet. Now that the rain has died down, I can hear the noise of the night creatures in the forest. A fresh, sweet smell lingers. The light seems to dance from inside the tent, creating shadows. I shine my own torch around, the sight of trees alien after our nights in the barren land further up the mountain.

I poke my head inside his tent.

'Hello?'

James is sitting beside Hugo, who has his sleeping bag drawn up to his chin. His reading glasses are perched on the tip of his pale nose.

'Yes?' says James.

'Any news?'

'Not yet.'

'Will he be able to make it down by himself?'

He steps out.

'Unlikely,' he says in a low voice.

'Is he going to make it?'

'I can't say any more right now. Go and get some sleep.'

I head back to the only place left to go: the mess tent.

The crowd has thinned out. Only Jonessa, Casper, Sara and Jacob remain.

'Why don't you go and rest in my tent?' I say to Sara. 'I'm feeling OK enough for now. We can take turns to stay up. I promise to keep you updated if there's any news.'

'Are you sure?' she says. 'I do feel sick with tiredness. I'm not going to be of any use unless I get some rest. I promised our nanny that I'd call the children the moment we got down and I want to be able to stay upbeat for them.'

'I'm sure,' I say.

'I'm going to hit the sack,' says Casper. He turns to Jonessa. 'You should come too. We'll be much more help if we've had some rest.'

'You don't mind, do you, Jacob?' asks Jonessa. 'We can take turns, perhaps swap with you in a few hours?'

'Sure.'

And then we're alone, just me and Jacob. Half-brother and -sister.

At first, neither one of us speaks. A wave of tiredness and nausea hits. Again. I don't trust myself to speak, let alone say the right thing. I don't want to start a big fight up here. I put my elbows on the table and my head in my hands. The red and white squares on the plastic tablecloth come into sharper focus. I see a splotch of ketchup that hasn't been wiped off properly. It has dried into a wizened, dark clump. Like the blood I have on my hands.

'I saw what you did,' says Jacob in a soft voice. 'I saw you kill Luke.'

I jolt my head back up.

'I beg your pardon?'

'You heard.'

My heart thuds. If only I'd called for help. If only it hadn't happened. If only . . .

'I'm not sure what you think you saw,' I say carefully, 'but . . .'

'I'm not stupid,' he says.

'If you're so sure of what you think you know, why haven't you said anything?'

'I was going to, but . . .' he stops.

'But . . .?'

'Hugo told me. About you. Who you really are.'

'Oh.'

'Yes, oh. It's not right and it's bloody unfair. You came swanning in to BVT and I can see quite clearly now that you had a very hidden agenda.'

I try to interrupt, but he's on a roll and won't let me speak.

'The thing you need to know about Hugo is that no one is special to him. I thought I was, once upon a time. Now, I have a crystal ball. I naively assumed that once I was embedded in the family business, that was it. Hard work done. I thought I'd forever bask in the light. I had *no idea* that the warmth would dim, that I would have to keep on trying to recapture it again and again.'

He looks almost close to tears.

'I didn't know,' I say.

'You must think I was born yesterday.'

'It's true. I really had no idea myself until a few days ago. You can ask Hugo himself when he's better.'

'If he gets better,' says Jacob.

'Why didn't you say anything sooner about Luke?'

'Because I haven't decided exactly what I'm going to do about it.'

I sense there's no point in begging him. Instead, I need to offer him something in return for his silence.

'I did you a favour,' I say. 'Luke had a file in his backpack. It's pretty damning, for you and Hugo. George, Simon, there's literally a list of people who have died on BVT's watch. Apparently, Simon was on the trip where a guy died in Barbados. Hugo made him cover it up, and according to Luke's research, Simon never got over it. It all comes back to BVT. Example after example of their negligence.'

Jacob doesn't reply. He looks like he's figuring out whether he can trust me.

'I also have some information George collected that was supposed to be shredded,' I say.

A horrible thought emerges. Did Luke try to kill George on Hugo's orders? No, it seems too far-fetched. And yet . . . people get murdered for less.

I voice my fears to gauge Jacob's reaction.

'It sounds pretty mad,' he says. 'Can I see the file?'

'How do I know I can trust you?'

He puts his hand in his trouser pocket and hands me my necklace, with my engagement ring and the St Christopher.

'Oh, thank God,' I say. 'I thought . . .'

I can't finish my sentence because the relief is overwhelming.

'If it makes you feel any better, I promise I didn't want to see George hurt. Luke really did take it too far – he spiked George's drink with Valium the night before the climb. He added in extra tequila whenever George wasn't looking for good measure. Mr Armstrong saw him and had a word, but Luke said that George knew, and it was just another prank.'

He sighs. 'I've been feeling guilty, but honestly, I had no idea that Luke would take things so far.'

The enormity of my loss and my terrible deed hits.

Jacob rummages around in his pocket again and takes out a tissue.

'Here,' he says.

'Thank you.'

I've run out of words.

'Christ,' Jacob breaks the silence, running his fingers through his hair. 'What a mess.'

What a mess indeed. I hate what I've become, but I have no choice but to continue this route. I wonder what George would have wanted. But then it comes to me, the answer, and the way it should have always been. Together, Jacob and I can destroy Hugo. A one-way ticket out of both of our predicaments.

From my tent, I retrieve the plastic wallet with Luke's intel and hand it to Jacob, knowing that once he's read it, he'll never think of his father in the same way again.

TWENTY-FOUR

Jacob

Mweka Camp

Deep down, Jacob always knew that the day of reckoning would come. As he reads the file, he understands how naive he has been. Hugo must be stopped before anyone else comes to harm. From Luke's notes and printed emails, it appears that Hugo strongly encouraged Luke to play dirty, '*to weaken his opponents*', as in George, '*if you want to be a worthy winner*'. To Luke, it added fuel to the idea that he would be Jacob's second-in-command, or perhaps even be awarded the top job.

Jacob lets out a deep breath.

'It's twisted,' he says.

All this time, he has carried the burden of immense guilt. It's sobering. He knew his father likes to play games, to see how far he can push people. But he never realised quite how far. Not only that, all the hush money paid out to various ex-employees is eye-opening.

Jacob can feel Florence's eyes upon him as he reads. There's a shift in energy, and for the first time, he realises that although they may never be best pals, they do have a common goal. Perhaps they could finally learn how to work together.

'Luke still had a choice in all this,' says Jacob. 'He made really bad decisions.'

'It doesn't make me feel better about his death,' Flo replies.

'No,' says Jacob. 'But it explains some of his actions.'

'Hello,' Sara calls out as she steps into the mess tent. Her eyes are red.

'How's Hugo?' both Flo and Jacob automatically ask.

'The same,' she says. 'I just came to get some biscuits and I'm going to stretch my legs. Can one of you look in on him in a few minutes?'

'Sure,' says Jacob.

When they're alone again, Jacob blurts out another concern on his mind.

'I think it's my fault he's sick. I just grabbed the pills I thought were the most obvious, *Monday's*. I don't want to be responsible for his death.'

'How would you be responsible?'

'I wasn't thinking straight. Sara asked me to pass his pills and I did.'

'I don't follow . . .' says Florence.

'I didn't check that's what she meant. There was another white container in there with a medical label, which I ignored. I just handed her what I now realise could have been any old drugs in the heat of the moment.'

'Well, unless it was arsenic, I can't see that you've done anything wrong,' she says. 'It probably wouldn't even have mattered if you'd given him Saturday's instead of Sunday's.

Surely the point of keeping them like that is that they're prepared in advance. It makes mistakes less likely, I would've thought.'

'Maybe. Do you think I should ask James for his opinion?'

Jacob doesn't know why he's asking for Flo's advice, of all people. But something about her reaction has put him ever so slightly at ease.

'It's too late to bother him,' she says. 'I honestly don't think that Hugo would carry around anything that would be dangerous for him. But I tell you what, I'll nip over and check them, if you think it will make you feel better?'

'I guess. They're in a washbag. A leather one,' he adds.

Florence disappears for several minutes. During her absence, he fights the urge to pick up his phone and doomscroll. He's relieved when the tent flaps open and she steps into the tent.

'You didn't do anything wrong. They were his prescribed blood pressure pills,' she says.

'Thank Christ.'

One less thing to worry about, thinks Jacob. His mind returns to the question that has bothered him since Hugo's shock revelation.

'Seriously, Flo, you can't honestly expect me to believe that it was all a huge coincidence you joined BVT?'

'No, it wasn't a coincidence,' she says. 'I was tricked. Headhunted. Flattered. Coerced. Bribed. However you want to look at it.'

'By Hugo?'

'Yes. With the help of Mandy.'

'When did you find out?' he says. 'And who is your mother?'

'Her name was Anna . . .'

The world seems to shrink, just Jacob and Florence now,

cocooned in this tent. As they talk and share stories, something becomes very clear: the two of them could make something good out of all this bad. They could work together to turn BVT into something very special. A company with decent values, one that embraces sustainable travel, a force for actual good. It could be their future. They could right any wrongs unearthed by George. It would be a real fresh start. If it wasn't for Hugo.

'I love the sound of a Japanese art called Kintsugi where broken objects are mended with gold. Imperfect but better. That's what we can do with BVT,' says Flo. 'Carve out the rot and make it work.'

'I've worked for this my whole life,' says Jacob. 'Hugo promised it to me. I could take you down any moment by letting everyone know what you did to Luke. I can prove it too. His daypack was in his tent when I went to look for you both. I know you left it by his body later, to make it look like he'd left on his own. How about we try making it work with me in charge and you as my second-in-command?'

'If you were so innocent yourself, Jacob, you'd have come over and done what you could to help Luke, but you didn't, did you? Because his death is convenient. He can no longer blab about the role you also played in George's death.'

He looks at Florence and, in her eyes, he sees Hugo's ruthlessness. He wonders if she can see the same in his.

'Luke was already dead when I went to check on him. You did that to him, not me.'

'It was horrific,' says Florence. 'And it also happens to be the second accident involving you, in one way or another. Plus, Jacob, you gave me an alibi by saying that you'd also overheard Luke talking about wandering off on his own. You'd be just as much a suspect as me, which is absolutely right as you're hardly innocent.'

Jacob doesn't respond.

'If the worst were to happen and it turned out he'd been given an overdose by his own son . . .'

'You said there was nothing wrong with the pills I gave him.'

'You don't know if he took anything else. You can't prove exactly what tablets you gave him. Sara will have been in too much of a state to verify anything you say.'

A silent understanding passes between them. Any accusations alone could potentially ruin them both.

'Fifty–fifty,' Florence says. 'Between the two of us, the company will be unstoppable. We can even change the name.'

'I've a better idea,' says Jacob.

He knows so much more than Hugo ever gives him credit for. To be a true success, to fully understand how business works, you must focus on those whose loyalty has been pushed to the absolute limit. The ones who could snap and abandon ship at any moment. For all Hugo's credentials, he hasn't clocked that loyalty can wither and die if it's not rewarded. The time has come for Jacob to cut loose from Hugo.

He lowers his voice to a whisper.

'Hugo is the true culprit behind Luke's murder. We have everything we need.'

They talk until late, barely getting any sleep, and thank Christ, in the morning the rain has finally let up. They have a workable plan.

'And how is Hugo?' Jacob asks Sara at breakfast.

'Stable. He's not well enough to walk, but he can be taken down by stretcher to Mweka Gate.'

His phone vibrates. It's an advert for a loan. Jacob wants to laugh. As he packs for the last time, he realises that now it's time to leave, he feels a strong attachment to the mountain. Down below, reality is waiting and he's not sure he's ready to face up to how much his life will change after this. But if his and Flo's plan works, he'll have enough to pay off all his loans, really start afresh. He'll be honest with Clarabelle too and tell her that they're not right for each other. Christ, if he's really lucky, he can persuade Joey to leave Casper, maybe even go public eventually. He's ready to take responsibility, let the chips fall where they may. Jacob smiles to himself. Maybe it's time to quit gambling too.

Sara stays behind to wait for Hugo's stretcher as Jacob heaves his bag on to his back. It's heavier than normal because he took some of Luke's belongings from his tent, including a book, his watch and his wallet to give to his family. As they start their final descent, Jacob finds that it's hard not to imagine that Luke is somewhere behind him, urging him to hurry up or staring at Jacob through the new, mirrored sunglasses that he loved to wear. He concentrates on putting one foot in front of the other and not slipping in the mud. The lower they go, the easier it is to breathe. Jacob can't believe that this is something he's taken for granted. Just like life itself, he supposes.

They all pick up pace. For a few brief seconds he forgets that Luke and George are dead. Maybe he can finally leave them to rest.

When they stop for another break, Flo sidles up to him.

'Are we really going to go through with it?' she asks.

Jacob takes a couple of sips of water to think through his answer.

'Thing is, Sis . . .'

They both laugh before Jacob continues. It feels strangely good, this tentative step into their fledgling relationship.

'I don't think we have a choice,' he says. 'I've sensed for years that one day things would come to a head. I gamble, too much. I'm used to risk. But I've never had to put everything on the table like this.'

'I see,' she says.

After a long pause she says softly, 'We both just wanted a normal father who loved us. If we'd had that, maybe none of this would've happened.'

It brings a lump to Jacob's throat.

'Look! A monkey!' says Casper, pointing up into a tree.

They all stop to watch it leap between the branches.

Once they walk again, they continue in relative silence, navigating down rocky steps, lined with lush green foliage, brighter than any ferns Jacob's ever seen. His knees are in agony. But on they go. Jacob looks at his watch. A couple more hours to go.

'We're here!' he hears someone shout.

Finally. He sees the sign:

KILIMANJARO NATIONAL PARK
CONGRATULATIONS!

Ben instructs them that they'll need to sign out and that they have time to shop for souvenirs. Apparently there are animal carvings, T-shirts and plenty of other bits and pieces, or they can have a beer, take photos and visit the restrooms before their transport arrives.

Around them, other groups are celebrating with music, singing and dancing, and Jacob feels a strong pang for what could have been. He imagines he's not the only one. It's nice not to feel frozen, he thinks, sinking down on a bench to enjoy the sun on his face. Joey joins him. She smiles and Jacob fights the urge to take her hand. If he plays his cards right, maybe one day soon they'll be together properly. Then again, he's probably kidding himself. They both thrive on danger and he's not sure they'd survive normality. And he's definitely not sure that Casper wouldn't kill him first.

'We did it,' she says.

'We bloody well did.'

They high-five.

Then they see the body bag.

TWENTY-FIVE

Florence

Dar es Salaam, Tanzania

The balcony net floats gently in the breeze. Back and forth, it dances. Outside, a tribute band plays an Elton John track by the pool. Joy. Merriment. By contrast, my life here, in this room, is quiet. We're waiting for all the formalities surrounding Luke's accident to be completed before we can go home.

It wasn't supposed to be like this, obviously. The last few days have been a blur. Jacob spoke to Luke's family; I couldn't do it. Meanwhile, I have to deal with the horrible fact that George's funeral is in a fortnight. Jacob, Hugo, Sara and I are here, waiting until we can leave. Everyone else has flown home. It was too upsetting to wait in Moshi, seeing the celebration parties held by all the other groups. We went through the motions. Ben and Samson gave us our certificates and we ensured that we passed on generous tips for the incredible team who helped us achieve our dream and supported us through the hardest times of our lives.

Hugo has almost fully recovered from his mystery illness. Jacob and I have booked Sara for a half-day spa because she deserves a break.

'Thank you,' she said. 'I'm sure I won't be able to relax properly after everything that's happened. And I'm desperate to see my children. But it will be a welcome distraction.'

She also expressed her gratitude that no one is going to drop her in it over Mandy's poisoning. Jacob told her we consider it to be a crime of passion.

'Thing is, I know I should leave Hugo, and I will. But I can't right now. He almost died.' She looks close to tears.

'You're too good for him,' says Jacob. 'And just so you know, I've heard from Mandy. She's definitely cut all ties with him.'

For our lunch meeting with Hugo, Jacob and I have booked the conference suite. We think he'll like that. We've ordered a luxury sandwich platter and a bottle of red. While we were at it, we put in a request for a fruit basket and asked that it be wrapped in cellophane and tied in crimson and black ribbon. It's all about attention to detail, every time, even for this occasion. Especially for this occasion.

The hours drag, but finally Sara is safely in the spa – a facial, then a massage and a pedicure; the latter should keep her trapped in the spa until the polish is fully dry. Jacob and I walk alongside Hugo – who is in a wheelchair – to the meeting room. He doesn't want to go, he makes a fuss about 'having plans', but, bad luck, because he's stuck with us. His children. We're the ones with his best interests at heart, we tell him. It isn't true, of course. Jacob and I have our own best interests at heart. We are his children, after all: we were taught to look after *numero uno*.

I pour three glasses of wine. This is all going to be very civilised. No histrionics.

'What I'd like to know before we get to the main agenda,' I say, 'is why my mother was so scared of you?'

'I've explained all this. She wasn't scared of me. We had an agreement, an NDA. I was loyal to Jacob's mother,' he says, looking at Jacob for approval.

'I don't believe you,' I say.

Hugo closes his eyes as if he can get me to disappear at will. Perhaps it's time for me to accept that Hugo will never tell me the truth.

'Please.'

He opens his eyes.

'Your mother betrayed me,' he says. 'She got pregnant on purpose. Anna wanted a child above anything else. But she wanted Jacob too, as well as her own baby. She also didn't like the thought that when Jacob got older it wouldn't be possible for me to keep her employed. Ivy couldn't have any more children. It is my firm belief that Anna wanted to stay in my life and she thought the best way to force my hand was by trapping me.'

'It doesn't sound like my mother at all!' I say. 'On one of the many occasions I asked about you she said there was no point in inviting darkness in.'

'Believe what you want to. But it was your mother who lied to me. She told me she was on the pill but she admitted afterwards that she thought I'd be pleased, that we'd all live happily ever after like one big, happy family. I might be many things, but I'd never have taken Jacob from Ivy. She is his mother.'

'And this is it?' I say, fury rising. 'This is all you have to say after not being part of my life for so long, then crowbarring your way in? Lies upon more lies?'

'I can't give you what you want, Florence,' he says. 'I can't give you the neat, tidy ending wrapped in a bow. It isn't how life works. Subject closed. Let's get to the point. I know you two have brought me in here for a reason. Spit it out. I'm tired.'

'We know you killed Luke,' I say.

'You what?'

'We saw you follow him,' says Jacob. 'We haven't said anything to the police yet because we're giving you a chance to tell your side of the story.'

'This is utterly preposterous.'

I place copies of Luke's findings on the table. Hugo picks them up and scans them.

'Proof,' I say, 'that Luke was blackmailing you.'

'It certainly looks that way to me too,' says Jacob.

'He wasn't,' says Hugo. 'And Luke's death was an accident.'

'If we tell the police that we suspect you killed him, they'll look into it further,' Jacob says. 'They could even learn about Gareth Snow and find him very interesting to talk to. Unless . . .'

We remain silent for dramatic effect.

'This is bullshit,' says Hugo. 'What are you after?'

'It's time for you to retire,' I say. 'If you go quietly, maybe Jacob and I won't have to tell the police anything.'

'You honestly can't expect that I'll just hand everything over to you?'

'You don't have a choice,' says Jacob.

'Plus,' I say, 'George's death may have been deemed an accident, but the culture of fear that had been brewing in the toxic workplace that is Blackmore Vintage Travel most certainly played a deadly role. I owe it to George to make sure you can't harm anyone else.'

'We've already had papers drawn up,' Jacob says, handing them over to him. 'They're ready to sign.'

Hugo laughs.

'Like I'm going to roll over and do as you say,' he says. 'Even if I felt threatened – which I don't – there's no way I'd sign anything without getting it checked over.'

'We're not letting you leave this room without an answer,' says Jacob. 'BVT has gotten away with too much and I know where all the bodies are buried. It ends today. Florence and I mean it. We've been in talks with Gareth Snow, who is prepared to spare the gory details of his unlawful dismissal once the merger between Blackmore Vintage Travel and Ethical Getaways is announced. We've even thought of a new company name, without Blackmore in it.'

'So you're getting into bed with that snake, Snow?' says Hugo.

'Seems so,' replies Jacob. 'I trust him more than I trust you.'

'You know it makes sense,' I say. 'There's no way BVT can survive this. Especially not after all that Mandy has to share, too. She's been feeding information to Gareth. Feedback is a powerful tool, according to you. I guess this is Mandy's way of letting you know that she's also had her loyalty pushed to the limit.'

Mandy told us that Hugo has been calling and messaging her since the climb, but she has held firm and cut off contact.

Hugo forgot that you need to treat people with respect, because sooner or later, however loyal, they will wake up one morning and realise they deserve better.

I take a sip of wine and sit back in my chair.

'It's a ridiculous plan,' Hugo says.

'There's no way you'll be flying home while there's a police investigation,' Jacob says.

'Oh, and by the way, we have a gift for you,' I say, handing him a small package wrapped in crimson, tied in black ribbon.

Inside, he'll find my St Christopher.

Jacob pours himself another glass of red.

'We have all day,' he says. 'But our offer expires once you leave this room.'

'Look, if this is about teaching me a lesson . . .'

Anger resurfaces.

'You owe me,' I say.

'You owe both of us,' says Jacob.

He looks at us and I think he realises that we mean business, because he takes out his favourite fountain pen from his pocket and signs our contract.

'You'll regret this,' he says, throwing the papers across the table. 'You'll be begging me to come back. It's not as easy as it looks, you know.'

'We could always search online for some of your top tips,' Jacob laughs.

'Look on the bright side,' I say, as Jacob and I accompany him back to his suite. 'You'll be known for doing good, because Jacob and I are going to clean up the company, make amends for the past. You'll end up being able to dine out on our success for many years to come. Who knows, you may even win a few lifetime achievement awards, thanks to us.'

I walk out of the hotel, past the pool and on to the beach. I make myself comfortable on a sun lounger, arranging my fluffy navy-and-white striped towels neatly, then order a pine-apple rum cocktail. I raise my glass and say a silent cheers to George and an apology to Luke. I take a large sip of the delicious coolness. A sort of peace, as much as I suspect I'll ever feel it, finally descends.

A woman makes herself comfortable on the sunbed beside me.

'Excuse me,' she says. 'Weren't you with that group on Kilimanjaro? The one where your friend died after a fall? You look familiar.'

I look at her through my sunglasses. She is wearing reflective ones and I can't see her eyes behind her glasses. It's somewhat unsettling. I gaze out over the turquoise sea, layers of green and blue. We're surrounded by palm trees. Still I don't reply, concentrating instead on a game of beach volleyball.

'I'm sorry,' she says. 'It was rude of me to pry.'

'No, it's OK,' I say. 'It's difficult to talk about. We worked very closely together. His name was Luke.'

'I understand. My condolences.'

I can't accept sympathy, I don't deserve it. Everything I accused Luke of, I've become.

We share snippets of our lives. Carole is a teacher and she climbed Kilimanjaro with a friend who had to return to the UK for work.

'I run a major travel firm,' I say.

It's nice saying the words out loud.

Then, for some reason, I get the urge to confess. It feels like a natural thing to do, sitting here, talking to a stranger. It's comforting. I now understand how Sara felt.

I take the plunge.

'I used to be a tour guide,' I say. 'Most of my stories were based in fact and history, but sometimes I'd embellish them a little to add a bit of spice. Especially to the ghost and murder ones.'

Carole laughs and admits she does something similar in the classroom.

'There was one story,' I say, 'where this guy assumed he'd given his father an overdose and made him sick, but he hadn't. It was someone else. Only that person had done it deliberately, over a period of a few days. The father in question always left a leather washbag containing his pills in his tent when he went to eat or for a bathroom visit. He believed he was taking his altitude sickness tablets like everyone else on their trip.' I pause and for my own benefit add a detail that isn't true. 'They were visiting the Andes.'

'Is this true?' asks Carole.

'Like I said, it's just a story. I'm not sure where I heard it.'

Although it wasn't my intention to kill – or hurt Hugo too badly – he undeniably started the chain of events that led to George's death. It was his culture of fear, after all. I wanted him to get a taste of failure for once. It's dangerous to take drugs that slow down your heart rate at high altitude instead of anti-sickness pills.

In the aftermath of Luke's death, I completely forgot about it. I meant to take them back before any real harm could be done. It wasn't until Jacob shared his fear and paranoia that he'd given Hugo the wrong pills that I had enough presence of mind to retrieve them.

Still, it's no bad thing for Jacob to carry the guilt. He has enough on me. I can't fully trust him, after all, because Jacob hasn't fallen too far from the tree. Who knows what unseen darkness lurks within?

'My friend reckons that your colleague's death wasn't an accident,' says Carole.

'I beg your pardon?'

'She reckons the police are going to question the entire group further.'

'First I've heard,' I say. Then, feeling the urge to get away from Carole, I add, 'I can't hang around, sadly. Duty calls.'

'I saw you,' she says, as I yank my towel off the sun lounger.

I think I might throw up.

'I'm not sure what you mean?'

'I saw you all on the mountain, one big, happy team. My husband, Simon, used to work for BVT,' she says, removing her sunglasses and staring at me.

She has clear, blue eyes.

Shit. Without her sunglasses, I immediately recognise Carole as the woman travelling with Ethical Getaways. A client, not an employee.

'You be careful,' she adds. 'That man is capable of murder, I'd say.'

As is his daughter, I think, turning away and heading back to my room.

Come evening, sitting on my hotel room balcony, a little tipsy after multiple mini-bar spirits, I remove the chain from around my neck and slide off my engagement ring. I throw it as hard and as far as I can into the flower beds. I hope someone finds it one day, and if they do, I hope they can use it for something useful. Maybe it will even bring them happiness. I don't deserve it.

'Goodbye, George,' I say out loud.

When I return home, I'll buy myself a pair of black pearl earrings as a late birthday present. They're supposed to be a symbol of hope. I've now read the full report by the private detective Hugo hired to follow me pretty much cover to cover, several times. Hugo knew about George because we were spied on so frequently. He didn't care about George, and he certainly doesn't care about me. For all I know, Hugo may have thought it would be character-building for me to suffer like I did. Things keep popping into my mind. Horrible ideas, like what if Hugo thought that by keeping up the pressure on everyone, George and I would've split up. Hugo said to me once:

'My dear, you must realise that the reason George is in a private hospital and getting the best treatment is because of me?'

Hugo thought he could buy forgiveness. Jacob's using Hugo's wealth to break free from loan sharks, and I've gained my freedom by discovering the truth. But the truth in my case is a different cage, and this is one I can't escape from. I'm capable of far worse than I ever expected. However, Hugo's exit from the BVT stage has given us a second chance. For me, it means that the world really is my oyster now, just like the one illustrated in the Blackmore Vintage Travel logo. I'm going to make a real difference.

I step inside my room and from my handbag take out the sleeping pills I switched with Hugo's anti-sickness ones, flushing them down the toilet. *Cover your tracks. Watch out for number one. Win at all costs.* It seems I am my father's daughter after all. When it comes to survival, I will lie. One task down, one to go. I get the story straight in my head, how it's all coming back to me that Hugo followed Luke into the darkness the night he died, then pick up the hotel phone and ask reception to put me through to the local police station. If Carole's right and the police are going to question us further, then I'll give them a suspect to focus on. Hugo's hardly blameless.

Afterwards, I raise a glass to my mum. I partly did it for her, for the way he treated us.

Later, while I'm waiting for news, I search online for any comments written using Hugo's not-so-anonymous username. There's no sign of the Anonymous Traveller. Hugo has finally been silenced.

Acknowledgements

Thank you for reading my fourth book. I loved writing it. As always, I'm hugely grateful to Sophie Lambert, my wonderful and insightful agent and Jack Butler, an equally wonderful and insightful editor. Their patience and expertise are invaluable. Huge thanks to the amazing teams at C+W, including Luke Speed, Anna Weguelin, Theo Roberts, Matilda Ayris, Kate Burton and Alice Hoskyns and Hillary Jacobsen at ICM. Massive thanks to the incredible teams at Wildfire and Headline, including: Areen Ali, Rosie Margesson, Elise Jackson and Rebecca Bader, as well as my copy editors Karen Ball and Sarah Bance and my proofreader Jill Cole.

Thank you to Lucy, Joe and friends for sharing their experiences of climbing Kilimanjaro and to Kate, for putting me in touch. I really appreciate your patience in answering all my questions, things like: 'What did you smell, how far away did the stars appear, what were the best and worst bits?' I loved all the photos and videos, so thanks for sharing them. Any errors are mine or are for artistic license as I noted during my research that experiences naturally vary when climbing Kilimanjaro. Route popularity, among other things, also change over time. One of the best books I read was written by a local guide.

Thanks to Jo and Andre for putting me in touch with Alex

Harris for climbing advice. Mistakes are, of course, are my own. Thanks also to Graham Bartlett, police advisor. Again, any mistakes are mine. Huge thanks too to Rona and Roy for reading early drafts. I love having this opportunity to thank everyone, but I'm always concerned that I will leave someone out by accident. I haven't (to my knowledge) so far and fingers crossed, I won't this time either.

My father died while I was in the process of writing this book and it made me think even more about identity and what makes us who we are. Luckily, my dad wasn't anything like Hugo. He was wise, kind, generous and taught me to believe in myself, to work hard. I'll always be grateful for the support from my parents and family.

Thanks to my wonderful friends who read my books and support local events. Also huge thanks to all my writing friends for their support and understanding, especially the Ladykillers. Big thanks to Liv Matthews for being such a wonderful writing pal and to Liz for introducing me to a wonderful place to work away from home. Big love to my Faber group, still going strong after eight years! Heartfelt thanks, as always, to readers, bloggers, reviewers, booksellers, librarians, event organisers and everyone who gets in touch. It's all very much appreciated. Thank you with all my heart. I'm truly grateful to be able to do what I love.

Thank you to my family and my husband and sons for their support, love and belief. I'm proud of you and I love you very much.

ABOUT THE AUTHOR

Karen Hamilton spent her childhood in Angola, Zimbabwe, Belgium and Italy and worked as a flight attendant for many years. Karen is a graduate of the Faber Academy and, having now put down roots in Hampshire to raise her young family with her husband, she satisfies her wanderlust by exploring the world through her writing. *The Perfect Girlfriend*, her first novel, was a *Sunday Times* bestseller. *The Contest* is her fourth novel.